[JYZE AND JYZE ALONE]

Annals of The Jyze Age

Jyzeburst

Jyzemelt

Jyze and Jyze Alone

Jyze in Love

Deep Jyze

The Jyze Millennium

Jyze of the Heavenly Year

Scat Jyze

Jyze and Jyze Alone

G.P. Sandefjord

Annal Three of The Jyze Age

Cover art by GPS
Published by House of Jyze
ISBN 978-0-9964173-3-4
Library of Congress CIP pending
www.HouseOfJyze.com

To Rob

a brother indeed in a time of need

Only you and you alone
can thrill me like you do.

    -- Buck Ram and Ande Rand,
    "Only You (And You Alone),"
    as performed by the
    Platters.

BOOK I

[The Jyze Moves]

1

Here begins the new year and the new age and anything else auspicious-sounding I can come up with. The ministorage place, about eight a.m. on a rainy Sunday morning, inside unit 161.

Granted the setting by itself is not too lively. The garagelike door is pulled two-thirds down. Outside, from my seated position, I see rainwater coursing by on blacktop, flowing left to right (which would be south to north) past the back right wheel and fender of the wagon. And that's about it.

At some point, though, a pair of high rubber camo boots and an upside-down face may appear. The owner. Fellow Mentoka refugee, demanding normality in all things, wondering what sort of weirdness is going down in 161 -- a vehicle parked next to a unit with the unit door mostly closed for a suspiciously long period and no sign of work ethic in action. Some snoozing taking place in there? Strictly against the rules.

What I'll say if asked is I'm just doing inventory. That'll be for the first offense. After that, who knows. But I do expect to be coming here for years, and starting in March or maybe April I'll likely be arriving on foot most of the time (after ferrying over from the city and then walking or busing up from the dock), and that too may strike the owner as dubious.

Well, no matter. I'm having fun. I'm back into it. I've regained some sense of life and purpose. Joie de jyze!

Last night another big date for the lady. At seven o'clock off she went, her new romantic interest, I'll

call him, or one of his cronies (who himself may be a
new romantic interest for all I know, and I wouldn't be
in the least surprised if that were the case) -- the
dude gunning the engine of his light green pickup right
outside the kitchen door. To which I say: fine. Am I,
the zen husband and putative former prime romantic
interest, feeling humiliated? Am I angry, distressed,
bewildered? Absolutely not! None of those. Instead
I'm galvanized into action. In a flash I load up the
wagon with boxes packed earlier in the week and haul
them over here. Then back at home I wheel the old
picnic table end-over-end down from the barn in the dark
and ready it for an early getaway (propped up behind the
carport cabinets, out of sight from the driveway). At
two a.m. or so the lady slips back in. At seven a.m. I
slip back out with the table (it's a very tight fit in
the rear compartment of the wagon; I have to drive with
one window rolled down and a corner of the table poking
out in the rain). And now here I am bellied up to that
same table for the year's first jyze session.
    The new regime. And my feet are chilling
(literally) on the cold concrete. But I'm lucky the
day's as warm as it is -- already close to fifty
degrees. (Holding forth beneath a single naked bulb
dangling about five feet up. Is it a hundred watts?
Could be. The light's not bad at all, except for the
sharp shadows it casts, because to avoid them I have to
contort myself in ways I can't sustain for long. -- And
how about sliding some cardboard under my shivering
feet? See what I can find.)

*

    -- Done. That's better. And while at it I donned
an extra sweatshirt I brought along just in case. And
then zipped up my coat and pulled up the hood. This
damp type of chill, it can get to you even when it's not
really all that cold. (And also broke out a packet of
fig newtons and a can of soda lugged here from home to
help celebrate this special occasion.)
    So I begin the first full year of my life in which
the woman who brought me into the world will not be in

6

it herself. Am I ready for this? On top of everything else? I'm hoping I am. I'm dedicating my breakout effort to her. And her devotion and generosity are helping to make this effort possible. And I do have a plan, oh yes I do.

Some elements of this plan are new. First, I'm no longer seeking to hang on at home for another four to six months. The new getaway date is far from certain, but I'm aiming for the end of March or even sooner. And as the key to this change (here's element No. 2), it's dawned on me I can take part of Mother's bequest in cash right now. It would just be a small part, say five K of the roughly seventy-five I'm expecting when the estate closes, but it would enable me to rent a place quickly and would also provide the kind of cushion I'll be needing (because Jyzer Ink's been getting little work lately; in the last ten days I've done one night of finaling and not a single lick of scoping).

Element No. 3, I'll devote myself to cranking out a draft of "Jyzer" over the next six to eight weeks while awaiting the arrival of the main bequest check.

And No. 4, sometime in early to mid March the lady will be visiting her parents for ten days or so on a mission to renew her driver's license (or at least this is her stated reason for making the trip). While she's away I'll do as much moving as I can -- hopefully some of it into a new office of my own in the city, preferably in the funky old historic quarter near the ferry dock, and maybe even, if I'm truly lucky, also into a loft/studio in roughly that same area -- and when she returns I'll present her with a fait d'accompli. The only task remaining will be distribution of the items which one or the other of us designates community property (chief among these the wagon itself, in which I've invested nearly seven K and she not a penny).

How accommodating will she be? Hard to say. Since the house and the property it's on and the note on the wagon are all owned by her parents I'll be a bit short on leverage. But she may worry I'll raise a stink with them (that's my one piece of leverage) and therefore she may let me off the hook fairly easily.

And well she should. Sometimes it's hard to remember she's the one who's pulling the plug on this relationship. I get too hung up on the vow I made to myself (and reconfirmed to her frequently over the years) that I'd stay on with her for the rest of my days no matter what. I have no doubt she really does want to put things to an end with us and wants me out of the picture sooner rather than later, but I should note she continues to refrain from coming right out and saying so. Instead I'm supposed to be taking the hint (this is her cultural way, or at least so I believe -- preserving appearances, minimal open expression of conflict).
-- And by god I am taking the hint. At all times I'm trying to look at things thus: I ought to be damn grateful she's setting me free. Because given what she's been showing me about herself lately -- especially the past several months -- I sure as hell wouldn't want to be living with her for the rest of my days.

I'm not saying I succeed in feeling this way at each and every waking moment. But I'm doing better at it all the time.

And having this storage unit is a big part of the reason why. It's not just a symbol of freedom, of security, of a new life -- it's all those things themselves. It's a genuinely existing place, mine, unknown to the lady, a home (of a sort) away from home that's gradually filling up to the point where more of the material basis of my existence resides here than there.

To wit: cartons line the three interior walls, in some places stacked six or seven high, as do also my large cabinet (containing the hard copies of all my writings and notes up to last year, among other things) and this picnic table (which still bears its original blue-and-white-checked vinyl tablecloth, no longer quite as spiffy as it was in its early days in the city but still looking good to me). Then in the middle of the U formed by the items stacked against the walls is a big mound of furniture and large boxes piled roughly eight

feet high, with a couple of good-size lamp shades
perched on top like antic hats. A narrow aisle, also U-
shaped, goes all the way around this central island.
(The fourth side, the open part of the U, is taken up
almost entirely by the roll-down garage door.)

Can I live with this setup? Definitely. I even
have hopes it will lead not just to a new life but to a
new kind of life. For the first time since before the
lady and I met I'll be able to travel -- and live --
light. I won't need a big apartment, to say nothing of
a "country estate"; a single room will do. And if I
succeed in renting office space in the city (small one-
roomers are currently available in a number of buildings
near the ferry dock for as little as $115 a month; but
of course right now I can't afford even that modest sum)
-- if I do eventually succeed at this, I say, I'll
consider my living and working setup close to ideal.

-- Brrr. Admittedly close to ideal is not ideal.
Most people would probably consider this plan a lot
closer to demented. ("Brrr," by that I mean even with
the cardboard in place my feet remain icy cold.) -- But
yes, I'm ready to go with it. I'm even elated. The
numerous potential drawbacks I'll worry about later.

Enough for the moment. The upside-down owner's
face has yet to swing into view and so if I hit the road
now I'll stay a step ahead of the game -- no demerits on
my record (except, that is, for the time last month when
I inadvertently padlocked the bolt on the roll-down door
in open position, a gaffe which I'll probably never live
down -- both owners, man and wife, to this day aiming a
sad silent cluck my way whenever I pass by the office).

(It is a new year. I ought to try to say a little
more about how it's gone so far. So maybe a postscript
a stop or two down the line.)

*   *

-- And now some fifteen hours later, say about
midnight, a break in the middle of my weekly shopping
run. Groceries. The usual supermarket, just a mile
from the storage place. The small cluster of black
plastic tables and chairs near the deli section, which

9

is closed at this hour, in the west-central portion of
the market, with three stacks of blue soft-drink twelve-
packs looming directly at my back and well above it.

Obviously this is the place. Fluorescent lights
and freezer hum -- just listen to that! Somewhere far
off a shopping cart jounces noisily down an aisle. Two,
three, maybe four other shoppers in this truly big "big
box." A few stockers. Distant country music.

How fine it is to be living in the age of the 24/7
supermarket! For a night worker it makes up for a lot,
it really does.

A twenty-minute drive straight down the roller
coaster of the old county road, headlights able to
pierce only a few yards ahead through a thick ground
fog -- floating along like a slow-motion tail-less
comet inside my own fuzzy bubble of luminosity. Not a
single other vehicle did I encounter the entire way.
And I want to note this: the new franchise burger joint,
which fronts on the massive new discount mart which has
sprung up over the past eight or nine months in the lot
next to the market where I now sit, is open for
business. The new traffic lights are still hooded like
hunting hawks, but the opening of the mart itself can't
be far off. This area, as everyone who lives in it or
nearby knows and talks about almost nonstop (or so it
often seems to me), is about to go big-time suburban
consumerist. My upcoming exit from the area is indeed
well timed.

(Parked next to the table is my cart, already half
full, mostly with huge "family size" boxes of cornflakes,
the house brand, on sale for the unheard-of low price of
a buck a box. I'd buy even more but now I must keep in
mind a new reality: don't want to be stocking up on too
much stuff I'd just have to turn around and haul to my
new living quarters later on.)

-- But the new year, what about it? We're seven
days into it already, or eight if we've crossed into
Monday a.m. And I must say I've failed to retain much
in the way of details about any of those days except
maybe the one now ending (or just ended). Gray and

rainy they were -- no doubt. Packed full of bowl games
and pro playoff games -- of course (but this year I
didn't watch or listen to a single minute of a single
game, not even by accident). I coughed, I snuffled, I
slowly recovered from my nasty Christmas cold. I read a
lot -- a whole lot, I mean really a lot, stacks and
stacks of reviews and magazines and quarterlies. No
newspapers. Lots of small chunks of books, continuing
with my usual practice in this recent era of skipping
from one to another, five pages here, ten there. Some
philosophy, some lit crit, some fiction, some collected
letters, some poetry, some protojyze, so forth and so
on. (It's true I'm gradually coming to feel a bit more
knowledgeable than before, for what it's worth.)

     Feast of the Epiphany, that was the 6th. At least
I noticed it. On that day I happened to be in the city
doing finals and I observed a two-man crew using a
rickety old wooden ladder to strip strings of white
municipal holiday lights from the leafless potted
ginkgoes lining the downtown avenues -- in the rain.
And later, after checking at the office and finding no
work, I took a long wet hike through the historic
quarter trying to locate an agency which had advertised
offices for rent, its ad giving a building name and
phone number but no address. I never did find it (it
wasn't listed in the phone book, and people on the
street seemed to have no idea what names attached to
which buildings, and most of the buildings themselves
were unlabeled as far as I could see). -- And enjoyed
not just the hunt but the enduring mystery. Would that
I have plenty of such in the months ahead to keep my
life, if not necessarily vibrant, at least usefully
distracting.

     (Once in a while a cart rolls by. Many of them
squeak as well as rattle. And most of the cart-pushers
-- all Cawks -- smile at me, and I smile back. I can
see why they'd be amused at such a sight as I present.
I am indeed myself tonight, "as is.") (Too bad no
restroom's nearby for washing up. -- In the back
somewhere maybe, but I don't want to make a nuisance of

myself trying to find it. It's not as if I'm planning
weekly supermarket jyze sessions.)
     Let's see, what am I? Have to think. Yeah, it's
enough to say I'm getting old. Jyze rules rule! And
yet not quite really old. And here I am starting out
another year and it's a year that'll be -- already is --
teasing me with a lot of unknowns. A teaser, a
titillator, a tantalizer, a tormentor, who knows what
else. The basic challenge is the achingly familiar one
of getting the Mentoka series written, but beyond that
-- a whole new ball game. I'm not sure whether it'll
really be new, though, actually, as opposed to a rerun
of old tapes from the pre-zen-marriage era. How
different a person am I now? Could I maybe do at least
a few things a little better than I did them back then?
     Answers will be forthcoming. Jyze this year will
find ways to keep itself occupied.
     And so it is. And so my shopping break comes to
an end. Back to pushing the cart (rattle, squeak).

2

     As of right now, tonight, I've cracked. Given up
on getting anything more done on the real work before
blowing this pop stand. Nothing to do at this stage but
to get on with the getting out. Day by day and week by
week until it's over.
     Or I guess the actual cracking point was this past
weekend when for three nights in a row the lady was out
messing around behind my back (except I knew she was
doing it, and she knew I knew) and I found myself unable
to squeeze out a single fictive word. Or maybe it came
Friday when brother Jeff called and I learned from him

that I could indeed ask for a "small" advance on the
bequest and receive it within a short period just as
he'd already done -- "small" in his case, as soon in
mine, being the previously mentioned five K. Or maybe
it came on the phone tonight when sister Barb confirmed
she could arrange such an advance for me and said the
check would be in the mail within a week to ten days.

     But no, the true emotional-whammy moment of
cracking hit earlier tonight. M.L. King holiday. Wind
whooing and isolated raindrops splattering on house
windows. I'm sitting in my brown armchair in the so-
called parlor sipping coffee and trying to gear up for
another go at "Jyzer." And suddenly I know I can't do
it. Just like that. Gonna hafta be outta here first.

     One other contributing factor. Today the lady --
this is still Dani, yes, or D, Mel, Skeeter, Stretch,
Lady U, among her many aliases -- today she informed me
her friend Marissa will be visiting us, not in March as
previously planned, but in the third week of February,
on or around the 20th. At the end of her stay, say
around the 25th or even before, the two of them will be
flying back home -- this she didn't spell out today but
it's been my understanding they'd be traveling together
-- and I immediately realized that would be the time
for me to make the major part of my getaway (which,
barring some radical change in the way she's interacting
with me, I won't be telling her about until the
getaway's an accomplished fact) -- and all this means
I've got just five weeks to prepare for it. And there's
lots to do. Still. Despite the lots I've already done.

     Even so I can't let such a long stretch go by
without plowing ahead in some way or other on the real
work. Can't. Unthinkable. Therefore I'll start typing
up last year's JIRT -- at the scope office -- and
hopefully that task will be completed by the time the
move's done and I'm ready to return to the JIFT again.
(JIRT, JIFT: I'm intending to stick with the same basic
jyze lingo all the way through this annal no matter what
and will assume the terms will eventually explain
themselves.) -- And also during the period directly

ahead I'll winnow down my stacks of Mentoka newspapers
to the essentials I'll need for "Jyzer" and the rest of
the Mentoka series (because I don't want to be hauling
all those papers around with me). (And so there goes
another nifty scheme -- a way of fictojyzing I wanted to
try -- but I don't think the loss will be too great. In
any case: nothing I can do about it.)

       -- Yes, I'm angry about all this. The furies I've
been going through. The conflicting internal voices.
The struggle to find a tolerable way of seeing it (the
whole schmear), understanding it, framing it. Sometimes
I'm on top of it and more often I'm not. I snort. I
grimace. I howl. I grit my teeth. How sweet revenge
would be! But no. But yes, and what a simple matter it
would be to tear the lady to pieces over this -- make
her suffer something fierce. But no. What right have
I? Who am I? Have mercy. Be grateful for what you
never thought you had a chance at in the first place.
All that. A better way to think of it, yes indeed. And
keep your eye on the ball. Think how you've got no time
to waste. Think how a change will be good for you --
even for her. Think about the opportunity for intense
unimpeded focus on your work. Think how few loves last
"forever." Think about your blessings. Think about her
growth, or movement anyway, in other directions. Think
of her various past betrayals, and in particular the big
one, and the consequent hollowing out.

       Yeah. And more. And on and on. Ooh it does get
funky down in there.

       Too much pain! Too much grief! -- But then isn't
life supposed to be about these things too? It's not
all just the pretty stuff. Not hardly! And who'd want
that anyway?

       -- And so now it's ten p.m. and here I sit at the
desk in my study (yes, still directly above jyze central,
which itself is also still known as, and serves as, the
library/guest room), and it's subtly different in here
because of the ongoing silent evacuation. Behind the
usual stacked bundles and boxes most of the bookcases
are empty. Half the things occupying the room a month

ago are gone -- a lamp here, a statuette there. The
desk surface is actually visible in some places. A
number of items from the shed now inhabit most of the
spots on the shelves here that would otherwise be
conspicuously barren. The holiday lights we put up four
or five years ago have finally come down and been packed
away, by me. And the heater roars (wall heater). Three
lamps glow. Jazz horns wail from the radio. The
washing machine rumbles downstairs. The windows rattle
sporadically from ongoing peltings of wind-driven rain.

First part of last week I was just about wholly
immobilized. Paralyzed. Groaning with comical self-
pity (if only I could've seen it that way at the time).
A tremendous effort it took to wrench myself out of the
torpor. But finally -- did. Called Suzanne at the
genealogy publishing house. Failed to get through for
two days -- delayed by a "fifty-year blizzard," it
turned out. More than two feet of snow blanketed their
area which hardly ever sees any.

It'll be months, she said, before the presses roll
for "Memorials." Fine. At least I had something to
report to Barb, brother Rob, Aunt Shar, et al. And then
the next morning brother Jeff called from Lahontan with
the news that it's time to start filling out the forms
for the investment group (and now, after talking with
Barb, I'm planning to call Lynn, our contact there,
tomorrow -- best to get moving on this too).

Most helpful all week has been a long poetic
rumination I read on Zen masters and their stoicism
before death. Me too, stoic in the face of all this
with the lady and in the face of that other death too.
(Right. Sure. Some stoic. -- But trying to do better
at it.)

-- And here's my row of antique picture postcards
from my father and grandfather's time, weird hues
almost like colorized black-and-white photos from half
a century earlier than that. These cards show the real-
world model for Parapet Bluff with its flapping USAn
flag, the Our Lady of Sorrows chapel, the Old Armory on
the Mezzu campus -- the fictive Mentoka world which I

sure do hate to step out of even for a moment. But
must. All this in here, this room, will soon have to be
closed down the rest of the way. This makeshift desk,
consisting of a maple door balanced horizontally atop a
pair of two-drawer oak filing cabinets, will just barely
fit inside the wagon -- I've already measured. The plan
is to haul this desk around the southern loop and
eventually deliver it to a new Jyzer Ink office in the
city (better still be some vacancies left when that check
from Barb arrives).

And now the chores. I'm just trying to do what I
said I would do and stay out of the lady's way. To
realize both of these ends tonight I should hit those
dirty dishes right now.

*   *

Thrown for a loop by another blown fuse in the
microwave. Only a day and a half later am I finally
staggering back to normal. (This aboard a state ferry,
a tiny two-seater canteen table because it's the four
o'clock run, which is always crowded, and the facing
bench in any booth I might've grabbed almost certainly
would've drawn an occupant, thereby making a jyze
session awkward if not impossible -- as right now the
engines labor mightily and we chug out from the dock,
bending left, aiming down the inlet -- nothing even
slightly unusual about any of this.)

It's also taken me most of the past two days to
shift modes from mixed JIFT/move-out to mixed research/
move-out.

(Every table here in the canteen is occupied,
mostly by shipyard workers in groups of two or three. A
few are white collar, most are blue. Newspapers are
open and rustling at many of the tables. Several
laptops in action. Not much talk.)

This morning I finally reached Lynn at the
investment outfit. The process of setting up my account
is officially underway. She tells me they'll be able
to meet my income-booster "requirement" (that's her word
but I can't think of a better one) of approximately
three hundred dollars a month. I told her it's my

intention to leave the principal untouched for at least
ten years. (I sure as hell hope I can live up to that.
Admittedly, though, the chances are slim.)

Had I started setting aside a thousand dollars a
year upon graduation from college and never missed a
year and had that money consistently earned five percent
interest, I figure the sum accumulated by now would just
about equal what this account will contain at the start:
seventy K. "The deep reserves."

It had been my intention to be jyzing this jyze up
at the shed yesterday morning with a candle burning in
old Mom's memory. The stripped-down shed. "The last
time" -- maybe. In any event things are moving fast now.
The endgame.

And sorrow. It's tough to come up with the words.
It's not that my spirit's broken or anything like that
(as Jeff was saying he feels Barb's lost her "zest for
life"); it's just that right now I'm too caught up in
various griefs and mournings. And having to be in the
same house with Lady U every day under circumstances
like these, that's not making things any easier. "Blows
against the Empire" -- such as it is.

This coming Sunday a group of Mother's friends will
be holding a "remembrance gathering" for her. Since I
don't know any of these people I'm not too sorry I'll be
missing it, but in any event I'm pleased to be aware
it's happening. (Why? I guess just because it shows
that people in the adopted city of her last two decades
really did care about her. But I already knew that.
-- But then I also knew, or thought I did, that Lady U
really -- no. Drop that. No bitterness! No self-pity!
-- Or at least keep fighting the good fight.)

This canteen seat commands an almost unobstructed
180-degree view ahead and at the center of it right now
stands the massively familiar cluster of downtown
skyscrapers, cloaked today in a pink-tinged haze. My
new home in the slow zoom. "New." Ha! (In today's
paper a story about the improving downtown real-estate
market predicts rents will rise ten percent this year.
And this story could all by itself make it happen almost

immediately, meaning the rent for a one-room office, if
any are available at all, could increase by ten or
fifteen bucks a month. If only I'd thought of asking
for the bequest advance a few weeks earlier....)
     -- And I hauled out the original, unexpurgated
typescript of "Jyzeburst" and that's another source of
sorrow. It didn't read as well as I'd hoped it would.
-- Or actually it was the opening month of last year's
"Jyzemelt" annal that disappointed the most. Too glib.
Too choppy. Too strained (in places). Not a total
disaster but far from the triumph I'd been hoping for.
     Even so the plan remains the same. If time
permits, tonight I'll start typing up the fifth entry
from last year. That's the one in which the news of
Mother's terminal diagnosis comes down.

                         *   *

     Just to be predictable: concluding now at a
certain blue table in a certain basement cafe with a
certain very fine bookstore upstairs, "the only real,"
also known in jyzeworld as the ORB. On the way here I
did do a quick loop through a newly revamped bar/
restaurant and found it inviting -- and with plenty of
empty booths and tables at five p.m. -- but no, I
thought, better to hold places like that in reserve a
while longer. Wait until I'm actually a resident down
here in one way or another, office or apartment or
maybe both. Or at the very least wait until I'm in a
better jyzing mood.
     How long to wait. Could be I'll have an office
rented by the end of next week, meaning another utterly-
at-loose-ends entry lies ahead (or utterly-at-tight
ends, as in leashed and despairing and helpless to do
anything about it). Or maybe two more, but I think
that's the outer limit. Then the transfer will be
underway. (True, I've already said it was underway as
of the moment I rented the storage unit almost two
months ago. So call this phase two of the transfer.
And I acknowledge several more phases will follow after
lining up an office. Finding a room to live in, for
instance. Completing the move-out. The last contact

with Lady U and her family. The initial adjustment to
living alone. The last severe pangs as involvement
begins with someone else -- maybe -- or as the period of
mourning the death of a love comes to an end, possibly
in a year or two or more. -- And maybe some surprises
lie ahead as well. Let's hope so anyway. And hope not
too many of them are the unwelcome kind.)
     Drop that line! (But is there any other I can
grab?)
     Think think.
     There's the grandmaster of all English-language
protojyzers. Finally, after a wait of maybe fifteen
years, the eleven-volume annotated "compleat works" is
coming out in paperback. The first three volumes are
here. Alas, they're sixteen bucks a pop. But could any
use of bequest money be wiser? It's all but a done deal,
the whole set. (No, there won't be other splurges like
this, or at least they'll be rare. I'm determined to
live within my means -- give it my best shot.
Subsistence-level living while the work on "Jyzer"
proceeds. No frills beyond an occasional meal out.)
     The virtuous life. Monklike devotion and
dedication. Fierce focus. And for fun: this jyze right
here. JIRT. The real stuff in real time.
     -- Just know. Just know I'll be able to do it.
Insist on it. And jyze too will come alive. This city.
This age. This life.
     Or else.
     (The elses are numerous indeed and powerful. Many
could do me in no matter how intense my struggle. But
this is not news or worth dwelling on -- except you have
to do it. Except -- when you don't. And you do
sometimes have some say in determining when you don't --
though never without cost. But of course nothing's
without cost -- except when you're very lucky.
Therefore: struggle fiercely and hope for luck. And
once in a while cease struggling and hope for no luck
just in case by a kind of judo this might do the trick.)
     And now, duty calls: let the struggle resume.

[Jyze and Jyze Alone]

3

    Blue table at the ORB cafe. It's that time again.
    I'm still suspended -- little money, no way to make
a move -- but ready to move fast when the check arrives.
    Today's news, delivered as Lady U grudgingly drove
me to the county bus stop: yes, she'll be visiting her
family "the third week in February," but with these
caveats: she won't go if they can't come up with a cheap
plane ticket for her, and she's not sure exactly what
dates "the third week" refers to. She'll know more
after talking with her mother tonight.
    This means she could be leaving somewhat earlier
than I'd been thinking -- before Marissa's visit begins
on the 20th, roughly, rather than after. Thus even more
so than before I've got my work cut out for me.
    And this item, "just in": all the way across on the
ferry this afternoon I listened to the spirited rants of
an attractive woman of Lady S's ancestry (in fact she
grew up in the same city maybe twenty years behind her).
Talk about deja vu! My new friend Nancy, who's caught
my eye a few times before on the four o'clock. Just
last night she bashed out a ten-page letter to EEO
alleging bias against her -- in her work unit at the
shipyard -- and today she filed it. Talk about stressed
out. All over again it was Lady S enraged by the plots
hatched against her at -- well, at a lot of places.
    I'm letting myself be drawn in a little bit just
for the hell of it. Why not? I need some practice in
dealing with unattached women. Can't forget I'm about
to reenter the bazaar now -- but also can't forget I
don't want any new entanglements for a good long while,

20

or at least not any serious ones (and unless I'm misreading this Nancy, serious would be the only real option with her).

Otherwise little to report except for the latest series of indignities visited upon me by Lady U herself, she of the eighteen-year entanglement currently grinding so painfully to a halt. Best not to dwell on such matters. Or just touch on one, the night of the big snowstorm when one of her current "associates" at work, Jason, drove her home in our wagon because she couldn't handle the slippery roads. I opened the kitchen door as the wagon pulled in, its driver's-side-door window steamed up so I couldn't see who was behind the wheel, but I assumed it was her. Wrong. First time I've been face-to-face with one of the guys she's now hanging out with (that's how I'll put it for now). "Well," he gulped, "I got her home safe." "Couldn't ask for more than that," I observed, not at all unkindly so far as I know. And then he came inside to use the phone -- unable to stop himself from staring at me, and looking pathetically young in his baggy skater gear and ball cap worn backwards -- and I nodded toward the basement and said, "It's down there," meaning the phone.

End of dialogue. The lady never even bothered to introduce him. "I thought you wouldn't want me to," she explained later with extreme nonchalance when I asked why.

Talk about being dissed. One diss after another. Two nights after that she went out somewhere with another of these guys and upon their return at two a.m. they sat in the wagon yakking away for an hour right outside the kitchen window. Yike! How dare she!

But I'm not complaining. Just biding my time. Nothing else I can do.

*

-- Went off for a coffee refill and heard a familiar voice coming from the next-door room where readings are given. Took me a moment to recognize it was the president himself, ours, this country's, his State of the Union address booming out live on the P.A.

Currently he's locked in a tense battle with the
reactionary new congress over balancing the budget and,
more fundamentally, over "control of the nation's
agenda." For the moment he seems to be prevailing.
More power to him, sez I -- but where will it come from?
     Never mind. Jyze. Turn away from the political
stuff -- for now. In the current era there's little one
can say about the center-right clash that's not yawn-
inducing. To myself in the saying of it most of all.
     A few more indignities I might as well touch on.
How about the new CD player Lady U bought for a hundred
bucks and hid in her closet? How about the bare-faced
lie she told me about how much she's got in her bank
account? How about the photos of herself goofing around
suggestively with "the guys" at the New Year's party to
which I wasn't even invited? (Worst of all, how about
the need I feel to sneak around when she's out so I can
check up on this sorry stuff? For if I don't, now that
I know she's deceiving me about any number of things,
how will I keep her from jerking me around even more?)
     Ugly ugly ugly. I hate it. Feeling reduced and
traduced like this. Burned. Chumpified. Helpless --
and that's the worst part. If I could've skipped out
several months ago we'd both be much better off by now.
     Which reminds me: tomorrow it'll be two months to
the day since Mother's death. In a way maybe it's good
that this fiasco with Lady U is keeping me from focusing
too much on the death, but more likely it's bad: because
I'd like to focus on it more and probably need to. And
can't. Being unable to is another kind of indignity.
     My intention, again, was to mention nothing about
any of this in these pages. It's sad, it's downright
disgusting that I can't stop myself. But this is how it
is. (I'd thought I would try to look at underlying
causes. Forget about what's happened the past year.
Anybody's likely to behave badly during a breakup. Lord
knows I've done it myself. From Lady S's point of view,
as an example, my actions at numerous points during our
two major breakups must've looked a lot like Lady U's
have to me. But if I could delve more deeply into my

history with Lady U maybe I could transcend the blame issue. How and why did we fail? Of course it was my doing as much as hers and on neither side was there intent to fail -- of course! But how did the relationship get so hollowed out the way it did? All of a sudden last summer she broke; she could no longer keep up the facade. Yet under different circumstances the one who broke might just as easily have been me. Except -- I'd vowed all along I wouldn't. I'm older, more experienced; it's more in my interest to hang in there even during the very bad times. For me finding a new gig anywhere near as good overall would likely be much harder. -- And so on. And enough of that. Where did this digression into the really sore stuff start anyway? -- Premature for sure, even as mere digression.)

So what do I do with myself these days? If I'm not working in the city I get up shortly before four p.m. (roughly an hour and a half after the lady leaves for work), I rustle up some breakfast and dawdle over coffee until six or so while reading in my brown armchair in the parlor (classic rock on the radio because during these hours the jazz station goes to repetitious public-radio news and I can no longer stand listening to "The End," the alternative-music station which the lady now plays constantly), and then I get to work on clipping pages relevant to the fictojyze from my huge stack of Mentoka newspapers (I figure all the stacks, including magazines, piled atop each other would be about fifteen feet high) -- and so far I'm about a fifth of the way through and the stack is shrinking by about three-quarters as I cull it -- and so the project is achieving its purpose. But I need to speed it up. Three weeks to go and many other things to do.

At eleven I stop clipping, tend to the chores, fix and eat dinner, retire to jyze central in the basement. There I read for an hour or two, then sleep until eight or nine a.m. (on the couch, beneath an unzipped sleeping bag with my feet wrapped in an old winter coat). Then after picking up the mail at the post office I head out to the shed and work on the packing and dismantling for

a couple of hours, unless I have to go in to the city
that afternoon, in which case I pack a lunch and hit the
rack early (in our upstairs bedroom, which the lady
usually vacates about half past nine) so I can rise
before one p.m. to shower and shave in time for her to
drop me off at the bus stop on her way to work.
     What a life. Love it.
     And at the office I use any spare minutes to type
up last year's jyze. In the past week I've pounded out
about twenty single-spaced pages. I'm still learning
the new word-processing program and this slows me down a
lot. And my right shoulder and left wrist are aching
because the workstation's not really set up for long-
distance typing -- as opposed to scoping -- and I have
to go at it in an awkward position. (And I'm realizing
that what I thought was purely a weed-whacking injury to
my right elbow may be partly computer-related, because
extensive keyboard work causes it to act up.)
     But the preparations for moving -- what a nightmare!
They literally keep me awake "at night," meaning during
those oddly scattered clusters of hours when I should be
sleeping. What am I forgetting? In what order should
things be done? What will go where? What items will
the lady and I both want to keep, and when it's time to
parcel them out, how can I minimize the friction without
giving up more than my rightful share? (Not to mention:
how can I get the things I want? How can I make her
feel some pain? Lots of pain? Just the right amount of
pain? -- But no, how can I overcome my stupid urge to
exact revenge? -- For in the long run it's not in my
interest anyway, and besides, who wants more ugly scenes?
Why not try to salvage a little dignity for both of us
by at least handling these matters civilly and fairly?
Why not indeed -- other than the urgings of bedrock
human nature. -- Or wait, no, I don't believe that
either. Or only partly and in a nonessentialist sense,
I'll say.)
     So lots of interesting moments ahead. No doubt.
(I did mean to mention too, concerning the nightmare,
that I wasted hours searching for the large portfolio

containing Lady V's and Lady S's paintings before
finally locating it moldering away behind a couple of
sheets of plywood up in the barn where Lady U had
stashed it without telling me and then entirely spaced
out the fact that she'd done so -- and this sort of
thing is happening way too often. Almost two decades'
worth of detritus, not to mention the leftovers from
previous eras we both brought into the relationship (me
especially), and for the past six years the lady's been
squirreling this stuff away while I've mostly been off
bringing in the bacon, and she's shifted and reshifted
the location of things until she herself has forgotten
where many of them are; and besides she can't be
bothered to think about such prosaic matters at this
time of high social excitement for her, and even if she
could I wouldn't want to be pestering her with
questions and setting off alarms.)
      I'm thinking now I'll say something to her just
before she leaves on her trip. "Since I'll have the
wagon to myself while you're gone I might start looking
around for a place of my own." Something like that.
Casual, offhand, as if I'm not too serious. This way at
least she won't be totally shocked when she returns and
finds the house half empty. Or a quarter empty anyway.
(And I could say then, "Well, didn't you tell me you
wanted the place in tiptop shape for Marissa's visit?")
      -- When Nancy came up on the ferry I was looking
through one of last year's J-books. She was interested
-- fascinated even. (Especially when she learned I was
"an educated person," not like "those foolish people"
tormenting her at work; and what's more I'd taught
college English for a year in her ancestral land and
could possibly prove useful, as she bluntly said, for
clearing up any mangled language in her future EEO
complaints.) But she wanted to know, why a pen with
such a broad point? It was so wide, it was almost like
an ink brush for calligraphy. -- Precisely! I cried.
"You got it! You knew! First one who ever did!"
      (How self-conscious was she? First she apologized
because her teeth were "dirty." Then she pulled out a

toothbrush from her backpack and, shielding her mouth
with one hand, brushed away. -- And she mentioned she'd
seen me on the ferry several times before, including
once last month when I was sitting in a booth across
from a shipyard couple who were making out like crazy,
and she said she found that kind of public behavior
disgusting and was sure it meant they didn't do any of
"that" at home because people who act that way in public
never do -- and she went on to fill me in on the sorry
histories of both members of the couple, who worked in
her unit at the shipyard and, as it happened, were among
those she was filing the EEO complaint against. -- But
I liked her anyway, Nancy, and was reminded quite a bit,
in both looks and accent, of Kyongae L. from that same
overseas stay. -- And I may never have mentioned this
before in jyze but over the years I've often thought
about Kyongae and missed her a lot and even wondered if
I might've been better off taking up more seriously with
her -- a true jyzer in spirit, at least potentially, if
ever there was one. -- And I suppose now it's more or
less inevitable I'll be swarmed by this kind of
regretful memory, self-deluded or not, and featuring
certain others probably even more than Kyongae.)

   (But this Nancy is divorced and apparently living
alone. Both of her kids are off studying at distant
universities, one pursuing an MBA and intending to go to
law school after that -- just like my father although in
reverse order, as I told her. Nancy herself has a
master's, or at least she hinted she does. Went to
college in the old country. And she asked for my phone
number at work in case she needs language help on the
complaint and I gave it to her and I wouldn't be at all
surprised if she called. And I said I'd be on the boat
again Thursday if she wanted to show me another letter
she'd mentioned she's working on. I even invited her to
have a cup of coffee with me right here, the ORB cafe,
rather than stand in the rain on a sidewalk near the
ferry dock rattling on about her EEO case as we were
doing. But she said no, she was tired and a big sinkful
of unwashed dishes awaited her at home; she'd see me on

the ferry on Thursday. But if only we'd met one day
earlier, she pouted, I was just the person who could've
helped fix up that ten-page complaint. How unlucky she
was! And then of course I had to insist that no, I was
the unlucky one not to have met her earlier. And back
and forth on who was the unluckier until finally we
broke through to a kind of parity and said goodbye.)

     Well, but see, I can't resist, it's just such a
trip to have a new character pop up in these pages and
take my mind off Lady U (about whom this Nancy as yet
knows nothing -- but only because she hasn't asked about
that sort of thing). So I can say some life may still
be left in the old boy. (Mother would've said it that
way. That's her phrase, often used playfully to refer
to Dad. This may be the first time I've ever used it
myself, and especially for myself.)

     Ups and downs. Ifs. Dangers. Desires. Alarms.
Anti-alarm alarms.

     It's back into this again. Whooee! And I'm not
even half packed yet!

4

     Wotta god-awful screecher. I've stumbled in on the
one-year anniversary of the artiest bar in town. Solo
female guitar-picker/vocalist. Back here eyebrows are
rising, eyeballs rolling, tongues sticking out -- and
not just mine. Others even more than mine.

     My new life. I might not like every last thing
about this place but it will definitely be part of the
circuit.

     And it's icy out there. Slippery as hell. You
gotta watch every step. Especially hiking the two miles

between home and bus stop, which I've done three times
in the past twenty-eight hours. Trade-offs: the road
shoulders are frozen and offer better footing -- unless
you step on one of the many frozen puddles, most of
which still lie hidden beneath snow. Since last
Saturday a hard freeze. I even dug out my old bicycle
gloves. And this morning watched an eagle banking,
swooping, gliding, diving -- first baldie I've seen this
year. Out over the lagoon. "And like a thunderbolt --
he FALLS."

The new life. I've gone around a couple more bends
since last jyzetime. The very next day an outburst from
Lady U as she dropped me off at the bus stop. For no
particular reason I had chosen this moment to broach the
matter of my investment in the wagon. If she wants to
keep the thing she'll need to pay off my share;
otherwise we'll have to sell it. Maybe she'll want to
talk with her father about this when she goes home in a
couple of weeks? (If she does go.) Explosion. She
doesn't like being reminded of unsavory breakup details.
But -- somewhere in there she did use the phrase "when
you find a place of your own." And also "we'll both be
living in poverty." These were her first direct
acknowledgments that a separation is more or less
imminent.

(And today vivid churning dreams about loving and
trying to repair things with -- Lady V. Frequently
she's popping up in dreamland these days. Not just as
a surrogate, I think. Back I go into a life in which
I'm engaging with, yes, emotions. Turbulent kind.
Knowing better how to detach myself -- maybe. In any
case my long and highly unexpected experiment with
extreme self-sacrificial loving is over.)

The second of the bends-inducing events, arrival on
Saturday of a letter from sister Barb informing me of
the details of the distribution of Mother's estate and
containing the advance check for five K. "Hope this
puts a grin on your face," she concluded in an otherwise
wholly businesslike communication. And a grin did
indeed appear. Out of the brier patch at last! (True,

today a note came in from my bank here placing a hold on
the funds until February 5. They're no doubt, and for
good reason, wondering what the heck's going on -- a
deposit this big in an account like mine with a history
so checkered. But no problem. I'm on my way now. I
can be patient a bit longer. In fact I have to be; my
getaway scheme requires it.) (And this is payday anyway,
end of the month, and I rushed up to the office to pick
up the check for Jyzer Ink since with the five K on hold
I'm practically broke -- and discovered I've run out of
deposit slips. So delays, delays.)

Saturday also the big storm, which itself was
delayed -- day after day, like living under a perpetual
tornado watch -- and then the freeze. Tall slices of
snow still riding even very skinny tree limbs five days
later with few signs of melting anywhere. (And yet on
Super Bowl Sunday I somehow managed to deliver another
big wagonload into storage. Space there now is running
so short I'm planning to build a platform in the high-
ceiling area at the back this coming weekend or next.)

Dreams: one shattered. No office in the best of
the historic-quarter buildings. Only two-roomers are
available and the rents in that building are too high
regardless, by half or more. This was my first call
seeking new space of any kind. But other buildings in
the area may still offer single rooms cheap enough for
my budget. An ad ran in the weeklies again, $115 and up
for unnamed "historic buildings." So far I haven't been
able to get through on it. Tomorrow I'll try again.

And circling ads for rooms, lofts, shared living
arrangements, apartments. Anything for $350 or under,
and out of the hundreds on offer overall, only about a
dozen qualified. A co-op just north of downtown: I'll
look into it. So far nothing in the equivalent turf
south of downtown, but I've only just begun the search.
(A basement apartment far to the north, about seven
miles, is tempting except I want to be within easy
walking distance of downtown. Seemingly I must choose:
either go for isolation and intense focus or embed
myself in a social situation, living with like-minded

people if possible. The frustrations of warding off
loneliness. And me what a couple of ads referred to as
"mature" now, I guess, meaning I'm no longer a kid. Do
I want to be around "less matures," not even to consider
"immatures"? And how about "anti-matures"?)

     Shipyard Nancy of the conspiratorial mind I still
haven't seen again. She wasn't aboard the Thursday four
o'clock as she'd said she'd be and I haven't been on a
four o'clock myself since then. Nor has she called,
apparently, or at least no message has made it to the
board at the office (dayscoper Amy may've, in fact given
the opportunity almost certainly would've, just blown it
off anyway). Unfortunately -- or maybe fortunately -- I
have no way to reach Nancy to see what's up with her.
If she's strongly interested I suppose I'll find out
eventually. So deal with it then.

     I've always tended not to look before leaping. Is
it too late to change my ways now? And me in no sense
prepared for the deep rebound?

     Then there's Rikki. She wrote too, and with
sincere apologies for the long delay. Nothing
flirtatious or aggressive or anything like that, except
for a promise to come visit me up here if it looks as
though I won't be getting down their way anytime soon.
(Mischa had predicted they wouldn't be seeing me again;
this letter implied any visit up here would be mainly
for his benefit.) And was it true, Rikki asked, that
I'd be moving soon, as she'd heard, presumably from Barb
but maybe from Jim Q. (who'd just taken Mischa to a
movie)?

     Don't know what to do about this either. What's
Rikki's situation with her seemingly absconded partner?
Do I want to be raising hopes which would likely turn
out to be false? What do I really want regarding love
and romance? When will I know? How will I know? And
how much should what I want matter anyway?

     These recent dreams, they've been about emotional
depths. What I had with Lady V, fierce engagement all
the way down. Enough, they've seemed to be saying, of
careful loving superficialities. To me this means my

unconscious must be listening to what I'm saying to myself anyway. But -- why would it want to do that?

(Also I'm moved to think about matters like these by the glum ponderings of a certain lit critic. In the long run we're all dead, as he authoritatively points out, and for that reason the traditional tragic view, agon and all, is the only way to go, so to speak. But what about temperament, I ask? What about emotions and "affect"? Why should the "long view" matter so much at the individual level? Emotionally it's beyond our ken anyway. Middle runs are the limit -- say twenty or thirty years -- and most people can legitimately (though of course not necessarily realistically) hope to live at least that much longer, even eighty- and ninety-year-olds. Why don't the heavy thinkers ever consider this? (As far as I know none do.))

Death. Art. Sex. Some woman who looks like a taller and more robust Rikki keeps charging over here to warn me I'm risking blindness by going at the jyze in this bad light. We're flirting, it seems. Or is that just my imagination? The hard part of this sort of thing, I'm creakily remembering, is estimating just what you can realistically hope for in finding and winning over a potential new lover or mate or partner. Snap decisions are required. Is this one a genuine contender? How far could it go, if any distance at all, and what would the pain quotient be for failure at any point along the line, and how would it be apportioned?

Oh yeah. Saloons. As far as I can see they don't really change a whole lot. This one I like mainly because of the gimmick it's trying to make it on, its flagrant artiness, as well as the crucial fact that the staff seem to have a sense of humor about it. A sassy transgender bartender. Style. And styling by my table right now, a dude in bizarre checkered pants, suspenders, a homburg with its brim rakishly turned down, and a twirled black half mustache painted above the left side of his lips but nothing above the right side. Decadence, flamboyance. Colorful canvases adorning the walls, original stuff, hip-hop scenes, certainly worth a second look. At least at a joint like this not everything's predictable.

Ugh. Think my spring has sprung. -- Not much to do at the office so I'll head on up and do what there is real quick and then type up some more of the old jyze, last year's, for a while.

*   *

For the first time ever deploying backup J-stick No. 6. This is because both the first-stringer, No. 5, and the second-stringer, No. 4, are clipped into the pocket of my workshirt, and that's locked in the bedroom upstairs where the lady is sleeping. Not for another hour is she due to awaken.

-- Which I've just done myself. Awakened. Feeling as groggy and loggy as the nib on this No. 6 is feeling (to me) stiff and unfamiliar.

But this is jyze central. And it's "bone-chillingly" cold out there, just as the grooveyard DJ was warning. Yowling for attention in the next room is Vinnie the semi-feral black cat: again we're letting him in at night for fear of what the cold would do to him. (Really now it's not all that cold here -- "mercury in the high teens." But elsewhere in the country records are shattering. Thirty to forty below in the Mentoka zone, with wind chill in the minus seventies.)

And I'm awaiting a call. Two calls in fact. One from Adam P., the realtor advertising generic offices in the historic quarter for $115. The other from Brad N., at the co-op I mentioned earlier, so we can set up an appointment for a grand tour of the place, hopefully on Sunday.

This co-op sounds good. I'm pumped. A group of local artists started it twelve years ago; they bought the top two floors of a three-story building a couple of blocks from the waterfront (and just ten blocks or so from my scope office) and converted them from old-style single-room-occupancy (SRO) hotel rooms to a series of studiolike living spaces. Brad (who kept yawning comically in the middle of sentences as we talked) said artists still make up most of the membership and they

range in age from twenties through fifties. The co-op
duties aren't too arduous, he assured me, citing his own
for this week as an example: answering calls like mine
about the ad. One chore a week that usually takes about
half an hour, monthly membership meetings, sitting on
the board one year of every three.

The next step is filling out a written application.
After that, if you survive the cut based on your answers
(and some of the questions call for what amount to short
essays), a live audition of sorts follows with a group
of co-op members. "Compatibility check." If you pass
that, you're in. Then you wait for a space to open up.
And at least one will become available later this month.
So far, Brad said, response to the ad hasn't been too
brisk, meaning my chances of landing a spot right away,
should I clear both hurdles, would be pretty good.

The more I think about it the more I like it. The
location is ideal. The communal aspects of co-op living
(including shared bathrooms and kitchens) don't bother
me too much, at least in theory, as long as the time
demands aren't excessive. Living with a rowdy gang of
artists could turn out to be a real plus. And at the
same time, a small office in the historic quarter would
provide a realm of privacy where I could focus on my own
work, and no one else at the co-op would even have to
know about it; and the office would have no phone or fax
or internet connection or anything like that.

It's still mainly a dream, sure. Lots of things
could go wrong. But just to have the possibility of
this working out means a lot.

(The co-op charges an up-front membership fee of
about sixteen hundred bucks which is refundable when you
leave, although it wouldn't accrue any interest while it
sat there. In years past coming up with a sum this
large would've presented a formidable obstacle for me.
This year, as of next Monday when the funds go off hold,
I can manage it. -- And thank you again, good ol' Mom.
How fine a legacy you laid on me!)

Yesterday I drove over to the bank to deposit my
paycheck, and since I was near the ministorage place I

took the opportunity to buy forty bucks' worth of lumber
for construction of a platform in unit 161. Had to
"poke along," literally, with ten-foot studs sticking
out both ends of the wagon -- front passenger window and
back hatch -- but only two blocks. No one got impaled.

Mama U called last night, so I should be learning
soon when her rascally daughter will be leaving for home.
Presumably it will still be around the 15th or 20th. By
then will I have at least one place in the city where I
can start delivering my stuff? I'm hoping so. If I'm
lucky I might have two. In any case the search for a
new living setup now assumes top priority.

What else? Out there in the big bad world we've
had the president announcing in his State of the Union
address, as I learned afterward from the news, that "the
era of big government is over." (No big-think comment
from me now on such an absurd statement. Some other
time maybe.) And -- not much else of note.

So back to the small bad world. Except in at least
one way it's not so bad after all.

To wit: my share of the estate turned out to be a
little less than I'd been expecting for the past two
months but still considerably more than Mother's
original estimate. It's $72,000, with a thousand or
two, maybe three, still to come when contingency
accounts can be released. (A year ago Mother was saying
$50,000 to $60,000. Then the market took off.) I'll be
investing $67,600 of this and deriving a monthly income
of $275 from the proceeds. This will pay for the
ministorage and the hideaway office (if I can ever find
one) with about $75 left over to apply to living-space
rent. I'll need a minimum net of, say, $500 a month
from Jyzer Ink nightscoping to be able to scrape by. On
average this certainly should be doable, and I'll set
aside the remainder of the $5,000 I just received --
maybe $2,000 or so -- as a contingency "cushion" to meet
the occasional shortfall.

Okay. That's it, the plan. I'm pleased with it.
Now to see if I can make it work.

[The Jyze Moves]

5

    Close up through the glass at dusk I see the bare
tree limbs of the triangle (at the heart of the historic
quarter) sinuously framing ranks of lighted highrise
geometrical shapes arrayed against a patch of indigo
sky. To the near side of these shapes, just across the
street, dark except for a few scattered windows, stands
a magnificent six-story granite-and-terracotta edifice
whose western facade forms part of the border of the
triangle (with its celebrated cobblestones and totem
pole and historic statues and iron-and-glass pergola,
which is a kind of glorified old-timey bus shelter).
This edifice is the very one where I'd originally hoped
to rent an office -- and now have done so!
    A lucky break and part of an unlikely chain of
events. (As the latte line inches ahead a few feet
behind me and heavy rush-hour traffic sizzles by outside
in the rain. And now a red-and-white aid van rolls to a
stop in the bus zone out there and its blinkers flash on
-- an emergency so the crew can hustle in here, it
turns out, and go mouth-to-mouth with some java. And I
notice my soggy backpack is the source of a little creek
emerging from under my stool. Uncomfortable low-backed
high stool. Narrow windowside speckled counter, looks
like formica. First time I've ever even tried sitting
inside one of these downtown franchise coffee shops.)
    A map of the quarter is on conspicuous display next
to my "venti" cup of drip coffee in hopes the staff will
think I'm a jyzing tourist rather than a fake-jyzing
vagrant looking for shelter. (Acknowledging the virtual
certainty they've not yet heard about jyze per se.)

35

[Jyze and Jyze Alone]

     Shining at street level, through tree trunks and
pergola columns, are the colorful neon lights of
nightclubs whose live music I expect to be able to hear
up in my new office. Shards and glints of those colors
(mostly from beer signs) reflect festively on wet
surfaces -- and all surfaces are wet now after ten
straight days of rain. Floods everywhere, including on
the street in front of our house way the hell over
yonder in the boonies. The main creek there is doing
credible imitations of raging mountain-wilderness rapids
and appears ready to take out four or five of the town
bridges (but even if they all go we'll still be able to
get in and out via the uphill church loop). In several
river towns to the south large logs, from collapsing
docks, have transformed into floating battering rams in
downtown streets. I mean this is serious stuff.
     And this also is serious, at least for me: a
deposit is down on the office. It becomes available
next Wednesday. Fourth floor, a carpeted nine-by-nine
cubicle, a small window to the outside up high and a
larger window up even higher offering secondhand
daylight from the triangle here via the windows of the
next-door office. 430A is my "suite" number. I may
even be able to sleep in there without too much hassle
should the need arise, using the same sort of "magic
carpet" style I now employ at the scope office.
     We don't officially sign the lease until next week.
Something could still go wrong. But I'm guessing
nothing will.
     How'd this happen? Lots to explain. First and
foremost and maybe best of all, everything's now out in
the open with Lady U. Well, not everything. In fact
far from everything, and especially, I'm sure, on her
side. But I decided to reveal my intention to apply for
membership at the co-op and to move out soon, possibly
even later this month. No sour grapes, no vengefulness
of any kind. And when she responded civilly I pressed
ahead and began talking about ways to divvy up our
meager "community" possessions, and this time she was
much more reasonable even on the matter of the wagon.

(Presumably she realized if she wants me out soon, as
she surely does, she'll have to return at least half my
investment in the wagon -- or so I've been implying, and
she's going for it. As indeed she should be doing
anyway just out of compassion and fairness and with no
prodding necessary, for example by reminding her that my
lingering at the house might seriously cramp her style.)
    We went all the way down the property list. Even
enjoyed doing so. No big hang-ups -- at least not yet.
Trade-offs! We're both getting most of the things we
want and/or need.
    This was just this past Monday. (She even cut back
on her aerobics so we could do the distribution deed as
completely as possible. She also agreed to provide a
good reference to the co-op or any other outfit or
landlord who might want one. And she seemed to
appreciate my suggestion that we present a united front
to her parents, telling them we're separating by mutual
consent. She'll be informing them of this when she goes
home next week.) -- But it broke up a logjam, yes. I
never did get a response from Adam P., the realtor,
about the generic $115 offices, but now, knowing I'd
have an additional three or four thousand dollars from
return of the wagon investment (half), I figured I could
justify looking into the next-best ad for office space
in that same area. Its list started at $165 a month,
fifty bucks higher. The wagon money, as I saw it, would
pay that extra fifty for a period of up to seven years.
    Oddly enough, the "next-best ad" turned out to be a
second realtor offering space in the same building which
had been my previous first choice. And unlike the one I
called last week, this one, a guy named Trevor, had a
"suite" about to open up. He stayed late the next day
to show it to me, I pulled out a tape measure and tried
to act like a bona-fide small businessman, and within
ten minutes the deal was cut (though, again, it's not
yet signed). And I like the interior of the building a
lot. -- But later for more on that. Or next time,
when, if all goes well, I'll be viewing it up close.
    Meantime I'm moving ahead on the co-op. A big

chunk of Tuesday night went to working up detailed answers to the key application questions. I've visited the place twice and I'm keenly hoping I'll be accepted there. It's just what I want. (And I'll try to say more about why later -- because soon I must be hiking up to the scope office where we're in the midst of an unusually heavy workweek.) Unfortunately the two other serious applicants at the co-op have friends who're members and one of the two even lived there for a while last year as a "subtenant." Yet I still have a shot, Brad told me, because I offer some qualities which the co-op needs right now (such as experience with city politics through journalism). The "compatibility check," in which applicants answer still more questions but this time in person for thirty minutes before a full co-op membership meeting, is this coming Sunday. I'm trying to gear up for it. Group auditions I've never done well at. Nerves. Tendency to freeze up -- stumble and mumble.

  -- And this disturbing news. The bill for publishing "Memorials" will be much higher than Suzanne at the publishing house had been telling us. By a factor of about a hundred and fifty percent! "Paper costs have been skyrocketing." I'm wrestling with it: put up a stink or not? The cost to me would be an additional five hundred or so, and the same for Rob, and Barb would have to approve as executrix before Mother's equal portion could be allotted from a contingency fund. Whichever way we go, dealings lie ahead which I don't at all relish. (Aunt Shar I won't even ask to contribute anything more; I'm too embarrassed by the many delays. And besides, we all agreed from the start that her limit would be a thousand.)

  -- But have no dread, Mr. Jyzer G. It's the new regime. A chance to be more active. Get away from the extreme isolation entailed by life with Lady U. (And she even had the gall to chitchat for more than an hour in the "parlor" with one of her new inamoratos as I lay in bed ten feet up the hall trying to rack up some badly needed sleep. "I couldn't help it!" she explained later. "He came early!" -- Then was out with him until past

four a.m. Well, I just hope she's getting something
good out of all this. I fear it'll backfire terribly on
her before long. But she's probably seeing it as her
last chance to score big out there in the unlimited
competition before moving on to master class. Which is
where I already am, no question, and have been for a
while, though I was scarcely even aware of it until very
recently. -- Or call it joker class, right.)

Reminding me: two more days in a row, including
today, I've listened to shipyard Nancy's near-maniacal
rants on the ferry. As she rattles on I think mostly
about the way her looks and mannerisms remind me of
certain friends of Lady S -- and once in a while, but
less and less often now, of Lady S herself. And Nancy
is a year or two older than I am, it turns out, though
she could easily pass for half her age. Astounding --
but it's much the same with Lady U. What age is she
going by with the twenty-year-old Jason, I wonder?

-- But yup, there it is across the triangle, the
likely new home of Jyzer Ink. Tastefully floodlit now
along the side street as well as in front. Looking as
historic as it truly is, which for this city is about as
historic as buildings that large can get. Or rather: do
get. It stands exactly where the city began, it turns
out, the site of the original timber mill. And it went
up just over a century ago shortly after the great fire
which leveled most of the original downtown.

(Now a couple of drifters are gesturing to me right
outside the glass. Buy them cigarettes? Coffee? Long
black hair, tough-looking dudes, quite possibly members
of the tribe from whom we Cawk invaders expropriated all
this land more or less at gunpoint a few decades before
that building over there went up. Or if not that tribe,
some other one with much the same story. But sorry
fellas, can't do it. Not a prayer. -- And just last
weekend a nasty murder under the viaduct a block down
the road from here, it's still making headlines. But
nowhere near as big as those inspired by the announced
departure of the pro football team from the domed
stadium which stands four or five blocks to the south --

they're bound for a sweeter deal in another city.
Deafening shrieks of pain and rage rock the metropolis.)
     Yipe. Late.

                    *   *

     Hard to keep up with all the changes. Another big
one's come down in the twenty-four hours since last
jyze. What's it mean? Won't know for a while. Could
be very bad news but maybe not.
     First, though, the symmetry. Structural. Another
coffee shop in the city, neobeat storefront "bar" type
this time, and I've again staked out a window table
(it's round, the tabletop, steel, the size and look of a
manhole cover) and to my right, peering through the "O"
of the shop's sign (it's the middle letter of three
suspended vertically in the window, red neon tubing with
metal backing, and I'd say the tabletop would fit snugly
over the "O", capping it) -- through that as yet
uncapped "O" I see, directly across the street, late in
the dinner hour, with no rain or glints or glimmers in
sight, but even so not a lumen less dazzling to my eyes,
the building which houses the co-op I'm hoping to join.
Three stories. A light shining in the co-op entrance to
the left at street level, with the darkened show windows
of an ultra-mod furniture store taking up the rest of
the ground floor. And directly above that store's
marquee, the twin windows of the room that would be mine
if I could figure out some way to ace Sunday's audition.
To emerge victorious. To crush the other contenders
(and thus, to be sure, be about as cooperatively, or co-
opily, incorrect as one could be, one would think).
     It's not likely to happen, so I'm trying to squeeze
what I can out of the place while hope still lives.
Ride that high before it goes phzzzzzzzzzz.
     But wait. The potentially bad news, blurt it out
and shove it aside. The firm that employs me -- through
which, I should say, I contract the services of Jyzer
Ink (their vendor 273) -- is shutting down. Selling out
to another firm. At this point it's not clear what J.
Ink's one and only active client at the firm (or
anywhere else), reporter Naomi, will be doing. Will she

still be taking grand jury? Will the old firm's
contract with the feds carry over to the new firm? Will
the new firm allow reporters to work with outside
scopers on independent "contracts" such as Naomi's with
J. Ink? If so will the page rates stay the same? As
yet no answers on any of these matters. But it'll all
have to be shaking out soon because the official date of
transfer is April 1st, only about six weeks away.

Another long-term alliance bites the dust. Sixteen
years this fall. But no tears or howls of pain over
this one. It went dead long ago. Even with Naomi,
pretty much. It's just business, or at least mostly.
(Or go ahead and say this gig too has hollowed out.)

So maybe I'll soon be looking for a job. At this
point I can't do much more than shrug helplessly. I'll
just have to find some way to keep going. (But it sure
does help to know the "deep reserves" -- Mother's legacy
-- are there if all else fails. This very afternoon the
official word came in from Lynn: they've got the dough.
If worse came to worst I figure I could live on that
money for ten years -- unless something even worse than
"worst" happened and, say, the stock market imploded.
And today it hit another all-time high. You can't help
but wonder if the months before Black Friday didn't feel
a lot like these recent ones. -- But better not be
thinking about such things. Think instead about a book
I've been reading on writing and aesthetics. -- Or
first, the co-op story.) (Except to say this book's
inspired me to reconceptualize the whole Mentoka series.
A bolder approach. May help get it off the dime.)

Brad at the co-op (the yawner dude) kept failing to
return my calls. He also failed to leave a promised
note on the door over there (glance across the street
right now; it's glass, the door, and you can see the
bank of co-op mailboxes inside it at the foot of the
stairs). So I just stood around outside that very door
until someone came out, and it was a member, Phil, short
stocky gray-bearded fellow, very friendly, and he kindly
went way beyond the call of duty and gave me a quick
tour of the premises and an application to fill out.

Later I phoned Brad again and he apologized (again)
and I finally did meet up with him three days after that
and he too gave me a brief tour. Using loans from the
city designed to increase the supply of low-income
housing downtown, the co-op bought the whole building
and remodeled it. The upper two floors are laid out
just about identically, each with a single long L-shaped
hallway, rooms staggered on both sides, a lounge/kitchen
combo at both ends, four large bathrooms scattered here
and there, hallway walls and common areas bedecked with
the members' own artwork. Overall the place boasts a
surprisingly clean and bright and colorful funkiness.
Under the terms of the city loan (soon coming up for
renewal) rents are pegged to a certain percentage of the
average downtown clerical worker's salary and thus must
stay low. Also a certain percentage of residents must
be low-income, a category I'd surely fall into.

(Two guys snoring on couches in the middle of the
coffee bar here. Reminds me of the ferry. But bizarre
electronic music. Too stark and cold, this joint. I
like the big new cafe around the corner much better. A
number of smaller places similar to this one here,
though, have been prospering in this area for a decade
or more, drawing a clientele of artists and all-in-black
faux bohemians and the like. -- But a newer generation
is also in evidence. Walking over here tonight I passed
a long line of college-age kids waiting to see a hot new
alternative-rock group. "Alties." The type Lady U's
hanging with these days. Baggy and saggy pants, long
outsize T-shirts and jerseys and nose rings and tattoos
and baseball caps worn backwards and hardly a jacket or
coat in sight even on a chilly evening. Five or ten
years ago I'd've felt sorry for them because to me the
whole scene looks so dull and defeated and dead-end.
But now they're in ascendancy and -- what? They don't
deserve a little sympathy? In any event I'm even more
out of it myself now than I was five or ten years ago
and what's more I don't care that I am. So let 'em be.
That is, as long as they're willing to reciprocate. And
by and large it appears they are.)

[The Jyze Moves]

    I met several other co-op members, including the
current president, Rebecca, and an amusing dark-haired
tile artist, Sophie, who sells clocks and mirrors she
decorates by hand to scratch out a living (same thing
Lady U tried to do for a while years ago, but in her
case the tiles usually adorned wooden boxes and
flowerpots) -- walked with them to the new cafe, which
they told me has already become the main hangout for
co-op members. Liked 'em both. (what else can I say?
Better let it go for now. But these were friendly,
intelligent, physically appealing women, somewhat
younger than I but not unthinkably so, with interests
and values apparently not too far removed from my own.)
    Those twin windows up there (glance again) -- dark
now. Twelve by eighteen feet, the room. No. 201.
Through gauzy curtains it offers a view of neon lights
across the street, including of course the red three-
letter sign I'm peering through right now. Traffic.
Lots of people strolling and trolling and lurking and
larking on nearby sidewalks. It was almost the (fictive)
Hotel Kiss Mine all over again up there except -- much,
much better. A splendid wooden loft in 201. It would
be departing along with the current occupant, I was told,
but yes, I could move my own loft in -- the one
presently serving as the inner sanctum in the shed.
    Next I'll see if I can reach Phil up there. He's
been out all week, traveling, but might be back by now.
I need all the allies I can get.
    And the obsessed shipyard Nancy. Actual name: Nan-
Gi. Coffee at the ORB cafe with her. Alas, as noted
before, it might get off the ground but I doubt it would
fly for long. Best to let it go. Turns out I've likely
just been scratching a little nostalgia itch.
    Everything's moving so fast. Too much is happening
and jyze is reduced to wildly scribbling out
chronologies. Jotting telegraphic notes. And it's
exciting, this interim period. Strictly a temporary
effect, I'm sure. Not to get carried away. But to
enjoy. Don't regress. Don't stew.
    And now: Cut! Wrap!

[Jyze and Jyze Alone]

6

    The new life. Looks pretty grim at the moment but
why not relish it anyway? Why not relish it for just
that reason? Might even make for a better -- which is
to say, a jyzier -- account of itself.
    Twenty minutes ago I laid out a thirty-buck deposit
on a furnished "studio apartment" at an SRO dive I
definitely don't want to be living in for long -- in
fact, not at all. First of March, however, is move-in
day for me there. Unless, of course, something better
turns up before then -- enough so to justify kissing off
the thirty.
    Monthly rent will be a fin short of four bills.
(That's $395.) Room 317, and basically it's the last
SRO hotel I lived in nineteen years ago all over again.
Another drug-infested loony bin. It's also the one I
lived in before that, twenty years ago. But it's
cleaner than those two earlier flops and it's secure,
it's got its own "efficiency" kitchenette and bathroom
with shower, and it's got location, location, location.
As, come to think of it, those other flops did too.
    (First of the locations this one has is negative
and thus also to relish by jujitsu force of will: mean
streets. Second, though, is positive, heart of the
artsy little hood I was jyzing in last session, in fact
just two blocks from the co-op and right behind the big
new cafe I like so much. Third locational aspect, also
positive, clinching the matter, is the shortness of the
walk to work: only nine blocks. And the distance to the
public market, downtown library, fairgrounds, historic
quarter, ferry dock -- all in about the same range.)

[The Jyze Moves]

     Five p.m. Friday afternoon. At this very moment I
was supposed to be picking up the keys to the new Jyzer
Ink office. But a snag arose, and it did so just as I
was loading my desk into the wagon. A call came in from
Trevor, the building manager (not realtor), saying the
current occupant of "suite" 430A has changed his mind;
he's taking back the notice he gave last week. And yet
I already have a payment down (though not, again, a
signed lease) for that very room. Trevor therefore will
see what he can do. He thinks something "roughly
equivalent" might be opening up on the second floor.
     I'm too stunned to say much. Should I sue the
bastards? Then again I have my heart set on moving into
that building. I even met the building owner, a frail
old gent with a good deal of weathered dignity. On and
on he declaimed about how he loves the building too much
to sell it, and I absolutely believed him. Certainly I
wouldn't want to sell it if I owned it myself.
     Still, up in smoke went my plans to be fully moved
in before Lady U returns on Tuesday (she's with her
parents now). All week I've been working toward this.
All month really. And on the rebound I grab at the SRO
dive just so I'll feel a little less at loose ends.
     Finish line of the daytime workweek. At a new bar,
what used to be a pizza joint, across an alley from what
once was a cinema, in an obscure corner of the downtown
public market. Window table with a bay view, afternoon
gray and drizzly after a week of spectacularly beautiful
days making up for the previous week of massively ugly
storms (which did horrendous damage throughout the
region -- worst floods on record in many places).
-- And for me too what a week.
     At the co-op I took it on the chin. Came in second
behind the guy who'd lived there last year. Nothing to
be too ashamed of in that, but nonetheless I appalled
myself with my nervous audition. Why was I so agitated?
Maybe because I've been wearing a backwoods disguise for
so long I can no longer show my true artsy self (or
truer anyway, unless I'm wrong) -- no longer show it
even to my own kind of folks. For days beforehand I was

on tenterhooks and then likewise for days afterwards as
I sweated out the verdict. Heartsick in anticipation of
what I regarded as almost certain rejection.

How good would co-op life have been for me? Maybe
real good. An antidote to my loner proclivities of
recent times. (Oddly I lost even though one of the co-
op founders had read my screed on urban ecology and told
the rest of the group, as I sat before them quivering
with gratitude, it was "one of the most important books
of my life." -- Which I'll admit doesn't say much for
her life. Evidently she's a neighborhood activist type
on the side. Probably I'd've faced some pressure to
return to some sort of civic involvement myself had I
not been rejected at the co-op's starting gate.)

Well, I'll be seeing them around, the co-oppers.
As noted before, many of them hang out at the big cafe
right behind the SRO hotel. Should be amusing. (And I
hope the tile-working Sophie is one.) -- But reapply
for the next opening, as Brad suggested when informing
me I hadn't gotten in? Not a chance. They want me,
they can come after me. No more am I gonna grovel.

-- And this wasn't even the biggest event of the
week. Lady U laid claim to that. Saturday night she
surprised me (as I sat reading in the parlor) by saying
if I still wanted to talk, now would be a good time.
After more than six months of waiting! "You said you
wanted an explanation...." Well, no, I hadn't said
that. But if she was willing to talk now, fine. So
would she mind telling me what the hell had been going
on for the past year and a half, let's say?

First off she admitted having made "a big mistake"
in being so nasty toward me for all those months. "I
see it now but I couldn't until just recently." Her new
line is that, though she also wants the breakup for her
own reasons, she's doing it mainly for my sake. "I felt
I was just getting in your way."

Some truth in this, I suppose, though I doubt her
real motivation had a whole lot to do with it. In any
event a sad talk. More than five hours of it, and
almost all focusing on her concerns. What should she do

with her life. Her idea for making CD holders. Her
belief that her job's in jeopardy because the camera
factory may soon shut down. With the money from the
sale of our house (really her parents' house, but
through them, in effect, as she doesn't fail to remind
me, hers) -- with that money she'll buy a condo, most
likely, maybe in one of the nearby harbor towns to the
south, maybe in the city. And she hopes the two of us
can stay in touch. So she says. (I sensed some doubts
but I don't think she's really regretting her decision
to move on. Mostly I think she finally got around to
noticing I'm trying hard not to be hostile toward her
and she's realized that an amicable parting would be
better for all concerned, including her family. She may
even have recognized that in certain practical respects
I could still be quite useful to her.)
     She insists she has no romantic interest at the
camera factory and never did. Or anywhere else. It's
more a mothering kind of thing -- "maybe because I can't
have kids of my own." If any of her new "buds" were in
love with her, she went on, it wouldn't be who I think
-- it would be her girlfriend Patrice, who's ten years
younger and has never even gone out on a date. In the
previous week she had visited the U's while on vacation
and called from their family home and sent a postcard
enclosed in a plain brown envelope (it came in that very
day) showing a naked young woman lying on the beach with
the comment "Looks just like you!" (It doesn't at all
except for certain generic so-called racial qualities.)
-- But more likely she's closer to asexual, as Lady U's
college pal Jo evidently was and as the lady says she
now considers herself to be, pretty much, though she
does admit she likes to be around men. ("Sex, who needs
it!" she cried. And insisted there had been none of it
with any of them. I don't think she's leveling with me
on this, but it doesn't matter a great deal just now. I
know sex has been important to her at times in the past
but lately it certainly hasn't appeared to be and in
general maybe it never has been all that much compared
with some other women I've known (especially Lady S).

[Jyze and Jyze Alone]

As could also be said of her art, except for dance
before her back injury, sex seems to be less than deeply
hooked into her emotions. But then again, this isn't to
suggest it hasn't been deeply hooked in at certain
previous times or couldn't be again -- as I think is
true of her other arts as well: painting, sketching,
maybe even theater -- though probably not tile-working.)
     Since I'd said I might well have found a new place
to live by the time of her return, she knew this Saturday
night of our talk could turn out to be our last chance
for repairing some of the damage done over these terrible
months. And I believe some was repaired. But -- most
couldn't be. Instead I was stunned all over again by the
extent of her insensitivity concerning much of what's
happened during these months. As I mentioned to her now
only in passing, when I'd needed her most she'd failed me
utterly. The dimensions of the betrayal! (My mother's
death -- about which she's still said scarcely a word.
The writing of the Mentoka series which I've had to
abandon, at least temporarily. The extended job crisis.
And going further back: my willingness to forgive her
after the Marco affair. My financial support of her
during most of the time we were together (though her
parents also helped plenty). My years of sacrifice for
her when she was seriously disabled -- basically nursing
her back to health over a period of several years. Oh
there are grounds for bitterness here, and bitterness
there is. But I'm doing the best I can to keep it to
myself and move on. And the very fact that she decided
to talk with me as she did means I must've succeeded at
least somewhat.)
     Next, though, I'll be telling her I think we need
to keep our contact to a minimum for a year or two so
some healing can occur. (Tuesday night I'll be picking
her up at the airport-shuttle stop. While visiting her
parents she's telling them of our decision to split up.
-- And I don't like the way she said she'd be explaining
it. "Things were fine as long as we saw so little of
each other." The usual nonsense. Fibs. Lies. Why
can't she just be straightforward with her family? But

-- she can't. Nor is this anything new.)
     Reverbs. Lots ahead.
     -- This new bar, it's all right. Poetry slams
downstairs. A rack of bound scripts of well-known plays
and movies. Writer-friendly personnel. Candles and
bare bricks and a couch, a warm and intelligent "server"
with short platinum hair and a glittery silver micro
skirt, R&B music rather than alt stuff ("alt cult" is
the term I've been hearing most often lately, though
"indie" is gaining too).
*   *

     Alone in the house for a week. Right here the only
clear surface anywhere in sight on which I could spread
the J-book. It's my study desk, and even this a few
hours ago was standing on its end in the kitchen, ready
for loading in the wagon. But for the moment I'm again
stymied. Therefore back to the study with the desk so I
could clip another stack of newspapers on it. And
therefore also my fingers on both hands are blackened
with newspaper ink. "Wretched ink-stained J-slinger."
     The house is all torn up. Everything out of place.
Mounds and stacks of this, boxes and bags of that. But
whether I'll be able to do anything with it -- even a
small portion of it -- before the lady returns I won't
know until day after tomorrow and maybe not even then,
because that's Presidents Day, a holiday, and I doubt
Trevor (who's trying to line me up a new office to
replace 430A) had that fact firmly in mind when he said
he'd call Monday. Tuesday is more likely. And that's
the day the lady returns. (Unless she manages to find a
seat on a later flight. At the last moment, after her
round-trip tickets arrived, the camera company gave her
a second week off and she'd probably like to stay over
for that week too if a ticket exchange could be arranged.
Or maybe not. Maybe a week with her parents would be
about all she could stand, especially under our breakup
circumstances. They, the U's, may be plying her with a
lot more questions than she wants to be answering right
now.)
     And we've got a new twist. I'm back on tenterhooks

again. I've always wanted to try living in a co-op but
the prospect of doing so anytime soon seems dashed for
now. I've also wanted to live in an artist's loft, and
suddenly a chance for doing this has opened up. An ad
appeared in both weeklies for sharing loft space in the
historic quarter for just $290 a month. Ideal! But I
hadn't caught the ad on the first day it ran and
probably not the second either. Most likely the offer
had been snapped up right away. Yet why not check it
out. I called, and a recorded female voice said anyone
interested in the space should leave a number to call.
I didn't -- needed to think first -- but called again
half an hour later, and this time I got a live voice.
     Max (for Maxine). Three years out of art school.
Seemed game. Invited me to drop by this weekend and
check the place out. I should've asked if I could trot
over right then. Why didn't I? Dumb. I'll probably
lose out because of this gaffe. (Today I called again
and left a message saying I sure hoped she'd hold off on
making a decision until after my "tour," which is set
for tomorrow at five p.m.)
     Oddly enough Max's space is in the very building
where I saw some loftlike activities going on a couple
of months ago on my way to the depot and fantasized
(even in jyze form) about one day living up there.
     This is the third ad I've come across in the past
month for sharing a loft in that area. I'm encouraged.
I doubt I'll succeed with Max but I do think my chances
of finding something else down there are pretty good.
And therefore I've decided to blow off the thirty bucks
I deposited on room No. 317 at the SRO dump. (Also last
week I checked out an artist's studio for a mere two
hundred a month directly above the restaurant where
model trains deliver the food (it's half a block from
the depot and about two blocks from Max's loft). But
this one turned out, as I was afraid it would at that
price, not to be a live-in. -- But talk about dumps.
Yeek! And danger. In that area and during the hours I
have to be on the streets a canister of pepper gas --
the kind Lady U always, or rather up until maybe a year

ago, urged me to carry -- just might be warranted.)

But what fun. A female loftmate probably about half my age. A cubbyhole office of my own a few blocks away (the G.C.H. Sandefjord Memorial Office of Jyzer Ink, I'm hereby christening it, in my benefactor's honor). A legion of artists lurking about and making life interesting. -- And yet the twenty or so square blocks around the co-op that rejected me are so lively right now I'd almost prefer living up there. Or actually either hood would be terrific. Low-rent inner-city digs. Free bus service throughout the greater downtown area until nine p.m. -- or is it seven p.m. now? And I've already amassed plenty of experience navigating the mean streets -- know how to steer clear of trouble. (Knock knock knock on woo-woo-wood.)

At the only real bookstore in town (ORBIT?) -- just two blocks from Max's loft and the same distance from the prospective Jyzer Ink office, right in between them -- I picked up the eleven volumes of the protojyze grandmaster. Elation! -- But what a heavy load they made. Trying to keep the double shopping bag dry in the rain. Moving fast so I could call Max again from the scope office before the hour was ridiculously late.

Excitement, yes. This is a fascinating time in the life of the jyzer. Transition. Uprooting. Reexamining everything. Seeing lots of possibilities and also lots of perils. Feeling lots of pain. Moods just as manic as all these antinomies suggest.

(Nor have I mentioned this. County bus service between here and the foot-ferry dock is being cut way back "because of low ridership" -- actually because of right-wing-engineered funding cutbacks forcing public-transit agencies to reevaluate service patterns. A year ago this cutback would've been calamitous for me, making my commute so much more fraught timewise as to be effectively impossible. No time for sleep, or rather nowhere near enough. So again I'll say it: I'm exiting the south-county scene just in time. And this new bus schedule starts Monday. If I don't have a place to crash in the city for a couple of hours during active

work periods -- say on the floor of my new office if not
in Max's loft -- this next month will be a real ordeal.)
    And getting back to that long talk with Lady U, I
do want to mention she said a few kind things. "You're
the person I admire most in the world" and also "You've
influenced me ten times as much as anyone I've ever
known, except my parents." I do believe they were
sincere compliments. True, one tends to say this sort
of thing when one is ending a relationship and wants to
make the other person feel better (and thus ease one's
own guilt, I suppose). Still, I'm grateful. It's a lot
better than the nastiness that preceded it for so long.
    -- Well, not living completely alone this week.
There's Fred the cat. Good old Marco surrogate Fred.
And here he is right now, padding through the mounds of
clipped and discarded newspapers, yowling. Needs
attention. Needs grub. Needs both immediately.
    And oh there's so much to do. A solid month's hard
labor still ahead before I can be truly outta here.

7

    Where was I? What had happened up to the point of
last jyze and what's happened since? I could read the
previous entry and track down at least part of an answer,
but that might not be too much fun. In any case I'm not
about to do it. No time for such frivolity.
    Cramped spot on the redwood table down here where
jyze began. Thunderous roar of the heater awakening.
(It drowns out most of the jazz coursing from the radio
in the ancient bureau-size console.) My left upper arm
pressing against my rib cage -- did I say left? I meant
right -- to be able to do this, what I'm doing.

The wagon's fully loaded and ready for a six a.m.
getaway. I want to arrive in the city at the hour when
it's least likely anyone will disturb the unloading and
I figure seven a.m. on a Sunday morning is probably it.
Or do the missions kick the "aggressor panhandlers," as
the media like to call them, back onto the streets that
early?

Only yesterday did I finally secure the cubbyhole
office for Jyzer Ink. Hank, the janitor, was working on
the lock to my new "suite" when I arrived -- No. 225.
Fine spot. Elation. It's a little larger -- ninety
square feet in all -- and a lot more interesting than
430A, the first room I was offered there. For a while
last week I actually was renting a third room, one with
a window looking out on the triangle, for which I agreed
sight unseen (after a moment's intense agonizing) to pay
an extra thirty bucks a month. But then Trevor yanked
this exceptional spot away from me (since it was worth
sixty bucks more a month, not thirty, and he had offered
it to me at the discounted rate only because I already
had a verbal contract of sorts, albeit for a different
room) and substituted No. 225 for it.

Crammed into the back of the wagon right now with
just inches to spare are the desk and filing cabinets
from the study upstairs. They've been in there once
before but that trip I had to cancel. It's been a crazy
couple of weeks that way.

And most of this latest week I was waiting for Max
to decide who'd be her loftmate. In the end it wasn't
me. "A real tough decision." In truth I probably never
stood much of a chance. I came along too late in the
vetting process. By that time she was burned out trying
to get to know people. I need to do better at pouncing
on ads the moment the papers hit the street.

The SRO dive I've put on hold. With Lady U no
longer bothering to be nasty I figure why not save
myself the four hundred in rent for March and stay on at
U Acres. I'd be here most of the time anyway.

I'm sorry about losing out on Max's loft. Yes,
I'd've liked living there. She's short, pudgy,

phlegmatic, but she does have a nice crinkly smile and a
winningly laissez-faire attitude. She welcomes
strangeness and is clearly on the lookout for
inspiration. We'd've been sleeping within a few feet of
each other up in the loft. Ceilings about twenty feet
high, bricky views through two good-size windows facing
west onto the street. A kitchen and right next to it an
ancient bathtub raised on cinderbricks like a junker car
-- these in the lower section of the studio.

So now I'm thinking any loft studio will do. I
have some flexibility here. If one opens up I might
rent it myself and look for a roommate later. So far
one or two loft-studio ads have appeared every week but
one. Be ready to move fast, that's the thing.

And it was three months ago today that Mother left
this vale of travail (sometimes veiled). Wouldn't she
be amazed to see what I'm going through now. (And Barb
volunteered that Mother would be delighted to know I'm
using a big part of the income from the money she left
me to rent a cubbyhole office dedicated in her name.
During visits up here over the past fifteen years she
said several times she thought I fit best in that very
part of town: the historic quarter. "Your kind of
place." -- Barb mentioning this when I called her to
talk about the jump in cost for printing "Memorials.")

A bunch of letters to write. First Aunt Shar, and
on this I'm shamefully late (she's in very poor shape
with leukemia). Then Rikki, who remains an odd sort of
temptation, a possible lover or mate, same age as Lady
U, mother of a great kid -- but I don't want to be too
distracted from the real work. And Tom T., who sent me
some scabrous paragraphs in reply to my request that he
be ready to provide a reference for the co-op. -- And
also I should write that prepublication promotional
notice for "Memorials."

No dread! Much better I should just let myself
enjoy this stuff, which I know I can do. Why worry?
How many years do I have left anyway? Be secure and jam
pedal to metal for the final curve, if that's what it
is, and the home stretch. Then hope for extensions.

[The Jyze Moves]

    The new world headquarters of Jyzer Ink just by
being slightly larger than expected will allow for the
presence of most of this wall of books currently looming
a few feet to my right. And thus one of my most urgent
problems is solved. Because the storage unit in the
home port is almost completely full. (And I'm proud of
it -- a makeshift loft platform! My own creation!
Boxes and chairs and bags of old clothes crammed up
there as much as fifteen feet above ground level!)
    So the first hope now is to come up with a loft
studio of my own either just north or just south of
downtown. If that fails I'll settle for an SRO kind of
arrangement for six months (the minimum lease at the one
where I still have the thirty bucks down). Very few
possessions. Lots of ferry trips to the storage unit.
    -- And I do continue to have a job. Have I even
mentioned this lately? It's a done deal: reporter Naomi
and I are sticking together no matter what. Of course
advancing technology could do us in at any time, but
that's a different kind of worry. (Yet I shouldn't fail
to note it's trashing Lady U's job right now. Just as
her boss was warning her months ago would likely happen,
demand is dwindling for recycled disposable cameras. In
a week or two she'll be laid off, probably permanently.
-- But she doesn't seem at all bothered by this and so
I'm not either. I'm guessing she has something lined up
through her friends in the nearest harbor town to the
south where we sometimes shop. That's the place she
most often talks about moving to. Among other prospects,
she's heard of a toy store there that will soon be on
the market and she may ask her parents to stake her in
buying it. -- And she did tell her parents about our
impending breakup. Apparently they took it well. But
who really knows. Maybe I'll find out a little more
when it comes time to deal with Papa U on the wagon.
Supposedly he's looking into the matter now -- how much
he should offer to buy out my share.)
    Do I seem emotionless about all this? Probably
do. Probably am, at least in some ways. Sometimes I
seethe, sometimes I exult, sometimes I mope, sometimes

I'm just plain numb. Mostly I try to focus on keeping busy and avoid thinking too much about all the losses.
     -- But I've stayed on too long here in the jyzosphere. Need to sleep some before setting off for the city. (Lots more such hauling lies ahead. Maybe six to eight round trips if I don't find a loft studio and maybe twice that many if I do.)
                    *   *
     -- And made it. This the first time ever from the G.C.H.S. Memorial Office of Jyzer Ink. On a Sunday morning at eight o'clock or so when the building is very quiet but nonetheless is -- well heated! (In fact only the low rumble of the heating system, it seems, keeps the silence from being complete.)
     Still dark when I left the house. "Pitch black." Black sweatpants too, green sweatshirt. The maple door resting on its side across the top of the passenger seatback pressing ominously against the right flank of my neck like a blunt horizontal guillotine. Vibrating. A risk but -- I was taking it.
     The usual loop, county roads down to the bridge and across to the freeway and then the fork northward. A sudden rainstorm at the bridge, pelting type, then as abruptly vanishing and soon you could see the mountains silhouetted against a band of incandescent orange across the eastern horizon. More cars zipping along than you'd expect at that hour and most seeming (to judge from the occupants' clothing) churchbound. Sunrise services? Flashing blue and red lights, one such car pulled over for speeding -- yay! (They'd passed me doing at least ninety. Were you speeding with them, Jesus?)
     And then the city. That awe-inspiring first view as you top a hill and round a bend out near the smaller of the two airports -- the skyline popping up almost like one of those intricate three-dimensional cardboard cutouts from a snapped-open book. And then curving down into the industrial flatlands near the historic quarter, streets virtually deserted. A big old expando bus lumbering along. The two ancient railroad stations standing oddly side by side. A couple of ungentle-

looking gents lurching across the street -- uh-oh, I'm
thinking, they're out and about. Turn left up by city
hall, roll steeply downhill a few blocks to the triangle.
Yup, already a dozen or more good ol' boys are wandering
around or rooted in place on the park benches. And a
big flock of squabbling pigeons and gulls, an early
bread tosser (out of sight around the corner but the
chunks of bread are flying into view like rice at a
wedding). And here's a parking space just ten feet from
the side entrance. Only this one space available and
it's in a loading zone but the zone's not enforced
Sundays and holidays and besides -- I'm unloading. So I
guess I did pick a good time to come.

Open the car door and -- birdcalls. A foghorn. A
hit of bracing salty sea air with some fish-whiff in it.
The triangle and all its century-old buildings looking
so freshly scrubbed they're still wet, all that ancient
stone and brick and ironwork.

Unload. First move all the stuff up to the
entrance, cautiously in the beginning but no one's
hassling me. Then open the side door using the push-
button combination (5-3-4-2: not too hard on the memory)
and move all the stuff a few feet inside the hallway so
it'll be protected by the locked door. Then move it
all a hundred feet farther around a couple of corners
to the central lobby, foot of the grand staircase (with
its splendid red-marble-below-fretted-woodwork walls)
right next to the ancient twin-cage elevators ("oldest
operating elevators in the city" -- Trevor). Then,
some via the stairs and some via the elevator, haul it
all up here, second floor (but close to thirty feet
above the first), far northeast corner.

What a relief. I can't begin to say how much
difference having this place makes. Already.

Two maple filing cabinets holding up the maple door
which will again become my desk. Three-tier oak boxes
for "in," "out," and "other." Two long, narrow desktop
cabinets, oak or maple, with sliding doors. Three-
drawer maple filing cabinet. Wooden folding chair and
folding tray and folding magazine rack. -- What's weird

is all this stuff is mine and it almost seems to make up
a matched set. Certainly it goes together quite well as
long as you don't look too closely. And who's looking
anyway? Just me. And old Mom's ghost. And we like it.
     Oh yeah, and here it is, already pinned to the wall
above the light switch: Jyzer Ink's city business
license. "Post conspicuously." So done! And now,
thanks to the huffing of the furnace vent, fluttering
faintly just as it used to do out in the drafty shed.
     -- This building, like many others in the area,
was renovated about a quarter century back. The main
idea was to dispel some of the antiquarian gloom of the
original interior by carving out a pair of central
atriums with skylights at the top. My room has two
large windows (each probably close to seven feet high)
opening out onto one of the atriums -- the northern one.
Both windows sport brown thin-slat venetian blinds which
are closed at the moment and will remain so most of the
time, because people walk by in the hallway right
outside and I don't want to be on display. But it's
enough to know these blinds could be opened -- and they
could; they work. (And the same's true of the ones on
the door window. It looks out into a small foyer giving
onto the main corridor. The door-window glass has a
large "225" painted on it in a quasi-Victorian style
suitable for the era of the building's construction.)
     Blue-gray carpet wall to wall. I just tried out
the spot by the back wall where I hope eventually to be
grabbing some zees. It should work well enough. When
everything's here I'll be entirely concealed down there.
(On the other side of that wall is something called a
wellness clinic. How noisy it'll be during the day I
don't know -- shouldn't be too bad, or at least in
comparison with, say, an illness (illth?) clinic. And
during the off hours I doubt anyone will be around.
-- And on Friday I did exchange hellos with an extremely
healthy-looking young woman, blond, almost surely a
medical worker of some kind employed back there.
Thought hmm, this place is getting more likable by the
minute. I'm certainly curious about what might be

happening in the rest of the building during working
hours. This floor by itself boasts some thirty offices
-- doctors, lawyers, an ESL outfit, several firms whose
natures aren't revealed by their names, and then about a
dozen personal names with no clues as to occupation.
Soon Jyzer Ink will be joining them all on the rosters
in the south atrium and the first-floor lobby.)

   Mail is delivered direct to your door -- shoved
under it, Hank the janitor told me, though he also said
he could "punch" a mail slot through the door if I
wanted one. Just talk, I think. Surely it would fall
low on his priority list. A building as old as this one
must kick up plenty of malfunctions to keep him hopping.
(Several areas down on the ground floor look a little
shabby -- scratched-up woodwork and such. Once you get
upstairs, though, the general condition is surprisingly
good. So good I couldn't believe they'd let a lowlife
like me rent here. Still can't. -- Although I've seen
some other tenants who look to be more my type than all
those doctor/lawyer roster listings would suggest.)

   This room. I'm expecting great things. Can work
here. Can be pleased as punch just to be here. Am!
And I think will continue to be. (That the heat was on
at seven a.m. Sunday morning is promising all by itself.
The modern skyscraper in which the scope firm offices
can't manage this, or at least not on Sundays that are
only borderline cold like today. If I were up there
this morning I'd be using a portable electric heater set
up in the leg space beneath my worktable to keep warm.)

   Gray walls. A transom window atop a plastered-in
door frame at the back of this room: it looks down into
the wellness clinic from about eight feet up. In the
corner to the right of the desk I'll be squeezing the
wood-frame leather armchair and hassock and a floor lamp.
Along the wall behind me now, the door wall, will be a
high bookcase; beneath the two windows in the wall to my
right, the west wall, will be a low bookcase. The red
framed bird mola I gave Mother a few years back will
hang on the wall above the desk. Not too much else in
the way of decor, or at least not at first. Don't want

too much clutter. Above all, KEEP FOCUSED.
     -- Tonight I'll be coming back here with a second
load. The antique revolving bookcase, the wheeled
wooden cart -- both from Mother's apartment. Must think
about just how much I can fit in without overdoing it.
     In four days, or three now, Mother would've turned
seventy-six. That no longer seems so old to me. Even
ninety doesn't. -- And this is leap year. Had she
been born a few hours later she'd've been turning
nineteen on Thursday. For me "Leap Day" this year will
mean twenty-four rent-free hours to futz around with.
     The big question right now is how private a life
I'll be leading. How isolated. What could I do to make
it otherwise and do I want to try to do any of that.
What will be best for the work. Can I tolerate solitude
better now that my hormones are (I would suppose) raging
less.

                    *   *

     Twelve hours later and I'm back with the second
load. And the bird mola is up! So too a framed poster
for a street fair featuring Mother's old turf for the
last eighteen or so years of her life, as seen from the
west: soft pastels, a slice of hillside including a
house where the memorialee and presiding maternal
ghostly spirit of this office used to live and the
"tombstone tower" atop the hill on the far upper slope
of which her ashes are now becoming an inconspicuous
yet inextricable part of the local scene. (It was one
of my favorite posters even before taking on so much
new personal meaning for me in the past few months.)
     With two-by-twelve planks I've now raised the
surface of this desktop to thirty inches even (just
measured) and I'm finding it a much better jyzing
height. These paragraphs are the test and it's passing.
With flying jyzer ink!
     This building is so quiet on a Sunday evening.
It's still churning out good heat, though, and the hum
to go with it on all six floors (I did a quick tour).
Only a few other folks around at this hour. "Movin' in

or out?" asked one. "Both" -- I should've said. The
old in-and-out. "Move 'em out, boys and girls, we got
work to do!" Yup, I'm loving the place. Forget the old
shed, forget the old jyze central (because this is the
new shed and the new jyze central rolled into one). No
looking back. -- Except I will look back, of course.
I'll even be back, back where I used to be, and soon:
in about an hour. But not for much longer or too many
more times.

8

   Aboard. But do I really want to be doing this now?
Damn right I do. True, I ought to be doing something
else. The Shar letter. The one I've been endlessly
procrastinating on. In fact this is when I vowed to get
it done for sure, the Sunday-night trip in. Even took
the ferry for just that reason. And yet -- cain't.
   Left hand dipping into a bag of popcorn. Hot on
here today. An unusual squeak. And I've been rushing
ever since getting up three hours ago. Decided not to
take a shower after all -- better to make it over to the
city as early as possible. Got work to do: my own. And
better to avoid Lady U who when I left was still closed
up in her room. Last night Zach fetched her at seven
and she didn't return until ten this morning. From the
shed I watched as she hurried in from his pickup (red).
By the time I shambled down to the house roughly twenty
minutes later the lights were off behind our bedroom
door. Silence. She must've had a strenuous night.
   In my face! First time since January she's been so
flagrant with an overnighter. Could be this is one of
her less-than-subtle ways of advising me to speed up the

evacuation. The other day she started moving her stuff into my half-empty study -- same message. "I could've kicked you out long ago," she pointedly reminded me. And: "My parents might be coming in April -- you wouldn't want to be bumping into them, would you?"

Whatever happened to her heart? I wouldn't've believed this possible. Or anyway: would've assigned it a low likelihood. And therefore I know her shame and/or guilt -- but most probably just shame -- must be great. She's bailed. Given up. Can't live the way she thought she wanted to. An act of cowardice on her part but also an act of courage. "I'm deficient," as she said -- keeps ringing. "At least I didn't interfere with your work" -- likewise. With no serious arts pursuit to bestow meaning on her life (after she'd lost dance/drama and pretty much given up on sketching/painting and the rest) she felt only emptiness, inferiority -- and probably resentment. Definitely resentment. Love alone couldn't do it for her. Not with her cultural and family tradition. Which is a major reason why I was always the one loving and sacrificing more. Simple truth, acknowledged on both sides.

-- And so to No. 161, the storage unit. The wagon was already loaded -- that was my task for Saturday night while she was out playing. An hour of shifting things around there so the stacks could rise a little higher. And during a break a hike to the hardware store across the street to buy shims. For lack of shims all moving-in work at the new office had ground to a halt.

That's the one and only, the real, the marvelous new office, No. 225, G.C.H.S. Memorial, home of Jyzer Ink. Next stop. Two packages of shims in my bag right here and two more in reserve at home. Ninety-six shims in all: oughta be enough.

Speaking of the hardware store, the big surprise of the week also happened there. A wild infatuation with bookcases, folding pine beauties made in a distant tropical land, three large and three small -- I bought. Over two hundred bucks' worth. Along with the "compleat works" of the English protojyze grandmaster and five

packages of work socks and a green hooded canvas jacket,
these bookcases constitute my impulsive inheritance
splurge. -- Oh, and one other very large pine bookcase
from the new discount mart.

All these bookcases because I really love this
office and want to do right by it. Want it to be a
place old Mom would've been pleased to think of me at
work in, not causing her to roll over in her grave
except with pleasure. (Can "cremains" roll over in
crumbly hillside soil? Sure! And no doubt many do!)

-- Week of her birthday. Week of Leap Day. And
for me week of driving. Except for the one trip with
Lady U to see old Mom twelve years ago I haven't driven
so much in, what, almost seventeen years, since the lady
and I first arrived in this area. From the stoplight by
the foot-ferry dock in the home port to the parking
space outside the side entrance leading up to the new
Jyzer Ink office (just two blocks from the city ferry
terminal, by the way) is 62.3 miles. Six round trips so
far, 750-odd miles. Off hours, light traffic, moving
fast, watching for cops. Thanks to the heavy loads
getting to know every bump in the road.

Pulling in now. "All passengers must go ashore" --
a distinguished P.A. delivery today, theatrical quality
almost compared to the usual. Some deckhands marble-
mouth it just the way I did the explanation of my work
habits during the "compatibility check" at the co-op a
few weeks ago. Yeah, I'm still shaking my head over
that. Wotta doofus I turned out to be at crunch time!

*   *

Mother's old kitchen clock, the big wooden one,
ticking away. I just hung it on the wall. Temporary
only in that spot but it'll fit in somewhere.

Shimming took longer than expected. Almost two
hours all things considered, including the effort to
determine just the right location for the revolving
bookcase with the canted dictionary stand on top.
Despite my vows I'm cramming somewhat. Snug fits.
Utilize every cubic inch at least up to a height of
eight feet or so. It'll still be fine.

[Jyze and Jyze Alone]

    This going down at my doortop desk with one of the
new three-tier foldable bookcases balanced atop each
end. A workspace five feet wide remains in the middle.
    Wonderful. I'm over the hump. Can't help myself,
I emit little yelps of joy. Guess in some ways I wanted
out of that relationship as much as the lady did. And
this building is just so terrific. I like to wander
around checking out the offices and gazing at the many
large colorized photos, framed and lit up, of century-
old urban scenes, most appearing to be enlargements of
postcards from that era. Saturday night I discovered
it's not always so quiet here -- a rock band struck up
around nine p.m. in the club downstairs and the stage
there seems to be directly below this office, or almost
so. Okay by me. Sound muffled just enough.
    That same night I moseyed around the triangle and
the adjoining streets of the entertainment zone. Not
carrying a pack or anything -- just stepping out of the
office for a break. I counted eleven clubs offering
live music and probably missed a few. Fairly good
crowds considering all the bad press stirred up by the
murder a few weeks ago. Just like the greediest
developer I'm already worrying street crime will take
this quarter down.
    Ten o'clock on the nose. Earlier a conversation
was echoing on the other side of this wall, the
acupuncturist and the lady from around the corner, the
hotline for people with head injuries, both non-Cawks --
yippee! This is more like it! And my hunch is they're
meeting down here on the sly. Neighborly assignation,
Afrusan woman and Asiusan man. No one else around --
except the new guy in 225. But he's cool, he's cool.
    Some mail on the carpet when I arrived. Previous
occupant Alicia H., vocation unknown to me. And phone
bills are still coming in for the one previous to her
and that's "Shannon M. dba Escorts International." So I
know I had at least one distinguished predecessor here.
A lot to live up to, by god. And I intend to do it.
    In the meantime I've been thinking. Maybe that SRO
hotel isn't all that bad. Maybe it's just what I need.

[The Jyze Moves]

A loft studio is my long-range goal but at this point
renting one on my own would probably be too risky. And
sharing one, as with Max, might turn out to be a pain,
especially in my current frame of mind. More and more I
want to be the JIFT-obsessed loner, at least for a while.
     Take off the gloves. Fiery eyes. Mr. Bold. No
more trying to spare everyone. Hiding my light under a
barrel -- why? At this "mature" stage? In this "era of
dysfunction"? Let fly. Do it while you still can.
     Walking around the quarter I knew I could. I'm
pleased with the setting. High energy. Becoming part
of the action. Mystery man. Churning out all that
great stuff.
     And the same night around one a.m. I drove the
streets of the area around the SRO hotel, which is just
about exactly a mile due north of here. Up one north-
south avenue, down the next; then up and down the east-
west cross streets. A lively scene, especially the
blocks immediately around the hotel, which is pretty
much at its center. Some signs of danger in isolated
spots but not as many or as bad as I'd been thinking.
It's still a happening kind of place -- reminds me a
little (maybe because the city weeklies have written
about it this way) of other hoods I've known that were
in the middle stages of takeoff into prime scene status.
     For a six-month trial, why not? Who knows, maybe
I'll take to SRO living. Things'll be different now
that I have this office -- a place to escape to. Not
like those earlier SROs. And I shouldn't forget I liked
many things about living in both of those.
     The ad for this particular SRO appears in the
classifieds every day. Don't think I'll have a problem
finding a vacancy there in future weeks or months or for
that matter years. My application and deposit are on
file and I told them, in canceling my hold on room 317,
that my new projected move-in time would be in April,
either the 1st or the 15th. All I really have to do is
confirm this and show them proof that (A) I really do
have a job but on the other hand (B) my income falls
below the city's official "subsidy" level. Martin, the

manager, said he'd need to see some "paste-ups." What
for? I asked. "To show you don't make too much," he
said. I didn't get it. The talk turned elsewhere.
Only later did I realize he'd said "pay stubs."

Just like the earlier SROs of my life the lobby of
this one features a manned 24-hour desk. But you can't
just walk in. You buzz and they query you via a tinny
intercom, meanwhile scrutinizing you from across the
lobby through thick glass doors. Virilio, the amusingly
yet also aptly named desk clerk I talked with, is a no-
nonsense sub-mafia type but also a sports nut. Reminded
me of the immortal Gus, the muscular heavy employed by
Miss N. as a bodyguard for her ballroom-dancing class
back in my junior-high days (except Gus wore a tux).

-- I'm about two-thirds moved in here at No. 225.
A space is cleared for the armchair, hassock, and small
table in the corner beneath one of the windows, but I'm
still using those items at home. Most of the reference
books are here, half of the binders are, but none of the
non-reference books -- and that's nineteen shelves'
worth. Still haven't begun the major dismantling job up
in the shed, which is otherwise almost empty. Still
have seven chapters of "Jyzer" to do the clipping for,
of thirty-nine. Have a whole roomful of papers to go
through. Need to move a few more large items to the
storage unit, including the largest, the loveseat. Need
to pack kitchen stuff and other miscellaneous items.
Tools, linen. And then finally clothes.

Just thinking. This is the kind of thing I have to
be focusing on all the time now. What do I pack next?
Where does it go? Will it actually fit there?

-- And I'll amble on. Have to write out my first
rent check and slip it under Trevor's door upstairs.
Figure out what to do with all this misdirected mail,
including a new shoebox-sized parcel for "Escorts
International." Wonder what's in there. Sez the label:
"ABC Distributing -- Another Great Value." Negligee
with nipple holes? Month's supply of French ticklers?
*   *

Twenty-four hours later, a muddle. Here or the

bridge drive-in? Or the old tavern maybe? Why such
indecision? Irritation. Lady U chirping away on the
phone upstairs. Still haven't begun the letter to Shar.
Things-to-do piling up. I tackle this and I tackle that
but the pile gets no smaller. On the contrary: grows
almost exponentially.

Or it's just a mood. A glance at the calendar,
draw a diagonal line through circled dates eight days
apart. Three more jyze sessions and I'm history around
here. Save the drive-in and the tavern for those. And
save jyze central too, the old one where I sit now, or I
ought to save it. Except here I -- am. Discombobled.
Fractured.

The detritus of all these years we've been together.
You'd think I'd turn up something exciting. Not so --
so far. For that matter any major move ought to kick up
something. And this is major.

Loose ends. I'm at them. Why?

(At the ORB cafe I caught a glimpse of the author
of an historical novel that has another Lady U in its
title. Young, blond, attractive, a strange but
affecting gait. Reviewers are rightly savaging the book
as a serious work of art. Nonetheless it's amusing and
sexy, I'd say, from briefly leafing through it. I like
the notion that a young woman of our era is writing such
erotically obsessed poetic prose about those female
protojyzists of ancient times, the greats of a different
land and vastly different cultural tradition -- Lady U's
tradition, in fact. My Lady U's as well as this other's.
And I like this new Lady U's family name too, although
it's a little too close to my Lady U's family name for
comfort. -- My former Lady U, that is.)

Two hours now she's been blathering away on the
phone up there. Cascades of laughter. It's Patrice no
doubt. Nor will I ask if they've become lovers. But
I'd be curious to know if the lady has the courage to
try it. And the desire to try it. Could be it'll
happen (or has). Nonetheless it would strike me almost
as oddly as my mother's trying it a few years ago when
her lesbian co-worker was panting after her, had old Mom

actually done so, which she didn't (as far as I know --
and I think she would've told me if she had).

"My" Lady U -- should I call her Lady Ex? -- is out
of a job and supposedly looking for another one. I see
little sign of the hunt and no sign at all of panic.
Probably her parents are staking her during this
difficult transitional period (used and abused for all
these years by an older man until she was finally forced
to drop him, as she's probably painting the picture, or
encouraging them to paint it for themselves).

Half past eleven. Bland dinner jazz playing -- the
kind we bicker about. She can't get it through her head
that I'm not really defending it. I just don't want to
be traipsing over to spin the radio dial every three or
four minutes. But neither am I saying all tastes in
music should be equally admired. Yes, I go for some
genres more than others, for some composers and
lyricists and performers more than others. Surprise!
And surely it's one thing to respect someone's right to
pursue his or her personal taste and another to share
the taste. How elementary can you get? (She's striking
back because I said some mildly nasty things about her
sudden fascination with so-called alt music. Said them
six months ago! Under extreme provocation!)

-- No no no, I don't want to be going any further
into this. Least of all tonight. Just carry on with
all these moving-out tasks.

9

Ceiling fans spinning, pool balls clicking. Smoke
and beer-whiff and sports play-by-play and a heavy rock
beat. Wood and plants. Lotsa backcountry folks.

[The Jyze Moves]

    Here we brunched the day of our very first visit to
this area to check out the house and property. Andy and
Tera raved about the food. I liked the place all right.
Lady U hated it. In six years plus, living less than
two miles away, we've come back here together only once.
It's just a stone's throw from the county bus stop but
I've dropped by on my own maybe three times. And it's
the only night spot -- only tavern, club, saloon, what
have you -- within six or seven miles of our house.
    Never mind. I won't miss it. Move on.
    A fine J-week! The whole time I was thinking I'd
soon be moving into the SRO hotel -- but figured I owed
it to myself to check out one more place. The hotel is
already a lock if I want it; why not a last look around?
    The city housing agency's ad for subsidized low-
rent units in a highrise apartment building just east of
downtown said they offered similar units in sixteen
other locations in or near downtown. I walked up to the
agency office this morning. Along the way I confirmed
my dislike of the agency's advertised highrise and the
nearby freeway-dominated area with its paucity of street
life. But in leafing through agency materials while
awaiting my appointment I noticed one of those sixteen
other locations was in the same area as the co-op I
tried to join, in fact right across the street from it
to the north. I asked Harriet, the rental agent, if a
vacancy might exist there. And -- yes.
    A prim chain-smoking older woman in a tightly
belted blue trench coat, she drove me over to check out
the place in her fancy new-model car. (It's what she
does all day long every day.) The vacant studio, 2-B,
is on the second floor of a restored three-story former
"sailors' hotel," as she called it, perched on the edge
of the bluff that runs along the waterfront in that
area. It's a corner room, large windows looking out to
the south and west -- a bay view and the viaduct right
outside with lots of cars roaring by but behind some
shielding greenery -- a fine back-of-the-docks feel to
the scene as a whole. Inside, a long hallway internal
to the apartment, a large carpeted room of, by Harriet's

estimate, four hundred square feet (the hall included).
Fully equipped kitchen nook, bathroom with shower and
tub -- holy shit! Wotta find! And fifteen bucks a
month cheaper than the much smaller and dumpier room at
the SRO hotel, which is just two blocks to the east.
     But would I qualify? And could I prove it?
     (Meanwhile here's dinner. About time. Two
apologies in the interim.)
                              *
     (Ooh man, did I choke that down. Stale relish,
near-rancid mayo, chunks of super-sour pickle hidden in
limp chopped lettuce. I must've been hungry all right.)
     Long story short: unit 2-B is mine if my credit
checks out. I slipped my paperwork under the wire ahead
of the other contenders for the place. An elated hike
around the downtown at ten a.m. A call home warning
Lady U the housing agency would be phoning her as my
current "landlady," a few suggestions about what to say.
And she'd do it, I knew, because the breakup is now
proceeding smoothly and this would make it even smoother
-- and faster. Her father's check for three grand is
in the mail. As I'd hoped, but doubted would actually
happen, he's buying out my interest in the wagon.
     Two hours' sleep last night but I was so excited
when I got home at one p.m. today I couldn't sleep
anyway -- and had to be up at four to call reporter
Naomi to ask her to fill out an employment-verification
form (confirming my earnings do indeed fall well below
the low-income line). Visions of how I'd live, puzzling
over what to take out of storage and what to buy.
Biggest drawback, the studio is unfurnished. It'll be
lots of work to come up with even the bare necessities
by the April 1st move-in date. But worth it.
     Will my credit check out? It should. No blemishes
in decades. The biggest worry is they'll hold my utter
lack of credit usage against me. No credit cards, no
loans, no nuttin'. As far as the credit world's
concerned I'm a nonentity (and that's just what I hope
to continue to be for them).
     The housing agency also inquires into criminal

records, including drug and alcohol offenses. While in
their office I've twice heard applicants being rejected
by phone because the records check had turned up
outstanding arrest warrants. And unit 2-B was vacant
because the previous occupant had flipped out on drugs.
During our visit a two-man work crew was putting the
place back together. The toilet bowl had been shattered;
it appeared the guy had taken a hammer to it.

To be allowed to scope grand jury I've twice had to
submit to an FBI security investigation. Given all the
antiwar and environmental activism of my newspaper days
I don't know how I passed, but I did. So I should be
all right for a low-income studio apartment.

Then again, as Lady U pointed out, credit agencies
make mistakes. The FBI too. And how about the Lady S/
Elgie snafu, the zen marriage with Lady U herself, the
shaky stories I've had to present to the IRS over the
years? So I'm not home free. I'm on tenterhooks again.
But should know the outcome in a few days. And if it's
bad, there's still the SRO place, which until just
twelve hours ago looked pretty damn good.

Exacerbated excitability and suggestibility. Well-
known symptoms of the condition I've been in for months.

*   *

One last jyze at the shed. This half a day later,
most of it given over to sleep. Sleep and newspaper
clipping. The end's in sight! Of all things, alas.

Or is it the last jyze up here? Probably I could
squeeze in a couple more if I wanted to. Up until
yesterday I was thinking I would, after all, leave this
inner sanctum in place, the reworked loft originally
built for the bedroom at our last city rental house and
now melded with the handmade desk and bookcases salvaged
from the shed at that same house. Too much work, I
thought, to tear all this out when I had no immediate
use for it and might never have any. I'd previously
decided to "go light," meaning to pack everything I'd
need for my work into the hideaway office (that is,
suite 225) and otherwise keep things in storage, living
minimally, material-wise, in a furnished room at the SRO

hotel or some similar dive, ready to move on quickly
should a cheaper loft-share arrangement turn up. And
the idea of living that way appealed to me. Still does.
     And yet the new studio changes things. Its appeal
is still greater. With that under lease I'll have no
need to live quite so lightly and minimally. For one
thing, I could easily see myself staying on in unit 2-B
permanently, and I do mean all the way to the end. For
another, it's unfurnished so I'd have to move things in
anyway, thus totally subverting the "quick and light"
approach. And for a third, this loft right here, when
reassembled over there, should enable me to use the
space -- which, though considerably more than the bare
minimum, remains just a single room -- use that space
much more efficiently. And I'd be needing still more
bookcases, and this loft is lined with them on three
sides. Wonderful thick-lumber bookcases which I love
to be in the vicinity of. And I could easily add more
shelves to the fourth side. And would, definitely.
(Pausing now to think just how I could do that. -- And
a reminder: don't fail to take the power saw over.)
     Or then again I might not get the studio. But if I
do. And if they don't have some sort of regulation
forbidding this sort of internal construction. But how
could they? We're just talking about a bookcase. How
can they stop you from building a bookcase? Albeit it's
a very big one, a walk-in, three-dimensional bookcase
with a desk and counters inside and a roof on top and a
bed on top of that and a staircase going up one side.
     I'd been in the midst of packing the last couple of
boxes of supplies and miscellaneous desk items up here,
deciding which should go to the office and which to
storage. Now I'll suspend that for another day or two.
     If this studio 2-B works out, time will be lost to
disassembling the loft. But time will also be gained
because I won't have to go through all my boxes of
Mentoka clips before leaving. Those I can move as-is to
the new abode. Call it a wash.
     Meanwhile. Excellent J-week, as I say. What
opened the way was finally getting the letter to Shar

written. What a mental block against doing it! And
what relief when it was done! Rushed it out at, of all
places, the franchise burger joint next to the new
discount mart as closing hour approached.

   Then again my doing it at that burger joint isn't
such a surprise because I've been putting in a lot of
time at the discount mart itself rounding up the
miscellaneous items I'll be needing in order to take up
living on my own. Lady U's being reasonable about
divvying things up but in many cases we have only one
item for both of us, or there's a personal reason an
item should go to her (her mother bought it for her,
etc.). Such as tweezers. Hair scissors. Can opener.
Coffee maker. Rice cooker. A dismayingly long list of
such things. For me too, as I don't think she yet quite
realizes. A ladder here, a pair of pliers there.

   The breakthrough came in that talk just before she
left for home. "I made a big mistake." Now she's
crowing near and far about the peaceful breakup we're
pulling off and she's trying not to be inflammatory. In
short, she's come around to my way of seeing things.
And so I'm glad I withheld my fire last summer and fall
when her provocations were much more than sufficent for
me to go after her. Yes, I commend myself for this.
I'm a good guy. I owed it to her, I figured, not to let
her blow herself apart, as she easily could've done. It
was part of the burden of being the older and wiser one
-- having taken the younger and not-so-wise but also
much, much foxier one (as no one would dispute) for a
long, long ride. And by and large a sweet ride for both
of us. Got to see the big picture here.

   So now I can be smug? This is the new stage I'm
moving into? Maybe so. Or I can reverse things and say
looking back I realize I was the one responsible for the
breakup. Unconsciously, pretty much, but things got to
a point where I began putting pressure on her either to
shit or get off the pot -- make art or get out of the
studio -- ball or get out of bed. I started withholding
myself, my love, my approval. And this went on for a
long time, a slow turning of the screw.

[Jyze and Jyze Alone]

    It's just I never thought she'd choose to go the
way she did. I thought she'd decide to make art/love
with renewed vigor and devotion, not get out of the
studio/bed. That was the shocker. But it's also why I
have to applaud her courage. One could say she called
my bluff and raised me a bundle. And maybe she was
surprised and maybe she wasn't when I wouldn't see that
raise, much less bump it up in turn. But after what
happened with Marco thirteen years ago there was never a
chance of that. And she should've known this. I'd made
it very clear all along. But I don't think she was
paying much attention.
    Why not? Because in truth (that is, not just in
cliche) we had grown apart. Or rather: she'd gradually
discovered, but had been unable to admit to herself, she
wasn't as dedicated to making art as she thought. The
loss of face -- to her parents and longtime friends as
much as to me -- was simply too great for her to admit
this. But as soon as I'm out of the picture she'll
start living quite differently, I'm sure of it. She's
already doing it when she thinks I'm not watching. And
I know she's happier this way and so I say nothing.
Yes, I can let her go and I'm doing it. (And it hurts,
goddamn it! But less and less every day as my new life
starts to take shape. Of course I know hard times still
lie ahead for me once I'm actually out there on my own.
The bonds haven't really been broken yet. Some of the
bleeding hasn't even begun.)
    But in a surprising shift, I'm now implicating jyze
itself in our breakup. My all-out effort to make this
love work pretty much forced me to shut off my
oppositional voice. For six years straight and for most
of fifteen years it was largely silent because I stifled
it anytime it started to speak up. But then the jyze
breakthrough. I could suppress the voice no longer. I
would start listening to it and going off in new
directions. If she wanted to follow, fine. If not, I
could no longer wait for her. I would never hurt her
openly or directly, I wouldn't take on a lover or do
anything crazy like that, but I'd start turning up the

pressure, and to have the strength to do that I'd need the voice of resistance, independence, defiance to be strong within me. Thus jyze. Was born.

Well anyway it's an interesting theory. Or maybe rationalization is all it is. In any case I like it. And I also like doing this jyze and I'm not giving it up. For anything.

-- What's new? Mama U is said to be making nasty cracks about me. "I think she's enjoying this." "I think she really hates men." (Lady U herself saying these things.) As for Papa U, he's being more understanding. He's talked with a lawyer and, as noted earlier, has cut me a check for three K to buy out my interest in the wagon. I figure I'm actually owed considerably more than that (I've paid almost seven K and also all the upkeep, and the blue-book value is currently about three-quarters of the original purchase price and we've put only 22,000 miles on the thing in four and a half years) but I asked D originally to tell him I'd settle for three K and I don't want to dishonor that. And I'm throwing in the shell of the shed for free -- though apparently they think it's worthless anyway. And I'm saying nothing about the fact that the value of this "U Acres" property has more than doubled during our stay here -- during which time I was supporting Lady U so she could, in theory anyway, do the upkeep on it. Technically I suppose they would owe me nothing for this but in actuality I think they do owe me something. But I'm letting it go.

Noblesse oblige? Maybe it's partly something like that. More it's just who wants the hassles. Who cares. By and large the U's always treated me fairly and generously. They just couldn't understand my way of life, much less approve of it. But they felt it wasn't their place to express disapproval, not openly and directly, and the indirect expressions I could shrug off and did, as did their daughter, usually.

-- Where am I? Shed-jyzin'! The kerosene heater once again pulsing out the therms because we're in a bit of a cold snap after a long warm spell. All those gnarly branches out there like desperate misshapen arms and hands reaching this way in supplication, with mostly moss for skin though in a number of shades and textures. Birdsong. Jonquils and daffodils thrusting into bloom. Horse trainers at work off in the distance.

A recent magazine article explores the notion of the so-called "Third Age" -- when one is supposedly no longer part of the sexuality scrambles. More commonly the term is applied to women, and often in a sexist way, so it says, but in any case I think it's not yet for me. I'd still like to appropriate the term, however, for a slightly different purpose. I'm just weeks away from embarking on my own kind of Third Age. Or already have done so. Or under my original 28-year Glennarian time scheme will do so next year. And for me the meaning derives mainly from the fact that I don't care too much anymore about adapting to another person's ways. The Third Age I do it, if at all, my way. (Horrible old crooner song of that title almost makes me want to take it all back. But am I gonna let that sleazy dude change my way of thinking one jot? Huh-uh. Not.)

This means giving free rein to my most perverse self. Irreverence. Try to do to me what you want, world, it's just gonna bounce off. Even as I'm going down -- though I hope I won't get to the serious part of that process, or regress, for a good long while. Call the era for that the Glennarian Fourth Age.

10

Last time for the room where jyze "burst into being." Or at least for the redwood table while it's situated in this room, because tomorrow or maybe Friday it will go into storage, though only temporarily -- two weeks from now this will be my main table at the new studio apartment.

It came through! My credit checked out! Naomi and Lynn (at the investment group) affirmed my income! It'll be neither too low to keep me from affording the rent nor too high to keep me from qualifying for the city's low-income housing subsidy! -- But what complications. Faxes flying back and forth, long-distance calls to cities in other states. You'd think I was applying to join a posh residential country club.

And all of a sudden I'm rolling in dough -- even more so. Papa U's three-grand buyout check for the wagon arrived. I'm planning to spring for a microwave, vacuum cleaner, floor lamp, maybe even a TV with VCR -- all at our local discount mart, the new one. It's the good life for me. Or the best I can manage anyway. Soon all this profligacy will abruptly cease and I'll be living on peanut butter again.

In fact I'm chomping on a peanut-butter sandwich right now. For the fourth straight meal, breakfasts excepted. This way I won't be out of practice.

Monday morning I again stayed in town late so I could put down my damage deposit and first-month's rent. Then a return to unit B-2 (not 2-B as I'd been thinking) with Harriet, the trench-coated chain-smoking rental agent who seems to have stepped right out of a noir film, so I could do some measurements. Three hundred eighty-four square feet including the bizarre internal hallway. A recessed area in the northwest corner almost the perfect size for my loft, with the long dimension flush against the windowless north wall. All week I've been mentally arranging furniture around it.

Also I surveilled the neighborhood by car in daylight. Liked it a lot. Discovered an art school (which Lady U says she might soon be attending) a few blocks away just off the waterfront. And one block down the hill and half a block north, crowds of day laborers were lining the street hoping to be chosen for jobs (because of the way I was creeping along in the car they thought I was an employer and dozens of hands started waving -- "Choose me!"). An attractively artified "P-patch" community garden is located in the same area. Two jazz clubs I often hear mentioned on the radio lie within a couple of blocks of the studio and so do two large billiard halls, a rock club, and a good number of galleries and funky bars and cafes and restaurants.

Racking up the miles on the wagon, usually at night and preferably at three or four in the morning when traffic is almost nonexistent. Probing with my tongue for the hole in the soft-drink can so I don't accidentally pour the stuff all over myself (as I did do once). Jockeying for position and cursing freeway game-players out loud if a rare clot of heavy traffic happens along. Keeping an eye out for drunks and drifters in the triangle as I unload items for "suite 225," the Jyzer Ink office, "the hideaway": my own little chunk of heaven on earth. Now knowing where to look for the building's hand truck and how to put it to good use.

And steadily progressing with the packing here at home. The lucky break of hitting on the new pad (B-2) means I must refigure moving sequences and details. The storage unit won't be anywhere near as tightly packed as I'd been thinking. Today I began actual disassembly of the loft in the shed. Gave myself a good scare when I somehow managed to whack myself on the left knee with the hammer; at first I thought I'd shattered the kneecap. But after a few minutes the pain started to subside and now I'm pretty sure the damage is minor. It'll be colorful though.

What kind of klutz do you have to be to bang your own knee like that? And just moments earlier I'd been congratulating myself on doing such a fine job and staying injury-free.

Meanwhile Lady U has turned grumpy again. Is she perhaps starting to wonder if she's making a big mistake in kissing me off? If so I see no other sign of it. Today we changed the name on various accounts, by phone, from mine to hers: power, cable TV, auto insurance, the phone itself. It was startling to hear the winningly

polite and chirpy voice of her business persona: I'd
almost forgotten about this side of her. It's effective
but I never much cared for it. Close to obsequious at
times. So take that, soon-to-be Madam Ex.

This room is crammed with packing goods and stacks
and mounds and heaps of things to be packed. The radio
that's playing is a backup, Andy's ancient console (and
the sound's great at higher volumes, it turns out --
much better than anything else we've been listening to
here, if only we'd known). Just about everything I'm
using now is a backup. Not this table or J-stick or J-
book, true, but the desk chair, lamp, lawn chair in the
parlor, table up there, blanket I sleep under. All
creaky moth-eaten moldy stuff. What a way to go.

Bought myself a new map of the downtown area in the
city and became engrossed in studying it. It's the kind
that labels individual buildings, clubs, restaurants,
shops -- action map for tourists, really, is what it is,
and a tourist of sorts is what I'm about to become and
I'll be happy to be one. It occurred to me if I don't
feel like walking from home to office or vice versa and
I don't want to ride the buses (at no cost during
daytime hours since both apartment and office, and scope
office too, are within the downtown free-ride zone) I'll
be able to jump on the waterfront streetcar. It'll be
like an earlier era in my life exactly twenty years ago
and five thousand miles to the west. -- But it'll cost,
I think, the streetcar, at all hours, unlike the buses.

And I can save over a buck a day by reading the
newspapers on the wooden split-sticks at the ORB cafe
and the house copies at other venues along what will
soon be my regular circuit or set of circuits.

I'm not failing to let Lady U know my new life
potentially looks pretty good. In subtle ways only, or
at least I'd like to think they're subtle. Like not
once have I said nyah-nyah-nyah.

What's happening with her? It remains a mystery to
me. Apparently she'll be returning to school, but this
time not for anything "frivolous," she informed me;
otherwise her parents won't support her. Teaching,

maybe, or commercially oriented art achool, perhaps a certificate in travel and tourism management. But she wants to stick around our current area (including the harbor towns), purportedly because her parents like it but actually, I'm sure, because this is where her new pals are. "Patrice and the boys." More astounding tales about weirdnesses at the camera factory as the shutdown date approaches. Excited talk about so and so being a lesbian, someone else bi, about "eating out" (cunnilingually) -- lots of laughter -- and I'm starting to think she might actually try to swing that way for a while. Seems to me she's got a crush on someone. But who? Patrice seems too obvious.

Well anyway, another ten or twelve days and I won't have to put up with any more of this truly insulting treatment she's laying on me. Dissing the howler! If she wants us to stay on friendly terms she'll have to start being genuinely friendly herself, and not just when she wants something from me. -- And take that too, Madam Ex!

A list of some two dozen magazines/reviews/journals I'll be sending change-of-address forms to. Right here. Oh so much still to do. How many runs to the dump? If I'm smart I'll check out the lady's favorite hiding places to see what she's trying to conceal from me that I might have a claim on. Or smarter yet I might not do that if I think I'll be okay and I've got all my major stuff. Who wants more battles? Depends on whether she's back to seriously dissing me or not. By and large I'd prefer to sail right on through. Unruffled.

Broke the news about the split-up to brother Rob on the phone and to Barb by letter. Also to Naomi, Shar, and Judy J., a clerk I scarcely know at the bookstore -- strange how the compulsion takes you over. Rob professed shock, though he then recalled I'd forewarned him of the possibility when we were together for Mother's funeral back in November. I frame imaginary letters to the U's. "This wasn't my idea; I didn't favor it and indeed I thought...." Pathetic stuff. But I do want to write them. Which doesn't necessarily mean

I'll be able to figure out how to do it.

     -- Best I not take any more time for this decidedly
unjyzey nonsense. Too much to do. The same'll probably
be true next week as well. But I'll catch up. Later.
The jyze rules require it. By the end of the month this
J-book must be full, or else.

11

     Nope, wrong. Still here, the table is. Jyze
central. At three-twenty a.m. on what's just about sure
to be my last free night at home.
     Tomorrow's Wednesday and I'll be driving in with a
wagonload to be temporarily stashed at room 225 ("the
hideaway") and then I'll do some scoping and then roll
home at four a.m. Same for Thursday. And Friday I'll
drive back in at three p.m. to pick up the keys for
studio apartment B-2 and start moving in.
     Last free night, by which I mean no moneymaking
kind of work awaits me in the city. I get to knock
around the house in sweats doing whatever I want, which
on this night happens to be mostly packing of one sort
or another. But also flip some nerf shots, leaf through
some mags, heat up a can of chicken vegetable soup with,
for what will presumably be the last time ever, home-
cooked rice as an ingredient. Lady U bestowed a portion
on me in exchange for my shopping for cat food for her.
     The celebrated "Comet Calvin," as it's known at U
Acres, is supposed to burst into brightness out there
tonight. This comet, spotted for the first time just a
few weeks ago by an astronomer whose nationality is the
same as that of the U family's ancestors and is
officially named for the astronomer, was renamed by Mama

U for her husband, Calvin, because of the intense
interest he's shown in it, as he does in most things
relating to the old country. The comet itself may or
may not be a dud (like most of the other ballyhooed
comets of my lifetime) but it sure is intriguing how
it commands symbolic significance in our little family
universe. Anthropomorphizing -- you can't help it. A
big, big change is going down around here and you
might as well say this comet is swooping in to confirm
it. No point in being in denial about it.

Horrible news from sister Barb: Keith's father,
driving out from the far coast for a visit before Barb
and Keith's scheduled departure for a month's travel
overseas, falls asleep at the wheel in the mountains and
dies in a fiery collision. Mother's old apartment, in
which they're finally beginning to feel comfortable,
again becomes an abode of death, this time with Keith's
family arriving to say their farewells. (And ever since
the news came down I've been flashing back to my own
impossibly innocent "honeymoon trip" across those same
mountains with Lady C, the night we nearly bought the
farm when I likewise nodded out at the wheel -- and was
revived in the nick of time by the flashing lights of an
accident scene for which we might easily have provided a
second act, like one terrorist bomb following another.)

And spring has -- sprung! Clouds of blossoms and
eye-popping rhodies. Legions of frogs sproinging across
the backyard. Honking geese. And ringing ears -- my
own -- from too much hammering in the enclosed space of
the shed as (just today) I completed the disassembly of
the loft. All the pieces are now stacked beneath a tarp
in the exposed part of the carport. -- Don't forget to
wear gloves when loading and unloading, I remind myself.
-- But except for a very sore and technicolorful left
knee I've come through the entire "deconstruction
project" surprisingly unscathed.

Finally all the shelves here in jyze central are
bare. All books, save the couchside stack of current
reading, are packed. Ditto papers, photos, tools, art
supplies. I'm just about ready to depart for good. Go

through the (antiquarian) vinyl record albums, pack some
dishes, throw my clothes into boxes -- I'm done.
     Last week Lynn of the investment group came calling
in our city. She took time out from a visit to her
sister to meet with Rob and me to discuss our accounts.
Everything's all set -- we each pay her five hundred a
year for doing the managing. Rob's plowing all his
income back into the fund until his kids hit college age
(still a few years off); I'm taking out about half of
mine for living expenses, just as planned, $275 a month,
or in other words enough to pay my rent on unit 161
(storage) and room 225 (hideaway) with about thirty a
month left over -- and that remainder should just about
pay for my utilities at unit B-2 (studio) (if that
bill's truly as low as Harriet assured me it would be).
     Now it's four a.m. and here come five straight
hours of public-radio news. Jazz stops. Jyze too.
     (Lynn and Rob became the first visitors to Jyzer
Ink headquarters. A short walk from the bookstore cafe.
Still a musty smell in the room because most of its
contents have come out of storage or from the shed.
Even so I felt proud showing off my new digs.)
     And this is it. No more the table here. No more
backwoods jyze. No more zen marriage. No more kiri
ribbons hanging on our bookcase wall -- I'm taking them
down right now. And with dry eyes. I'm relieved to be
moving on. Nostalgia is not grabbing me even though it
might seem it is (because what else can you write about
at such a time). If any sobs or moans or shrieks of
pain, later for those.

*   *

     Stopping by the ORB cafe after the last drop-off at
the hideaway. Late, an hour before closing. When I
went up to buy my coffee I caught Ken L., the guy who
runs the bookstore's speaker program, munching on a
freebie cookie behind the counter. He and I have never
met and we never say hello but we've sure seen plenty of
each other. The man may personally know, that is, be
acquainted with, more writers than anyone else in the
world, but me he doesn't know in that sense and he's

seen me far, far more than any of them and possibly more than all of them combined. And doesn't even suspect, as far as I can tell, what he's missing out on.

I might be doing this up at room 225 but it's packed tight right now. Three extra wagonloads which I rolled with a tremendously satisfying clatter down the long L-shaped side hallway with its bumpy brick floor, and each day at the same time. Jenny the Asiusan night janitor (and she's friendly too, young, appealing, as in "Jenny Jenny Jenny, won't you come along with me"), she knows it's me before I round the last bend and come charging into the elevator lobby where she's seemingly always vacuuming. Into the ancient iron cage which so snugly accommodates the hand truck and up one floor, out and another lengthy L-shaped push, but much quieter because it's atop carpet this time. Lights on in No. 225 so the poor plant (the philodendron from our bedroom at home) can get some, then a quick stop in the men's room, then unload and back down to the wagon for the return trip to U Acres and start-up of another cycle.

Almost always I find a parking spot near the side door. Friday and Saturday nights are the exception -- only then is the entertainment zone really cookin'. Usually at least one triangle habitue will come up and offer to help me unload -- stagger up or lurch up -- for a price, of course, and when I decline they tend to demand the wages anyway. Tonight the drunk van pulled up a few feet in front of the wagon and started shoveling guys in. But so far never a sense of any real danger. And I like the grittiness of the area -- it's one of the main reasons I'm drawn here. "Reasons." Not a whole lot of reason or rationality involved in it. Much more love and desire. (Say instead.)

At most I'll have a couple of hours' work at the scope office tonight. That's why I can linger so late down here as I'm doing now. And I'll want to leave for home a little early so I can get some sleep before tomorrow's unusually early one p.m. departure to pick up the apartment keys at the housing agency in the city.

Today I did the final cleaning of the shed. Swept

it out. Marveled at the setting, the forest and the
grape arbor and the barn and the yard as seen up close
through those seven splendid hand-cut and hand-mounted
windows on a fine sunny morning. Then down at the house
I advised Lady U to put in a claim on the shed before
her parents arrive and decree some other use for it.
But she didn't seem much interested. Again she was
grouchy. who knows why. Almost certainly a whole lot's
going on with her I'll never know about, to say nothing
of the motivation therefor.

I agreed to take the wagon in for servicing on
Tuesday. She hadn't cared about this before but now she
suddenly did. This means my move might be stretched out
an extra day. But what difference will it make? Better
to keep the lady as appeased as possible.

What did we divvy up today? Mother's fancy blue-
and-white dish set. Last of the LPs. Sharp knives.
And agreed to make a special run to the dump next
Wednesday, a pay run. And discussed a newspaper article
on physical fitness, which is what she seems to care
about most these days. She's even reading a book about
it, "Smart Exercise." What she'd really like to do now,
she says, is become a certified fitness instructor, but
she's sure her parents would decline to foot the bill
for the schooling. Not enough prestige in it. They
want her to get a master's in something they can boast
about. And she wants to stick around the area, so she's
looking into nearby schools even though none of them are
much good. Just wants to hang with her new friends and/
or lover or lovers, it looks like to me. She's not
being very smart about anything, I'd say -- but it's all
beyond my purview now. Good luck to her. Yeah.

-- And closing time here. The back corner already
dark, chairs going up on the other tables, soon all but
this one. Then this one.

*   *

Here's what I intended to do last night. Scope-
office jyze. Then when I sat down to do it I hadn't
even pulled the cap off the J-stick before I knew I'd
soon be fading. And so let myself do that immediately,

85

but stretched out on the carpet, for just two hours so I
could hit the freeway at four a.m. (And did.)

Tonight I'm livelier. And facing not even the
small amount of scoping I expected. A few minor
corrections to punch in, and those already done, and the
entire job's printed, and it's not yet midnight.

I stopped by the broiler (usual one) for a burger.
In almost seventeen years of going there I had never
before arrived by car. Now it's about to become, for me,
a neighborhood establishment. It's right on one of the
primary routes to B-2 from here. In fact that's where I
picked up the map of my new turf. "A Mosaic of City
Life." An excellent little production.

I'm excited about this move, yes. (It starts
tomorrow!) I'm also wary. Shudders of trepidation.
Trepidate nothing! But I can't help it. It's not just
that everything's going way too smoothly. It's not just
that I'm well past the peak age for exploiting the
advantages of a "happenin' 'hood" (as the map actually
calls it) like this one. It's not just the difficulties
I've had before with living alone. Nor is it just that
I know I'm truly up against it as far as cranking out
something I can be proud of with the Mentoka series.
Nor is it just that emotionally I'm in such a battered
and bruised state as a result of the personal
catastrophes of the past year.

So am I about to say it's also not just the effect
of all of these combined?

I don't know what it is! Superstition? Uncanny
instinct? Pro-forma expect-the-worstism? Am I just
fearing the unseemliness of seeming to land too quickly,
as it were, on my feet? Of seeming to be too
superficially wounded by the death of my mother and the
"you're a liability" ultimatum from my sister and the
end of the living-together gig with the woman I dared
for almost two decades to call the love of my life?
Could it be a twisted kind of survivor's guilt?

-- Tonight I again drove around the new "happenin'
'hood" just to deepen my feel for it. Fifth or sixth
time I've done it. And each time I've hit on a couple

of notable new features. Tonight it was an all-night
cafe at the far northern tip of the district (which
boasts at least two other all-night eateries I know of)
and a steep brick road coming up from the waterfront
with a fancy jazz/billiards nightclub and a funky rock
venue facing each other across the street in the middle
of the block. So many clubs and cafes and galleries in
the area, so much live music! I tell you it's ideal!

Last night I pulled into the alley right behind the
"old sailors' hotel" that's my new home and tried to
figure out exactly which room was mine. The back wing
of the annex in which B-2 is located is built in a sort
of sawtooth pattern, as it would appear from above, so
that each room becomes a corner room, in a sense, with
at least ten or fifteen degrees of bay view. I think I
identified B-2 but I couldn't be certain. I think it's
the one just above alley level (not the second floor)
looking out on the alley itself along with the interior
courtyard whose existence up to that point I hadn't even
noticed.

What a big transition this is! Maybe the last such
major segue of my lifetime. I hope so, or at least in a
way I do. For sure I don't want to go through another
move like this one. The complexities! More than two
hundred boxes packed! (First I had to assemble most of
them, wiping out a dozen rolls of packing tape.
Exhausted several markers just writing contents labels.)
Stocked up on all items needed for the single life in an
unfurnished apartment, or rather on all the ones I could
think of, with some not yet actually bought but just
located. -- But a TV with built-in VCR is paid for, and
it's not one made by Dad's old employer (he would be
miffed). And a microwave. Those are the two big items.

Rip of the packing tape: signature sound of the
period.

Lots of grim moments too. Muttering and cursing.
I especially fail to enjoy listening to Lady U chirp
away on the phone to these guys and/or gals she's
hanging with these days. The seductive voice. The pure
joy. The excitement. But then there are also the

moments when I'm chortling away to myself as if I've somehow pulled off the scam of the century here and without even trying. To have my life all shook up like this: just exactly what I've been needing! And how horrible it is, such a truth! -- Yet not really. It fits right in with the way I've always felt life is and been delighted to think it so. Or just say that's one angle on it. At a time like this you need a lot of slants and you've got to keep shifting from one to another or otherwise you're stuck with a lifeless static picture and the grimness starts seeping back in.

    -- And an eminent American literary critic is about to die in his own words (in real life he's long gone). Last night I turned page 800 of the last volume of what I'm thinking of as his protojyze. Less than a hundred pages to go. I must say as a protojyzist he's less than scintillating. In its social dimensions his life could scarcely be more different from mine. He's gruff, tyrannical, sententious. Yet I'm liking him in a way I never did before. Behind all those poses he's just one more wanna-be writer who's trying the best he can to churn out some good stuff and touching in his inability to do so at the level he aspires to. I can identify with him here. I figure that at least in this one sense we're peers, this critic and I. I even feel sorry for him as he asks himself over and over why he's bothering to write -- and the asking itself is more writing. For some reason he never seems to think of this. It appears he needs -- reasons! To write!

    (I have a similar problem with a certain contemporary novelist's long essay in a current monthly mag about his difficulties with continuing to write novels. The culture no longer thinks novels matter, says he, and therefore he's too depressed to write. Just feeling sorry for himself, I'd say. Pouting child. You write because you love to write! -- And if sometimes you feel sorry for yourself because no one wants to think what you write matters very much, you at least have the good sense to consider that the responsibility for this shortfall may be your own.)

[The Jyze Moves]

    And here on the conference table, next to my
growing collection of maps and postcards, is someone's
copy of a glossy fashion mag. "What's Hot Now! Secrets
of Style!" You want to know about what really matters
in this culture, look no further. (But of course and so
what. I just hope I don't suddenly have to know about
such things again myself just to be able to cope.)
    Tonight in glancing through a city guidebook I
discovered that the historic building in which Jyzer Ink
is now residing was for many years around the turn of
the century widely considered the most beautiful in this
part of the country. Before its construction, a city
founder's home stood on the same piece of land, right
next to the original sawmill. The city's last lynching
(in public anyway) took place on a maple tree in the
founder's yard about 113 years ago, I think it was.
    Catastrophes. Major disruptions in my own puny
life (though it's not so puny to me, of course, except
with certain long-range lenses in place). I'm just
thinking how the current series of such disruptions
began right in this office some eighteen months ago with
the loss of my salaried job. Oddly enough -- call it
irony! -- I just learned this week that the new
conglomerate firm will be making its office here, this
same suite 1740, though the name on the door will be
different. Most likely this is where I'll still be
working. "Jyzelby the Sole Prop.," yeah. And if not
here, almost certainly four stories down at the office
of the other firm. (Have I mentioned it yet? The
merged firms will go by the other firm's name.)
    In short, this job turns out to be the one constant
in my life. And this building, by using my J-stick as a
measuring device on the downtown map I see it's almost
exactly equidistant from my new apartment and my new
personal office. Walk three short blocks west (slightly
downhill, toward the bay); then walk either seven blocks
north and somewhat uphill and I'm home (unit B-2) or
walk eight blocks south and a bit more steeply downhill
and I'm at Jyzer Ink (room 225).
    Of such walking I'll be doing a lot. I hope! I

intend! I figure I've got about three years during
which, without adding any income at all beyond what I
receive now, I can afford to maintain this downtown-
straddling life with an outpost at each end. I can't
imagine a better physical setting. I can't imagine a
better setup for living as I want to live. It's
flabbergasting: all of a sudden here I am. All I've got
to do is walk out that door and start doing it.

12

     Home again, U Acres. Yawning. Five a.m. But must
do this. "One last round in the House of Jyze." The
room itself, but barely recognizable. My stuff's all
gone and our old TV's been moved in from the "pantry" on
the other side of the bookcase wall, the shelves of
which on both sides are now entirely empty.
     It's been D-day all week, so D-week. Neither here
nor there or actually both here and there but mostly in
between. (And don't mess with Mr. of that name --
because that's me.) (And Ms. of her own D name? Same
advice!) Roaring along in the wagon. So much time for
thinking but scarcely an idea's popped up anywhere. For
ideas the shower is much, much better.
     A big symbolic moment. A short while ago I pried
the five keys to the old life from my key ring and
worked onto it the two remaining keys to the new life
(for B-2 and the lobby mailbox for B-2; the ones for No.
225 and unit 161 and my scope-office lockbox were
already on there). In a few hours I'll turn those five
old keys over to Lady U and that'll be it. Then she'll
be dropping me off at the foot ferry one last time.
     Close to three thousand miles I've put on the wagon

in the past couple of weeks. A fine little vehicle.
The way I'm seeing things at this point, I'll miss it
more than I will the lady herself, at least for a while.
In any case it's a good bet I'll never have another of
either, live-in lover or wheels. Live-in lover may be
a little more likely than wheels.

Last night at eight I left with the final
wagonload, every nook and cranny crammed with stuff,
some items sticking out the windows. "Like the Beverly
Hillbillies," the lady observed (a favorite all-purpose
analogy of hers ever since we moved out to this area).
For once no rain. Each night for six straight nights I
unloaded in the alley outside the courtyard gate and
just a few feet from my new pad, but then had to haul
everything the long way around, usually in rain varying
from light to extremely heavy, through the open interior
courtyard with its locked gate at one end, locked
basement door at the other, and two short but slippery
staircases in between, and then down the long zigzag
hallway to B-2. How many round trips between wagon and
room, I wonder -- maybe close to a hundred. Without the
building's pro-type hand cart I might've given up. (Or
no, not true. But sticking to the program would've
been a helluva lot harder.)

On four of those six nights I also had work at the
scope office, but luckily nothing too demanding or time-
consuming came up. April Fool's Day fell somewhere in
there. April Fool's Week is what it often felt like.
Keeping an eye on the sky for "Comet Calvin" but never
seeing it or even hearing a single word about it, other
than some of my own. It just streaked across the
firmament and left scarcely a trace. Apparently.

But what a moon. As if to make up for the comet's
flop. Full or close to it and achingly lovely and each
night at two or three or four a.m. I was driving more or
less straight at it as it hung near the southern
horizon, often swathed in swirling mists or streaked by
brushstrokey low clouds. Rainstorms marauding about.
During one pelting storm the cars plowing along kicking
up spray and mist reminded me of old newsreels showing

wartime convoys plunging through massive storms as U-
boats (ha!) lurked nearby. Or maybe better to say ghost
riders galloping through the clouds. In any case:
impressive. I felt like such a rookie out there, being
so long away from serious driving. How it can stir the
competitive juices at times -- I'd almost forgotten.

Tonight at midnight in the city a last vehicular
run to the big supermarket just west of the fairgrounds.
Stocking up on the heavy stuff. A dozen large cans of
veggie juice, eight large jars of chunky applesauce.
Noting the city prices are considerably higher than what
we hicks pay out here. -- And soon I'll no longer have
a legitimate reason to play the rube. Now I'm back
where I belong and I can be an authentic rube again,
relatively speaking, at least for a while.

But this is it. End of a monthslong evacuation.
It's demanded my full and undivided attention at nearly
all times. Now everything of mine's out of here that
could conceivably be gotten out. A year ago I would've
thought this impossible. And a whole new kind of life
is set up. I'm damn proud of this fact. I've picked
myself up off the floor and come storming back.

And how clean the old jyze central is! Swept it
myself. Didn't vacuum, though; left that for Madam Ex.
It's her vacuum cleaner. (I've got my own now back in
unit B-2, a brand-new nineteen-dollar three-in-one
model. I like its looks but I don't know yet how well
it will work, if at all. But if it's a bust I can
always borrow the building's industrial vacuum, a
massive bulldozer next to any ordinary model not to
mention my own little hand-held miniature.)

The lady's up there right now asleep in our bed.
Our lovers' bed! Over the years we gave it a pretty
good workout even if she now so sadly likes to imply I
was the only one who was ever truly into it. This past
week I was thinking about that as I slept there for the
last time -- a two-hour nap. At B-2 I'll still be
crashing on a previous lovers' bed of ours, albeit a
different one: the red futon atop the creaky loft. So
there will be some continuity. And half of us -- the

Madam Ex "better half" -- will be hanging on here at U
Acres, at least for a while, to maintain our rep, such
as it is, between the sheets on the bed upstairs.

     Will miss the cats. The birds. The various other
animals. Certain trees. The creeks. But in general
I'm not all that unhappy to be kissing the place goodbye.
(Noticing that a notorious radical bomber and tract
writer, in today's news proclaimed caught by the FBI
after evading them for well over a decade, has lived
since the mid-seventies in a remote backwoods area in a
handmade shed exactly the size of my own shed here, the
one I'm giving up and the feature of this rural life I'll
miss most: ten by twelve feet. And this bomber, by the
way, if that's who the arrestee truly is, is almost
exactly my age (three months older), grew up in the same
burbs I did, went to college in the same state and to
grad school in the same region, descended on the same
distant metro area I did after graduating and became a
college teacher there just as I did. And underwent
further radicalization there as well, no doubt, much as I
did, except for whatever reason he crossed the line into
violent resistance -- spun out of control, I'd say.)

     Little Ms. Hardbody -- what else will she do with
her life? She's starting to bone up for the Graduate
Record Exam. I noticed a stack of books again, well
hidden. Shocking: Lady U taking a renewed interest in
books. Then a look at the titles and I could see why
she was hiding them. Fantasy stuff, science fiction.
This is one way being out of my clutches might do her a
lot of good: she'll no longer feel she must suppress her
true interests. -- Nor did I ever want her to. But I
couldn't help expressing my own slant on the world, and
that of course included the arts and pop culture.

     Yes, it's over. I don't want to say I have no
regrets. I have plenty. And yet: on balance, do I
really? Would it be better just to try to avoid
thinking about such things? True, all too often
thoughts are popping up -- seemingly more or less
spontaneously -- oho, you'll be sorry, Madam Ex; aha,
take that, Madam Ex. Some yearnings for sweet revenge.

Mostly they're not so fierce, though. Even at their
peak last fall I still managed to wrestle them down or
trick them into exhausting their strength on diversions
and decoys.

Squirming. No comfortable place left for jyzing
here in the original jyzeroom. Not even good light.
Pathetic, sez I. If she wants to live like this, making
the best room in the house into TV central, I should be
happy I'm outta here.

But oh how I loved her once. And there's no
denying it: the ache rises again and again. As did
other aches for other lost loves in other eras -- and
those still do so even now, from time to time. Love
love love. Live for love. I did -- couldn't help
myself. Nor am I sorry about it. But now: trying to
regear and regroup. Wondering what, if anything, might
lie ahead for me in the love realm.

And unable to keep my eyes open any longer. Sez
Jyzemaster G to the House of Jyze: So long, and not
just for a while. Now I'm taking it out into the world.

*   *

*

*   *

Pinch pinch. Could this possibly be? Plainly not.
Yet plainly so. Which is contradictory as hell but then
-- isn't that what amazement's all about? Or can be?

Sitting by the open windows in my new crib looking
out on the waterfront, the bay, the western sector of
the city, the islands, those spectacular jagged peaks.
Gorgeous cloud-streaked sunset just starting to strut
its rosy stuff. Any moment now a ferry ought to be
chugging by down there, maybe even the same one (a
passenger-only vessel) I rode over on an hour ago. Also
a twin row of multihued plastic garbage barrels and a
big blue dumpster stand just across the alley, but
before long they'll be obscured to my eyes by the vines
growing laterally along the iron-grate fence from the
courtyard. This fence rises about four feet outside the
window and reaches to about a foot below eye level from
where I sit so that no part of the bay view is blocked.

And if the vines, now just budding, should grow too high and too leafy and start to get in the way, I can go out there and clip them. Can't use my former favorite clippers, though, because in a last-second magnanimous gesture, forgetting all about these vines, I let Lady U -- enough with the Madam Ex lingo sez I -- keep them.

No matter. Who cares. Spend a few more bucks. The things are useless for anything else. I've already realized this. And not for the first time either.

And traffic rolling by on the viaduct about a hundred feet away, two lanes in each direction, all from my perspective right at the same level as the top of the fence, with the roadway canted slightly toward me. I'm looking at the arc where the elevated viaduct curves away from its straight run along the waterfront and angles to the right -- northeast -- down toward the double-mouthed bluff-side tunnel that takes it to the main north-south highway which skirts the big hill about a mile due north. And grass on the other side of the cement alleyway (with a row of parking spaces to the left, or south, of the dumpster) and maybe it's the human-waste-product fertilizer provided by the local homeless and day-labor population that makes that grass grow so vividly green and thick. There's even some gravel where the alleyway, paralleling the viaduct, curves uphill to the right into the next-door vacant lot, only a small corner of which is visible from here.

Beauty and squalor. True urban grit. This combo I really go for. This is where I want to live. Pinch pinch. Why did I have to wait so long for this?

On the far side of the viaduct stands a brick warehouse, five stories tall, my ground-floor window here roughly level with its fourth floor. Beyond that building rises a fancy structure of similar size which is probably the new port headquarters. My slice of bay view opens out just north of this edifice and runs for maybe fifteen degrees until it collides with an upscale apartment house of seven or eight stories. I can also see little pieces of several piers on the waterfront about two blocks away and maybe a hundred feet down.

[Jyze and Jyze Alone]

    Surges of a weird euphoria as I gazed out at my new
home turf from the ferry as we rounded the point and
glided in. The area bounded on each end by a large hill
with a famous landmark structure standing nearby: now
mine. Both buildings in which I'm renting clearly
visible from the boat at times, including these windows
right here. The historic building in which Jyzer Ink
now offices, only the top stories were in view and those
only briefly, but still, there it was, with the gorgeous
antique white skyscraper rising forty-plus stories just
half a block behind it. Bipolar. Magnetic north and
magnetic south. My beautiful bipolar disorder.
    The dysphoria part will hit too. I know it and I'm
ready to ride it out when it does.
    The drive down to the home-port ferry dock with
Lady U at the wheel. Not really an amicable parting
but not all that unamicable either. More like cool.
Numb. Affectless. Almost as if I were a neighbor she
didn't like too much but didn't want to get on the
wrong side of -- giving him a lift into town because,
say, his pickup broke down. Except -- not even that
friendly.
    We talked about the home-port library and how lousy
it is, about my need for a pair of stackable ice-cube
trays for the freezer compartment of my fridge here,
about an invitation that arrived yesterday in my B-2 mail
for an open house at the art school she's interested in
-- which stands on the waterfront right behind that
upscale apartment house I mentioned earlier -- and which
I may well attend myself (the open house, that is). In
fact the woman living in the room next door is a student
there. (And her brother lives in the other room next
door, on the other side of mine. They're B-3 and B-1,
I'm B-2 -- B-2 as in the massively expensive supersonic
bomber, yes. Those are my only two immediate neighbors
because we're all three in a kind of pod at the end of
the long zigzag hall and across the hall is the north
wall of the building, sort of. It's hard to describe.
And below us only a crawl space. And to the south, at
my back now but visible through another window, and with
yet another window looking out on it closer to my kitchen

nook, the courtyard with its shrubs and benches. And
above, in the unit directly overhead, a guy who walks
around quite a lot late at night. From my loft bed less
than twenty inches beneath his floor I'll no doubt
become intimately familiar with his pacing patterns and
probably much else about his daily life.)
    Curious parting. Just -- "See you." Both of us.
And we will be meeting again soon, in fact next Saturday,
so she can sign some tax forms. That'll be the occasion
for my first ferry ride whose main purpose will be
visiting the storage place. Meet at the "jingo heaven"
lounge half a block from the dock, five p.m.
    A week ago tomorrow I signed the last papers at the
housing agency and then came over here to pick up the
keys. Listened to a no-nonsense spiel from Mindy, our
big-shouldered building manager -- but she's got a sense
of humor. "People say I shouldn't be living in this
candy-ass town. I should be from Hell's Kitchen."
Usually wears shades even in her dark office by the
front entrance. Sexy, probably about Lady U's age,
likes to box (that's as in the sport of fisticuffs, not,
say, boxing bonbons). And in her job she needs to be
tough. Probably she's thrown a few punches in the
course of carrying out her duties here but I didn't ask.
    Oooeee this is the life! And I've got so much work
to do. Right now this apartment is jam-packed with
boxes, lumber, furniture, all set down and piled up more
or less at random. It'll be a long time before I'm
truly settled in. Putting up the loft in its altered
form could take a month all by itself.
    And so much exploring to do!
    A further good sign. I'm walking past the little
lookout park north of the public market an hour ago, or
more like two now, carrying a bag of apples and bananas
bought at the market produce stalls, and someone walking
toward me catches my eye -- and I catch hers -- our
hands reach out and clasp and we spin halfway around
from arrested momentum and she says, "Aren't you --"
"Hey, Sophie isn't it? From the co-op? All those
clocks by your door?" "Yeah -- and you're Gun-Gun-Gun

-- uh --" Sounded sort of like the name I was called
for a while as a toddler (because it's what I called
myself since I couldn't say my own name properly):
"Gunnah." Sophie the tile artist! The very one I've
been fantasizing about for weeks. What luck! The
perfect way to run into her. And on the day of my
official emancipation! "No doubt I'll be seeing you
around, homey," said I, and I hope that's so. (This
after telling her I'd just moved in about two hundred
feet north of the co-op.)

     Not that I'm forgetting my words of wisdom to
myself. Don't plunge in. Keep priorities straight.
But something good just might happen here. If it
doesn't develop naturally I might look her up after a
while. My type, I think. Even just to have an
acquaintance or two in the hood is very good. Phil
from the co-op I might look up too, and the woman who
raved about my politics book -- I even brought over a
spare copy for her to replace the one she lost.

     The "B" in B-2 stands for basement, I finally
figured out, but because the building is constructed
right on the edge of the steep hill or bluff overlooking
the waterfront and I'm on the side of the building
facing that way, B-2 is more like a ground-floor room
and is actually half a story above the level of the
north-south alley carved into the side of the hill. The
older part of the building, originally erected ninety-
some years ago as a hotel for working men of all kinds
-- not just sailors, as I was first told -- and refurbed
into apartments seven years ago, stands directly across
the courtyard. I'm in what's called "the annex," added
during that same refurb period and integrated with the
original building, a single entrance serving both
structures where they come together on the hilltop side
along the first of the city's numbered avenues -- what
I'm thinking of as the "edge road."

     The founding spirit of this area, which in its
earliest days after the first wave of Cawk invaders hit
was a little town of its own, used to live directly
across that same edge road from our main entrance. He

later put up a large redstone structure there, five
stories tall, and it's still standing today, unoccupied
but as magnificent in its way as the building Jyzer
Ink's just moved into at the other end of the bipolar
zone and almost exactly the same age. The east-west
street which the south side of our building here faces
(across from which stands the co-op) is built atop what
was a ravine cut into the hillside to serve as a sluice;
when a much larger hill dominating the area immediately
to the east was reckoned to be impeding progress around
the turn into the twentieth century, that whole hill was
blasted to bits and the bits were pumped down the sluice
out into the bay. And that's why the entire hundred-
square-block district in which I'm taking up residence,
except for this bluffside sliver on its far west, is now
as flat as an engineer's level could make it.

(Might I clarify any of this a twist or two?
Probably not in this lifetime.)

I first became aware of this part of town about
fifteen years ago when it began developing a reputation
as a funky arts district. I first passed through it
almost two decades before that, in my late teens, while
walking from downtown to the fairgrounds during my first
visit to the entire region. But my only memory of it
from back then is the way the fair itself looked as I
approached it from these streets.

I mean it: I expect to live here the rest of my
life. They'll have to haul me out of old B-2 feet first.
Not too soon, I hope. I'd like to have a decade or two,
even three, maybe even more than that, to enjoy this
setting. (Mindy said an eighty-three-year-old tenant
died here a few months ago -- her first death as a
manager.)

So now I can just walk to work. First fix myself a
bite to eat if I can figure out where the utensils are,
then do exactly that: hike over to the scope office.
Lots of scoping to grind out tonight and I'll be running
on just about zero sleep. But elation will fuel me at
least for a while.

Pinch pinch. Jaw hanging agape. How did this

happen? How did such bad luck turn into such good luck?
And what will the next turn be, and when? Who knows --
so savor, kid. Your unexpected moment. The late
flowering of Jyzemaster G, starting today.

13

    New hood hang. "The big cafe." Fine spot except
for the gimmick that draws in the geeks and the nerds
and no doubt lots of truly strange people as well: the
rows of computer monitors and keyboards. Every last
one of them is in use right now -- at half past five
on a Friday afternoon. The happiest of happy hours.
    And am I one of the happy ones? I am. Still.
Though what a seesaw J-week it's been, and for sure in
more ways than one. More ways than four or five, most
likely, if I wanted to try counting. Which I don't.
    Big square room, this place, probably a hundred
feet on a side, high ceiling with bare rusting iron
beams, some sort of cement-screed floor. Informal
bohemian feel except for the computers. Lots of artwork
on the walls, eclectic and sometimes seriously bizarre
music playing. The space is divided into quarters, more
or less, with few partitions between them: one quarter
for computers only, one for the cafe counter and kitchen,
one for live performances (with several couches and easy
chairs and a grand piano which I listened to a classic
bird's-nest-haired guy tune yesterday), and then this
one where I'm holding forth now, the cafe seating area.
Blond wooden tables, odd-looking chairs with too-small
and overly bendable backs (the part you rest your spine
against, if you're masochistic enough, about the size
and shape of a scrunched-up human face). And the entire

western wall from four feet to maybe ten feet up
consists of industrial windows looking out on what I
think of as "the middle road" with its four lanes of
one-way traffic heading south toward downtown. It's
become my preferred nighttime avenue for walking home
from work because it's well lit and has abundant foot
traffic on both sides even at two a.m.

Seesaw, first, literally, as in see the man saw.
And hammer. And mess up again and again even after
measuring twice, and nonetheless the loft is almost
fully reassembled in its newly re-revised form, the
steps now mounted on the opposite end from the doorway.
The leaning loft of B-2. It creaks, it puzzles the eye.
It looks at once jerry-built and formidably solid, and
is both. All the hammering, I worry about alienating my
new neighbors before I even know them and so pound away
no more than four hours a day and only in the afternoons
when most or all of them seem to be out. This limited
work window drives me crazy because it's hard to think
about anything else until the thing, meaning the loft,
which will also be my bed and home office and most of my
home bookcases, is fully up and usable.

But then maybe it's good to have something to be
obsessed with. I know it is, in fact, because otherwise
I'd be going even crazier trying to fight off an
adolescent crush I've developed. And in my very first
week officially out of harness! It's just too
embarrassing. Fool!

Sofie is the crush. Same Sophie as last time, but
she spells it with an F, not a PH, and it's short for
Sofiya. Co-op Sofie. The very next day after last
jyzing about her I bumped into her again at a little
stationery shop just up the street, and she agreed to
join me for coffee here at the cafe. A bold move on my
part to ask her. Sofie of the tile-work mirrors and
clocks. "Just say my days as a thirty-something are
numbered!" Looks a bit like -- may the gods help me --
like the smoldering-eyed actress who married the
greatest (albeit the most hateful) of the great crooners
of my father's generation. Short black hair (Sofie

again now), a little above medium height, good busty
figure in black tights and white T. Trying to live on
sales of her art alone. The small coffee bar right
across the street from the co-op is currently featuring
a display of her work. Colorful handmade tile clocks,
sixty bucks. Interesting mosaic-bordered mirrors too,
and several portraits, made with tile alone, of famous
female artists. Clearly she's good at it. And
obviously works hard, because I see the lights shining
until late most nights in her second-floor window. But
-- she has a boyfriend. He's a set designer at a
college several hundred miles from here and he's there
most of the time, but they're planning to live together,
or she's talking about it anyway. When, I don't know
for sure, but my guess would be at the end of the
academic year -- so perhaps in a month or two.

   We get along easily and well. Sparks, or I thought
so. She picked her way through a pile of women's
clothes we found dumped in the gutter near the battered-
women's shelter (I found a Bat hat for myself, as in the
crime-fighting superhero duo). "I never buy clothes
anymore," she said. "I get them all from dumpster
diving." Also reminds me of Jean B. of Mezzu days, she
does, in some ways, especially the natural smoldering/
sultry/sloe-eyed look; but this Sofie's more poised,
steadier, warmer, not such an outrageous tease. But does
often put her hand on your arm when she talks. She even
came over to see my room -- my first and only visitor
thus far, building employees and agency inspectors
excepted -- though on the pretext of checking out the
building as a possible place to live with her boyfriend.
Anyway I'd like to think it was a pretext.

   Her visit to B-2 was brief, sorry to say, and I
haven't seen her since. "This room wouldn't work for
me," she sniffed. "I need bare floors." As I walked
her back to the lobby I fumbled out something about
understanding she's already partnered up but maybe we
could do lunch or dinner or take in a movie one of these
days just for the heck of it. She responded in a
puzzling way: didn't say yes or no, but at my mention of

"partnered up" she blurted something about that not
being relevant, or started to; then she seemed to have
second thoughts about saying this and stopped in
midsentence (I forget the exact words).

Meaning what? I don't know. Later that day I
signed her guestbook at the coffee bar, scribbling a few
laudatory sentences about her work and including my
phone number (I do have a phone now, and even an
answering machine, though only one person has called me
so far: myself, checking out the machine from the scope
office). But weeks may go by before she reads that
guestbook message.

And so the struggle began. What to do. I couldn't
get her off my mind but I didn't want to pester her and
I didn't want to betray my own vows concerning a new
kind of life. Everything revolving around love and
romance? No! Don't let it happen!

So: wait and see what she does. It would be easy
for her to concoct an excuse for contacting me if she
wanted to. We live just a couple of hundred feet apart
-- have I not mentioned this happy fact a few times
already? I'm new in the hood and know no one except her
and three or four other co-oppers (and we both made a
big deal of these key facts as well).

But -- no contact so far. "No risk, no honor."
That goes for both of us, I guess. Is she too taking
figurative cold showers and grateful to plunge into
other obsessions? Wondering what to do? Seesawing?
Not too likely but then again not totally unthinkable.

My unstable newly separated self. This may be only
the first in a string of oddball infatuations. Only now
a week later do I feel I'm beginning to come out of it.
Glad at least I haven't embarrassed myself with her as
far as I know. And if she walked in the cafe door right
now (I'm trying not to look but this whole time I've
been hoping she would) of course I'd try to hang on to
my cool, such as it is -- which is to say, isn't.

Lots of seesaws in this Sofie episode, but taken
together they count as only one of the larger of the
major array of same mentioned earlier. And I'm not

saying I'm anything less than delighted to have an idiotic high-school-like crush to be on the brink of flipping out over. Nor am I saying I'm anything less than agonizingly frustrated.

So next? I'm grateful too I've had much else to keep me distracted. All this newness. The exploring. The effort to shift my schedule back to one in which I can sleep seven or eight hours a night and all of them in a row (for the first time in seven years). Crashing on an air mattress on the B-2 carpet beneath my mother's dual-control snow-white electric blanket. Searching obsessively (again) for items I suddenly feel I must have for launching the new life, not to mention a few real necessities. Pondering how I want to arrange my furniture, what little I have, and how I want to improve the room -- build a light stand for the bathtub, a flowerbox for the west windows, more closet shelving.

Numerous trips to the hardware store just two blocks away (and flashing again and again on how much more one appreciates standard urban neighborhood shops after living out in the boonies). Splurging -- as if outfitting myself, I've often thought, for a long stay in a wilderness cabin, not really at all sure why this or that item suddenly seems so crucial. But then on the other hand, why do without it? A nifty "Red Army" pocket watch, for example, surprisingly inexpensive (on sale for thirty bucks), now attached to my bag with an eighteen-inch length of small-gauge chain (as my keys are attached to a belt loop with a similar length of the same chain, bought from the same hardware store). Also frames for various photos and paintings -- and one, to hold brother Rob's "Possession" watercolor, I'm still searching for, defeated so far by its odd dimensions.

-- I'll get back to the seesaws, but later. Unfortunately reporter Naomi took a rush job today which I must tackle tonight. And tomorrow will be lost for settling-in matters because I'll be meeting Lady U in the old home port at five o'clock. I haven't seen her either, any more than I've seen Sofie -- in fact twice less -- but I'm not anguishing over it. Not even

slightly. And I did talk with her briefly on the phone
to confirm tomorrow's meeting. She didn't seem to be
missing me at all. Said she was hard at work cleaning
the house in preparation for her parents' upcoming visit,
but then later in a different context she blurted that
their visit had been put off until June (apparently
entirely forgetting, too, that a month ago she used
their alleged impending arrival in early April as a prod
to hasten my exit).

    Tonight she's coming into the city -- this area, in
fact -- to see another live-music performance of her
currently preferred "alt" variety, with -- well, I don't
know with whom she's coming. Nor do I want to know. But
one of these days I expect to bump into her on the
streets around here and she'll probably be running with
some twenty-year-old kid in skater gear with his (or her)
hand riding her ass. She especially likes one of our
neighborhood venues just a diagonal block from here, and
I often make a special point of walking by the joint, not
so I might by chance see her but so she might by chance
see me. I do want to stick it in her eye a bit how
pleased I am with my new life and how terrific it is and
how too bad for her she's not part of it.

    More unstable behavior. No doubt. Shameful indeed.
And much more of it still to crop up, I'm sure -- crop
up only then to be stomped down again, right.

*   *

    -- Starting now, some six hours later, the new
upwelling of -- what? We'll see. A quick burst of it,
a gush only, because this joint will be closing soon.

    It's the same joint. Digital cafe, I think I'll
call it, or digi-cafe for short. A seat at the window
counter this time. A high stool, cool air coming in,
foot traffic streaming by on the sidewalk outside, the
crowns of their heads bobbing along a few feet below my
eye level like more or less furry coconuts riding the
surface of an unusually clear brook. Friday night --
the hood is jumping. The live-music venues -- throbbing.
Panhandlers and drug peddlers hard at it up and down all
the main drags and many of the side streets and alleys,

and definitely not least the one outside my B-2 windows.
(The next three avenues to the east of the one here I
haven't visited yet tonight but the scene's likely much
the same over there.)

The jazz band playing here just calling it a night,
probably heading off to a jam session elsewhere.
Upstairs the constant clicking of pool balls sounds like
a roomful of castanet dancers. Huge operation up there.
I'm taken aback by the number and size of the pool halls
in this area. And by the number of nightclubs offering
live jazz. Almost as much jazz as all other types of
live music combined. (Though much of the jazz itself is
in a fused state with some of those other genres.)

Comical all this Sofie blather of mine. Next week
it'll probably be someone else -- maybe even one of the
digi-cafe waitresses. Or servers rather. The one with
big brown eyes (and technicolor spiked hair) smiles at
me a lot, even from back in the kitchen, and I'm
reminded so much of Maruko of pre-Lady U days I want to
-- to -- no, not weep. Cheer! (Not that Maruko looked
anything like this one here, but Maruko's eyes and mine
first met when she was working in a kitchen and I was
sitting in the cafe outside.)

-- Now they're going around snuffing out the
candles. And I'm not even half finished with my
schooner of root beer. That's what they sell the small
glass as, a schooner. I like it. Prairie type maybe.
Covered wagons rolling west, dust clouds rising, skulls
of fallen oxen grinning up maniacally from trailside.

So I'll carry on back in B-2. "The crib on the
edge." (Taxicabs prowling in the garish yellow crime
light out there. Punks goofing. -- "You're such a
goof!" cried Sofie, and warmly, when I fed a quarter
into the parking meter "to keep you legal" as she
lingered over her pile of discarded clothes in the
gutter below. "You should've given that to me!" -- She
has no money, she moans, and her bills are so high, over
a thousand a month -- did she say including her wheels?
Or not including her wheels? In any case she needs
those wheels because she must hustle to sell her clocks

and mirrors and tile portraits to pay for the vehicle
itself, among other things. One such other thing being,
I would imagine (oh yes I would!) a big phone bill to
her boyfriend. -- And one by one the screens here at
the digi-cafe are going blank. A single candle's still
burning and it's just for my benefit -- now snuffed!
These last jyze strokes by feel alone, or almost.)
*   *

    -- Reminds me of an antique photo I saw last week
showing the new home of Jyzer Ink in half-completed
shape, most of its inner structure still visible, the
upper stories just a skeleton like the ribs of one of
those same oxen scattered along the prairie-schooner
trail, sticking up bare-bones from the sand.
    The loft I'm talking about. The one and only,
right before my eyes. Rising out of sawdusty chaos --
but its ascent interrupted for the weekend. I've nailed
down only half of the planks that'll make up the
platform and sleeping surface on top. A few more lie
haphazardly athwart the crossbeams with big gaps between
them, conspicuous as missing (what else?) teeth. (Was I
going to say eyeballs? Kneecaps? Left elbows? -- And
I almost wish my left elbow really were missing at this
point, it's become such a nuisance. It's now in far
worse shape than the right, which seems to be healing.
The course with these elbows appears to be paralleling
that taken by my bad shoulders of a few years ago --
first right, then left, with no apparent reason for the
shift. And come to think of it, the drill's been the
same for my Achilles tendons, but in reverse: first left,
then right, and now maybe left again.)
    It's been a long one. The day. Began with Stu, a
maintenance man from the housing agency, knocking at
nine a.m., sent by Mindy (the pugilist manager) to
provide the missing window "blockers," as they're called,
metal bars to prevent someone outside from raising, or
rather further raising, a window that's cracked open.
Woke me up and then had no blockers to offer. Cutting a
stick to size would be best, he kindly suggested.
Mindy's advice was simply never to open the windows, but

it gets too hot in here for that. Stu says every now
and then somebody will try to crawl in one or another of
the building's ground-level windows (which level all
mine are), not so much to rob or rape but just to get
some sleep. "Gimme Shelter." Sight of a stick will
dissuade them, he thinks, not draw their attention even
more. The blockers would be fully concealed.

    A train whistle. I hear them at least as often as
I did in Mezzu days and at their closest they're just
about as far away as they were then: a block and a half.
In this case they're down at the base of the hill. But
here the sound effects also include foghorns. And the
clamorous thumping of empty trucks as they hit some sort
of bump or crack on the southbound lanes of the viaduct
while careening around the bend at high speed. Those
lights streaking by at all hours, except rush hour when
they, or the vehicles, usually creep by. People driving
in all four lanes can look right in my windows, though I
expect they're normally too busy with negotiating the
curve to do so. Rush-hour or accident-induced gridlock
would make for exceptions. I don't worry either way --
can't help but flash them a little skin every now and
then. That their curiosity might not go -- unrewarded?
unpunished? -- could also work either way, I suppose,
but probably tending toward the latter. No, certainly
tending toward the latter. Like a finger in the eye.

    As for the seesaws -- getting back to those -- did
I mention manic moods? They should count for plenty.
But they're all interior and they're even interior to
the interior in many cases, droning away in there or
raging or grinding or bubbling as I try to stay focused
on other things. Like scoping. Like hammering. Like
planning. Like dreaming. Like reading -- last night a
book-length essay on blues and the heroic spirit with, I
noticed only today, a Ray W. blurb on the cover. Yes,
the same Ray W. who so disruptively introduced Lady C
into my life near the end of those same nose-to-the-
grindstone Mezzu days, in fact bringing down the curtain
on them with a big whomp. And has anything been the
same since? I say no. But it's true I could -- do --

assert that about many things and those things come from many different incidents in many different eras.

Five bananas I've eaten today. I overstocked on them -- as I'm sure on a good many other things, out of sheer pique -- and now it's a mad rush to gobble them all before they go bad. Four still left. Not a whole lot of yellow showing on any of them. Mush inside. Try to gently pry them open "howler style" (Lady U's jesting term for the practice) from the non-stem end and they burst in the middle and start oozing.

What else of jyze note? How about the evening I caught the last set at the jazz billiards club? Like a dream come true, dropping by on impulse at well past midnight, the joint almost empty and the band working hard to please mainly itself or maybe a musician's squeeze lolling somewhere out of sight. A vintage Afrusan gent in frayed suit and rakish fedora was holding down a barstool to my right, an earthy Eurusan waitress was counting her tips a few stools to my left and every once in a while absentmindedly scratching an itch beneath her fishnets, lower inner left thigh -- for some not so inexplicable reason that one little last-named detail particularly clings (and pings).

Each time I come in the building here I check my mailbox and answering machine. So far not a goddamn nibble on either, other than, as mentioned earlier, my own (this is turning into infinite solipsistic regress). "Glen's electronic shadow here saying if you've got a message for my real, noncyber self, you're on at the tone. Feed the shadow." -- The first answering-machine greeting I've ever composed. (Best to terse it up pronto, I'm thinking now.)

Boards leaning against walls. Boxes stacked literally to the ceiling. Sawdust tracked everywhere and rising in drifts in most of the corners. The power saw squatting on the kitchen floor like a giant black frog with steely eyes and a mouthful of shiny sawtooth fangs, its electrical cord serving as a leash. Bags of nails, rolls of scrap carpet, packages of shims. The ever more handy shims. Thank the cosmos for shims!

And shedding light on this page, one of my two new floor lamps. This is the life! And I finally figured out how to take a shower without flooding the bathroom.

But -- seesaws. Still more of them to report, and I'll get around to doing that sooner or later. Or perhaps much later. After I figure out where to sleep tonight -- which patch of floor to clear -- and then do the clearing and then, with zero delay, the crashing.

*   *

Did clear, did crash, did awaken at the sound of a strangely familiar voice -- my own! -- speaking in ponderous electronic-shadow form at seven a.m. after four rings of the phone -- but I guess it was just a wrong number. Or another computer calling, maybe, but programmed to speak only to noncyber selves. In any event the shadow could entice no message -- no feed. In unit B-2 I remain unreached and untouched by the outside world. Except for Sofie. The one brief visit.

Did return to the digi-cafe for breakfast: a half-price day-old cinnamon roll and coffee. Did read a newspaper for the first time since Thursday. Did stroll down through the public market (wonderfully vibrant shortly after noon on a Saturday, street musicians and buskers of many other types drawing big crowds), did take in the bluff-top waterfront view from the small lookout park nearby (trying to triangulate with my similar but much more obstructed B-2 window view a few blocks to the north and maybe thirty or forty feet higher). Did buy a magazine at the main newsstand before leaving the market. Did then hike on down the edge road and, a block north of the triangle and Jyzer Ink, stop in at the map store and buy three maps, two depicting my new stomping grounds and, when overlapped, fitting the territory almost perfectly, with most individual buildings named thereon, and the third map covering the whole of my usual ferry route with water depths noted and obscure geographic features identified.

And then did trek on up to "suite" 225 where this installment's going down. For the past week I've had to neglect this place but I'm still greatly pleased with it.

110

Truly a top-notch hole-in-the-wall jyze hideaway. (And
just moments ago I met a fellow who works in the
neighboring wellness clinic, one Keenan D. "Well, hi,
neighbor!" cries he in a surprisingly high-pitched voice.
Likely gay, but not the one I met before. The other's
partner perhaps. I told him I'd be here mostly in the
evenings and I didn't think I'd be disturbing his
business in any way -- since in effect we're subleasing
different parts of what was once the same large many-
roomed office -- a true suite -- and I joked that I'd
pound on the wall if the yelps of aspiring wellness
originating over there become too distracting. -- He in
ratty jeans and a worn and patched plaid shirt.

Happily for me, most folks around here dress very
informally, in many cases even during official business
hours.)

Again only a brief stop -- to water the plant and
then why not jyze just a jot or two. Another half hour
or so until I head over to the dock to catch the ferry.

(Not bipolar disorder, I should call it, I was
thinking during my peripatetic "did this did that"
stroll down here, but bipolar order. A rigorous
philosopher of deconstructionist bent might not think
too highly of my viewing things in such simplistic
binary fashion -- I don't myself! -- but for the current
setup it can't be denied: the fit is good. If not
forever and thus essentialistically or foundationally,
at least for now. At least for a while. Please!)

And it's true, as I passed beyond the public market
and the strength of the polar pulls started reversing I
noted I was suddenly feeling different. I hadn't known
my spirits were down (must be the Sofie thing, most
likely) but I felt them lifting as I neared the historic
quarter. Happy to "get away" -- to have a place I can
go to and call my own. Yeah! A crowd gathered around a
tour guide in the triangle, learning about the original
Cawk "pioneers," skid road, the eponymous chief (whose
bronze bust stood sternly and, so it seemed, pointedly
silent next to the motor-mouth guide) and the pergola
and the totem pole and the antique white skyscraper
(once for a very brief period the world's fourth-tallest

building), about the bricks, the burning city, the high
tides gushing out of toilets, the miraculous raising
(not razing, because the fire had already done that) of
the entire business quarter, as it was called then.

So many daytime things. The biggest change of all
for me right now is the righting (as well as the
writing, yes) of my upside-down world. I hit the bed
by three, rise by ten -- and those are both a.m. I'm
on the streets when shops are open and lots of people
are out and about and the sun might even be shining.
All this is taking some getting used to. It's like
returning from the wilderness -- another form of it.
Nocturnal wilderness, backwoods wilderness: both. And
the reclusion of a long-running inward-turned love
relationship -- returning from that wilderness too.

But now I leave to revisit the last-named two of
those wildernesses -- partially. Under public
chaperonage, as it were. Lady U. And I still haven't
gotten around to mentioning some of the best of the
weekly seesaws, so I'll be back yet again.

*   *

Aboard the ferry, auto kind, already chugging
through forty-six fathoms, or atop them rather, if this
new map ("not to be used for navigational purposes") is
to be believed. A late jyze start on this voyage
because I had to exchange a few words with Lenny, then
Alison, then Haskell. Here's where my real friends are,
to the extent such limited ties can count as real
friendships. And I say they can and they do and I hope
this will continue to be the case. Though I also have
to say it's not very likely it will.

Grinding past the point, the navigation light
bobbing on its buoy a few hundred yards offshore. The
map calls it a "head." This turn we're making now, I
could be observing it from a distance of a mile or so
out my B-2 window. From there I can monitor the
progress of these ferries most of the way across until
they're about to disappear into the Z-narrows. (Take
this map away from me before I'm tempted to name some
proper names in flagrant violation of the jyze rules.)

Partly cloudy day, warming up again, just breezy enough to make the sailboats frisk a bit. Weekend boaters just like Dad used to be -- you can tell by how wobbly they are.

So then seesaw the third. Is what? Nine days ago my first brokerage check arrived in the mail. It was in the batch I picked up from our driveway box as Lady U and I were leaving for the last drive to what was about to cease being the home port for me. Or at least I thought it was a check at first, from its looks. But then I decided otherwise -- because after all the deal was, as set up with Lynn at the investment group, they would be depositing the quarterly stipend directly into my bank account. This checklike piece of paper, I figured, must be merely an acknowledgment of deposit, its appearance designed to make me feel good in the absence of a real check. I very nearly threw it out. But then over the next week I noticed my checking account balance as disclosed by the ATM (which I was hitting up regularly for new infusions of cash) was failing to show the expected $825 bump. Finally it dawned on me that the "acknowledgment" might've been a real check and I launched a frantic search for it. Fortunately I hadn't been quite so stupid as I might've been -- I'd tossed it into a box of papers to be filed. I did find it. And a close reading revealed it to be -- indeed -- a real check. Yesterday I deposited it.

(Turning now into the maw of the narrows -- that other point out there, I finally know its name -- and it's probably, like the town I'm bound for today (but hope I'm no longer bound to, or at least not to the degree I was for all those years), named for a crewman aboard the Cawk sailing ship that first put this area on world maps and not for any distinctive physical features which may be present -- and no doubt some are out there, though from here I can see only wholly unremarkable ridgelines and even more unremarkable evergreens.)

Seesaw the fourth is related to the third. I miswrote earlier -- one piece of mail with my name on it did come in at B-2, and that was an express delivery of

some kind. The only time my room's been buzzed. At
first I thought it must be something from Sofie -- good
news! Instead it was a letter from sister Barb
enclosing a copy of a K-1 tax form from the accountant
handling Mother's estate. It indicated there would be,
after all, taxes to pay for last year on something
called an intervivos trust even though this same
accountant had suavely assured us back in November there
wouldn't be. Fifteen hundred in taxes on dividends,
five hundred in taxes on capital gains. Yikes!

(Rounding Point Such-and-Such -- not an actual
name. Only eleven fathoms of water here, whereas midway
in the crossing we passed over an area with between 111
and 130. This means it's just about deep enough there
for the tallest building in the city -- some seventy-
five or eighty stories -- to stand on the bottom without
breaking the surface.)

-- So the time had come to do my taxes. I'd been
feeling flush up to this point, having more bucks left
in the bank than expected after engaging in so much
frantic "outfitting." But then another shock: my total
taxes for last year, which I'd estimated at about $700
still owing (partly because unemployment comp is now
taxed and partly because Jyzer Ink had yet to pay any
taxes, its gross receipts being so negligible as not to
require quarterly prepayments) -- my taxes, or rather I
should say Lady U's and my taxes, the return being a
(zen) joint one, would be almost double my estimate --
close to $1300! Since I already owed the lady roughly
$450, and she'd agreed to pay half the taxes (very
begrudgingly, I might add), this meant her half would
come to about $640. Instead of getting a hundred-dollar
refund from me, as she was expecting, she'd have to
cough up another $180.

I decided I wouldn't ask her to do that. Basically
I didn't want to go through the hassles. Instead I'd
tell her I'd absorb the $180 myself. She wouldn't be
receiving a "refund" from me on her loan (used to buy
plane tickets and pay various bills back when Mother
died) but at least she wouldn't have to pay more.

[The Jyze Moves]

     On the phone she seemed to take this news well
enough. But in a couple of hours I'll be showing her
the return to sign. At that point we'll see where
things really stand.
     As we pull in. (Twelve fathoms.)
                    *   *
     Approaching a double-length entry, this one. At
least it improves the odds I'll have a decent sheaf of
pages done before it's time to move on to Book II at the
end of the month.
     "Jingo heaven," the lounge. Same old place.
House bourbon and water. But an unfamiliar weekend-
afternoon waitress. Nasty short skirt too. But I
suppose up until the past few months it wouldn't've
looked nearly so nasty to me as it does now.
     Today I won't be visiting the storage unit. I've
decided it's too early in the new life for that. Later
on I'll have lots to do up there and also, most likely,
lots to haul in one direction or the other or both. I'm
figuring I'll try to go through one ferry coupon book,
ten rides, every three months -- because at the start of
the fourth month after purchase the book expires.
     Maybe the best news of all from the new frontier is
my sense that living on seventy bucks a week won't be
too hard. I'd thought it might feel oppressive, and I
suppose it still might when the weather turns bad again,
but for now it definitely looks doable. Most days I
should be able to scrape by on under three bucks, not
including grocery costs. The key here is having good
cafes at both ends of my turf (both poles): cheap
coffee, free house newspapers, unlimited sitting time.
I'll make myself a box lunch to eat at whichever office
I wind up in, hideaway or scope, and on most days I'll
rustle up dinner at home. Grocery costs will be low:
surely under thirty bucks a week. The phone is just
short of ten bucks a month, laundry about five.
     The main budgetary question right now is how many
subscriptions should I keep going. Easy to read most
mags and journals at the bookstores and newsstands, but
then I can't clip the good stuff. If I buy all the

individual issues containing clip-worthy items I'll pay
a much higher per-issue price. Will potential clips
seem useful enough often enough to justify shelling out
for subscriptions? And even if the subs look desirable
from this perspective, can I afford them?

   -- But what an eighter it was. My first full day
back living on my own was Good Friday. Of course
everyone's out partying for that. Of course! (It was
also the day of Sofie's reception at the coffee bar --
wish I'd learned about it early enough to attend.) Then
Saturday night the time, appropriately enough for me,
shifted. "Spring forward." (I say yes, fool, do it now
if ever!) Then Sunday, by the usual calendrical course,
was Easter. At the scope office the small countertop
Christmas tree (artificial, naturally, in harmony with
everything else there) reappeared bearing a string of
glowing garish-pink bunny lights. Resurrection symbols!
And all these days were warm and sunny. Delightful
waterfront air. Baseball season opening. "You gotta
love these guys." Signs everywhere so insisting --
remnants of last fall's pennant fever. (In fact several
of my final week's commutes with full wagonloads
coincided with the baseballers' opening homestand, the
parking lots surrounding the dome packed to bursting as
I curled off the freeway nearby, cheers heard on the
radio seeming almost visibly to lift the dome roof like
the top of a drummer's foot-operated cymbal.)

   Recalling life in my former home city way back in
another incarnation. The new bipolar zone here with its
many night spots and nearby waterfront is like that and
even better in a way because less tacky. Where else in
the entire country could I find a setting like this?
Nowhere I know of. Nothing in that former city like the
public market or the digi-cafe. (The digi-cafe also has
a political conscience, I've neglected to mention.
Sunday nights it features not just live blues but also
a political forum. This Sunday's is "Liberalism v.
Progressivism." Yawn. But maybe I'll check it out
anyway.) -- Recalling overseas days too, the last six
months of small-town isolation, desperately fantasizing

about the return to my home country to live in some
funky city neighborhood with a bookstore nearby, a cafe,
a little nightlife, a few people of similar cultural/
political persuasion, a language in which I might even
be able to communicate occasionally. Well, yes, this is
it beyond my dreams, then or ever.

     Love and romance -- the catch. Sex. Already I'm
way too horny, even at my "mature" stage. Are the old
gonads still capable of taking over my life? I say no.
Not that I want to give up these good things (love,
romance, sex I'm talking about -- and yeah I'd like to
hang on to the 'nads as well and have them be active
too) but I want to keep all this under some kind of
control. That's all. (But to succeed at it I may have
to become an authentic blues hero, at least to myself.)

     Five to six. It may seem I'm building dramatically
toward this meeting with Lady U, former self-proclaimed
(that is, by me) love of my life. Yet as far as I know
there's no reason to, and certainly I've not been trying
to. Already this over here is the misty past. So much
I gave up in an attempt to make love work! Who knows,
maybe I'll feel the call -- someday -- to do it again.
But I'm thinking not. I'm thinking do what I must to
keep the new bipolar order intact. Seesaws, fine, keep
things in motion, they give you something to jyze about.
But hang on, Jyzerman, if you possibly can, to what
you've now finally -- astoundingly! -- got.

14

     Just so irritated right now. Annoyed. Pissed off.
Maybe I can jyze myself out of it, though I doubt it.
And this on the day of the long-awaited unit-warming

party.

I arrive at the office -- mine, Jyzer Ink's -- and find a photocopied handwritten note on the door saying it's been, as I make it out at first, "redkeyed" and if I have any trouble getting in I should call Hank or Trevor at such-and-such numbers. I try my key and it doesn't work. I'm locked out. And I'm carrying two big bags of items I've brought on foot all the way from B-2 to stash at the office, I need to pick up some other stuff, I have plans to hang the last of the framed pictures (I've brought tools for that purpose) and to get some editing done.

"Redkeyed" -- what could it mean? Sounds like I've failed to pay the rent or something. Maybe put up too many pictures and aroused some inspector's wrath. Or could be someone's broken in (the previous tenant, possibly, or the escort service, or someone out to get one or the other of those or both) and the building managers had to change the lock to keep them out. I'm worried that something (or everything) of value I had in the office will be gone.

Fuming, I head over to the phone booth at the ORB cafe to call Hank and Trevor. I get only their answering services and they, of course, can do nothing for me beyond taking a message. I lose four bits on the two calls. I gain, however, upon rereading the note as I talk with one of the operators, a better fix on the word "redkeyed." It's actually "re-keyed." Two rather eccentric flowery loops stemming from the "e" and the "k" intersect with the hyphen to create what at first appeared to be a cursive "d."

I return to No. 225 to see if I can make my old key work after all in a lock which has been "re-keyed," whatever that means exactly. Or maybe Hank's wandering around somewhere in the building, as he was one other late Saturday afternoon at just about the same time. No luck on either score. But this time I notice the same note, photocopied, is taped to the doors of a number of other offices, though by no means all. One out of every three, say. This would suggest it probably went up buildingwide or floorwide -- I haven't checked upstairs -- late Thursday night or early Friday morning and it remains up only on the doors of offices whose occupants, for whatever reason, didn't show up on Friday, like me.

What a pisser. What kind of low-rent operation is this anyway? How come no advance warning? How come no advance apology for causing such obvious inconvenience?

I hike over to a local bar. Such a splendid afternoon and my mood so black, just like the rear corner of the barroom itself, which I can testify to because it's where I'm holed up right now with all the stuff I've been carrying with me from the start (the bags are stashed along the base of the wall behind me so they won't be too conspicuous). Glary windows up front, dancing leaves visible on the trees outside and beyond them big complicated clouds drifting along. The waterfront in all its early-spring glory.

Doesn't take much to tip me into fury these days. It's part of the new-life syndrome, no question about it. Griefs I had to suppress before are now resurfacing to haunt me. Overextensions, miscalculations, overcompensations. Over under around but not often enough on. Wild scattershots.

And my ridiculous Sofie infatuation. Has it even peaked? Yet I haven't seen her all week, not once, and so far as I know she's never tried to get in touch with me. What's going on? How could I have been so wrong about her?

(A woman rolls her bicycle by, into the "employees only" room. The cafe section next door is gearing up for the dinner trade. My eyes have adjusted to the odd combination of glare and gloom: jyzing here is almost like taking notes near the back of a darkened movie theater with a small but very bright screen at the front. Cola drink in a classic green hourglass-shaped bottle. Grungy alt/indie music pounding. Of course we're well into the post-grunge era now but lots of the authentic stuff is still around, especially here in what was once a prime grunge venue in the grunge capital of the world.)

[Jyze and Jyze Alone]

Sofie ducking me, I guess. Who knows. I was proud
of myself for holding out so long before trying to get
in touch with her and then yielding in a very low-key
way. A long article in the afternoon newspaper about a
married couple, immigrants from Sofie's Balkan ancestral
land, the wife maddened by the husband's seeking a
divorce, she offs him and chops up his body into seventy
(count 'em!) pieces for dumping in a nearby river. In
the photo she looks quite a lot like Sofie. I clip the
article and scribble a brief note on it, trying to be
funny. "Maybe you missed this? It's sure to come up at
the next meeting of the Daughters of [her old country].
-- G." And then as if in afterthought: "How you been?
Everything okay? Still game for dinner and/or a movie?
If so, let me know when's good," with my phone number
following. I slapped a couple of pasties from a new
motif book on the envelope -- surely she'd like those --
and shoved it under the co-op's front door.
That was Wednesday. This is Saturday. Nothing.
(These co-op people, what a disappointment. I've
caught glimpses of one other member I recognized out on
the streets and then later saw fixated in front of a
computer screen at the digi-cafe. After all the trouble
I went through trying to complete the obstacle course
leading to membership couldn't they at least welcome me
to the hood? Sofie herself is on the membership
committee. "You had some very strong support," she told
me. "You shouldn't be so hard on yourself." -- I'd
been panning my performance at the "compatibility check"
before the assembled co-oppers. -- Yeah, well, where's
that "very strong support" now? How come Sofie's not
telling them to drop over and say hello? "We want that
dude to apply for our next opening! We need someone
like him around here!" -- What, am I dreaming?)
Yet strangely enough I love my new bipolar setup
every bit as much as before. More, even. I gasp
sometimes, it's so perfect. It's just I'm -- I'm going
through a phase, that's what. I'm insecure or
dissociating or something. It sounds almost normal, not
to mention predictable: a guy's given his walking papers

by his longtime partner, right away he falls hard for
another woman who's literally the first one he runs into
on the first day of his new life. Just to prove to
himself he can still do it, I suppose. Isn't so
terrible and unlovable.

But unlovable is what he is. Probably terrible
too, at least in spasms, but surely unlovable because
you just can't love again so quickly, nor can you be
accessible to love, that is, you can't let yourself be
loved.

Just look, don't touch. And look discreetly.
Appreciate from afar. Try to get used to a new role, at
least for a while and probably for quite a while.

As for getting laid, forget it.

For the unit-warming party I bought flowers at the
public market. I'd been thinking about it all week,
flowers and booze. "If nothing works out with Sofie
I'll invite her spirit over" -- and I'm still intending
to do just that. Can't help myself. First, tulips, the
main fresh-cut flower on sale at this time of year, a
bouquet of stunning glowy red hue. Undeniably sexual, I
observed to the saleswoman (lewdly, crudely, rudely,
shamelessly -- unlovably!). Back to the room with those
and then in passing through the market again an hour
later on the way down here I spotted some lilacs for
sale I hadn't noticed before and the altered poet's
phrase from last year jumped into my head: "When lilacs
last in the jyzeyard bloom'd." Postbellum grief, that's
the diagnosis here. So I had to have them too, meaning
four more bucks on top of the six for the tulips. And
ten for the booze. Then hauled them all back to B-2 and
restarted the hike to the hideaway.

Maybe I'll take up steadily with Sofie's spirit and
relegate the woman herself to some different corporeal
dimension or parallel universe. (And thinking this for
the first time a couple of days ago spurred some new
ideas for "Jyzer." As a result I'll now be splitting
the Lady S character in two and loving the spirit of the
half who's the dancer friend in love with the hapless
jock. It's Ryu Mija again, a new and improved avatar.)

[Jyze and Jyze Alone]

     Those wonderful public-market crowds. Such fun it
is to weave my way slowly through them. The indigenous
South American mountain musicians with their haunting
flutelike instruments. The many languages being spoken.
The color, the smells, the excitement. (All of which is
so abstract as to say nothing. But I'll have plenty of
chances now to get detailed and particular. No hurry.)
-- Saw a bird land about seven feet up a brick wall by
the old furniture mart as I hauled the lilacs home, and
then it seemed to vanish. I wondered if I was imagining
things. Was that "bird" a leaf blown by the wind? But
no, on further inspection I spotted a tiny gap between
two bricks where the mortar had fallen out and the bird
had squeezed through. I knew this had happened because
suddenly its head was peeking out from the hole as if a
cuckoo clock had struck the hour. A nest in there.
Ancient bricks, one of the very fine particulars found
throughout this whole area. And so many of them! And
each an individual brick not to be confused with any
other, each possibly sheltering a cuckoo's nest, among
so many other possible kinds of nests and things and
beings! -- This was near a corner which has been a
pleasant surprise to me, a three-way intersection on the
"low road," as jyze calls it, a block west of the edge
road and two blocks south of unit B-2. Steep east-west
streets, an interesting "view tunnel," a rectangle of
bay framed by the sides of two tall buildings, a brick
street surface below, and the bottom of the viaduct on
top -- completing the frame -- with the upper parts of
trucks and buses zipping by above the viaduct fence all
headed in one direction like huge tracer bullets (cars
not visible from my angle).
     Hard at work every day. Loft up. Shelves up.
Most boxes unpacked. The project of making a cart for
the TV, though, I've decided to put off. Several others
too. I've wearied of the carpentering. Time's a-
wasting. I want to get back to the real work.
     -- But first weakened and bought some small jars of
cheapo watercolors along with a rubber stamp saying "X-
rated" and various colorful lesser items (including

those three dynamite motif books) during a trip to the
downtown art store planned for the sole purpose of
finding a frame for Rob's painting. Another lesser
item: a book of postcards featuring self-portraits of
female painters, including several of the worthies
depicted in tile by Sofie and hung in the co-op hallway
near the door to her room. I very nearly sent her the
book. But managed to restrain myself. -- And didn't
find a frame, so instead wound up cannibalizing one
which Lady U had herself cannibalized from another of
Rob's paintings. It's a perfect fit, as I knew all
along it would be. Now, however, I need a new frame for
the lady's newly de-framed painting -- but that can
wait. And will. And should.

    Our meeting, by the way, the lady's and mine, the
one eight days ago now, was wholly unremarkable. I did
sit in a booth in the cafe section, instead of the usual
spot at the counter or in the lounge, explaining to Vi,
the server, my old pal, that I was about to meet my ex.
First time I've ever called her that, I believe, other
than here in the JIRT. Half an hour later the lady
herself showed up, noticeably makeupless, in blackjeans
and T-shirt, fifteen minutes late (no apology), and she
treated me in a perfectly normal way. I explained the
situation with the taxes while forking down a piece of
cherry pie ala mode. Showed her the forms. She said
she appreciated my willingness to pay the unexpected
portion. (I forget now what she ate. She complained
about how high the prices were, though they were nothing
out of the ordinary. I took it as being part of her act
proclaiming how poor she supposedly is these days.
Thanks to my previous unconscionable snooping I know for
a fact she's doing quite well financially. But am I
making anything of this? Absolutely not.)

    After forty minutes or so -- I talked about my new
life, the hood; she about her effort to study for the
GRE and her plan to have someone named Ben from the old
gang at the camera factory mow the U Acres lawn (though
he's "not too reliable") -- we went out to the car in
the lot next to the ferry dock and she presented me, as
promised, with a sack of mail and the tattered sleeping

bag and blanket I'd been using on the couch those last days at the house but hadn't had room to carry with me on that final trip in. I stuffed all this into the very large white canvas bag which I'd brought along -- the one her mother gave me for commuting purposes and which has unexpectedly proven so useful during the move.

"Well, call," she said, "when you're ready to give me the grand tour."

"Sure," I said. "I'll do that."

And the only surprise, she put an arm around my waist and leaned in, gave me a perfunctory little hug. I returned it in pretty much the same spirit.

"Well, see you," she giggled, shrugging, her hand already moving toward the driver's-door handle.

"See you," said I, stepping back. I stood by the totem pole and watched as the dusty gray wagon circled the lot and reemerged at the exit not far from where we'd just parted. At that point I waved as I'd done countless times before when she'd dropped me off at the dock on my way in to work, and she waved back, drove on, went around the corner onto the main drag at the light and then out of sight behind the antique shop.

No tears. End of scene. End of a long era. (And if anyone should've been disappearing behind -- or into -- the antique shop, it was, and is, me.)

I'll carry on with this later. Been sitting in one place too long. Up to the scope office now.

*   *

All right, I'm freaking but I'm here to pick up the spirit of Sofie E. and escort her over to the party in B-2. It's the coffee bar, the same window seat by the big red neon "O" as a couple of months ago, directly across the street from the co-op (where the Sofie spirit still dwells if the nameplate by the buzzer at the entrance door can be believed, and maybe she's even over there right now in fleshy as well as spirit form). It's also, this coffee bar, now, half a block from my new home. "The jyzeyard."

And my spirits -- speaking of spirits -- were just dealt a double boost as I walked over here by a

124

roundabout route. Thriving Saturday-night edge avenue
-- I can't believe it. Traffic crawling along in both
directions as far as the eye could see. Long lines
waiting outside a number of clubs, including four or
five right in this block. But two blocks south of here
I was striding along and a woman maybe in her early
twenties leaned out a car window and called, "Hey,
what's your name?" And then while I was still thinking
ooh wotta nice fluke, another one, different car, "You
wanna ride?" Carful of raucous young women.

So a double fluke, so what. So it was dark, who
cares. I needed this.

This and a lot more.

Then I laid out three bucks for an ordinary bottle
of mango-peach smoothie (cheapest item on the menu) so I
could sit at the window table here at the coffee bar and
imbibe spirit of Sofie. Her clocks and mirrors mounted
on the walls. Small clock number 22 is the one I like
best, $38. When I complimented her on it while we were
in here a couple of weeks ago and said I'd like to
barter something for it, she pretty much laughed off the
idea. (That woman in the ill-fitting black maxicoat
standing with her back to me at the counter right now,
she could almost be Sofie. Just came in. But I'll
pretend I haven't noticed, just in case that's who she
is. I don't think I'd want her to know I'm in here
doing the jyze thing about picking up her spirit. No.
At least not the incarnation who's been ignoring me.)

Her biggest mirror is going for $450. Or hold on,
no, that's the second biggest. The biggest is not for
sale. All have tile-mosaic borders, though none are
anything like as intricate as Lady U's tile-mosaic bird
that sits on my desk in the Jyzer Ink office I'm still
locked out of. That's the only example I still have of
the lady's -- Lady U's -- work as an aspiring tile
artist.

Grrrr. Return of the furies. Just long enough to
note that the end of my spending spree might somehow be
related to the ease with which I fall into black moods
these days. Reminds me of the bad period overseas

almost exactly twenty-one years ago when the money ran
out. But -- how different that was. What am I
thinking? An entire hemisphere of difference!

Here I have three K in readily accessible savings.
But I'm determined not to touch that. In my checking
account sit just enough bucks to cover the three rents
due on May 1 ---

*

Surprise. The woman at the counter I thought might
be Sofie? Yep, Sofie she was. In the flesh. And I
hate to say it but -- but there's nothing there. Not
even a flicker of interest on her part. Lots of sneezes,
though, caused, she said, by her asthma. And went on:
"What was it you sent me in the mail? I didn't get it."
Didn't understand it, she meant, and so I explained
about the ancestral angle and reminded her that we'd
talked about our ancestries at the digi-cafe.

Her blithe reply: "I didn't read it. I thought the
people in the picture looked sort of familiar. I'm not
a big reader. I look at pictures."

She obviously didn't want to stick around, so I
didn't try to detain her further. "But take another
look at that article -- it'll blow your mind for sure."

"I have this big pile of mail to read, four days'
worth" -- said as she wandered off, pulling the big
black coat tightly around her. Right out the door. Not
another word.

As for the "dinner/movie" query, nothing.
Apparently she didn't read that either. Or just as bad,
or probably even worse, did read it.

Shattering. End of my little fantasy.

Spirit of Sofie, I'm leaving you right here. Carry
on in my absence, which will be permanent.

Such intense radiation of "don't hit on me" vibes
have I rarely been subjected to, ever.

*   *

Still frazzled. Bursts of hysterical laughter and
howls of dismay. Out loud! And I do mean loud! But
I've poured myself a stiff drink and turned on the jazz
station and the unit-warming party is underway

regardless. Off to a rousing start.

There they are, the lilacs that now in the jyzeyard bloom. And the bouquet of red tulips. And the one red tulip extracted from the bouquet and installed in Mother's favorite red single-flower rose vase; that one was supposed to mean something big tonight. But not what it's turned out to mean. Standing there mocking me! My pathetic delusions!

Waiting for me when I came in the door was my very first answering-machine message not planted by myself. How funny, I mused, if it should be Sofie with a heartfelt apology for snubbing me at the coffee shop. "I don't know what got into me. Must've been the stupid allergy. Let's have us a late dinner right now. It's on me!" More likely, though, it would be Hank or Trevor, the two probable villains with whose answering services I'd left my number and a message that tried hard not to sound too irate about the re-keying. -- Punch the button and it's an all-too-familiar male voice booming out, presumably in response to the fact that I now have an answering machine for the first time ever, "So, you really are resurfacing!" It's cousin Kar. He and Elaine, his new romantic interest, want me to go pub-crawling with them in the historic quarter.

Why not do it. Under my new straitened emotional circumstances I might as well give it another shot with Kar. (Elaine I've never even met.) -- But not right now, no. Maybe next month. As I was starting to say back there before disaster struck, for the rest of April I'm broke. Luckily I still have lots of food stashed away, and most of it's not the perishable kind like, say, those mushy bananas.

So here it is, B-2. And what a terrific unit to be unit-warming! Four lamps are shining. The central section of the main room, between the kitchen partition and the chair and couch by the windows (I'm sitting in the chair, the old green armchair with a couple of cheapo Indian rugs thrown across it to disguise the worn spots) -- the central area is cleared of everything. Otherwise I could not have my very own indoor nerf court.

The hoop and backboard are up too, attached in easily
removable fashion to the loft's southeast corner post
some eighteen inches below the ceiling. For certain
truly important visitors I might want to take down the
whole assembly and stash it in the back end of the
closet, behind the sliding door. (That's where the TV
is already hidden, and that's even without visitors.
For a while, maybe a long while, it'll be staying right
there. I think I'd have to be desperate for a surrogate
social life to take it out. And I'm certainly not there
yet. Even if it may sometimes seem otherwise.)

All the books and clothes I brought over are
unpacked but none are in the right places yet. Except
for the shirts on hangers in the closet I haven't even
figured out what the right places will be. None of my
desk or art stuff is unpacked, but the boxes are shelved
in the inner loft area. All kitchen stuff is where it
should be, though I've yet to wash a dish (or launder
any clothes). I did take out the garbage for the first
time today, three big bags' worth. I also broke down
most of the reusable cardboard boxes and found places
(mostly under and behind the couch) to stash them.

For the past five or six nights I've been sleeping
in the loft on the red futon Lady U and I used up there
atop those very same planks when we were living in the
last of our city rental houses about ten miles north of
here. As noted before, the guy in unit 102 sleeps
directly above where I do, probably no more than three
or four feet above, and that's assuming he has a bed and
not a floor-level mattress or futon. It's almost as if
we're in bunk beds. I hear him up there quite often but
so far nothing he's done has truly disturbed me. I'm
trying to learn all over again how not to bump my head,
shoulders, elbows, hands against the ceiling in such
close quarters. Last night I bumped something against
it only twice, the closest I've come so far to complete
noncontact. I know he can hear me up there. Seems like
shortly after I bump something, no matter what it is,
against the ceiling I hear him stomping off to the
bathroom -- almost every time -- and then a toilet flush.

Right now he appears to have no love life, thank god,
and I suppose he's thinking the same about me. In a
sense, though, one might say we are each other's love
life. (Who is he? I don't know. I've never seen him as
far as I'm aware. But building manager Mindy told me
he's looking for work these days, so there's no
particular time when he'll be out of the apartment and I
might as well hammer away to my heart's content. In fact
it seems he's just about always up there making the floor
creak. Fortunately he seems to keep pretty much the same
night-owl hours I do.)

Aw man, this is some party. Pour me another!

So far I've had exactly two phone calls (not
counting my own and the ones last week I was unable to
answer). The first was an accident: it was cousin Greta
trying to reach her brother Kar, whose number she'd
sought from information because she'd lost her address
book. Somehow the operator gave her my number instead.
So pleased was I to be talking with another human being
that I went on and on until she practically had to
scream for the hook. But she's a rich lawyer and it was
all on her dime, so why not. And I like her. (She was
calling Kar to warn him that he's carrying a recessive
gene for hemachromatosis, which their sister Kjersten
has recently been diagnosed with. It's way too
complicated to try to explain in here, but I and my
siblings could have that same gene. Apparently it's
often found in the northern Euro-tribe from which we all
descend on our fathers' side.) -- Greta also sent me a
postcard soon after calling, and that was the first and
thus far the only piece of mail I've received here (not
counting two Mentoka weeklies which arrived just today
-- meaning my mail addressed to the old U Acres house is
now being forwarded). And Greta finally did reach Kar
and gave him my number, which explains how he was able
to ring me up tonight.

Well. The lilacs blooming. Beautiful. I had
intended to reread "When Lilacs Last" today so I could
toss a few literary allusions into these pages, but
unfortunately my copy of the collected works is locked

in the re-keyed Jyzer Ink office. In any event it's a
handsome bunch of cuttings here, a mixture of darker and
lighter colors all of which could be called lilac or
slightly off-lilac perhaps. And the lower parts of the
cuttings are stuffed in my big insulated polyurethane
mug (hailing from the most recent Mentoka trip) because
the one large vase I brought over from U Acres had
already been claimed by the tulips -- all except one.
    The damnable Sofie. She could've been at least a
little happy to see me. "Hey, thanks for sending me
that article." I can almost hear it. "I meant to call
but I've been so damn busy and on top of that I got
sick." And then, who knows: "Say -- how's your room
coming along? When you gonna let me see this amazing
loft of yours? You got it up and ready for action yet?"
    Ha. Ha ha.
    -- Not a single painting or poster on the walls
here. Nothing. I'm biding my time. Before too long
I'll be putting up some big swatches from a roll of
drawing paper I bought at the art-school store. I'll
have my own concoctions/creations up there and nothing
else but. This is something I've always wanted to do.
Rob's stuff, Lady V's, Lady S's, Lady U's: the Jyzer Ink
office walls are better for all those. Here I want to
go a little crazy. There I may go crazy too -- I hope
so -- but I'll be trying to be sane and serious as well.
    What about the mags? I still don't know. A big
stack of them is in place in just the way the same kind
of stacks piled up at U Acres, on the heavy wooden end
table, but I've scarcely made a dent in it. Maybe I'll
be easing off on the periodical reading now. Scanning
at the newsstands instead. I think so.
    I have started in on the "compleat works" of the
English protojyze grandmaster. Volume one, page one.
It's up there in the little nightstand box I made for
the loft, atop which sits the small black radio with the
digital clock and alarm; and above that, mounted on a
two-by-four, hangs the wall lamp whose tan shade reaches
all the way to the ceiling. The lamp's for reading in
bed until I fall asleep. Back to that again, and I'm

enjoying it. And it's almost time for it now again
tonight, except I'm probably too far gone to take in
more than about three sentences.

But before closing up this J-book, a few other
details concerning the new life. The breakfast at a
twenty-four-hour cafe, the dinner at a nearby tavern.
The many explorations, usually conducted in the rain
(with uncanny bad timing the rain always seems to start
up in the late afternoon just as I'm finally ready to
lay down my hammer and hit the streets). The long
digression on this area as an arts district (on May 6th
the city art museum will conduct a guided tour of the
studios of forty local artists, the cost ten bucks for
non-museum members like myself, and I was thinking of
signing up just so I could pop into Sofie's studio,
since her name's on the list of artists to be visited --
break into song and dance maybe with some sort of over-
the-top plea, falling to my knees at the end with arms
spread in goofy supplication: "Please! Please!
Please!"). The sadly lame "Liberalism v. Progressivism"
forum at the digi-cafe. The house of blues that turned
out to be defunct. The first waterfront-streetcar ride.
The chair repairs. The tax forms filled out and mailed.
The determination not to become just another lonely guy
on the make (not to mention an aging and half-loony
lonely guy on the make). The realization of the
importance now of "re-engaging with myself" and how this
notion came to me. The new emotional seesaws. The
discovery of an excellent brand, entirely new to me, of
butterscotch pudding. The accidental meet-up on the
street outside the local market with my longtime josh-
around buddy Rick, a worker at the public-market
newsstand (and I've never seen him anywhere else but
there before this week) (but he now lives way up in the
north end of town and if he can scare up the bucks, he
says, he'll probably be moving to Mexico this summer).

And the jazz station fund-raising drive driving me
crazy all week. The discovery of a likable edgy postmod
restaurant/bar just a diagonal block northwest of my
likable edgy postmod B-2. The witnessing of aid-car

workers grimly pulling on rubber gloves before going to
work on a fallen fossil vagrant (which is not the term I
want for him but it's what arrives). A brazen laundry-
bag-toting cocaine pusherman come-on in broad daylight
in the courtyard outside my windows here. A telephone
solicitation (the second I've received) which this time
succeeded in selling me on signing up for daily delivery
of the city's morning newspaper starting tomorrow for
just $1.25 a week, including the Sunday paper which by
itself goes for two bucks at the newsstand -- but this
low-cost subscription deal will last only thirteen weeks
before the price doubles.
    Can't say anything more about any of these items.
The unit is now officially unit-warmed and I gotta climb
up to my own rack before I collapse. First, though, a
last note of appreciation for these fine lilacs so
lusciously and lilacly and yet also sort of
lilacadaisically or maybe even daisalilacally abloom.
And those tulips way over there. And this lone one
here. (And my buzzer goes off. Right now! Someone at
the door! Could it be her? -- But no, some drunks.)
    Good lord, what a night.

15

    Last time for an old way of signifyin'. Came back
over here because I thought I could gain some
perspective. Also some symmetry of a sort. Now I find
I'm running late. If I hang around too much longer I'll
miss the last bus back to the dock.
    "Over here" being storage unit No. 161. Way the
hell across the water not so far from where I used to
live back in a former age not too long ago. Sun

slanting in. Soon it'll be lighting up the back wall of
the unit -- wonder how long it's been since the last
time it's done that. Certainly a first for my tenancy
here. (In the distance, sounds of a high-school
baseball game, sharp rap of bat on ball, cheers. Now
also a chain saw, closer. Drowns out baseball and
everything else. Tree massacres. Clearing land for
another mall just maybe? Or would it be for condos? Or
maybe a mall/condo combo? A truly ginormous big box?)

It's a trip. The one thing I hoped to retrieve
over here I can't find. Now I'll have to buy one -- a
multiple-outlet circuit-breaker "power strip." Then
next trip over I'll find the old one. Or it'll turn out
to have been in the apartment all along. -- Which is
fine; I can use two power strips anyway. May even need
two. And one of my regular hardware/garden stores from
the old days is right across the street here, near where
I'll be catching the bus back to the dock.

(New pocket watch coming in handy now -- the first
time it has, really, though over the past couple of
weeks I've invented all kinds of excuses to haul it out
and crack open the lid. Also I've let it run down
twice. It requires winding every twenty-four hours.
Twenty-five hours, it's dead for sure.)

So the perspective. Yes, there is some. And yes,
it helps. I'd almost lost sight (amid all the
giddiness) of what my larger purpose for the new life is
supposed to be. "Fierce focus." -- Or would "loose
focus," I ask myself, serve better? So-called willpower
by itself never created anything -- and surely did block
the creation of much. But better focused I do feel
regardless. More balanced, yes. Back on track. Even
if the track is a bit rocky and overgrown with brush and
maybe washed out in a few places not yet visible up
ahead.

When I first wrestled this table into place for a
jyze session in early January -- to be exact, eight days
short of four months ago as of this coming Wednesday --
my current living arrangements would've seemed an
impossible dream. (They still do.) How colossally

lucky I've been! Lady U and I even remain on speaking terms! (Haven't spoken for a couple of weeks but I'll be calling her soon. Because I want my mail!)

A special section appeared in the Sunday paper examining the city's thriving downtown, with much of the focus (that word again) on the area in which I've just become a resident: the hundred or so blocks directly north of the central business district. Next month a big new cruise-ship pier and conference center will be opening on the waterfront two blocks straight down from B-2. In short, I'm ensconced in the middle of it all; and unless I screw up royally or my health does me in nobody can kick me out for thirty-odd years and maybe not even then. That's how long funding on the building in which I live is "committed," as they say.

Yes, over these four months my spirits have been way down, way up, way out, way in; they've been way here, way there, way everywhere. Not surprising at all, any of this, and surprised by it I haven't been, except occasionally (you still fantasize you can control it much more than you can). The breakaway. The transition. The move-in month. The settle-in month now just about ending -- today I'll be slipping my May rent under the office door in both bipolar locations as well as here in storage land. And my new checks bearing the B-2 address arrived in the B-2 mailbox. And one of the big supermarket chains welcomed me to the area with a mailed set of coupons for free butter, eggs, soda, and other staples. (But their local store is too far away, atop the big hill a mile and a half to the north, near where Naomi lives. Several other supermarkets, however, are located at the base of that same hill by the fairgrounds and those I can walk to, and have.)

(Whack! A yellow post-it, after gently flapping in the breeze for the past couple of hours, finally worked itself free from the filing cabinets stacked by the entrance and fluttered over this way and nipped my right ear like a mischievous canary. "Drawer #5," it says. Artifact of the time I was labeling Mother's file drawers in her little back pantry the week after her death, just prior to going through them with Barb.)

This is my first return to unit 161 since move-out
week. Too much to do in too short a time during my last
visits back then; I had no choice but to leave the place
in a huge mess. So this afternoon's gone mostly to
cleaning up and reorganizing (and searching for the
power strip). I lifted my not-so-trusty old mountain
bike up onto the loft (the storage loft platform here,
not to be confused with the loft I sleep atop in B-2 but
equally handmade by the same ace carpenter and to his
eyes almost equally magnificent). -- Figured I wouldn't
be riding that bike this year. In the future, maybe,
when I start needing new distractions or ways to get
away from what I can scarcely tear myself away from now:
the new bipolar turf.

And here's Mama U's extremely trusty giant white
canvas bag. In it I brought over the malfunctioning
power saw and some other items I have no current use for
(for example, a tea kettle usurped by a better one into
which I can more easily pour a measured amount of water
for coffee and which bears white-and-black Holstein
markings -- and this one here cost me only four bucks
anyway, back in the early move-out days when I was in
somewhat of a panic, as I can admit now, and snatching
up the first example of any seemingly needed item which
happened to come along). And a small shade for the
bathroom lamp with extender arm which just last night I
figured out how to repair -- before then I'd been
thinking I'd have to buy a new one today. So I'm a few
bucks ahead of the game. But I'll probably find a way
to blow those -- in fact I'll devote myself to doing so
if necessary. That's what this money is for. And this
big-spending era: it will very soon be coming to an end.
(Again. On which more later.)

Some lazy cheeps out there now. No more chain saws.
Sound of the garagelike roll-down door of someone else's
storage unit banging closed, just as mine will be doing
in a few minutes.

What else? A handful of the old county bus
schedules but for a route I've never used before. Just

leave them here; I can pick up more on the way home.
I'm still planning to come over here ten times every
three months, or roughly once per J-week, at least for a
while. (Now ink running out. Perfect timing. Quit.)

*   *

Some four hours later. It's not such a good idea
to wait for that last bus. It puts me at the dock too
late to catch a foot ferry that will get me over to the
state ferry dock in time to catch the seven-forty to the
city, which means I have to wait in the dreary transit
terminal an ungodly two and a quarter hours for the next
sailing. And did so tonight. Barely able to keep my
eyes open a good part of the time and the rest of the
time -- unable to. Conked out on three different
benches, each extemely uncomfortable in its own unique
way. And at all times the big lamp shade I was carrying
with me was propped nearby. Like the proverbial drunk
wearing one atop his head as he emerges from a party, I
garnered lots of amused attention.

So I finally made it across and now here I am
holding forth in the offices (singular, though, and in
more than one sense) of Jyzer Ink. No question it's my
favorite place on earth right now. It's as fixed up and
comfy and funky as I can make it. Paintings on the
walls all around, sketches, posters, mostly the work of
the three big loves of my life (yes, including the one
who just dumped me -- I'm not so aggrieved I'd kick her
work out of my gallery). Atop the glassed-in bookcase a
memorabilia shelf featuring a big photo of old Mom at
the not-so-old age of twenty-five, maybe even twenty-
four, with an idiotically smiling little blond kid at
her side: me. Just all kinds of good stuff in here.
If you glance in through one of the hallway windows
(which you can't do unless the blinds are open, which
they rarely are, and they aren't now) -- but if you do,
the dominant feature is the antique rotating bookcase
with the big fat dictionary spread open on the canted
stand atop it -- almost like a scene out of "The
Barristers of Bleeker Street" or something similarly
establishmentarian.

136

Anyway, it feels good to me. I like working here
and have been doing so every day. I've taken my first
nap here, on the carpet with the lights out. I've
leaned back in my armchair and discovered that even with
the blinds closed I can see through them at a sharply
oblique upward angle all the way to the north-atrium
skylight five stories up -- could see the sun, maybe, or
almost, at the time of year when it's highest overhead.
(This business of turning over my schedule after so many
years of sleeping mainly during daylight hours still has
me circadically discombobled. At certain unpredictable
hours, never the same from day to day, I'm likely to
become almost irresistably tired. Doesn't matter how
much sleep I've logged the night before. Wonder how
many more weeks or months or maybe even years before
I'll be fully adjusted to the new regimen.)

-- The triangle dead tonight. Sunday nights it
usually is. No music coursing from below, live or
otherwise; probably no one else is present in the whole
building. (I've now collected roughly two dozen five-
for-a-buck postcards featuring different photos or
paintings or sketches of this building. I've also put
up a large print of a painting of it as it looked a
hundred years ago -- it faces the window behind my
armchair. One of these days I'll leave the blinds open
so everyone can gasp at this room's fineness. I do like
the infinite-regress aspects of having that print there,
as when I stand out in the hall and gaze at it through
the window and imagine myself standing out in the hall
of the painted building gazing at the doubly-painted
painting of the building, recursio ad infinitum.)

Here my rent check for Allen W., building owner.
All three rents I'm paying today -- first time for this
trifecta as a normal matter. Combined total of $631.
And I've done a lot of mulling the past week and decided
exactly how I want to handle the cost of living this new
life. Without going into too many details -- well, I'll
just put it this way: I'll be trying to survive on fifty
bucks a week. That'll have to cover everything except
rent, utilities, phone, daily newspaper subscription,

and maybe ferry coupon book. To be able to pull this off I figure Jyzer Ink will need to clear an average of $750 a month. So far it's been doing a little better than that, but then so far Naomi hasn't fallen sick or taken any vacations and business has been good. It's chancy whether the average month's net will reach $750 in more normal times. Iffy. Gonna be tough.

I'll withdraw fifty bucks from the ATM every Sunday night. That's for the week's groceries, laundry, coffee, clothes, entertainment -- the works.

-- So here I am about to start into the last five pages of the first book of this third jyze annal. Can I make it all the way to the end tonight? Maybe but also maybe not. In any case I want to get what at least seem to be the final comments on a distinct era tucked away in a volume I can then put aside for a while. Start afresh with a new volume for the new era. In this case it'll be the new daily life in which I'll no longer be spoiling myself as I've been doing this current month. I'll be adjusting still, to be sure, but doing so while just living. Put paid to the transition period. May 1st, two days from now, the real new era begins.

Meanwhile what a bizarre eighter it's been. It divides neatly in half: the four days when I was broke and the four when I was unexpectedly swimming in greenbacks. These latter the result of a phone conversation with Barb prior to her leaving (with Keith) on their Southeast Asian travels. The final distribution is almost three times what I'd been planning on: not $2,000 but $5,500. So why not be good to myself just a little bit longer? Buy that new belt I've been needing for five years. Try out a few more of the neighborhood eateries because I may never get another shot at discovering which are good and which aren't, just in case I ever need to know (I'm figuring in a good week during a month when I'm ahead of the game in saving up for my next quarter's taxes, and my unexpected expenses total no more than ten bucks, I may be able to eat out once).

Most important of all, take advantage of a sale and lay in a stock of shoes that'll last a decade or two

(with judicious use of shoe goo). Four pairs of low-
cuts, two my standard type (both khaki color, by the
way) and two the usually much more expensive but now
marked-way-down moccasins (so-called; they look exactly
like the standard model except leather replaces canvas)
(and these are dark brown). And also take a flyer on a
pair of dirt-cheap soccer shoes, likewise dark brown but
with nifty black trim.

Oh the happy feet. The crowing toes. The exultant
calluses and proto-bunions. -- Because I'm walking more
than ever now, at least three miles every day and often
considerably more. (Though in a big drenching rainstorm
I did take my first free bus ride from one pole to the
other of the bipolar zone, straight down the edge road.)

Meanwhile it's gotten to be midnight straight up.
Don't want to leave any later than now considering I'll
be walking home carrying this big white lamp shade.
"Look how goofy I am! Mug me! Who's first?" (I'll
also be carrying the lamp itself and a couple of smaller
lamp shades and various other items in the big white
canvas bag while wearing my usual large black backpack,
not slung over one shoulder but the standard double-
strap way. I just may set a new all-time fool's mark
for vulnerable conspicuousness during this little
journey.)

-- So here goes.

*   *

Unscathed. Made it. Though I was panhandled five
or six times and a couple of them weren't too congenial.
But I know how to look at least moderately nasty if I
need to and I have the good fortune of being physically
fairly imposing. Regardless I know I'm taking risks,
especially when my hands are fully occupied as they were
tonight. Probably I should be carrying some protection
with me -- maybe even the pocket canister of pepper gas
so often urged upon me by Lady U and her parents -- but
I just can't get myself to do it. Not yet anyway.

A funny moment right at the start. As I walked by
one of the bars that pretty much surround the triangle,
a flower peddler who goes from bar to bar throughout the

quarter was coming out. A quick-witted one. "Rose to
go with your lamp shade?" she asked. I chuckled over it
until the first "aggressor panhandler" concentrated my
mind on other things outside a fancy late-hours
restaurant. That was some seven or eight blocks up the
long gradual incline of the "low road."

I love walking home by that route. Parts of it are
darker and more dangerous than the edge road or middle
road and the panhandlers are nastier but even they can't
completely ruin the trek. While cursing them beneath my
breath I remind myself this too is how things are and I
don't want to be forgetting it or how relatively
fortunate I am or how outrageously unfortunate they are,
and to a large extent (in both cases!) by a matter of
explicit societal design.

-- And so it's the jyzeyard again. Not the old
one but the new one with the big white lamp shade now
cockily enthroned on the armchair opposite. And the
lilacs -- the very ones which last eighter right here in
B-2 bloom'd -- have all fallen to pieces. Here on the
side table within arm's reach in their Mentoka cup. Oh
so wilted. Intentionally I've kept them on display like
this and the tulips too so that the appropriate lesson
might pound itself home. Flower power -- teach!

The tulips were more dramatic about it. Still are.
The blooms grew fuller and fuller for a few days and
then the upright petals started to tilt away from the
center while still remaining attached at the bottom. A
few more days and they were hanging straight down, each
bloom looking like a reversed umbrella after a brutal
windstorm. Then individual petals started falling off.
At this point about half are still attached -- but
withered and wilted -- and the rest are lying corpselike
on the rug at the foot of the bookcase (but the corpses
resembling those of gossamer-winged creatures, perhaps
miniature angels, it might almost appear).

For one day I was sorely tempted to send Sofie a
photocopy of a terrific essay I came across about
looking at pictures. "Even if you're not usually a
reader you might want to check this out." Managed

heroically to restrain myself. After that it was a
little easier each day. Only yesterday, though, did I
decide the all-clear could be blown on Sofie.

How lovely, how wild, how preposterous and pathetic
the Sofie crush was. (Nor have I seen her again. And
what if I do in the future -- what then? Just try not
to make a fool of myself as I did before. Did she ever
owe me anything? No. So remember that.)

The story on my being locked out of the Jyzer Ink
office, somehow I failed to bring that up when I was
there -- tonight, earlier -- but maybe just because it
turned out to have so little to it. Hank's mistake.
And he apologized profusely and came up with a couple of
extremely fishy stories which to me meant he really did
want me to think well of him (but he's a bad liar) so it
wasn't at all hard to let the thing drop. He gave me my
new keys and they work fine.

Brother Jeff called. He's "firing" Lynn and her
outfit because, as he said, "I like my investments a
little less liquid. I like to be able to look out the
window and see my investment sitting there." In other
words, real estate. Let's hope that's it anyway and not
a truckload of prime weed or a suitcaseful of cocaine.
-- A good talk with him though. He and Barb are in
agreement: I'm just an urban kind of guy and I'll be
much happier living in the city again. Not for a moment
would I dispute either of those notions.

Each day I try to get one more settling-in task out
of the way here in the jyzeyard. The list of same has
turned out to be longer than expected and I'm still
nowhere near the end of it. Tomorrow's will be to
complete the installation of the reading lamp on the
handmade shelves perched on one side of the counter
supporting the bathroom sink (the lamp will fold out a
couple of feet toward the tub so I can live the true
leisurely life, reading while soaking). Then the
flowerpots, of which I have seven to fill (and
eventually I want to do little paintings on them as
well). Then stacks of desk papers to go through. An FM
aerial to put up. A lamp for the dressing area behind

the bureau and between the staircase end of the loft and
the closet. On and on. And this week I'll be doing my
first load of laundry and making my first major grocery-
shopping expedition.

Each morning upon rising I pluck an album from the
old vinyl collection and play it on the old -- even
older -- portable stereo. One each day and most are
blues. At least a hundred albums to go through this way
and then I'll start over, I guess, especially if I don't
succeed in improving the radio reception. The jazz
station is on right now, the medium-size black plastic
radio softly holding forth on the loft bookshelf less
than a foot behind my head so no one will be disturbed
at one a.m. (though all my nearby neighbors stay up late
anyway, I think) -- but the sound's bad. Staticky, a
little out of register at times. In stormy weather it's
so hard on my ears I shut the thing off.

My J-book overfloweth. Literally -- extra pages
starting right here. And still so much of interest, I
do believe, remains unjyzed. A touching joint card
("Not a Bookworm") from Barb and Keith. This lifted my
hopes on being able to maintain relations with Barb. It
also spun me into a panic because she mentioned she'd be
sending my final distribution check to Lynn. No!
That's for my cushion! Without that I'm sunk! So I
called and that's when I found out the distribution's
much larger than anticipated -- and she hadn't sent any
of it to Lynn yet.

The cushion will total $7500 or so, and that of
course doesn't count the "deep reserves" of roughly 68K.
My pie-in-the-sky aim is to leave the $7500 untouched
for at least three years. And the deep reserves I hope
will survive fully intact for at least a decade,
possibly even somewhat enhanced by interest earnings and
a rising stock market if I'm lucky.

(What I was planning to say to Sofie if I saw her
during those first bad couple of days after the run-in
at the coffee bar: "Hey girl, how many times you think
the postman rings?" -- Thank god it never happened.)

With the news of the extra $3500 and the impression

that maybe the pathetic Sofie crush had finally blown
itself out I thought: why not a new beginning for the
new beginning? Like the false start of a race, just go
back to the blocks and wait for the gun again. Not hard
to do since no one else will fire it but me. "A Gun for
old Gunnah." (Or for old "Gun-Gun-Gun -- uh," as Sofie
called me. -- And scratch that irrelevancy right now.)

     I refurbed one well-worn pair of low-cuts with
superglue. Took the hinged lids off two of the cedar
boxes and turned the boxes on their sides one atop the
other and framed them with good-quality one-by-fours and
wound up with a serviceable stereo stand which also
holds all my albums. Microwaved some fish fillets, the
first time I've ever tried that (and the last as well,
for sure). Stocked up on the tasty new butterscotch
pudding. Sent in the quarterly taxes two weeks late
(thought they were due the 30th but no, the 15th) -- so
how big the penalty? Or am I so paltry a player they'll
just say I'm not worth going after? But no, computers
aren't instructed to think that way, not usually; more
often it's the other way around, that is, this player's
so loaded that going after him would be politically
dangerous, but the little guy we can crush without a
qualm. That's just Capitalism 101, the government unit.

     Barb told me she too was elated the first month
after the breakup of a long-term relationship. (She
didn't specify which breakup or what happened the second
month. She hit the wall, I'd guess. And I myself, in
this second month on my own, am keeping an eye out for
walls galumphing my way, from any quarter and at any
time but preferably not at too great a speed.)

     And this update: nix with the subscription renewals
on mags, reviews, quarterlies. Just no way I can afford
them. It's more important to be able to live within my
income. I'll read what I can while standing in the
various venues (the two big downtown chain bookstores
are especially good for this). Which means no more
clips. Guess I'll have to acknowledge I've already got
enough of the damn things. (Storage unit 161 is piled
to the ceiling with boxes full of them and what good

have they done me so far? Just misled me into thinking
I was accomplishing something worthwhile by piling them
up.)

     "This is the life -- if only I had someone to share
it with." Too often I'm thinking some variant of this
sorry smarmy thought. I've decided it's a sentiment I
should ticket for suppression in all its harshest forms.
(I tried to write Rikki but found I couldn't. I did
send off cards to Jim Q., Tom T., and cousin Greta, and
I called Rob in hopes we can get together soon. But I'm
antsy about Rikki. In part because of Mischa, much as I
like him, and in part because I just can't picture
myself going at it with Rikki up in that loft. I don't
know if I'd have the heart or the self-discipline to
turn her down if that seemed advisable, as it very
likely would: that's the really hard part. I'm nowhere
near toughened up enough.)

     I washed dishes. One evening at Jyzer Ink I nearly
gagged on rancid liniment fumes seeping in from the next-
door wellness clinic, but they haven't reappeared. Here
at home (the new home!) I discovered from the tenant
list posted next to the buzzer panel outside the front
entrance that the person living above me, supposedly a
male according to Mindy the manager, calls himself
"Claire Voyant." I had a little run-in with the
distinctly unfriendly older Cawk woman in B-5, some
forty feet up the hall, over an errant newspaper delivery
that wound up in front of her door and therefore, as she
angrily let me know, was her property, and now I'm
thinking she's probably tetched in the head and I might
need to be rethinking the newspaper subscription too.

     And that oughta be enough particulars if not way
more than enough. And I'm all jyzed out anyway. This
J-book -- this liminal era -- is now closed.

BOOK II

[Life of the Jyze to Come]

[In memoriam G.C.H.S.]

So I go into the scope office the very next night
-- the night before the new era is to begin once and for
all and for real -- and the bombshell hits: Naomi's
pregnant again. Kid due in October. A cartoon
announcing this is taped to the front counter in the
reception area. I didn't even get personal notice!

For a day I was reeling. Especially for about two
hours. Glass of wine at the digi-cafe to flip the
catastrophe on its back by celebrating it. The
meaning's clear: within six months I'll have to find
another job. No way is this enough time to finish
"Jyzer." Almost certainly any new job will have to be
minimum-wage or close to it -- what else can I expect to
come up with in my near-vintage state? And with no
decent meet-the-public clothes to wear -- oooeee, am I
in trouble. Probably I'll have to give up the Jyzer Ink
office and maybe the storage unit as well. Already.

For real. -- But wait. What about the money in
the bank? Not the investment-account principal, also
known as the deep reserves; that I dare not touch unless
the end is near. (And maybe it is? Maybe now's the
time for the big gamble? I'm thinking about this too.)
But first the cushion money, the two grand in my savings
account here and the five and a half soon to come.
Scarcely out of the blocks and I'm using the cushion?
Well, but what else is it for? Why not now? Or October
rather.

And maybe I'll luck out again. Maybe reporter
Verna will handle grand jury while Naomi's gone and
maybe Jyzer Ink will bring in some money through scoping
for her, though certainly it wouldn't be as much as I'd

been counting on from Naomi. And maybe Naomi will
return a few months after the birth as she did for the
previous one, even though this will be her third kid
and all under the age of five (or maybe the oldest is
six or seven now, I'm not sure; I haven't paid a whole
lot of attention to her family situation) (and that's
mainly because Naomi's always seemed to prefer keeping
it private). -- But then we'd be back to the way
things are now, except with my cushion much diminished.

Might even be good: I'd have more free time for my
own work at a point when I can definitely use it.

So a note asking Naomi whether she plans to return.
"Please say it's so!" And up to now, a whole week
later, no reply.

Obviously the long delay bodes ill. Yet I'm still
hopeful. Clinging to the last shred. If I lose, I
lose, and start looking for work before not too much
longer. Maybe before October so I can keep the cushion
intact (to protect me from what new bombshell?). Maybe
a gamble and devote all my time to "Jyzer" for six to
eight months while living off the cushion -- then
scramble like hell.

So, meanwhile, this inauguration of the new volume.
Got to, got to, just got to jyze it up. A jyze tribute
to Mom, among other aims. Starting out here with
Mother's Day half a week away and me taking a break
almost at the start of the first serious marketing trip
of my new life. I'd intended to stop in at a certain
nearby 24/7 cafe but now that's become much fancier, it
appears, with sit-down service and crispy-clean white
tablecloths on every table. Or maybe it's been that
way a while and I just haven't noticed (I have a hunch).

In any case I've hiked a block farther along the
trail leading to the nearest real supermarket and
pitched camp here at another new restaurant. It's an
offshoot of an old quasi-punk bar, which still exists
and adjoins it with an open interior doorway between the
two. Another postmod eatery much like the one in the
building studded with banged-up jello molds near my
apartment and likewise notable for its relaxed

industrial-arty atmosphere and ironic sense of humor
about its own bad food. Grease is still grease no
matter how you spin it, but if you spin it as grease
you can charge more for it: that seems to be the basic
(greasy) shtick in both of these joints.

Quite a week though. J-week I mean. -- I see much
more clearly now that after six or seven action-packed
days you build to a kind of critical jyze mass, meaning
the amount of material stored up is just too much to
permit a detailed chronology of the period or even allow
you to remember what order events came in, the ones you
can remember at all (and many, of course, you can't). A
diary or journal account is no longer possible, yet all
these remaining events are still clamoring to express
themselves one way or another. So you jyze.

And I will. More. Right now, though, I need to,
again, move on down the line. Too much coffee, I can
scarcely sit still anyway. (This almost in the shadow
of the city's No. 1 tourist icon, the giant white golf
tee with the disk-shaped restaurant spinning on top.
Literally spinning, yes, although quite slowly. And
we're literally in the shadow also, maybe, or at least
would be very early in the morning and if the sun were
to rise a little farther to the north. Clearly the
angle's not quite right.)

*   *

-- Arrgh, did I ever overestimate how much I could
lug home in my big white market bag. Just a mile or so
-- shifting the bag from hand to hand, shoulder to
shoulder while also wearing a full backpack and carrying
my jacket because I was overheating like a junker car
with a dry radiator -- lurching laughably along.

But made it. So now can stretch out in my nest of
poverty-level view chairs with my feet propped up and
basking in the sun. And watch a big dark stormbank
pushing in out there across the water.

This nearest real supermarket, as I may have noted
before, is a letdown. It's not all that large and it's
expensive compared with the ones I'm used to. It
doesn't even carry a number of items found in abundance

at the backwoods "big box" belonging to the same chain.
My favorite brand of vanilla pudding, for example. Even
so I save a bundle on most items compared with what I'd
pay at the even smaller markets within a few blocks of
B-2. Nor did I fail to yield to temptation: blew fifty
bucks rather than the thirty I'd intended. The usual
sorry rationale: "stock up while they're on sale." Need
to come up with some better counter-rationales, as it
were, which I can deploy before I get to the actual
counter for the official tally.

The supermarket and the commercial zone around it
define the far northern border of my normal workaday
turf. I figure I'll make it up there a couple of times
a month. A good cheap burger joint, a blues bar, a
movie theater, a number of other enticing places,
including a small bookstore with a good magazine stand.
I walk right by the arena which is throbbing with pro
hoops these days. (One anomaly about the old quasi-punk
bar I visited earlier is that it now offers three large-
screen TVs tuned nonstop to sports and its walls are
plastered with huge posters featuring pro hoopsters.
But then in that hood I suppose you have little choice.
"Go Pro Hoops Team!" signs and banners are everywhere.)

Meanwhile the shrubbery outside my window here has
sprouted a full array of leaves. These undeniably add
something to the overall B-2 aura, even though I'd
already thought it couldn't be beat. Ninety-year-old
brick wall across the courtyard, I gaze at that a lot.
Something there is you gotta love about a ninety-year-
old brick wall. It looks still better when I'm playing
scratchy blues from the very early days, say the female
grandmaster of that same era moaning about the life of a
brickyard worker. (Or anything by her. Maybe she
doesn't even moan about brickyard workers. But she sure
does moan about empty beds.)

This room's just about set now. The old jyzeyard.
Blues here -- fresh daily! The one big exception is the
interior walls, which will remain unadorned for a while
until I can come up with something of my own making
worthy of going up there.

            [Life of the Jyze to Come]

     Not a cut flower in sight. Over at the coffee bar
the clocks and mirrors are gone, replaced by the oil
paintings of this month's hot new artist. As for last
month's cold old artist, she's totally dropped out of
sight along with her art. So long, heartache! To help
nurse myself through the hard times I've stationed three
sets of potted flowers on the B-2 windowsills: a small
set of three, a medium set of three, a big "set" of one.
Violets, pansies, a geranium, miniature roses. Pottery
that's squarish and warmly earth-toned on three matching
trays. Reds and purples and whites for blooms. Just as
I hoped they would, they do quite well at cheering me
up. I water them with the old ceramic-chicken pitcher
(this is the one I gave Mother; Lady U kept ours).
     -- Speaking of whom, I met her again yesterday in
the storage port (nee home port) and picked up another
big bag of mail. This was supposed to happen the
previous day but she didn't show. I had to blow off
seven hours, including more than an hour of pacing the
dock waiting for her. Pleased with her I was not. Her
excuse when I reached her by phone later (after trying
unsuccessfully many times from the dock) was that she'd
lost track of what day it was. Over the weekend she'd
scarcely slept at all while helping her good buddy Zach
fill a big rush order of cameras on a private contract.
     Dissin' the ex. But what can I do about it? She
said she was really sorry and to express her contrition
brought me a container of home-cooked rice to thicken
up my soup. And as a bonus, in a way, I was greeted in
the transit port by a big contingent of marching bands
and strutting pom-pom girls along with a cheering crowd
of thousands -- me and the Olympic torch, which these
days is slowly making its way around the country. It
happened to be riding across to the city on the same
ferry I was. Media helicopters, fireboats squirting to
the skies, rainsqualls gusting in -- it was quite a
scene. Well worth a little abuse from the ex, I'd say.
Because if she'd come when promised the previous day I
wouldn't've seen any of it.
     We talked for forty minutes in the jingo lounge.

[Jyze and Jyze Alone]

From her the same kind of tales as during earlier
visits. Her frisky young "pillow boys" (my term) just
making so many pesky demands on her. Jobs so hard to
find, schools so stingy with info on costs, the house
so needful of cleaning before Marissa and company, the
prospective buyers, descend for their inspection tour.
How poor she, Lady U, supposedly is, though of course
she's really not. She's even paying pal Ben thirty
bucks a shot to mow the lawn! (Very same lawn which
caused me to whack out my elbows last year -- and
today's grocery haulage no doubt set back the healing
process on those a few more weeks or maybe months.)

     But not to complain. Just a few more tugs on the
sagging old heartstrings. (Aw....) I continue to do
the absolute best I can to let her go graciously,
heroically shrugging off provocation after provocation.
Reminding myself as much as I can -- hey, didn't I have
it incredibly good with her for a long, long time when I
really didn't deserve it at all? For most of our
eighteen years wasn't I a grinning old lech lucking it
out? Yup. Yup. I got mine and then some. Even if
it's an abominable bumpy ride for me from here to the
grave I'll still say so. -- But had better do this now
while I can because later I may not be feeling up to it.
As truth to tell these days I already often don't.

     What I need now is patience. Perspective. To show
a little class, right. I'm not a desperate pathetic
aging guy on the make -- no which way. Needful to take
a cold shower at times, yes, but more some long hot
baths. Just hop in there and melt into neo-eremitic
undesiring acceptance while flicking the yellow rubber
ducky to and fro in the mist. -- And the tub is ready
for this. The cedar shelves are fully installed on the
sink counter (glued together for the most part, clamped
and vised for the past two weeks; and the lamp folds out
on its elbowed brass arm to within a foot of the tub at
just the right height for reading). The only things I'm
worried about now are whether (1) the huge volume of
collected works by the French essay grandmaster will be
too heavy to prop above the water for long periods using

my hands and arms, especially with my bad elbows; (2)
the noisy bathroom ceiling fan will get on my nerves
(though it cuts out with the overhead light); and (3)
I'll be electrocuted by the fold-out lamp, which is of
manifestly inferior workmanship.

   More gambles, that's all. If that's what it takes
to go out with a splash of sybaritic/neo-eremitic self-
indulgence, so be it. (An article in a magazine devoted
to the wisdom of idleness convinced me on this.
Wriggling your toes beneath the bath faucet as hot water
trickles down on them, what better life could there be?
A book in hand, a cool drink. Heat-flushed glistening
pink body weightlessly afloat, slightly staticky jazz
wafting in from the next room....)

   -- Snap back to it. Time to hit the road. So I
can get down to the hideaway (that is, Jyzer Ink office)
and do some editing and then hustle on up to the scope
office and punch in some corrections -- maybe even crank
out some work of the moneymaking kind (if there is any).

*   *

   So a couple of nights after hearing about Naomi's
pregnancy I was thinking, well, at least that just about
covers everything that could go wrong. Moments later
the whole building started shaking like crazy.
Seventeenth floor, scope office -- earthquake! Curtains
swaying, building creaking and wheezing. I rode it out
crouched beneath a door frame. Close to a minute of
lurchy rock'n'roll and it seemed an eternity. Hardest
to take is the uncertainty as to whether what you're
experiencing at the moment is as bad as it'll get or
maybe just a sprightly overture preceding the main event.

   After it died down, the janitor and I flipped on
partner Una's radio and listened in as the city went
nuts. Real damage, however, was minor. (The current
janitor, a decidedly weird longhair Cawk who looks sort
of like my old Mezzu buddy Ken D., was vacuuming halfway
down the main seventeenth-floor hallway when the quake
hit. I saw him with his eyes rolling wildly as if he
were hearing voices from above. Then he burst in and
started babbling about flying saucers and psychic

153

predictions, the coming apocalypse and much, much more.)

     -- This now, this jyzequake, going down in the hideaway. Quicklike. The building's set of married janitors working just outside: Jenny and Tuan. With both of whom it's very hard, sorry to say, to break through the "sir" treatment. Maybe it would help if I asked about job openings in their maintenance outfit. (But I'd have a tough time landing such a gig. They pay a couple bucks above minimum wage so they're in demand. For me it'll more likely be flippin' franchise burgers.)

     Always something going on around here. Next day the headline read "BIGGEST QUAKE IN 30 YEARS." -- And lots of other things are happening. Thursday night a major fire gutted the top two floors (mostly artist studios) of a six-story building which I'd walked by on my way home less than an hour earlier (it's a block west and a block north of here, on the lowest part of the low road) (though an even lower road, I should note, runs along the waterfront). And all week a wrecking ball was pounding away day and night at a building half a block from the scope office to clear ground for the new symphony hall, partner Una's office window providing a superb view of the action. And a near-riot broke out at what I'll call a sub-alt dance joint Sunday night just as I was walking by, two blocks from home on the edge road, when cop cars swooped down on parking-lot drug peddlers. Hundreds of partiers poured out of nearby clubs to razz the polizei. (And how admirably diverse were these razzers, racially speaking. Surprising, this, and also how scantily dressed the women and girls. Lots of lookers too. My jaw was dropping. All this right here and me basically out of the game? Oooeee, the pangs sometimes.)

     And a decision's come down from mover-and-shaker level (made by exactly whom it's unclear but obviously it's the bunch that truly matters) -- a decision not to build the new baseball stadium in the big parking lot next to the railroad depot (again just a few blocks from here). Instead it'll go in half a mile farther southwest in the industrial zone. This is good from our

historic-quarter standpoint because our lives won't be
disrupted as much and the odds improve that the area
will be able to hang on to the arts-oriented part of its
character. -- Or so people say. Media talking heads.
And I'm convinced.

    -- When present here at the hideaway I now leave my
door open a crack almost always, except when napping,
and the room is much less stuffy. My old iron "Liberty"
doorstop with the patriotic Uncle Sam figurine standing
tall atop the pedestal does the heavy work (him of
course resplendent in red-white-and-blue top hat and
tails). -- Tonight, alas, it's let some fruit flies in.

    Jim Q. wrote. He's okay. Though he didn't mention
it in his brief letter, from Barb I learned he totaled
his car during a long desert jaunt he and Mother at one
time had hoped to make together (as he told me last
December). -- And I finally did succeed in writing
Rikki and Mischa. Invited them up. I'm as curious as
anyone else (Barb, say) to see what will come of this.

    And...and...aw, I've got so much good stuff.
Discovered I can score excellent bread for a pittance at
the public market. Often bananas too -- along about
four o'clock on Saturdays the produce prices start
plummeting. My first time I came away with thirteen
good-size bananas for a buck (and at the supermarket
today they were seventy-nine cents a pound and a loaf of
decent bread was over two bucks, whereas I paid a dollar
for a much better loaf at the public market Saturday)
(but can I count on being able to do this regularly?).

    -- Hung old Mom's wooden clock high on the B-2 wall
so it's visible from the loft bed as well as from most
of the rest of the room. Doused my flowers with miracle
fertilizer just like on TV. Hit on the useful phrase
"weep with frustrated lust." Received my first piece
of mail here at "Suite 225" not addressed to Alicia or
the escort service: from Aunt Shar. Gave a persuasive
street cartoonist one of my calligraphy markers so he
could complete his knockoff Road Runner drawing. Said
he, doing a little jig: "Beep-beep! Beep-beep!"

[Jyze and Jyze Alone]

17

Lift those blinds and let some sun in. -- Yes,
there is some out there! -- And spin a disc of the old
champ's blues. Get the blood moving again. (Though by
the luck of the draw this is my least favorite of his
albums, the one in which he affects an odd sort of
stuttering babytalk on several tracks.)
     Lounging around in my bathrobe midafternoon on one
of my no-scoping-work days. The regular ones. A
Tuesday it is. But for the entire jyze eighter past, no
work. Sometimes it'll be like this. So far the weekly
average is holding up all right.
     But -- as I feared, reporter Naomi might not return
to the job after this next birth. At least nowhere near
as soon as she did last time. Possibly she'll take a
year off. Doesn't really know yet -- she and Larry
haven't had a chance to talk it over. She was leaning
toward a full year but now her childcare provider is
offering a good package deal and she's reconsidering.
-- This she told me when I contrived an excuse to call
her. She never did reply to my note. But she's
promised to let me know the moment the decision comes
down.
     A year is a long time to hold out on a cushion of
seventy-five hundred dollars. Especially considering
that my rents by themselves total more than six hundred
a month. Maybe I could do it, though, because Jyzer Ink
would probably get some scoping work from reporter Verna
during that period. Naomi thinks so anyway. Under the
government contract grand jury must be scoped in the
firm's office for security reasons, meaning Verna can't

156

do it at home (and partner Una has said she'll be
strictly enforcing the terms of this contract, for fear
of losing it). Verna wouldn't want to scope GJ herself
at the office, so she'd use Jyzer Ink.

Or I'm hoping she would. Because this income
combined with the cushion and the quarterly "deep
reserves" interest check would probably be enough for me
to squeak by until Naomi's return.

If something doesn't work out here -- well, I'm not
panicking. Not yet. As long as possible I'll focus on
the fictojyze (JIFT). Undertone of worry, sure, but as
much as possible I'll ignore it. Try to take advantage
of what I've got while I've still got it.

-- Added a pot of yellow marigolds to the row of
windowsill flowers. The petal kind, like miniature
daisies but without an eye in the middle. Vine leaves
shimmering outside -- should I open a window? Right
now? I've been thinking on it. (Getting restless
though. Usually by this time I'm outta here.)

The routine. It's shaking out pretty well. This
is Tuesday so I must be drinking coffee at home. Sawing
through cinnamon-raisin bread. Gobbling cornflakes in a
bowl along with a sliced banana and four or five sliced,
half-thawed frozen strawberries. Reading the newspaper.
(The dispute with the woman in B-5 over just whose paper
it is that gets delivered every morning still defies
full resolution, though I do know I'm paying for the
subscription. If the paper's lying on the carpet closer
to her door than mine tomorrow morning -- again -- I'll
probably put in another call, my third on this vexed
matter, to the subscription office. But if the woman is
truly demented, as I suspect, the only solution may be
to give up on home delivery, as it's called. I know I'm
not about to get up at six a.m. every day -- after
crashing at four a.m. -- to meet the delivery person in
person out in the hall or up in the lobby.)

Meanwhile I'm shorn. Self-shorn. Still fine-
tuning the 'do: did it again just an hour ago. For one
thing I've realized I need to change my appearance a bit
to distinguish myself from the hardcore street dudes

who haunt my daily course on all three major routes from
pole to pole. Not my idea of a virtuous thing to
undertake, this shearing, but other people just about
force you to. No point in bucking it. And it was time
for a trim anyway. And I'm still perceived as a vagrant
regardless, I'm sure, not by everyone but by enough that
I can hang on to my newly refurbed sense of inner-city
authenticity ("street cred").

But routines. I need them to enable maximum focus.
Also I like them just for themselves. A shopping day, a
laundry day, a bath day. Nerf time, watch-winding time,
plant-watering time. Up time, sleep time, reading-in-
bed time. -- No fanaticism though. Half the enjoyment
of having routines is being able to break them. And at
breaking them I've always been pretty damn good.

Nor have I succeeded yet in cutting my overhead to
the level I can afford. Not quite. (That level: an
ultra-thin membrane away from bone.) I should be taking
fifty bucks from the ATM every Sunday, so what do I do
out of sheer cussedness? I take sixty. Cackle with
glee -- ha ha ha, fooled myself! Take that, Mr. Tight-
Ass Budget Curmudgeon! Soon, though, I'm hoping, I'll
stop getting a charge out of such flaky doings.

-- Still must make my box lunch. Cherry tomatoes
are this week's treat. Triple-decker peanut-butter
sandwich, chunky applesauce scooped from a jumbo-size
jar into a small lidded plastic container, a few corn
chips, a small oatmeal cookie, a can of cheapo store-
brand no-cal soda, a piece of hard candy (cherry
cherry). Hey, why shouldn't I feed myself right? Do
all I can to shore up morale. And the cost of this
lunch is a dime or two under a buck.

Living alone you're always well advised to be
looking for ways to keep the morale as high as possible.
All the little boosters add up, though you're still sure
to be blindsided by bad stuff from time to time. Then
you grind it out and give the inevitability of
homeostatic mood change a chance to rescue you. (And
sometimes just a glance at a flower preening on the
windowsill will flip the mood. Or pinning a "Bad

Artist/No Funding" button on your shirt. -- And I
promised I'd try to find one of these same buttons for
Darren, the street cartoonist who peddles his work
outside the art museum, right beneath the falling hammer
of the big black John Henry-like "kinetic sculpture"
with its endlessly swinging hammer. -- This being the
same guy, Afrusan himself, to whom I gave the
calligraphy pen last week. I see him most days if it's
not raining. Gradually I'm building up a network of
compadres along the newly beaten pathways.)
                    *   *
    -- Holding down the top floor all by myself at my
longtime favorite public-market coffee shop. That's how
late it is. And yet the spectacular view. Bright. At
this moment an old-time clipper ship cutting across the
bay close to shore, although under diesel power, its
sails furled. And of course a ferry chugging in, this
one as it happens hailing from the province of my former
life -- storage province now, as previously noted.
(Clipper ship just showing off, suddenly cutting back
the other way.) (But as a boy how I loved clipper
ships. Yeah! Carved a model of the most famous of them
all from a block of balsa wood, then meticulously
painted and rigged it. No wonder I've wound up living
on the waterfront of such a splendid harbor!)
    -- Where many others will visit this summer.
Didn't I say this city's hot? Makes the cover of one of
the glossy national news weeklies: "Everyone's Moving
to" -- our city! Jyze City! (Then eleven pages of what
I'd say must be some of the worst writing ever for a
magazine with a readership in the millions -- almost as
if they'd let the J. City Chamber of Commerce ghost it.)
    And this just a few hundred steps down the
bluffside "low road" from home. Sun permitting me to
don my shades indoors and make like I'm in full control
of whatever it is I'm wrestling with over here in the
corner. (Tooting ferries and a golden oldies tape, a
certain iconic rock'n'roller pleading with us to wear
his ring around our necks.) Spiffy new chairs up here,
a new carpet, new blinds (now pulled up), new paint job.

Just as it did when I lived in that far province, this
remains a regular stop of mine, once a week at least,
for coffee and a cinnamon roll -- a bigger, fresher,
tastier roll than the digi-cafe's and at half the cost,
and coffee refills here are free whereas the digi-cafe
has halted their freebies as of last week: a buck for
the first cup, like here and the ORB cafe, but four bits
now on the refills. My romance with the digi-cafe has
cooled considerably, and I'm not even talking about the
part that hangs on the chance of seeing a certain tile
artist there. (If I ever do run into her again I'll gin
up a puzzled look and say, "So-So-So -- uh....")
     First floor is where I usually wind up sitting in
this place. A wooden chair at the big circular center
table with miscellaneous newspaper sections mounded in
the middle. I'm just one of the irregulars like, say, a
group of pretty damn good writers and painters used to
be a few decades back. Or for that matter like the
former three-dot columnist for the city's morning paper
who still is. These days he's close to fully retired, I
believe, but I saw him poking along outside the front
door just the other day. Hope I'll last long enough to
be doing something like that myself -- in fact that very
thing -- and in these very precincts -- at his age.
Poking along. I'm practicing already.
     Not much in the way of mail today. Lynn at the
investment group wrote confirming my change of address.
The letter was forwarded from my former street address
in the far province, but this was no surprise (except
that the forwarding had actually occurred, since only
the former P.O. box had previously forwarded anything).
Lynn had also sent an identical letter directly to my
new address here and added a note saying she was mailing
a copy of that letter to the old address just in case.
Lynn has become far and away my most frequent and most
conscientious correspondent, supplanting E.Z. from the
auto dealership. (Lynn was it for today. But yesterday
was big with a couple of forwarded magazines -- the
first for any magazine or review or journal.)
     From this seat I can see where the elevated viaduct

roadway starts curving away from the waterfront right before it passes outside my B-2 window and bends down into the tunnel. Can also see a large portion of the new cruise-ship pier that's about to open, including several dozen slips in its protected inner marina, all empty at the moment, and an angular structure standing out at the tip of the pier which I take to be the metal sculpture "inspired by the idea of a lighthouse" I read about in the papers. Or it may be something else entirely. But whatever it is, I'm provisionally deciding I like it as sculpture.

Art. The obsession. Someone -- maybe even lots of people -- once wrote that only obsession produces great art. Personally I don't believe it, but I'm taking it to heart regardless. The thought's given me a boost several times in the past week alone and thus is already proving its worth. (Likewise the thought that I don't want to open myself to the kind of criticism a recent reviewer laid upon a certain serious yet popular novelist for sounding so sour about contemporary life -- "carping of a bitter old man." No sourness about such life here. No recoiling at new ways just because they're not the old ways. Not even because they're not as good as the old ways if that happens to be the case. You affirm despite what you know and despite critiquing as befits the needs and you don't forget the good or the bad old ways and then you poke a bit further down the road and see how things look from there. -- Today's hokey sermon now concluding. "Open the door and out pour the people.")

*   *

Door open, but not a church door, except in a sense. "Jyze sanctuary," i.e., the hideaway. Coming up on nine p.m. A short while ago I finished putting in my four hours, which is the absolute minimum to be devoted to the real work each day. Then ate the lunch I made (and described) earlier. One of the cherry tomatoes was half rotten, it turned out, but otherwise this lunch was okay. Up to the standard. I may tire of eating more or less the same thing every day (how could I not?) but it still tastes pretty good and fills me up the way it spoze to. Under current conditions I can't really be much else but a bare utilitarian about food. -- Or no, a little short of bare. A figleaf or two. But probably few outside observers would think me anything but bare.

Every day this loop. Down and back. I'll be very surprised if I ever tire of it. (The serious kind of tiring. Not the kind where you just need a brief break from it.)

-- I look up and there's Mom. There's the fluted white tower atop the hill. It's coming up on six months now. I'm still talking with her a lot and dreaming strange dreams. In an exceptionally noteworthy one the other night I had to carry her naked body from room to room in an unfamiliar house in search of a bed I could never find (no doubt in recompense for not being there for her final weeks when Barb had to bundle her around her, Mom's, and now Barb and Keith's, apartment). But the body in the dream wasn't old; it was quite young. Everyone was amazed at this, as if she'd made a miraculous recovery, but I wasn't. -- Oh of course, oedipal nonsense. What was interesting about the strangeness was something else: the sadness and beauty. (And next month the twentieth anniversary of Dad's death. Twenty years ago today I was living in an SRO hotel maybe eight blocks from that same fluted white tower atop the hill after returning from abroad -- what I look back upon today as the most intense and extraordinary month of my life. Then the whole thing collapsed, and a year later along came Lady U.)

*   *

And the quick walk home straight up the edge road at one a.m. The loop is now looped. Surprise, B-2's much warmer than expected. Squint inside the old inner sanctum (the loft room should I call it?) at the display panel on the answering machine, but no surprise, it's double zeroes. So far as real people go, that one message from cousin Kar (which I still haven't answered, though I'm leaning a bit more towards doing so) is it.

The life of the long-distance jyzer.

[Life of the Jyze to Come]

    (But no, I'm not really saying it must be this way.
Just that it's likely to be for a while, and probably
quite a long while, for me, damn it anyhow.)
    I'd been thinking about stopping in at a saloon of
some sort on the way home. Plenty exist to choose from,
and some are very appealing. But tonight time was a
little shorter than expected and the prospect of laying
out three or four bucks for a drink a little more
dissuasive. For that same amount, after all, I could
buy a whole case of cheapo no-cal cola. One libation or
twenty-four? The answer is so obvious I'm surprised I
didn't rebel and go for the one libation. (But maybe
it was more a matter of the question itself being bad.)
    So here I am, back in the chair where this jyzeday
began. Noticing the first early gut-rumblings for
dinner. As of yet I haven't decided what it'll be
tonight. Maybe just toast and veggie juice. Last night
I cooked up a storm. Some nights I like to fast or
semi-fast.
    Fast, but as in speedy, is also what the walk home
must be. Yet I realize now I was exaggerating or
overestimating the dangers before, back when I first
moved in. From what I'm hearing now they've decreased
significantly in the past few years. Even so you're
well advised to be quite cautious. Single young males,
young males in pairs, young males in groups of three or
more, boisterous larger groups that are mostly or
entirely young males, cars just poking along and/or with
loud music playing and a preponderance or a unanimity
of young males in them -- look out. Make sudden turns
if necessary, cross streets in the middle of the block,
even reverse directions. Do it all without faltering.
Stay out where the lights are. Go where the people are
as long as there are more than a few and they're not all
young males. Be unpredictable, but not in-your-face
unpredictable.
    Pause. The racial aspects. Yes, sometimes you're
wise to make decisions based partly on race. Clothes
too. Age, definitely. Gender, definitely. Musical
taste. Posture. Gait. Openly displayed weapons or

objects that could become weapons, such as baseball bats, say, or breakable bottles.

    -- Yet I enjoy these walks, especially if no rain's falling. (Soon I'll be back to carrying a fold-up umbrella in my bag at all times.) I like walking past the bars and nightclubs. The many ways the streets of my new home turf are artified: the custom-painted trash cans, the historical markers, the stone bus-stop benches (sittable and yet the stones are attractively odd-shaped, almost like boulders you might come across by chance while hiking along a mountain trail). The bas-relief historical tableaus lining the street-level sides of the phone-company building. The several low-income hotels with people chatting or watching TV in the lobbies or hanging around outside to get some air and/or to scope out the action. The all-night restaurants. The numerous art galleries. The storefront studios, often with goings-on observable inside (maybe silhouetted by curtains). The record company "world headquarters" (a tiny storefront, though its offices upstairs in the same building are said to be quite large) and the three major rock-concert venues with their long sidewalk queues on many nights. (And on Thursday through Saturday nights as long as I don't leave the scope office after two-thirty a.m. I'm likely to find considerable foot traffic along both the middle and high roads. So now I'm making a special effort to leave by that hour. Long stretches of the edge and low roads are deserted by then and potential mugger locations are numerous, so I try to avoid those roads entirely late at night.)

    -- I think sometimes: what if my legs give out? As noted before, my left Achilles tendon is still bad from the rupture decades ago and the right is still shaky from the bike spill several years ago as well as from sheer overwork in compensating for the bad left. Either Achilles might start deteriorating further with all the walking I'm doing on hard surfaces. I've noticed new stiffnesses; at times I have to make a conscious effort to correct for the slight occasional left-leg lameness caused by unexpected spasms of Achilles pain.

     -- And thinking: will any drama be left for these
pages? Probably not much new will be happening. And if
that's true, from the jyze perspective is it good or is
it bad? Could go either way, I suppose, but I'm hoping
I can make it good. Lack of drama, after all, is a big
part of what gave birth to jyze in the first place.
Then suddenly a lot of dramatic things started happening
-- dramatic only on the personal scale, now, to be sure
-- and they didn't ease up, really, until quite recently.
Say until right about now. And I'm having a little
trouble getting used to the regression to norm.
     I'll just keep trying to feel my way ahead.
Nothing new there. If lacking something big to focus
on, pick something small. Or lots of things small. The
supply is just about limitless. (And I'm referring not
to just any small things but to ones which mean
something to me, the jyzer, Jyzer G -- this Jyzer G
right here -- and preferably things of recent or even
contemporaneous origin, that is, as they're happening.)
     -- My first B-2 bath, by the way, speaking of one
small thing that meant quite a lot this past week, was a
rousing success. I thought so anyway. The lamp worked,
the tub was comfortable, the fan wasn't too noisy, the
hot water never ran out, the rubber duck was unsinkable.
Not a single serious problem surfaced (blub blub).
     Nothing else crucial to mention. No letters
written but several I'll be trying to churn out this
week. Continuing curiosity about what will happen with
Rikki. It seems my romance mechanism must have someone
to focus on and since she's the only live current
candidate it focuses on her. Well, and why shouldn't
it? Romance away -- fantasize to your heart's content
-- but don't let any big expectations build up, no more
on her side than on yours.
     Sounds wise. And about things like this of course
I'm ordinarily not at all wise, so that means this
advice-to-self is essentially irrelevant except maybe as
a temporary feel-good bromide. More to the point, I'm
nobody's idea of a good catch these days except maybe
another arts type of roughly my own vintage with low

expectations and without kids. Nor do I want to be
suppressing any qualities or traits which I know might
make me appear to be something other than what I am,
which is, again, a bad catch.

     -- What am I trying to say here? Probably I'm
trying to warn myself not to yield to the temptation to
use romance as a way to avoid the real work. It's even
more tempting than the long hot baths.

     So many obstacles. Such complexity. The heart can
be one shifty and tricky organ, oh yes it can.

18

     On this one the jyze gods granted a three-day
extension. I was worn out both long term and short. I
thought I had lots of scoping work to do (though it
turned out I had none). I was not hot to trot. The
weather had been miserable for weeks -- so bad its
cumulative psychic impact had become front-page news in
both local dailies. In short, I needed a break.

     I'll make up the lost days, I swear I will. One
six-day J-week (always handy for catchup purposes) plus
one standard Gregorian seven-day week and I'll be back
on track for the originally scheduled jyze eighters.

     So am I refreshed and bursting with energy again?
(If not for the first time ever.) We'll find out.
Everything's new and different now. I can't predict
anything. (Which won't stop me from trying -- except
maybe it will this time.)

     What's good, the three-day delay put me into a more
interesting temporal zone. Memorial Day weekend. Only
the opening day of it, but somehow we're no longer where
we were. We've got traffic backed up on the freeway (a

bridge over which I just hiked across), much of it bound
for either the big folk-music festival at the
fairgrounds or the twenty-fifth-anniversary street fair
at the public market. We've got sun, in patches (but
for the second day in a row at least some). Patriotic
festivities unfolding. Memories of those who died on
battlefields. Not the bad guys or the innocents; they
don't count. The good guys. Our guys. The righteous
warriors of the BUA: Bellum USAum Aeternus.

Me, I've wandered up to the easternmost corner of
my jyze turf. Partway up the second tier of the western
slope of the central hill. A coffeehouse I discovered
when I was lining up unit B-2 with the housing agency,
whose offices are just a block and a half north of here.
A coffeehouse as a coffeehouse should be. The finest I
know of in Jyze City and close to ideal. All those
celebrated literary java freaks of centuries-old lore
would surely rejoice over a joint like this.

Southeast corner location. Maybe it's a former
furniture store or auto dealership or speakeasy, I don't
know. But it's old, it's funky, it's dark in places and
light and airy in places, it's got ancient brick walls
and floor-to-ceiling bookcases looking about fifteen
feet high along the east wall (calls itself a cafe/
bookstore though I doubt it sells many, if any, books).
Weathered wooden library chairs. A sidewalk-cafe
portion, a long high-counter portion, a wide low-
platform portion, and best of all a balcony where it
appears they'll let you sit forever (at least on a lazy
Saturday afternoon like this one). Triangular, the
balcony, with panoramic window views to the west and
north, though partially blocked by massive highrises
standing lower on the hillside. Lean my head over the
railing and I'm looking straight down on the high
counter ten feet below. A bus roars by just outside,
its large blocky black number (151) visible on top. A
guy's chaining his bicycle to a parking meter and now
removing the front wheel. Five other coffee-sippers up
here at this moment, one a gent a few sizes bigger than
me hunched over a tiny laptop and pecking away so

arduously you almost want to offer to take over for a
while -- give the poor man a well-earned break.

All that's needed up here is some better art of the
visual kind. In fact no visual art's in sight (which is
where it ought to be if it's visual, yes, if there were
any). Why is this? Just for fun go to work on some of
these columns and railings. Mount canvases of various
shapes and sizes on the intriguingly elaborate brick
wall at my back. -- And the coffee, it's a little
expensive and I don't know yet what the refill policy
is. Will find out right now.

*

It's not so good. Four bits the medium cup. But
they'll give you a glass of ice water for free (with
cubes!) and I ordered one up and I have it right here
and I'll nurse it for a while.

Yes, this is how it is now. I'm still getting used
to it, along with much else about my new life. "The
facts thereof."

Thursday, though, I stumbled into an epiphany zone
that stretched on and on. Looking back through the
shelves of my own protojyze I found much I can be proud
of. And along came a new hardcover, my favorite among
living neoprags answering his critics, and not only did
I break my budget and buy the thing but I clipped and
framed the author's dust-jacket mugshot and hung it
right next to Lady U's sketch of the greatest blues
grandmaster of them all -- him with cigarette dangling
from his lips and funny little caricatural hell hounds
howling on his trail and still he's belting it out. And
lots of other good things on that day. I even did some
laundry, my very first load at the new apartment.

However. An ominous moment when the stereo
turntable ground to a halt. Made me heartsick. By
jostling this and tightening that I managed to get it
spinning again, but at age twenty or so the contraption
is obviously nearing the end of its useful life. Any
time I turn it on could be the last (and dread flares
with each flop of falling vinyl). Maybe it could be
repaired, but the expense would be unthinkable. Yes,

Mother's enormous console is parked in the storage
unit, but I have no way to haul it over here and I doubt
I could come up with one; and even if I could, the
monster would take up a large portion of B-2's nerfball
court. Not a trade-off I can endorse at this time.

   This is how the future bodes to be. Things
gradually falling apart and no way to replace them.
(Unless a quantum change occurs. And maybe one will.
Personally I wouldn't bet on it, but I've been wrong
about such matters before. Not recently though.)

   The daily blues album. Just a small part of the
evolving new way of life. A different disc each day:
slap it on as I'm preparing my box lunch and making
ready to sail out -- hit the road to the hideaway. But
first jump around a little to, today, the champ. Again.
What it's tight like. The poodle he wants to play with.
Great stuff! While watering the flowers and raising the
blinds to let a little sun in. Packing the bag. Making
sure the key ring is hooked to my belt loop and my
shoelaces are double-tied just so.

   Whirls me into the right mood, that spinning vinyl
does. Nothing I'm likely to come across on the radio
can do it like that. Morale matters!

   -- The other story about things falling apart this
week, we've got the old reporting firm officially
dissolving. By next jyzetime they'll be history.
Nobody tells me anything (Naomi might, but they don't
tell her either) so I really don't know much about
what's happening. I see lots of bare shelves at the
office. I see furniture with stickies attached saying
who's claiming the piece (I assume that's what they
mean). I know what's going down is actually a merger
and I know the other firm will be moving into our firm's
current offices on the seventeenth floor and the new
conglomerate firm will be taking that other firm's name.
In the past I've worked with several members of that
firm (one I like, one I don't, the others -- enh).

   But, but -- what'll be happening to Jyzer Ink? All
I know is Naomi will be merging along with the rest and
the new firm will honor the old firm's contract with the

feds and by the terms of that contract all their scoping work must be done in secure conditions, that is, in the scope office itself, and Naomi will be the one reporting most of those jobs at least for a while, and Jyzer Ink will still be doing her scoping. Therefore the new firm must find some way Jyzer Ink can continue setting up shop there. And if that's so, it's also so that I personally should be able to continue pushing my own stuff through their computers and printers (while providing my own paper and toner, to be sure).

Could anything go wrong here? Of course! Lots! Nobody's guaranteeing Jyzer Ink a thing. As a vendor it's close to powerless and I as its sole prop. am a virtual nonentity ("Jyzelby") and so far I've been left in the dark on just about everything. But personally I've still got two K in the bank and five and a half more on the way so I refuse to worry -- that is, I'm ordering myself not to. And I suppose for the most part I'll be able to obey this order -- keep those anxieties in check. Wait and see how things shake out.

-- So here I sit in this laudable coffeehouse. And wouldn't Rikki like this place, I'm thinking, and not just for its continental feel. (But no word from her yet. Expect nothing -- especially since I'm not sure I'd want anything.) I figure I'll wander up this way from time to time. The extreme eastern tip of a shallow isosceles triangle whose long side is the waterfront. Walk, walk, walk, I, within that triangle. (Another good new potential jyze venue has surfaced in the northernmost corner of the same triangle, or tripolar order, call it: a cinema cafe, open twenty-four hours.)

With the weather improving, jyze should be able to introduce a little more variety of setting into these pages. During bad weather it's pretty much confined to the same old venues: unit B-2, room 225, suite 1740, storage unit 161, and the cheap-coffee cafes of this same tripolar zone during the hours when they have a high ratio of seats to customers. In good weather, however, it can move outdoors. In theory anyway. No doubt jyze will assert its own preferences. I'm noticing it's often

taking perverse pleasure these days in shattering my
plans and predictions for it.

-- And it's hard to leave this joint. Not just for
me; seven or eight others are lingering up here now --
eight -- nursing a cup or a glass of whatever, reading
or keyboarding, gazing out the windows. Ages are mostly
in the younger brackets but this doesn't seem to matter
much (or put it this way: in few other places would it
matter less). The music's all right, some turbocharged
folksy stuff at the moment. Banjos and a zither, I'm
thinking, urged on by a maniacal electric bass. -- Now
reggae. But a good sound system. Wish the digi-cafe
were more like this and less internet-oriented. All
those zeroes and ones and ones and zeroes. But holy
shit, my man, you cannot ask for the moon. You like
this coffeehouse here so much, you can hike up to it
anytime. It's probably about the same distance from
unit B-2 as the hideaway is, a little over a mile. Not
as likable a walk, though. Downtown backwaters.
Freeway-dominated concrete wasteland. Maybe that's one
reason why it feels so good when you get here: you've
made it through more or less unscathed (depending on how
much long-term pulmonary scathing those abundant freeway
fumes can rack up on you or in you).

Some fresh-cut roses in a vase down below -- not
there the last time I peered over the railing. Creamy
yellow with red borders, very handsome. Hey -- some up
here too, right behind me! When did they sneak 'em in?
(Just far enough away I can't sniff 'em without standing
up and leaning over, which I'm not yet ready to do.)

Short guy in well-worn jeans at the next table now,
maybe my age (bald spot, a little gray), he's smoking
and he's reading "the indispensable paper" (as it bills
itself) from the far coast. Shiny brown oxfords give
him away -- so too the magazine he brought up with him
which I see isn't the mildly progressive political one I
at first took it to be but something about "smart
investing." No doubt the very type of thing I should be
poring over myself these days. But I refuse to be smart
that way. Better to go down my own way than to go up

the "smart investing" way.
    -- Fish out the clunky pocket watch by its chain.
Push button to flip lid open. Purple face in there,
exotic imprints in cyrillic alphabet. 3:05 it says.
-- But how happy I am to have this watch! How glad I am
I blew the bucks back during the binge period! How wise
I was! What foresight I displayed! (Yet will any of
the "smart investing" mags ever pursue this humble type
of uplifting story? Never!) (Not only that, but also
this week I invested a fin and change in a used copy of
a book I enjoyed twenty years ago, and it was thirty
years old then. A rave "reconsiderations" review in the
idleness magazine spurred me to do it. So that's lined
up after the neoprag. The "wise idleness" book. And no
more buying of books for a while. Probably a long while.
If I can be wise in such a way. -- And I can!)
    Now pack it in and sniff them roses up close.
                    *   *
    -- The way I used to call room B-2 the jyzeyard --
scratch that. That went out with the imbecilic Sofie
crush. Out forever, just as Sofie is apparently gone
forever. (In fact the co-op has a sign on its door
seeking new members and I'm wondering if Sofie's moving
out. And I'm more disgusted than ever with the co-op
itself, which still hasn't tried to contact me despite
my "very strong support" there and their urging me to
reapply for the next opening while they were showing me
the door -- that same one -- after the rejection.)
    As for the jyzeyard in B-2, that's out because this
obviously has to be the jyzeyard right here where I'm
now sitting. It's the building courtyard directly
outside B-2's south windows. It's in the slot of this
U-shaped building, the surface stepped down and tilted
to the west where it opens onto the alley through a high
gated chickenwire fence painted glossy black and
speckled here and there with white birdshit. The yard
itself is partially patioed in a vaguely double-diamond
shape (seen from above) and it has a single wooden bench
at the back of the lower and farther westward of the two
diamonds (but just about exactly in the middle of the

yard) and that's where I'm holding forth at this moment.
Eight or nine feet directly to my right are Mariana's
windows (her, the art student, I've seen only once more
since Mindy introduced us the day I moved in, and that
one time was from my windows as she passed by out here
-- but I hear her quite often, singing softly as she
strums her guitar, murmuring on the phone, listening to
her radio or TV, calling out things to her brother Kevin
right outside my door) (him I also rarely see).

And then ten feet farther west along that same
wall, my "dining area" window, small and square and
relatively high up, maybe six feet, with a rose-colored
open-mouth fish swimming in a square of incandescent
blue glass propped up on the sill next to a row of
colored glass bottles. Another twelve feet or so over,
at the far corner of B-2 and also of the whole wing, are
my larger windows, through which (with the blinds open,
as now) I can see the corner of my brown loveseat (love
-- ha!) and the potted miniature rosebush from the
market garden shop. Just outside that window a spindly
courtyard tree rises about two and a half stories. Pink
rhodies shimmer on surprisingly robust bushes four or
five feet to both sides of the tree trunk.

Supposedly some wild parties rock the yard out here
when things really get cookin' in the summer months. So
Mindy told me. I'll believe it when I see it.

The older part of the building, to my left, is
about the same height as the new annex in which I live,
but the ceilings are so high over there it has one less
floor, four as opposed to the annex's five.

-- But what a day. What a sweet day! I even broke
down and bought myself an exotic breed of impatiens at
the public market, which about shoots my budget for this
week, and I'm talking about the auxiliary one which I
called into being (at the ATM) after springing for the
"wise idleness" classic.

-- And the market, the market. I could wander
around there for hours every day. Huge crowds --
tourism is way, way up this year, and the market throngs
are not all tourists either. Thousands of people live

within a few blocks (myself included -- yippee!) and I'm
beginning to recognize some of them and exchange brief
greetings with a few (though mostly just nods). Live
sidewalk entertainment galore -- a mean steel guitar
today, a hundred feet farther down an even meaner seven-
member steel band. A clown, a one-man puppet theater, a
piano player, a balloon sculptor, a string quartet.

(This past week city voters rejected funding for a
proposed commons park which would've abutted this
district to the northeast, roughly a mile from here. I
had gradually come to favor it but the opposition also
had a good case. It would've been one more very
expensive jewel for a crown already boasting many.)

-- And my social life? None. I'm continuing to
adjust to the likelihood of this being a long-term or
even permanent condition. It's not that I couldn't find
myself a lover (unless I'm jiving myself), but that the
effort required to win over one with whom things might
at least have a chance of lasting would likely be so
great that little time would be left for anything else.
No change there. The kind of woman who's apt to go for
the kind of man I am now is less likely than ever to be
one I'd go for myself. Simple fact. Nor is it really a
question of being willing to lower my standards (such as
they are). I'm open to anybody.

-- Nah, I don't want to keep pounding on that one.
Just try to maintain my balance, that's all. Realize
the disappointments will be legion. Write them off in
advance (as much as possible) and try to carry on with a
good attitude about their inevitability. "Develop other
interests." But also keep the very same interest and
pursue it through the real work, which is to say: love
that quirky fictojyze antiheroine or subheroine.
-- Alas, an obvious conflict lurks here. Pursuing it in
your JIFT also makes you ache for it in real life.
-- But this is the price you pay, so -- pay it! Whine
not!

-- A few days short of two months ago I was hauling
all my stuff through this courtyard, scores and scores
of loads. And six months ago yesterday Mother died.

[Life of the Jyze to Come]

Here I sit in a place and condition I could scarcely
have imagined for myself a couple of years ago, say.
(Yet I did occasionally imagine myself living downtown,
breaking up with Lady U, old Mom passing on, so what am
I suggesting? I didn't imagine all three happening at
once? Of course I didn't! I had other things to think
about rather than consider every last imaginary permute
and combo! Just as now! -- And better go start
tending to some of those other things before I break
into sobs.) (Just kidding.) (I think. Or make that
not merely I think but I assert fearlessly.)

19

    Well, this right here'll do just as well as the
next place. Better even. Maybe lots better.
    The pocket park is where it's happening this
afternoon. Warm and sunny and we locals who are not at
work are out in force soaking up the rays.
    I've nabbed a little corner of the concrete wall
shoring up the sandbox and the top end of the kids'
double slide which issues into the dark gray dunes four
or five feet below. One kid is working the slide right
now, his Afrusan papa and Natusan mama (reverting to
Mezzu Silver lingo, this Eurusan is) hunkered down on
the far side of the slide.
    Those old gents shooting hoops on the concrete
half-court in the far corner of the park, I could take
'em all one-on-one with both hands tied behind my back
and -- no. Just trash-talking. Those guys can play.
    Such a fine day to be perched outside atop a grassy
knoll. Downhill some six or eight feet to my left three
drifter dudes sprawl in the shade, two reading beat-up

paperbacks, probably from a two-for-two-bits rack. Bare
feet and thrift-store clothes. A park claimed by the
downtrodden. We the salt of the earth. Whooee! And in
danger of sunburn too, some of us. A few. (Might be
another night worker or two out here. I'm less
conspicuous as one of those myself these days -- less a
paleface -- owing to my fairly well established new
routine that has me out and about in the early
afternoons, as now. -- Closer to midafternoon though.)
     Core of the district, this park. Two blocks east
of the B-2 building but on the south side of the street,
occupying the northwest corner of its block, maybe a
sixth of the block as a whole. Just to the south is the
small grocery store where I buy only an occasional item
because the prices are sky high. Just past that, the
hardware store which proved so useful in my first weeks
of settling in (but I haven't been back there in the
past month). Clothes hooks, watch chains and key chains
and wood glue and lots of other small items on which I
now depend came from there.
     And at my back across the street to the north, the
SRO hotel I almost rented a room in (and to which I
wound up forfeiting my thirty-dollar deposit). Across
the alley to the west from the hotel, the back side of
the digi-cafe. And that pretty much hits all the nearby
high spots as I know them.
     (The couple and their kid are leaving. They're all
right -- friendly folks. Loaned them one of my pens.
They picked the right guy to ask: my bag's always
stocked with a dozen or more backup pens and markers of
various types and ink colors. Her vernacular, though,
could corrode titanium. I now know this: she's on
probation and someone's about to be either sued or
strangled. More details maybe next sunny day.)
     -- Can feel the back of my neck sizzling. "Until
the pink skin on the back of my neck turns cherry red"
-- then I'll move. And I'm guessing "then" better be
right now.

*

For all those long winter months while dreaming of

sitting outdoors in the park you forget about little
details such as how the sun can scorch you. Even here!
Especially here, in fact, this city, where it's so hard
to build up antibodies against its effects.

    -- So I moved maybe a body length or two down the
knoll to the base of a small shade tree. This spot's
okay except I have to sit in an awkward posture with my
legs stretched out uphill, which means my back presses
too hard against the tree trunk and its jaggedy bark.
But I guess I can take it for a while. (If I pointed my
legs in any other direction they'd either be sticking
out onto the sidewalk -- where the foot traffic's heavy
-- or disturbing one of the paperback readers (whose
soles -- all six drifter soles actually -- rest nearby
now, and I'll just note they all could use a manicure).)

    So what kind of six-day J-week has it been? Most
excellent. Full of those kinds of small and essentially
meaningless personal events from which I love to try to
wring a little significance.

    On that same personal scale one of these events is
actually quite big. It's the last day of May and this
means at midnight tonight the court-reporting firm which
in one way or another has paid nearly all my bills for
the past sixteen and a half years -- and most of Lady
U's as well, except for her half of the rent, which her
parents always covered as a kind of apology for her many
health problems as well as her more or less permanent
student status, and no doubt they're still covering her
rent at U Acres now -- that firm ceases to exist.

    (Trying a new position with legs tucked under me,
left flank pressing against tree trunk.)

    What else? (I'll get back to the old firm's
demise.) (WACKAWACKAWACKA, a flock of maybe a hundred
pigeons just materialized from nowhere as a vintage Cawk
lady in black standing about fifteen feet to the
southeast tossed out a bagful of crumbs -- sounded like
a chopper coming down right on top of us. I'll bet I
wasn't the only one who had to fake being cool with it.
Were any war vets present they might've freaked right
off to cloud-cuckoo land.)

What else (again)? Well, a live phone message, my third -- no, fourth (Kar, Jeff, and Naomi were the others) -- and it was Lady U herself telling me it's time for another mail pickup. When I get back to her she might even say she'd like the grand tour now. Or maybe not. Whatever, it's fine with me. (This week I again realized if I'm to be consistent, not to say smart and/or wise, I'll accept all the way down that no one's to blame and nothing significant remains to be understood regarding our breakup. I always said -- in fact we both did -- and maybe most people do, or should, about whatever relationship they're in -- I always said it was inexplicable that the thing worked as long as it did, "a miracle." Thus nothing can be pointed to as the cause of its ceasing to work. The "miracle" expired, that's all. Miracles will do that.)

What else besides the love postmortems? Well, I can say Jyzer Ink's name finally went up on the hideaway building's main registry board in the elevator lobby and also the smaller board serving the second floor. Hank the janitor showed up one day with a couple of ductworkers who were trying to find a way to coax the air into circulating a little better so as to cool down our floor. (I wasn't the only tenant who was overheating. But just last week I liberated dayscoper Doris's old desk fan from the scope office -- it's scavenger's choice down there now -- and set it to work atop the filing cabinet next to the cracked-open door, which the "Liberty" doorstop prevents from being blown open more than about six inches even with the fan turned all the way up, and now I rarely feel overheated in there.) -- So I told Hank my ego was hurting because my business name still hadn't gone up on either board. He said he thought something could be done about that, and the next day it had been. The right spelling too, not "Inc." "So what's this new outfit in 225? From the name, some kind of press-clipping service maybe?")

But the key to the week was a spontaneous budget review. This I fell into less than twenty-four hours after begrudgingly authorizing myself a ten-buck raise

in weekly allowance, from fifty back up to sixty. Fifty
just wasn't hacking it and I was finally willing to
concede there was no way it could. Then I got to
wondering whether sixty could do it -- and for half a
day or so I'd felt euphoric about my new flushness and
the majorly enhanced subsistence-level lifestyle it
would support. So now I tried to itemize everything I
spend money on, including every single food and food-
related item right down to toothpicks (roughly half a
cent to deploy one per day). I discovered that if I
stay with the same basic menu -- which in truth is very
far from extravagant as it is -- I'll be spending over
fifty dollars a week on food and drink alone, and that's
not counting anything I might order in cafes or
restaurants or delis or mom-and-pops.

Obviously this won't do. I need more than ten a
week for "incidentals." Doesn't matter how well-stocked
I am. Therefore I'm cutting back on everything except
bread and potatoes. Bread, it seems I can get unlimited
day-old stuff at the supermarket for thirty-nine cents a
loaf, and some of it's just as good as any bread I buy
elsewhere at regular prices. (I just need to figure out
when's the best time to show up at the supermarket -- if
they have a particular time for culling the "day-old"
bread from the shelves and putting it in the special
rack. -- "Day-old" in quotes there because I'm sure
that bread's on the shelves well over a day before it's
culled -- probably more like a week or ten days.)

And then potatoes. At present they're going cheap:
$2.49 for a fifteen-pound bag. That's around a dozen
meals. It's hunter-gatherer times all over again when I
trek off to buy one of these bags and then haul it home
more than a mile slung over my shoulder like a deer
carcass. "Like a sack of potatoes." Too bad the free-
ride zone for city bus service doesn't extend up to the
north pole, as I never tire of thinking. (This weekend
I'll check out food prices at the one accessible
supermarket I haven't visited yet. It's at the other
far extreme of my bipolar turf, the southern one, but it
is within the free-ride zone. Unless, however, things

have changed radically since the era of city living with
Lady U, when we often visited that market for its
abundant ethnic choices -- all for her to choose from
and then later mostly for her to consume -- it's likely
to be the most expensive of all.)

(Couple of Afrusan hoopsters in a push-shove
altercation right now just past where the pigeons were
swarming. Going on and on. Loud and nasty. They might
slash each other to teriyaki strips but nobody's about
to take too much notice for the moment. "Best not get
involved.") (And that's for sure -- if you can defend
it morally. Meaning, in essence, if you have a choice.
This being life in the big city, obviously enough.)
(And now they're taking it back to the hoops court. And
the studied show of indifference in my area here can
again become something a little closer to real
indifference.)

-- So as of tomorrow, first day of June, I start
the new austerity regime. Watch every penny. Be
grateful I've got enough elements of the good life in
place to be able to afford this psychically. It's
simply a question of priorities. Would I rather eat
fish once a week, one option, or eat fish once a month
and a big potato one extra night a week the other three
weeks so I can drop in at one of the poetry-slam clubs
on open-mic night if I don't happen to have any scoping
work at the office that night?

Assuming there will be an office. Assuming there
will at least sometimes be scoping work.

(Last night was our district's infamous "Bad Art
Ball." I wanted to check it out even though the
"donation" was five bucks at the door. But Jyzer Ink
had scoping work. That work had to be done in an ad hoc
way too because the computer system's being revamped and
my station's set up in a new, much smaller space and I
had to tilt my head at an odd angle for hours and this
is why the interior of my neck is annoyingly sore today
to go along with the sizzling sunburned exterior.)

-- Couple of Cawk cops just moseyed up on horses.
They're scrutinizing the hoops group into which the

fiery disputants reblended. A fly is fascinated with
the ink coming from this J-stick. The pigeons are back
and in the same mighty force. A yellow tractor the size
of a pickup truck is noisily and fumily parallel-parking
just behind me, about seven or eight feet away across
the sidewalk. Buses are squealing to a halt at the stop
on the far side of this tiny park by the grocery store
and then roaring off. Another vintage Cawk lady, this
one in red sweats, is painting her nails purple while
stretched out under a blue umbrella just behind the
sullied soles of the paperback readers; looks like she
brought maybe half her room contents out with her,
including what appears to be a gerbil in a cage. The
cage has fuzzy pink bars and shiny ribbons of various
pastel hues tied in bows to each bar. My guess is she
lives in the same SRO joint I almost wound up residing
in myself -- maybe even the same room 317 for all I know.

        -- Before coming here I did breakfast at the digi-
cafe: the one day a week I've rationed for myself there.
(Four more Cawk cops on horseback ride up now, looking
like a posse from days of yesteryear except for the
anachronistic lumpy blue-meanie outfits. "My baby loves
the western movies....") -- Mostly lowrise buildings in
our immediate area here but one highrise of maybe thirty
stories looms at the other end of the block and another
almost as tall stands right across the street from it,
both part of the ongoing upscaling, that is, gentrifying,
of the hood. Lots of highrise condos on the drawing
boards according to the business pages. ---
                    *   *
        All right, let's see how this goes. Strolling past
the park at the north end of the public market -- on my
way down to the hideaway, thinking I'd finish up this
week's entry there -- I spotted an empty table out by
the overlook. On a day so fine why not here? With all
kinds of folks out to catch some late sun and traffic
roaring by on the viaduct below and a couple of big
freighters lumbering across the bay, tugs attached to
both like suckling piglets with hind legs churning. And
of course a ferry, a matched pair of tour boats, several

sailboats and some other craft whose functions are
unknown to me swooping or slicing or chugging this way
or that. And wharves, cranes, seagulls, dry docks,
wakes, clouds (but only a few), mountains, haze, street
lamps (unlit but here one stands resolutely just a few
feet away), an airplane, some sort of glider pulled by a
boat. And whatnot. Or better: whatnaut.

   This is the largest of the tables. Wooden, solidly
built, firmly anchored. Plenty of carved initials and
here's "Patooty 6/29" -- someone's sweet Patooty I
suppose (and where's my own jelly roll? Where oh lord
oh where?). Of all the tables this one is the farthest
from the nearby restaurant (a long row of fancy folks
chomping away behind abundant window glass over there
maybe thirty feet to the north) and it's sort of
isolated out here, a little jyze island. Very nice.

   Yeah, good things happening. All week. For one, I
finally put some sheets on my loft futon. Clean
pillowcases, the works. Splendor in the loft (though
admittedly lonely splendor) night after night after
night. And I built a custom bathboard, one that fits in
snug so it won't dump a load of books if I accidentally
nudge it. ("Made him a bathboard / so he could soak
just right.") And on my trip over to the storage unit
(the first in several weeks) I discovered a cache of
perfectly usable, if ancient and well worn, henleys,
work shirts, and jeans and this delighted me not just
because it'll eventually save me some money (if I live
long enough) but also because now I can stretch out the
periods between laundry days a couple more weeks.

   And then -- what? Yeah, well, I found a way I can
keep using the crippled stereo for my daily vinyl blues
hit. That's a lot all by itself. I have to do
everything manually and to a degree far beyond what the
owner's manual means by manual operation -- for example,
lift the tone arm by hand, pick it up by hand -- in fact
do everything except spin the turntable by hand. (Had
this scheme not succeeded I couldn't've listened even
once this afternoon, far less the half-dozen times I did
listen, to the honey-voiced boogie grandmaster tearing

into her biggest hit of them all: "Cleo's Boogie." And
did that ever bring back the days of pounding the piano
in the basement at 636 in Gatewood. Walking boogie
bass: my specialty in that distant era. -- Sometimes I
forget the degree to which boogie-woogie imprinted
itself on my soul. -- And then what a hoot to remember
again. -- But also to remember, alas, my right hand was
not so hot and kept refusing to get noticeably better.

    -- Here I look up once more and find everything's
shifted into a whole new configuration out there in the
harbor, and on such a large scale! I turn around and
all the skyscrapers have stayed exactly where they were,
but out on the water the floating horizontal skyscrapers
are forever creating new bayscapes to admire.

    (Right about here, and at just about this hour, a
pretty damn good rock band was playing before a large
crowd last Sunday. A portable stage was set up, cameras
were whirring, a video was being filmed. The band --
Somebody and the Somethings, sounded like "My Rag and
the Cinders" but that seems unlikely -- played the same
cut over and over, as the film crew worked on different
angles, and one phrase from that session has been
echoing in my head all week: "You've got it made / in
the shade / Mr. Jade." (Or you think you do. Or
something. Other words setting it up. And I'd never
have believed I could forget any of them.) -- But a
memorable scene regardless. Actually quite beautiful
with its bay backdrop reflecting the setting sun
seemingly rising toward the elongated and upside-down
mountains (more like stalactites). Me the solitary guy
from an earlier generation -- anachronistic isolato! --
but not yielding an inch in my admiration for what lay
before me, the band with its sappy jinglelike phrase
very much included.)

    -- And: I've shifted into a new reading program.
Not that it's really a program; I just started reading
some different things I've been wanting to get to for a
long time. So the poor English protojyze grandmaster,
he's been demoted from the loft to the bathroom, and
more specifically toiletside. I'm sorry, but not even

this celebrated diarist, good as he is, is good enough
for the loft. The nuggets in his unabridged works are
too widely spaced (especially in the first couple of
volumes). By and large I'd say his writing should be of
interest mainly to historians. Way too large a chunk of
it describes political developments of the day from his
perch as a fairly important government insider. I mean,
sorry, but who cares about that stuff? It has little
intrinsic interest outside its own time. So I say you
gotta liven it up, buddy. Gotta inflect through kinky
self. Protojyze it again, Sam! -- And I'd recommend
you frag some of those never-ending gerundial run-ons.

Can I give advice to a grandmaster? And why not?
For one thing he's just a kid when he's doing the
protojyzing, launching the first volume at scarcely half
my present age. He can use a few tips from an older,
more experienced jyzeslinger. In the volume I'm reading
now he's been at it for only half a year and he clearly
has much to learn. -- I'll grant, though, he shows lots
of potential. Unfortunately he doesn't seem to realize
the careerist track he's set out on with his day job
augurs nothing but headaches for him and ensures that
he'll squander most of that raw talent.

To assume his former place up in the loft I've
summoned the French essay grandmaster. The big fat $75
collected volume. And I'll admit he too is taking off
very slowly and shakily, not to mention overly formally
and antiquarially. But I'm giving him a chance. If he
too proves unworthy of the loft, others are clamoring to
take his spot. (All those massively grand and classic
tomes I meant to tackle in earlier eras but didn't get
around to: surely I could find a few that would still --
or should I say finally? -- work for me.)

Down in the armchair, meanwhile, for dinnertime
reading there's a newly published anthology of personal
essays by USAns. The lengthy introduction is quite good.
However, as I'm seeing right off the bat with the very
first contribution (and with the French essay
grandmaster's work too for that matter) there's no story
there. No action. Nothing much developing from chunk

to chunk. Thus the unexpected is not unexpected enough
and the personal is not really personal but rather
abstract (as in abstracted from life to the point it's
lifeless) -- or simply bloodless.

    Now, protojyze is different and of course so too is
jyze itself. Here we can do everything the personal
essayist does and far, far more. (And without a doubt
we'll keep trying to do just that. -- Acknowledging,
however, a danger posed by any personal life which --
like mine at present, for one -- is totally lacking in
the kind of dramatic story which I've just stated
categorically the personal essay must employ to engage
the reader. The danger is that these jyze sessions here
will devolve into nothing more than a series of loosely
linked personal essays on inherently dull topics. Can
jyze find some way to navigate this desert? For right
now, with Lady U out, Sofie vanished, and Rikki not
biting, the crossing of the sex/love/romance wasteland
itself may be the most intrinsically dramatic material
available to it.)

    The actual most exciting moment of the past week --
of the past couple of months, really -- came when I,
this jyzer, burned some toast and B-2's fire alarm went
off. For about a minute it shrieked and howled at ear-
splitting volume as I frantically tried to figure out
how to silence it. Luckily the alarm is easily
accessible because the spot where it's mounted on the
ceiling happens to be almost directly above where I
swing up into the loft from the steeply canted bookcase
stairs. I'm well aware it's there because various body
parts frequently bump against it as I crawl by. -- So I
was getting nowhere with the alarm, envisaging fire
engines roaring up, axes splintering the B-2 door. And
the shriek was ravaging my ears because I was so close
to it. -- And then as suddenly as it started it stopped.
Seemingly of its own accord. I guess the smoke thinned
out enough or possibly the battery went dead. (So next
time I'll be well advised to turn on the kitchen and
bathroom fans before trying to mess with the alarm.
Waiting to do that until after it stops sounding, as

today, doesn't accomplish much.)

    -- Of course all this time here at the park bench
(including right now, back in the present) I'm again
roasting in the sun. Little precancers vibrating with
anticipatory relish. They know they'll eventually be
getting me if nothing else beats them to the punch, it's
just a matter of when, and here I am voluntarily giving
them a boost and speeding up the timetable. -- Recalling
something I read, a doctor commenting to a decaying
forty-year-old that human teeth and for that matter the
entire human body are "designed" by evolution to last
less than forty years. I, of course, am wearing out
just like everyone else who's entered the beyond-design-
life phase and probably at a somewhat faster pace than
many. All the little aches and pains, the malfunctions,
the weakenings and the slippages and the salt-and-
pepperings and the abundant additional evidence of wear
and tear -- I'm just very lucky I can usually still do
pretty much what I want to do physically and do it at
pretty much the rate I want. Where there's been too
much of that wear and tear on one part, I'm still in
possession of another part in reasonable working order
that can compensate. My bodily redundancy has not yet
been severely compromised. -- Knock on flesh!

    Also this week, and maybe last week too, I
triggered some massive unexpected pleasure by rereading
certain protojyze passages of my own composition from
roughly nineteen years ago. I wanted to check out just
how things were with me back in the days immediately
before Lady U came into my life and transformed it. I
found they were a whole lot like they are today and in
several respects even worse. Of course I knew this
before, but not in the detailed way I know it now.

    -- There goes the replica sailing vessel. Motor
power again. Up here kids are leaping about like frogs
on lily pads from tabletop to tabletop and one might
land on mine at any moment. And I'm getting hungry
anyway. So onward. And farewell you presumably sweet
"Patooty 6/29" you.

20

Epiphany territory. Sun shining through the trees
of the triangle and lighting up this page. Late sun of
a happening Saturday evening. Just came strolling down
from unit B-2 by a circuitous route -- or no, more a
wandering, divagatory route -- which took me through a
laundromat-cafe, an artsy bar, the public market, a
couple of plush hotel lobbies, the city's central square
(which is also a triangle even though it's called a
square, just like here), the ORB cafe, the fast-food
joint at the ferry dock (for a chocolate cone -- not the
flavor I was hankering after but they warned me the
vanilla was too soft to hold its shape in the cone; it
would've worked all right in a dish, they said, but who
wants a dish on a day like this -- other than a dishy
jyze dish, that is. Or so I'm hoping anyway).

Oooeee, the town's jumpin'! Yeah! Because the
day's so gorgeous and tomorrow's game three of the pro-
hoops championship series -- played right here in Jyze
City! At the arena on the old fairgrounds! Lots of
tall people wandering the streets just like me (but many
much taller). Also many more Afrusans around than usual
-- which is something this unusually Eurusan and Asiusan
town -- by USAn standards -- should aim for as a new
norm to have any hope of becoming the truly cosmopolitan
burg it already likes to boast of being. Also elevated
trains whizzing by, packed to an extent you hardly ever
see in ordinary times. Bursting with gamegoers.
Groaning with foreplay pleasure.

(And here comes the band. This one bound for the
rock club before which I sit, facing it, my back to the

sun and to the back of the shirtless young Cawk dude
hunkered down directly behind me on this double-sided
bench. Deep in the darkness of the rock club I can just
make out the stage which stands more or less directly
beneath my office -- on which stage last night none
other than Swamp Mama J. was belting one out as I walked
by on my way home. -- And a door south of the rock club,
the sidewalk-cafe portion of a new retro lounge, which
used to be a rock club itself, every table now occupied,
mostly by hoops fans from the city just outside of which
I grew up, that is, in Mentoka styling, Centropolis,
a/k/a C-town. Or from the perspective of Jyze City in
this playoff finals week: the Bad Guys. -- The retro
lounge luring in the so-called "cocktail nation" crowd
with music which was mediocre enough, sez I, the first
time around half a century ago -- but I'll try to keep an
open mind since I'll also have to be listening to this
stuff through the floor of No. 225.)
     Yesterday a couple of benches to the north of this
one here a fine hour or so when, before going up to 225
to work, I read a chunk of the aforementioned "wise
idleness" book in a semi-intoxicated state as a sun-
mottled crowd streamed by, the sidewalk-cafe sitters
lolled and sipped and chatted, the bicycle rickshaw man
shilled for customers, a horse-drawn carriage clip-
clopped by (I often encounter these carriages emerging
anachronistically from a shiny new parking garage a
block north of here where I presume they harness up
after the horses are trailered in from boonies much like
the ones I called home until recently) -- ah, such a
splendid afternoon and such a splendid book! -- Just as
a bicycle messenger leaned in to inform me, about the
book, before pedaling off. The guy had read it "a while
ago" (like me; but my "while" was probably longer than
his lifetime). Still: I was startled with pleasure!
     Says the author of this same book about the most
celebrated author (poet and playwright) of them all: "He
merely lived, observed life and went away." That's all.
Nothing more need be said. The essence.
     But -- an ominous note. Tough times ahead at the

scope office. My early warning system tells me they're again suspicious I'm doing exactly what I'm doing and have been doing for well over a decade, which is to say, of course, using their office for my own nefarious late-night purposes, i.e., fictojyzing, and more to the point using their machines to print up my own stuff, JIRT as well as JIFT and plenty of miscellaneous items as well, with no intent to pay them anything for doing so, ever.

How do I know this? Long ago I set up a couple of odd-looking decoy files in reporter Naomi's computer directory and just let them sit there. I rigged them so I'd know if anyone looked into them, including the date and time it happened. I always check these files before starting work, and thus last night I discovered someone (probably dayscoper Amy) had invaded both files that same afternoon at 1:51 and 1:54 p.m. (Few of the reporters, Naomi included, know how to access their own directories, much less the individual files in them.)

The previous night I'd run off a clean copy of a volume of my own protojyze -- about 430 pages. I provide the paper and toner but can do nothing to disable the page-meters on the printers. Amy must be keeping an eagle eye on those meters now that I'm the only other printer user. And even if I weren't she'd still suspect me of being the villain.

And I was. And how! I figured during this chaotic transition period I could probably get away with printing a lot more of my own pages than usual. In the past week I've run off close to a thousand. (As noted before, none of this costs the firm a penny. Their printers are all covered by a long-term maintenance contract whose cost is based solely on the age of the machines, not on how many pages go through them. And my pages make up a tiny fraction of the total.)

-- Regardless, I figure they can't prove anything. I'll just have to play it cool for a while. Lie in the weeds. My hope is Amy will soon be out of there anyway, maybe in the next week or two. If they do accuse me I'll simply sigh deeply and say this is probably another of her attempts to make me look bad (of which, as

everyone from the old firm knows, there have been many).
Now more than ever she's out to get me because it
appears when all the dust settles I'll be the only one
of the longtime scoping crew still working in that
office, herself included. (Talk about irony.)
     How'll it all shake out? Won't know until next week.
A slight chance I could take a fall here and before long
be out job-hunting. If so, I'll say it was glorious
while it lasted. I got mine. They exploited me and I
exploited them right back. Kept things nice and even.
Any ethical system which failed to comprehend the
righteousness of my actions here would be a poor ethical
system indeed (and boss-oriented to boot).
     -- Sun's sinking beneath the old brick steam plant
a diagonal block to the northwest and so I've put on my
jacket. Black denim type with the right shoulder worn
threadbare from carrying the backpack mostly by one
strap on that shoulder for so long. Listening,
meanwhile, to scads of boisterous rivalry talk, my
current city vs. the city of my youth, J-town vs. C-
town. Hey, I could add a lot of cents' worth here!
     (Several of these people seem to be reporters or
sportswriters. Media circus -- well over a thousand
"medians" in town to keep the world up to the minute on
this crucial event.) (But no, I'm not putting it down.
I don't like some of the things going on in organized
basketball connected with its immense growth in
popularity -- for sure I'll never pay to attend another
pro extravaganza -- but hoops is still my game. I've
been following it and playing it all my life and still
am doing so now. It's just that at this point the
nerfing I do in my room with a makeshift one-third-size
(guessing) hoop is probably closer to the pure game than
the pro version is. -- But purity, right, that's not my
thing either. I can still enjoy hooping it up this
nerfy way, that's all, and I do.)
     Upcoming, meanwhile, is the city visit of Lady U.
Tuesday we met at the dock in the storage port (she was
only ten minutes late this time) and at my request she
brought along one of the small expandable window screens

from the shed. Then we motored up to the drive-in
across from the storage place and conversed there for an
hour. Mostly I'm just feeling sorry for her now, the
choices she's making. Faking it all these years must've
been even more of a strain for her than I realized at
the time. (I mean regarding full-bore commitment to the
arts and specifically the ones I went for -- which now
she could suddenly care less about. It was all for me!
She actually says that!) (I even started thinking, holy
moly, it's possible she might soon come to regret all
this nonsense she's caught up in now and want us to get
back together. -- And how would I handle that? Would I
give her a shot? It occurred to me I might be proud of
myself if I could. But -- not likely. Far from it.
Very far.)
     -- Nightlife starting to crank up already. Not
even full sundown yet. (My nightlife tonight will
consist of a coffee stop at the ORB cafe, some revising
at the hideaway, a nose poke-in at the laundromat-cafe
to check out a strange sort of hybrid blues show that
will be going down in their large back room -- a show
which I might consider attending if the door charge were
five bucks or under instead of eight -- and then a soak
in my B-2 tub. Another delicious chapter of the supreme
neoprag replying to his critics.)
     New also this past week, a stop at the primo alt-
music cafe for coffee and croissant (at eleven a.m. on a
Wednesday when I was the only customer, even though this
week's edition of a national neolib magazine features a
long story about it: purported center of the alt-music
universe). And a stop at a poetry deli for the Tuesday-
night "salon," an hour's sit in a small smoky room there
as local poets occupying spots all along the talent
spectrum boldly or shyly or apathetically read their
work and I as a relatively veteran observer new to this
particular scene tried to figure out how I really felt
about it.
     The younger generation out on the town. Here's a
cluster of 'em boistering it up in the sidewalk cafe
about ten feet away. Nose rings, brow rings, lip rings,

metastasizing tattoos, clunky and/or baggy clothes, in-your-face neopunk rawness and rudeness. Doesn't do anything much for me but then of course it's not supposed to. Quite the contrary. Therefore I must grudgingly say I admire their success at carving out their own generational space. I'm also grateful that thanks to their good work I don't have to feel quite so bad about leaving my own youth behind.

Scoping's been no fun at all for the past week. Last weekend the other firm, the former competitor, was moving in and the office was total nonstop chaos, day and, alas, night. All the machines I normally use are now crammed into one small room and Amy's seen to it that my workstation's virtually inaccessible. Headaches and backaches and eye aches are the result. Also disgust. Naomi and I are committed to muddling through, though, and I'll keep trying to do so if Jyzer Ink isn't given its walking papers.   (The new bunch seem all right. I haven't run into any of the reporters I know from past years but the office staff is friendly enough. To them I'm the mysterious grand-jury guy of a certain vintage who supposedly knows all the city's nastiest secrets.
-- And I am that! Or know a few of those secrets anyway.
-- Can't say what they are here in the J-book, of course, or for that matter anywhere else, or the feds might haul me before a grand jury myself. Then again if something truly disturbing came up I'd probably take my chances regardless. Maybe. Depending on a number of factors. A judgment call for sure.)

-- Why the window screen Lady U brought me? Unit B-2 gets stuffy and hot when the temperature outside climbs above seventy-five or so. But if I open the window, flies from the dumpster (now totally hidden from view, if I'm seated, by the fence-clinging vines) -- the flies come swarming in, yes, as I discovered on the day when the pest-control squad showed up to spray and I had to keep the window open for an extended period to clear out the fumes from the spraying (almost a paradigm case of the Law of Unintended Consequences, at least from the pest-control vantage).

(My worst mistake of the week: I froze three tubs
of margarine. Margarine you don't freeze, as I
should've known. Almost eight bucks wasted.)

-- But yes, the new austerity subregime is working
well. I've cut my consumption of all the (relatively)
expensive stuff exactly in half. So far no hardships at
all. Funny thing is, I've always loved bread and
potatoes. Even as a kid. And I can sneak in enough
little tidbits of the more expensive stuff to provide
some variety. Truly spicelike.

So it is that this will be the very first week of
the B-2 era I've succeeded in living within my budget.
Apparently. One more day to go and a fiver still wadded
up in my pocket to carry me through. Nor do I see any
reason I shouldn't be able to pull this off most weeks
(and I'm determined to keep trying for all weeks).

Meanwhile the suspicions which I in turn suspect
the scope office is harboring about me will force some
changes in my work regime for my own stuff. For a while
I'll have to do all my own writing and revising by hand
or on the computer screen, not printing anything out.
How much harder this will make things for me I just
don't know yet. I'm hoping to be able to adjust.

-- Periodical subscriptions running out one by one.
What's most frustrating about this is the impossibility
of knowing which ones will still be coming in. By the
time I realize I'm no longer receiving a particular
publication, the issue(s) I've missed have vanished from
the stands. Therefore I'm glancing through all of them
while they're available there and reading on the spot
anything I don't want to take a chance on missing.

*   *

-- Now a live kwikjyze postscript from the digi-
cafe. You can't beat this. The green armchair (with
matching hassock!) in the four-armchair cluster just
inside the entrance. Live jazz thirty feet away, five
pieces, big thumping string bass complete with fancy
hand-carved wooden rubber-stoppered pegleg. Clear line
of sight and sound. I could even have nursed my glass
of water here for as long as I wanted and not paid

anything. And in the future might just try to do that,
if broke. But tonight I've still got the fin -- or did
-- and so a small "schooner" of root beer.

     Ambling back from the hideaway on this exceptionally
rockin' night I lurked outside half a dozen clubs
listening to live music. The one I liked best was the
jazz club half a block south of here, east side of the
street. As on a couple of occasions earlier in the past
month, the singer working the mic inside and I seemed to
establish eye contact through the open door and I could
fantasize away to my heart's content -- and did. "Chick
warbler." This one even looked a little like a favorite
of mine back in college days.

     -- The week just past, to repeat, would've been my
parents' fifty-fifth wedding anniversary. A party right
here and right now in their honor. Flickering candles.
(And the thought outside the entrance as I flipped
through free lit while listening to an eighteen-year-old
mother talk, an infant babbling in her arms: in theory I
could've been that kid's grandfather. Or strictly from
an age standpoint, his great-grandfather, but only if I
and my kid and his/her kid all started up reproductively
as early as humanly possible.) (And to the hypothetical
great-grandson's pretty mother: Hey, mama, maybe I'm a
little vintage, but if you wanna play, I say okay.
-- But I said this only with my eyes, and only when she
wasn't looking. Don't want to be creeping anyone out
here in sproutsville.)

     This probably in lieu of that hot soak I was
thinking of earlier. Yearning for. But this is better.

     -- In most of these sentences I'm reacting, I'll
note, not thinking. Though I don't dislike thinking, I
do sometimes truly enjoy reacting without thinking.
(Mad applause now -- and I'm pleased to hear the band
will return for another set.) In any event genuine
jyzance often partakes of reacting-not-thinking. It
also at times disintegrates the self in the same way
sexual jouissance does -- pleasurably frags it, and then
the luminous fragments coalesce loosely into a new self
that is the same self all jyzed up and reconstellated.

[Life of the Jyze to Come]

(Well, this is one way of putting it. Clearly far from
a definitive one.)
     Such excitement here, it's almost too much for me.
What could be better than this? I'm almost ready to say
-- honestly now -- to hell with sex/love/romance. I'm
getting into the swing of the new good life -- the life
of the jyze to come, so to speak -- and now that life's
rolling in! The jyzer, he's chuckling and chortling.
(Hard at work on a sidewalk in the historic district
near the triangle, the jyzer's street-artist pal Darren.
He needs to clear twenty bucks tonight or he'll be
eighty-sixed from his room tomorrow morning. Cartoons
five bucks apiece and he's got a boxful of coin
donations -- that word again.)
     Flashing eyes. At me? A few. "What's this guy up
to? Could that be one of those hot new digital
notebooks he's playing with?" -- These days I'd say
more male eyes flash at me than female. Gay eyes maybe,
but how's one truly to know? Regardless I detect little
sexual or romantic interest emanating from any of them,
male or female, gay or straight or otherwise. How over
the hill am I anyway? (And is this the theme for the
year? When will I move on from brooding over my sad
fate of becoming reproductively, not to say
jouissantically, irrelevant?)
     -- Guy just came around with a jar, "Tips for the
band?" I shook my head even though he did avoid using
the D-word. Happy to say, he quickly moved on.
     All this and we're still in the June shallows.
(I'm recalling how a year ago I was going on and on
about the June shallows and the June deeps. Over there
in the far province where ruminants graze and nature
reigns supreme, though certainly to nowhere near the
degree it was reigning just a few short decades ago.)
-- Now here on the excellent house sound system comes a
trio of perky sisters belting out a favorite tune of my
mother's from back when I was maybe seven or eight:
about a choo-choo from a town near where she was born --
she herself one of a trio of perky sisters -- and her
mama was born near there too, as was her mama's mama.
And how this tune got ol' Mom "all hepped up," yes it

did! And me too! (Going at it now where post-hip retro
digi-culture reigns supreme.)
     -- Bottoms up with the schooner. And hunger's
starting to roar. I forgot about, as I often do, the
likely imminence of hunger: no doubt because (at least
in part) I'm so out of sync with the cultural norms on
mealtimes (and so much else). -- So maybe one set of
this quintet is all I'm meant to absorb tonight. First
swing a couple of blocks south on the next avenue over
-- edge road -- just to see what's cookin' down that way
on such a cookin' kind of J-town night, and then beat it
on home for some real home cookin' of my own.

21

     Only an hour until game time. We're all into this
now -- even the guy I joined on the elevator just for
the camaraderie (usually I take the stairs). "Ready for
the big one?" "Refuse to lose!" "Just do it! Dang!"
(The stairs for a last dollop of exercise after the
brisk hike down, like a sprint at the end of a jog.)
     For no obvious reason the urge was strongly upon me
to roll out this jyze at the railroad station, but for
that an hour wouldn't't've been enough. (Had to listen to
my main Centropolis blues-piano man groaning out "Nobody
Knows Centropolis Like I Do" a second time before I left
B-2 and that queered it for sure. -- But maybe I'll
head over to the depot after the game.)
     J-town vs. C-town. Our local boys here storming
back against "the best team of all time." Our local
boys' backs still against the wall. The city going
bonkers -- all week. Hoots and shouts and honks echoing
in downtown canyons of steel and glass and still lots

and lots of brick and stone too. Hysterical celebrity
sightings. Bars and clubs at both ends of my turf
doing gangbusters business at all hours.

     A fun kind of week most definitely (and yet most
intangibly as well, true enough). Lady U had to
postpone her visit until this coming Tuesday but brother
Rob filled in for her. I have now entertained in unit
B-2. Had to dig deep in my trick bag for the many-
bladed pocketknife with which to extract the cork from
the wine bottle -- the right nostalgic libation too,
same brand as the one traditionally broken out for our
youthhood family holiday celebrations -- but did. And
out that cork popped with a hair-flattening FWOOP. And
for dessert a true strawberry shortcake. Shortcake as
conjured by a master baker at the public market.
Height of strawberry season, half a flat for two bucks.
Every single day all week long I was slicing and
dicing, coring and -- what? Scoring. Exploring.
Roaring -- with delight. (With lust too. Oh the
beauties, human female kind, flocks of them every day
and some so spectacular -- many in town for the games
and stripped down for the weather -- I mean world-class
looks and shapes and jiggles commandeering the streets
-- so sensational, yes, I was all but forced to loiter
in certain prime spots and see how unobtrusively I
could ogle from behind my shades. And must say: after
a dozen years as a certified scoper I do know how to
scope 'em out, I do, I do.)

     What may be most epochal of all, though, jyze is
now out of the bag (same trick bag) with someone besides
Lady U and old Mom. Rob knows. I'm committed now --
got to make this stuff work. (Rob in all seriousness
saying he figures the only chance posterity will know
about his writing is if he can ride on my shirttails.
Which is asking a lot of a big brother. The way I see
it is that for either of us to have a chance we'll have
to depend on jyze, whether JIFT or JIRT, his or mine,
proto or ur or the complete and utter thing itself.
Starting, perhaps, if all goes well, with "Jyzer." Or
then again maybe with "Jyzeburst." Either would be more
than okay with me and I'm sure with Rob also.)

[Jyze and Jyze Alone]

    And so the hideaway armchair. The radio perched on
the table next to it. Blink, it's 4:01. Digital clock,
like magic don't you know. (And perched atop the radio
a greeting-card-size print of a painting depicting the
J-town train station as it looked at night sixty years
ago, abundant smoke from steam locomotives billowing up
and this very building in which I now sit standing aglow
off to the far left side -- or maybe it's not this
building, but it certainly looks like it.) -- These
days I'm arriving down here every afternoon sometime
between two and four and then working until six or seven
in this very armchair using the cherrywood reading tray
I gave Mother for Christmas a couple of years back.
Really digging the whole gestalt. This is how it's
gonna be as long as I can hold out. And that's all
there is to it, there is no more.
    Yesterday the means for doing so, holding out, if
not forever, for at least five more months, arrived in
the mail. The big check, the one for $5,500. That
plus the already existing $2,000 in the cushion account
plus whatever J. Ink can eke out from reporter Verna
while Naomi's out of action -- that'll be it. (And as
of yesterday I'm advised I may have to do all grand-jury
scoping on a laptop computer kept in the office safe
supposedly to protect classified info. Its keyboard is
so small I don't know if it'll be possible for me to tap
fewer than five keys with any one finger-strike. So I
may have to lobby for some changes. Again.) (And
meanwhile I'm being supercautious about printing my own
stuff. No one's said anything to me, so I'm now
thinking I'll be able to survive the scare. My guess is
no one listens to Amy anymore because she's cried wolf
so many times and about so many different people.)
    It was Barb who sent the check. She's back from
her overseas sojourn with Keith and again talking about
quitting her job because her anxiety level's too high.
Do I have any ideas, she asked in her short cover letter,
on how she could find scoping or transcribing work?
(Don't I wish. Then I'd know how to go about finding
more for myself as well.) -- Rob and I talked a lot

about Barb last night. Trying to understand why she
sometimes acts so strangely, not to say outrageously.
Where it comes from. For a while Rob thought he'd found
a way to get along with her but then about five years
ago she started in on what's turned out to be a long
series of nasty insults. The latest, this past
Christmas, came in an irate letter demanding that Rob
tell Gail never again to send her a Christmas card
signed "Gail and Walter" (Walter being her beloved
ferret). Astounding. How intolerant can a person be?
And yet it fits right in with a lifelong pattern. Rob
and I are now back to seeing eye to eye on this.

    And I, giddy to have that big check come in, spent
ten bucks from it on another used copy of the "wise
idleness" book for Rob. -- Also I learned that this
same book was not just a best-seller when Mother was
entering college but a selection for a mainstream book
club! Took me a bit aback, that item did. True, much
of the author's outlook is patrician and conservative as
all get-out. But I refuse to let any of this prevent me
from saying it's a marvelous piece of work -- and surely
not brought into being through sheer idleness.

    -- Oops, a glance to my right and -- game's on.

*   *

    Halftime now. Looks bad. J-town down seven and
lucky to be that close. Nor is the radio receiving
well. To make the play-by-play broadcast minimally
intelligible I have to keep my little finger pressed
against the receptacle for the microphone jack (thus
converting myself body and soul into an antenna soaking
up the micropulses of the intercity rivalry, my old
self versus my new self -- or better to say the main
city of my adult life so far versus the main city of my
father's adult life in its entirety. Or just go with
the Old Bull v. the Slightly Less Old Bull. Oh yeah!).

    This being Sunday I can wander around half-naked
out there in the hallway. Jump too (in my new brown
"moccasin" sneakers which are already beginning to
unravel).

    In her letter Barb also mentioned that Rikki had

suggested she, Barb, return to school to pick up a
teaching certificate and then find a job instructing
immigrants in ESL. (Another idea I could try.) Barb,
I've noticed, always finds an excuse to mention Rikki
(whose name Barb insists, no doubt for impeccable moral
reasons, on spelling in the more traditional way which
Rikki herself has rejected, i.e. Ricki, a variant of her
given name, Erica, before she officially changed it to
Rikki). Barb clearly would like to see me get together
with this woman. But the woman herself continues to
fail to find an opportunity to write or to respond to my
invitation. (Rob notes his problems with Barb started
about the time she began getting serious about religion.
Barb seems to favor Rikki because she, Erica, was raised
Catholic -- in the biggest cult of them all, I'd say --
and she's "good-hearted," though I'm no longer sure (if
I ever was) what that term means to Barb. I worry about
exactly those two qualities in Rikki, religiosity and
"good-heartedness" in the sense of excessive moral
uprightness and concern. My hope is she's rejected the
cult or lapsed from it and she's "good-hearted" mainly
in the sense of letting affection and sympathy at least
occasionally prevail over stern moral principle. And
even then I fear we wouldn't hit it off.) (It's not so
odd that I should go on and on about her even when I
doubt anything's there for us. Simple fact is I have no
other live prospect even to think about. -- Rob seeming
startled to hear this. He remembers earlier big-brother
incarnations, especially the one of his, Rob's,
community-college days when he and I lived together for
a year and I was madly juggling love interests -- and
thereby driving poor Barb, who was also living with us
off and on during that period, to even madder indignant
moralizing overreactions, at least as I saw them, which
is also how Rob saw them, as he affirmed this week.)

*   *

It's over. The city of my youth and my father's
adulthood rules. A valiant comeback effort by our J-
town stalwarts falls short. The heartland prevaileth.
     -- Today, as it happens, being Old Bull's Day, that

200

is, Father's Day. And: "It was twenty years ago today /
Papa Sandefjord taught the band to play." Or bought the
farm rather. Twenty years ago on Thursday, actually, as
Rob and I observed in our toast to the O.B. (And a
toast also "to friendship and brotherhood" -- and, not
said then but I'll add now, "to all things jyze and
jyzelike.") (And another thought coming to mind as we
talked: my urjyzings and protojyzings taken as a whole
might easily be subtitled "My Hunt for a Mate." Now the
question is whether the jyze series itself will one day
demand the subtitle "My Renewed and Belated and
Downright Preposterous Hunt for Yet Another Mate.")

(Rob, by the way, confessed to having been blocked
in his protojyzing for the past several years, except
for a single hundred-page binge inspired by his visit to
Mentokaland. This is what brought up the talk about
jyze. -- Because jyze, as I explained to him, was the
answer to my own protojyze blockage. That blockage was
intentional, true, or at least at the conscious level it
was. But some of the contributing factors were the same
as the ones for his, including feeling that my personal
life at that time offered little new to write about.
And both of us had been engaged in a project of readying
our respective overall protojyze for publication -- if
anyone would ever have either one, his or mine -- and
thus found we couldn't protojyze away with the same
unconstrained spontaneity as before. -- Jyze being,
among other things, the defiant act of protojyzing
anyway in the face of that constraint, but with certain
operational rules in place designed to prevent the act
from becoming obsessive or all-consuming.) (And Rob
with his wild long hair and octagonal gold-framed shades
looking as good as I've seen him in years -- arriving in
sandals, knee-length cargo shorts, old T-shirt and
carrying a big jug of wine and loaf of bread and hunk of
cheese. Not to mention a stick of real butter which he
forgot to take with him when he left.)

And what else? Just an AIDS cure -- it appears.
Not a certainty yet but very promising. Which in turn
could mean the end of the darkest portion of the current

mini Dark Age. (That a yet darker and not at all mini
ecological Dark Age almost certainly looms just a few
decades down the road -- if that far -- well, it can't
totally squelch the celebration if this AIDS cure turns
out to be for real. -- Though it's expensive. Will its
cost eventually be brought within reach, somehow, of the
tens of millions of victims or potential victims who
presently couldn't possibly afford it?)

And -- speaking of darkness -- I was thinking how
(dredging up an old favorite image) my venture into this
new life here in J-town is a lot like the proverbial
emergence from a dark theater into a dazzlingly sunlit
afternoon with crowded sidewalks and streets, rich
earthy smells, cacophonic sounds. For a while I can do
nothing but stagger about with eyes tightly squinted,
basically feeling my way, with a daunting distance to go
before I get to where I want to be. (This analogy being
especially apt because I really am emerging after a
dozen years from at least some of the literal darkness
of my upside-down nightscoper's life.)

The level my current life's on, let's see, I think
of the two things that made me happiest this week and I
blush. I was able to buy two dozen of those terrific
red-and-black brewery coasters at the source itself, the
brewery (which has taken over the space at the public
market occupied until a few months ago by my favorite
used-book store -- a sad story in itself). And I paid
just twenty-four cents for the coasters. A penny
apiece! In this day! In this age!

And I clipped the cord from my shades, meaning
sunglasses. Little call for it anymore now that I'm
rarely chasing ferries and so don't need to fear the
glasses will fly over the ramp rails into the drink.

And...and....

Cousin Kar got RIF'd. No longer does the eco-
outfit he was working for need a platoon of dubious
"salmonid specialists." This happened in the very same
week he announced his upcoming wedding. (Rob told me
all this. I still haven't called Kar. But also still
feel I should. Which doesn't necessarily mean I will.)

[Life of the Jyze to Come]

    And. And. A voice from the past. Tera, of Andy
and Tera, former owners of "U Acres," left a message
saying she and Andy are back in the area -- wondering
if I'm the Glen Sandefjord they think I must be just
because of the rarity of the surname (and as far as I
know they're right to think that). They got my number
from information, she said, and they were searching
there because the number for their old place is unlisted.
Tera wants to know how her plants are doing. I know
they've all long since bit the dust, and I know why.
But I decided to let Lady U do the explaining since the
plants were under her care, and so I gave them her
number. They're her friends and her parents' friends,
after all, not mine. (Ironic, though, that Lady U and I
were sure Andy and Tera's marriage would never survive
the extended close quarters of their five-year around-
the-world sailboat jaunt, and here they are back in town
in fine fettle and we're the shipwreck.)
    Anything else for the wrap-up here? Could mention
the other book I bought during the spree triggered by
the arrival of the big check: the one for myself. It's
a how-to manual for getting married in the very land
where Lady S and I did in fact do just that -- her
ancestral country. It's something I sure could've used
back then. Nor should I forget, as Rob reminded me,
that this marriage may still stand. (I've remembered
this all by myself from time to time. Now being free
again should I summon my possibly current, and certainly
former, wife, Lady S, to my side? Perhaps so we could
reunite and face old age together? She being already
almost there, I guess I can bear to say, being nearly a
full decade out in front of me. But, though it might be
a trip to see her again...I think not. And I think she
also would think not, though maybe not at first and
certainly not for public or family consumption.)
    And...and...and now, clap this thing closed and
head out into the despondent unvictorious untriumphal
streets of this city that yet still remains the unbowed,
the terrific, the virtually unexplored JYZE CITY. Yay!

[Jyze and Jyze Alone]

22

     See if I can make something happen down here. In
here. The loft room. "Inner sanctum." Still a big
mess because I just haven't been able to face the task
of going through all this stuff. And tonight I'm in
that same kind of state as I face this page. But this
page I can face. Because it's J-day.
     What else is it? The deeps of June. A few days
past the solstice (on which hangs a tail -- no, a tale,
damn it, and that tale is part of what's hurting). And
it's the end of a jyze eighter in which all three of my
current romantic interests, such as they are -- which
really means they're not current at all but former, and
in at least two of the cases, former only -- did put in
an appearance of one kind or another, and in each
instance stirring up some fresh pain.
     So big deal, I know. Aches and pains, old ones,
new ones -- what else to expect? (And that one's in
there too, the wild-card pain of "what else.")
     Fifty minutes past midnight. Hunger this time not
forgotten -- soon imminent. I had different kinds of
plans for yesterday and today, or notions of possible
plans anyway, but they got sidetracked. Instead I paid
yet another visit to the summer and fall of twenty-six
years ago. This time it too was painful, and remains so,
but I just can't help myself, I have to reexperience the
whole thing. An earlier trio of romantic interests back
when it wasn't all just in my mind.
     (I'm thinking fish sticks tonight. Will have to
preheat the toaster oven. Thus will need to turn on the
fan and open a window. -- Which reminds me: half the

plants in here are dying from mite infestations. The
magnificent exotic impatiens is just barely hanging on,
a single red flower bravely waving like a Veteran's Day
poppy. -- But not dying from neglect, no.)
     Lady V, Lady S, Briana T.
     Lady U, Sofie E., Rikki H.
     (But a good week for reading. A contemporary novel
from the remainder table and more "wise idleness" and
some critical writings on autobiography and memoir --
suddenly so fashionable these days -- and a philosophy
quarterly, essays by a couple of literary heavies
weighing in on the current state of the novel -- it's
bad but not hopeless, they soberly aver -- and then a
selection from a shrinking array of the usual periodicals.
And I should note: the two main fortnightly newsprint
book reviews seem to have stopped arriving by mail as of
this week.)
     So where to start? Lady U, I guess. Her visit
came off uneventfully. No heart in it either, so what's
to describe. One memorable line she delivered while
perched on the old loveseat a few feet behind where I
sit now (in the loft I built so we could rest just right,
the lady and I, lo these many years ago, and she could
study in the space beneath it, her desk set up precisely
where I'm now scrawling out these jyze laments): "It's
one of the tragedies of my life that I couldn't make it
work with us." That's what she said. And it's true, I
believe, but she didn't really seem to be feeling the
"tragedy" part herself and I doubt she really believes
it. In my reading it's just the line she's taking that
for the moment works best for her across a broad front.
And for sure it's a lot better for me than any number of
other lines she might've, and at times has, taken, and
might still take again.
     I walked down and met her as she drove off the
ferry. I took her over to the hideaway for a quick look
and then showed her around my new hood up here on foot.
I served her a big dish of fresh strawberries
meticulously sliced by my own hand (she took a pass on
the ice cream I bought especially for this occasion, her

favorite brand and flavor in a previous era). I assured
her I'm a happy camper these days, delighted with my new
setup (which of course is no lie), and that she has
nothing to feel guilty about in dumping me as she did.
In doing this I hoped I could at least induce in her a
few twinges of genuine regret over having given up on us
but as far as I could tell no such luck.

After she left I spun down into a seriously bleak
state. The cord of life between us has been severed.
Nothing there. After almost nineteen years.

(My newest analysis, which admittedly is a lot like
some earlier ones, is that it all started going down the
tubes when she began losing interest in making art of
any kind. After that it was virtually inevitable she
would eventually turn elsewhere. Now for entertainment
she's got indie music -- "indie" being the term she's
come to prefer; "alt" is out -- and a bunch of beer-
guzzling friends a decade and a half to slightly more
than two decades her junior. I guess she's having a
good time. I don't even want to know at this point.)

So there's that. I don't mean to suggest it
doesn't hurt because it does hurt. It hurts plenty.
But I can take it. It's just -- so sad.

*

More immediately painful, actually, was the
incident with Sofie. While showing Lady U the community
P-patch garden I noticed a handbill announcing a summer-
solstice observance to be held there on the 20th, so at
the proper hour on that day I moseyed down and found a
group of maybe two dozen celebrants gathered around a
refreshment table, some sitting on chairs and blankets,
as a troupe of mimes in whiteface entertained. One
person was down on her knees in a flowerbed and I
recognized her immediately from a distance -- Sofie. I
had no idea she was involved in the garden (though in
retrospect I realize I should've guessed: the tilework
on the elaborate entrance gate looks a lot like some of
her work I've admired on the large mirrors).

Out of sheer instinct I pretended not to see her.
How could I do otherwise after she'd ignored me for so

long? And to my amazement and despair she continued to
ignore me. At one point as I watched the mimes she was
troweling within inches of my shoes but still without a
word of greeting. So I guess her silence during those
excruciating minutes reflects her own sheer instinct
with me.

After wandering around for a while admiring the
garden (truly -- as much as I could, given the black-
dominated field my vision had become) and speaking with
no one (nor did anyone try to speak with me) I strolled
as casually as possible back out to the street. And
when finally sure I was beyond sight from the P-patch I
leaned against a car hood in a state of shock and
disgust and burning pain for I don't know how long.
Maybe ten minutes? Twenty? Then the steep uphill walk
back home, step by step by step.

Murderous. Lethal. I hadn't believed it could hit
me again. But then I really did come to know what I
previously only thought I knew. And after the dismal
afternoon with Lady U the only thing I could think now
was: deep reclusion. Deep as it goes. That's what
comes next.

(Isn't this some sad sob story? But wait, there's
more. Though not as bad. Maybe even good and maybe
that in itself will prove to be bad.)

*

-- Earlier in the week I tried to write Rikki. I
still hadn't heard anything from her. I'd happened upon
an essay about fairy tales I thought might interest her.
But in an hour of flailing I found I couldn't push the
letter past a fatuous opening paragraph (which I must've
copied out with slight variations half a dozen times or
more). Simply couldn't write her again with nothing to
go on from her. Yup, as I'd said before, it was her
move now. To me this confirmed it once and for all.

The very next day a letter came in from her. Not
much life in it. Most of the text had been written a
couple of months earlier and abandoned in midcourse,
never finished. Now she tacked on a few lines at the
end, including the news that she and Mischa were about

to leave for her home state (bordering Mentoka!) for a
month's vacation but when they returned she'd start
checking around to see about trains to my city. Mischa
missed "the Glunk," Mischa would like to see "the Glunk"
(I brought this "the Glunk" business on myself last
winter, proposing it to replace "Uncle Glen") -- and
she, Rikki, would like to see "the Glunk" too, of
course, but this she presented as a rather blatantly
delayed afterthought, as if she wanted to be sure I
realized that's exactly what it was. Tepid interest,
let's say, if any. But perhaps about mid August they
might be showing up to stay for a few days or a week or
however long right here in unit B-2.

    I'll try not to work myself into a state over this
potential visit. I will admit, though, I'm already
thinking about it a fair amount. Where the hell will we
all sleep? What can I do to keep them entertained? I
like Rikki quite a bit, so how can I prevent myself from
liking her more, or too much? (Recalling now it's been,
again, almost nineteen years since I've been with any
woman other than Lady U -- and it's been slightly over a
year since I've been with her, or anyone, sexually.)

    Deep reclusion. Or maybe not. "The Glunk" -- can
I be reasonably sure something bad won't happen if I let
a romance get started here? (And probably I don't need
to repeat I'm far from sure Rikki'd be interested
anyway.) -- But say she is. What are the risks? For
that matter what are the benefits? -- But then I'm so
far gone in the habit of believing romance is benefit
enough all by itself (making my world go round and
lighting up my life) I don't think I can seriously
respond to the question.

    I can mull. And no doubt will, plenty.
Unfortunately I have no way to get ahold of Rikki while
she's on vacation. She could've given me one, yet for
some totally unmysterious reason she didn't. But if I
could I might just be very straightforward with her --
somehow. Saying just what, I don't know. -- Naw, I
guess that wouldn't work. "Rikki, what you think, we
about to get carnally involved?" In truth it would be

an embarrassment not to become involved in that way if
they really did travel so many miles to see me. I'd
feel almost obliged to bust some moves on her. In fact
I would feel obliged to, period. It would be too much
of an insult not to. So I guess what I'd do is simply
say right at the start, "Well, Rikki, while you're here
we'll pretty much be living together, so why not have us
some fun. But if you want to draw a line somewhere, go
right ahead and do that and you can be sure I'll respect
it." -- At which point she'd probably run screaming for
the next train out of town, dragging Mischa behind her.

     -- Granted I'm not exactly hot stuff anymore. I
don't know how to do what it takes to get where I want
to go. Don't even want to do it. (Yet I do.)
     -- Or an imaginary love might be a better bet.
Loving a woman of my own invention who may also be, in
part or perhaps even wholly, or as wholly as I can make
her, a woman from my past. In truth (wow, lots of truth
proclaimed here tonight!) -- in truth this is pretty
much what you're doing anyway in loving a real-life
flesh-and-blood-and-jouissancer, or at least to a much
greater extent than you'd ever want to, or dare to,
admit out loud or maybe even just to yourself at the
time. The analogies are inexact but, to repeat, Lady U
is Lady S, Rikki is Lady V, Sofie is Briana. (Actually
what little I know of Sofie is almost entirely Lady V,
and Lady U herself is more a mix of Lady S and Lady V,
and Briana remains one of a kind to an extreme degree --
too extreme for me -- just as always -- but then come to
think of it that's equally true of Ladies S and V as
well if not even more so, and especially V, so what the
heck am I trying to say here.)
     -- Plainly I've pissed away this jyze session. A
new crisis at the scope office I haven't even mentioned,
partner Una intercepting a note of mine to reporter
Naomi and brusquely commanding me (in a note of her own)
to like the laptop or lump it -- but then basically
meeting my needs anyway in assuring me I'll be stuck
with it for only a month or so. (More likely it'll be
for two or three months or more but so long as there's a

limit I can bear it. To do any job on that damnable
machine will take, I'm estimating, a quarter to a third
longer than doing the same job on the existing desktop
system. But Una's now saying that system is not secure
enough, even though we've been using it to scope grand
jury for at least ten years and the feds have never
squawked about it before and are not squawking now.)
-- But beyond these few sentences I refuse to go. Save
the gripes for some future session if necessary but hope
they'll all be outdated by then and so this will be the
end of them right here.

     And this final note: I've been seriously thinking
of looking for a part-time job for the fall. Twenty
hours a week at seven bucks an hour would nicely fill
the gap until Naomi returns -- if she ever does.

23

     WHOOM! The first one finally went off and I doused
the lights and watched for a few minutes. Then flipped
the lights back on (or one lamp actually) and here I am.
     Independence Day. Fourth of. It's going on out
there now, the big fireworks display over the bay, and
by leaning about six inches to my left I gain a terrific
view of it from the loveseat here in B-2.
     Jazz station meanwhile playing loud (though not
loud enough to get in the way of the WHOOMs). This week
I gambled $7.98 plus tax on a rabbit-ears antenna on
sale at my usual drugstore (north-pole branch) and the
damn thing works! Life's a lot better now!
     Yes it is. And in more ways than one. Seems I'm
back on track. I've reached a new phase -- or whatever
it is. "Massive rededication" pays off. All else has

gone or is going by the wayside, pretty much. The
fierce focus again, only fiercer. It feels good.

(First just at dusk a jet swooped and swirled out
there, dropping pyrotechnical ordnance and releasing a
streak of incendiary exhaust made up of interwoven
strands of red, white, and blue, and of course all of
this was a ghastly reminder of ugly wars our USAn tribal
confederation has forced on others, and all of the
exhaust was, and remains, massively polluting to boot.)

Is anything else good other than the way the real
work's going and the mundane daily life along with it?
No. Not that I can think of.

All kinds of jockeying at the scope office. Looks
to me now as though Naomi might not even return after a
year, or ever, she's so disgusted with the new setup.
Doubt is also widespread that the new firm will be able
to win the grand-jury contract when it comes up for
renewal in October. All of which means the odds are
growing I'll have to be looking for that new job before
much longer -- possibly even next month.

(Still busily WHOOMing out there. Nearby buildings
are pulsating with reflections as if from lightning
bursts mixed with revolving police turret lights. A
fleet of small craft is bobbing on the bay and also
several larger boats, one probably being the same tour
vessel Lady U and I and her parents were aboard in that
same area for a previous Fourth about a dozen years
back. -- And WHOOM WHOOM WHOOM WHOOM WHOOM, that's
gotta be the grand finale getting underway right now.)

*

(Yes it was.)

-- I was about to say: Darren the street artist
hustled himself up a twenty-nine-hour-a-week job
throwing sandwiches together at a franchise sub shop
near the hideaway building (mainly so he can provide a
bed for his new honey) (and those "Bad Artist, No
Funding" buttons came in and I gave him one) (but the
enamel craftsperson at the public market who promised to
make me a couple of "Beware of Bad Artist" buttons has
dropped out of sight). I figure when the time comes

I'll be able to find some kind of rinky-dink job like
Darren's, minimum wage and low stress. If I can, I want
to be able to hang on to all three of my bases (B-2, 225,
161) and also my income-producing deep reserves. If
possible! (Meaning I still must be able to put in five
or six hours on my own work every day. Otherwise
something will have to give.)

So that's how it is. And I say it's good enough.
It's all I need.

The stocking-up seems to be working as it's
supposed to. It took a while but I'm now at the point
where I've laid in plenty of everything that's not
perishable. This means I buy things only when it's
convenient to do so for one reason or another: either
something's on sale or wheels are available (as when
Lady U visited) or I'll be in a certain area on some
other mission. True, I don't like being in thrall to
coupons and supermarket flyers, but it sure does beat
being in thrall in the ways I'd otherwise have to be
without those savings. So instead I try to take pride
in shaving tiny fractions from prices and keeping the
larder well stocked. I even get to buy a few minor
treat items every now and then. Imported cheapo
drugstore gingersnaps: all by themselves they can take
the sting out of a lot of the petty slights and
indignities one must endure to go on living the good
life on subsistence-level income. (The new butterscotch
pudding can do it too. And at a projected rate of
consumption of one pudding cup every six days I have
enough of this right now to last well into next year,
in fact a week or two past their sell-by date.)

-- A few feet to my right stands the big white
tabletop fan, rotating type, the twelve-incher. This
week the first spell of noticeably summerlike weather
finally hit and I cranked the thing up, also for the
first time, and it moved the air around in here pretty
good. I now think I'll be able to survive the very
worst of the dog days, even up there in the loft. (I'm
gazing at it now -- at the clock, the lamp, the book
box, the dangling windsock fish -- oh what a splendid

construction this loft is! -- And Mindy the building
manager, by the way, agrees. She accompanied the pest
exterminators on their rounds this time and caught a
glimpse of it (through her shades) and said it was even
more complicated than her own loft, and since then for
the first time she's been speaking to me with what to
my mind is at least a modicum of respect. "Taking off
the gloves," so to speak. (She keeps her boxing gloves
in the office and I've seen her pounding ferociously on
the padded tarp she's hung on the wall there with an
anonymous silhouette, unmistakably male -- and
rightfully so! -- outlined on it.) -- Far preferable,
this new respect she's showing me, to her usual mean-
streets cynicism and disdain and open suspicion you're
out to screw her over in some nasty underhanded way.)

     As for the prospect of my doing some cavorting one
day with Rikki up there atop the loft, I know no more
than I did before. But I did hit on a possible way of
sleeping all three of us in separate places in this unit
at once, should it be necessary. I'll simply lay my air
mattress down in the long internal hallway between the
kitchen nook and the unit door (which sports a little
peephole -- have I neglected to mention it before now?).
I swear to god I'll make some good use out of that
absurd hallway yet. (Should I ever want to shrink my
operations to a single base I could line the hallway
with floor-to-ceiling bookcases on both sides and then
suspend a row of overhead shelves from those. It's not
unthinkable that one day I could have all my books
crammed into this one measly little so-called studio
apartment. Book-lined it would be, and closer to book-
stuffed, but maybe not unlivably so. I intend to do
some serious thinking about this -- but probably spaced
out over the next several years. Or let's hope so
anyway, since I don't want to be shrinking my operations
at all if I can help it.)

     What else am I mulling? Let's see. (Now I'm
mulling what I'm mulling.) There's this: should I
attend Kar's wedding? An invitation came in with a
handwritten note from the man himself. No mention in it

of my failure to respond to his plea that we go pub-
crawling (if he ever asks why, I figure I'll just say my
resurfacing is turning out to be a bit more complex than
anticipated). In the note he says Rob and Gail will be
attending, as will Greta and Mort (aunt and uncle), and
I could ride over on the ferry with those four and he'd
have someone pick us all up at the dock. But I don't
know. I hate to waste a whole day and don't much like
weddings, especially third or fourth weddings, and I
hate the thought of being trapped there. And really
now: how many Kar weddings should a cousin be obliged to
attend in a single lifetime? -- But I've still got a
week or so to, yes, mull it further. The big day is the
21st, I think it is, of this month.

     And cogitating on how to handle the "Memorials"
publisher's failure thus far to send proofs or get in
touch with me. Are we being jerked around here? Will I
have to try to do something about it? I can't let old
Mom's memory down. (But oh how I wish I could otherwise
just flush all this genealogical nonsense.)

     And all this jyzealogical nonsense? It's still
comin' atcha from the same brown loveseat, with the fan
and lamp and end table to my right, windows to my left
and behind me, splintery wooden footstool and green
armchair and loft straight ahead, and we've now moved a
minute or two past midnight and into the day on which
Lady U turns yet another year older -- or a full year
past the unthinkable age, I'll say, as I don't doubt
she's regarding it herself. And for the first time
since her cake bore twenty-two candles I won't be there
to watch her blow them out. The balloon people of the
past couple of years will probably still be around but I
won't. And don't that take the cake tho. Snicker
snicker. As if she'd even cut me a slice in the first
place. (Help. Eject from this paragraph -- emergency.)

     (Perhaps I'm being besieged by memories here simply
because this week I broke out my old "Remember" bag from
overseas days -- dark blue with white rope handles and a
humorous botched-English legend printed beneath the
"Remember" on the side pocket -- the legend now mostly

worn away, however, to the point of illegibility, and of course I can't remember what it was, or at least not verbatim -- and used it, the bag, for my grocery run since it's easier to carry than the huge white canvas one. And it did indeed work well for the purpose and I intend now to press it into regular service. -- And I bought that bag within a few weeks of the time when Lady U would presumably have been huffing and puffing over her cake ablaze with twenty-one candles.)

    -- But oh the patriotic jazz! Now it's Ray C. again, "America the Beautiful" (and a damn fine version too -- except I wish he'd pluralize that first word, just a tiny little subversive hint of an "s" to imply praise for all the Americas and not just the one that's arrogated the name to itself). And just today, as the "Remember" bag goes into service, a pair of khaki low-cuts goes out of service. Hole in the sole, flapping heels. I'll try shoe-gooing them later to coax some more wear out of them, but I should note that under the greater walking pressure of my new regime this pair lasted only about three months. No longer, therefore, will I be leaping around beneath the nerfhoop wearing shoes -- instead I'll be leaping around there barefoot only. Or at least as long as my skin remains renewable.

    (Skin. Renewable. Moles. Danger. Article in the "indispensable paper" science section yesterday. Only one mole in two hundred thousand becomes cancerous, the experts say, but that's all other things being equal, and for me they're surely not. I'm at the moles' mercy, that's all there is to it. Third-stager molestation!)

*

    -- Where was I? Another emergency, this a lesser one featuring a fresh two-liter bottle of no-cal cola, just sent me flying for the bathroom. While unscrewing the plastic cap I heard an unusually loud hiss and immediately knew why from long experience with this particular poison: ice in there and lots of it. So rush the thing to the bathtub and close the shower curtain before unscrewing the cap the rest of the way because an explosion's coming to rival those roman candles out over

215

the bay. And did it blow! -- So now I start worrying
about the refrigerator. But a quick check shows nothing
else on its shelves frozen that shouldn't be (except for
the one remaining tub of margarine in the freezer itself,
and there the fault was and is all mine).

The previous big problem of the week (other than
the shoes giving out) being the mites. They're attacking
all the flowers and plants. I went after scores or maybe
hundreds of their tiny webs with a half-cent wooden
toothpick. So far all the flowers along the windowsill
to my left appear to be doing okay, with the ravaged
exotic impatiens bringing up the rear and most likely an
exception -- a goner. Still lots of blooms in sight on
the other impatienses (some peach color fringed with red,
others red splashed with a white internal star: all very
pleasing to the eye) and also on the fancy geranium
(white-bordered red blooms). My pride and joy, these,
all three types. Won't give 'em up to the mites without
a fight.

-- Beyond the blooms, solid green pressing against
the lower half of the west windows. I've thrown in the
clippers, so to speak, on the vines -- they just grow
too fast. Streetlights up there, a double set,
yellowish and very bright, the better for the drug
dealers in the alley trying to count out the right
change. (But crime is way, way down, here and all
around town, and for that matter nationwide, even beyond
demographic expectations, and I'm noticing that most of
the streets in my extended hood, "from pole to pole," do
feel a whole lot safer at night than they did, say, on
those widely scattered occasions several years ago when
I traveled the same routes.) -- And if I stand up I can
look in half a dozen of the artist-studio windows on the
upper floors of the old brick five-story building on the
far side of the viaduct. Real artists working at real
easels often visible late into the night, eccentrically
framed by their large windows. My very first night here
that sight fascinated me and radiated the right kind of
feeling and has done so ever since. Of course I have no
way to know whether any of it's truly real -- could be a

kind of stage set or a series of them, a phony creation
of realtors fearing that gentrification is undermining
the artsy local color that gives the district its cachet
and keeps rents and real-estate prices skyrocketing --
but for now anyway I choose to go on believing.

     -- And then last week I blew off the last ferry
coupon in my book, which expired as of Tuesday, and I'm
not planning to buy another book for a month or so,
possibly just prior to Rikki and Mischa's visit, should
there actually be one, since a ferry trip to the storage
port might be something relatively inexpensive they'd
enjoy. As for myself, I'm tired of that double-stage
cross-sound round-trip jaunt -- having made it roughly
fifteen hundred times in the past six-plus years when it
was still the home port for me over there -- and if I
buy another coupon book I'll feel pretty much obliged
to make it up to ten more times, depending on Rikki and
Mischa, within the three months before the book expires.

     And speaking of inexpensive voyages: for the rest
of the summer bus fares citywide will drop to just two
bits on weekends. Therefore I'm thinking of visiting
several spots which a full bus fare would put beyond my
budget, and I'm thinking Rikki and Mischa and I can go
wild (unless, of course, again, they don't show up).
The zoo. The locks. The arboretum. (I'm even mulling
whether to attend a low-cost matinee showing of an old
French film out in the Yuke this weekend -- the drawback
being I really do want to devote every available minute
to the JIFT. I've already made the key decision: I
won't even bother to try to have a life other than the
life of jyzing, not now and not for a good long while
and maybe not ever. That's why I didn't make an effort
to set today's JIRT session in some new venue. I've not
given up on doing that for future sessions but as a
"jyze rules" priority it's tumbled considerably. -- And
JIRT can take it. JIRT should be able to function just
as well when no special efforts are made on its behalf,
other than, of course, the all-out effort to crank out
the requisite number of pages when J-day rolls around.
-- So I'm no longer particularly looking to explore my

new turf, to say nothing of the territories beyond.
Later for all that. For now, the fierce, the fierce,
the truly fierce JIFT focus.)
                             *
     (Just peered at the legend on the "Remember" bag
under a bright light and it's not quite illegible after
all. Here's what it says: "This bag is fashions [sic].
Both illastration [sic] and fresh of feeling. Born in
the young power." And right there the last words for
tonight, pounding home all the ones that went before.)

                          24

     Lunch all packed and I'm ready to go, except not
dressed. But...but...this is one of those terrifically
good days. Fan spinning, blues playing, sun shining in.
"I've Got What It Takes" -- and she does, on the album
of classic streetwalker blues, sassing it out right now
when it counts. Walking of streets directly ahead for
me as well. This time it'll be the loop-de-loop.
     Riding an upflow of JIFT ideas. Thank you, O
fellow transplanted local scribbler, for your meditation
on the so-called homesteaders of the Mentoka zone and
parts west and the roots of the militia/"Don't tread on
me" spirit (in a magazine piece from a couple of months
ago I'm just getting to now). You're helping me see my
own family from a genuinely new angle which illuminates
a lot. The "low-class" roots of certain traits on my
father's side -- the aggressiveness and the eye for the
ladies coming down from great-grandpop Bendyk, it would
now appear, he being the poor immigrant who married the
boss's daughter -- a more restrained form of the same
wildness that led to great-uncle Roar's tragic troubles.

And to gramp Perry's. And to Dad's. And to brother
Jeff's. And to mine too, maybe I can concede or even
claim, since I do feel some pride in looking at it this
way. (Rather than in the snobby moralizing way coming
down from Mother's side and gram Barbara's as well.)
     Yeah, could be the key. Get me off that dang dime.
     The whole week's been like this. Exciting
discoveries. I do believe it's all falling into place
now. (And by the way, this JIRT jyze right here, much
as I love it and see it as the key breakthrough of them
all -- what would I do without those two words, "key"
and "breakthrough"? -- I'm also viewing it now as just
a series of kwikjyze postscripts to the main work.)
     And what really matters, I'm firing on all
cylinders. Eat, sleep, jyze -- that's it. And walk the
streets, of course, to haul the flesh from the site of
one of these functions to the site of another of them
(or their subsidiaries such as shopping for grub) but
not necessarily always in a perfectly straight line, no.
     "Fine film of sweat." Nineties today. High summer
and high tourist season. Other locals may hate having
these huge crowds of foreigners and outlanders clogging
up their usual lifeways, but not me. Emphatically not!
     Liveliness everywhere. Walking down the "low road"
into the public market via its back door: how I do look
forward to it every day, including even those days when
I wind up not doing it. (And today's the same.) Who'll
today's buskers be? Those gospel doo-woppers, they
always lift my spirits no matter how low or high they,
the spirits, may already be. (It's a triple combo, I
think, of loving the blues and doing all that barmy
barbershop harmonizing as a kid and going through the
high years of doo-wop as a pop-music-addicted teen.)
     At the garden shop all bedding plants were half
off. I sniffed around and came up with some small but
fiercely colored snapdragons to replace the mite-
devastated violets and violas. Right here they now hold
forth, on the sill, catching a little direct sun. (And
next to them stands the big stack of newspapers at this
point mounting from the floor almost to sill level and

ready for discarding. Time to sack them up in grocery
bags and haul them out to the wooden recycling shed next
to the dumpster -- which when I stand up I can see
squatting out there beyond the fence and the shrubbery,
other side of the alley, its mouth gaping open a couple
of feet like that of a toothless blue hippo with an
unusually flat upper jaw -- the shed of course nowhere
near as fine as either of my personal sheds of bygone
days, but still it's always a pleasure to have a sturdy
wooden shed heave into view outside one's window.)
    -- And the rate of newspaper discarding will soon
double. A major change here. Monday starts my "home
delivery" of that notorious but "indispensable" far-
coast newspaper. "All the news that fits our fits."
It'll cost four bucks a week, for which I'll be giving
up my evening cup of coffee at the ORB cafe (and thus
coming out ahead three bucks a week, in theory anyway,
since that coffee's a buck a cup and I've been going
there daily, seven days a week).
    I've been wanting to cut back on coffee consumption
anyway. And trying to get ahold of a house copy of that
same paper at one cafe or another has turned into a
daily annoyance I'll be glad to skip. It all came to a
head one night this eighter when I sat in the ORB cafe
waiting for the guy at the next table to finish reading
the single remaining house copy. I'd seen him many
times before, a large, corpulent, stinking street dude
who carries around big duffles of newspapers and lingers
for hours over the house copies of various papers, from
time to time blithely clipping any article he takes a
fancy to and adding it to his collection. This time
when he tore off the whole front page of the arts
section of the "indispensable paper" right before my
eyes I'd had enough. I leaned over and told him the
rest of us didn't appreciate his doing that. He took
furious sputtering exception to my interference with his
freedom to do as he pleases in this free country of ours
(he's a right-wing nutcase too, clearly, and wears a
worn military ball cap bearing the name of a celebrated
aircraft carrier) and we got into it a little bit. No

fisticuffs, but something drastic might've happened if I hadn't decided it was time to ease on out of there rather than create a bad scene for the cafe itself and its staff (my buddies or semi-buddies, most of 'em).

-- Anyway, the change. I'll still be stopping by the ORB cafe but nowhere near as often, and I actually prefer it this way because I'm able to get more done at the Jyzer Ink office. It was starting to bother me, the way I was wasting time at the ORB during those breaks.

Getting late. Almost five! Time for a shift.

*   *

Whew, plenty hot down here, even in the shade. Even hotter than up in the residential zone of the tripolar turf, which is to say: hood central. Must be because the bricks and cobblestones of the triangle absorb lots of sunlight.

O pretty girls. O hormones. O temptations. O advancing years. O new insights -- and will any of these clear me a new path through the tangled grove?

I'm thinking maybe so. If the gleam is genuinely back in my gaze as I suspect it might be. (A glance in the mirror to find out, but the only handy one was a shop window which, mercifully perhaps, didn't reflect enough detail.) -- And how long was it gone, the gleam? Don't even want to speculate. Better to say I went through a long spell in which I intentionally ignored or suppressed it, possibly even to the point where it (for all practical as well as natural not to mention depraved purposes) vanished.

(This time perched on a bench in front of the pizza joint. From the doorway emerge bunches of scantily clad folks wickedly licking ice-cream cones. It's a rare moment on a weekend in this midsummer month when you see not even a single big cluster of tourists making the guided tour of the area on foot, the first several stops of which are up here in front of the totem pole, the pergola, and, of course, the arched stone entrance of my own "National Historic Landmark" building -- but this is one of those moments. We're into the dinner hour now.)

-- Yes, I believe I'm feeling closer to my father.

221

[Jyze and Jyze Alone]

In a sense I could say this is the crowning moment, the
past few hours of this day right here, of my long
investigation into my Mentokan roots. Though the roots
of the investigation itself go deep, no doubt straight
back to my infancy in certain ways -- and a good thick
bunch to my last year in college and first year in grad
school -- and another bunch to the battles of the
antiwar years -- this current investigation actually
being sparked, I'd say now, by the events of the summer
he, Dad, died, and especially by two incidents then:
first, the trip to Turtle Rapids and the nearby Buena
Vista overlook to scatter his ashes; and second, the
subsequent discovery of the little black book containing
indisputable proof of his bad, bad, baaaad skirt-chasing
(commiseration-hunting?) ways that continued right up to
the month, and maybe even the week, of his death. (I
mean without the evidence of that little black book I
never would've believed it myself. But in retrospect I
don't doubt it at all: everything falls so neatly into
place, and I'm talking about all the way back to the
days of the wartime overseas affairs, the three
simultaneous pinnees at three separate colleges, the
"Snake" article about him in his college paper -- and
what splendid irony that his own eldest son, offspring
of the "good" side of that same rambunctious drive,
meaning the married side, would one day be the editor of
that same paper. Truly a snap-shut detail for any
memoirist worthy of the trade.)
     No doubt I'll be further exploring the
ramifications of all this for months or even years to
come. Surely for years!
     Meanwhile it's time to march upstairs and get some
work done. -- Hauling this unexpected quart of
strawberries. Just four bits, could I possibly say no?
(The opportunity opening up because I stopped at one of
the public-market produce stalls to buy a banana. The
ones I have at home are still a little green. I can no
longer do without a daily hit of banana.)
                    *   *
     Four hours later and it's Jyzer Ink. The desk this

222

time, my main workplace for the past couple of weeks (as opposed to the previous main spot, the brown armchair, three feet to the right -- west -- of the desk).

Still flying. Yup, I am, I am. What a splendid day. Surely a landmark itself. (As only now at this unusually late hour -- almost ten p.m. -- does the live golden-oldies music start pounding down below.)

In my work I'm suddenly back to loving Lady V. Might as well be in my life too, I guess. So all right: V, I'm loving you again, you hear? (Pretty powerful spell she exerted on me given that we last set eyes on each other a few months short of twenty years ago.)

No action of any kind on any other love front. -- Well, no, not quite true. I mailed off a package of clipped articles (all having to do with scholarly work on fairy tales, which is her field, albeit in a different language; and in one of her letters she did say something along the lines of "you can see what an escapist I am") -- yes, to Rikki. And I just thought of another action on the Rikki front. One day last week I awakened with the idea of brushing up on that same ancestral language in which Rikki does her research and she and Mischa do most of their communicating (I recall almost nothing from my high-school courses in it) so I could wow them when (and if) they came up. What better proof that "the Glunk" is just the kind of man they're looking for? -- So I hit the foreign-language section at the bookstore, flipped through a couple of refresher books, and immediately dropped the idea. And what better proof that "the Glunk" is the wrong man for them?

(But maybe not. Who knows. I also scoped out an ethnic restaurant where that same language is spoken -- this was a couple of weeks ago -- and I'm often thinking of things we might do while they're here, sometimes even including X-rated things with Rikki alone should we be able to clear some privacy time. So yes, maybe I am after all "the Glunk" of their dreams.)

As for the hideaway here, a few little newnesses of the current J-week to mention. For one I've got both small portable fans whirling, one aiming into the leg

space beneath the desk and the other pushing stale air
past the cracked-open door out into the foyer, and I'll
say this combination makes for good working conditions:
as good as I could ever hope for. Right here and now --
and every day -- it's like this. (Glancing up, a dose
of Lady V's watercolor "Homage to Our Pumpkin Castle,"
with Lady U's unnamed yellow-eyed tile bird hanging to
its right and Lady S's oil painting "Gramma Mountain"
to its left. I'm mighty pleased.)

Philodendron cuttings are rooting in small glass
veggie-drink bottles atop the large filing cabinet. And
behind me, Mother's antique rotating wooden bookcase, I
want to note I use it a lot, not just to look up words
in the monster dictionary spread atop the hinged support
piece but also for reading or editing my own stuff while
standing up, sometimes just to take a short break from
working seated at the desk or in the armchair but other
times for hours on end just for the sheer pleasure of
it. (Here I'm writing by double desk lamps, one on each
side, both enamel red and both bought the same day about
a dozen years ago, one for Lady U and one for me. But
she never much liked hers and let me have it during the
split-up distribution. Intriguing detail? Damn right!)

One day I happened to get here early enough to meet
the mailman. He was surprised to learn I'd moved in
four months ago and promised to stop leaving mail for
Alicia H. and the escort service, whom he assumes to be
one and the same. (A likable Cawk longhair of roughly
my own vintage, this mailman: we knew instantly we
spoke the same language. Even before speaking we knew.)

What else about this office and its environs? Not
much. I recognize the faces of most of my neighbors and
many other building residents, I regularly say hello to
some of them, but (other than manager Trevor and janitor
Hank and the married cleanup crew Tuan and Jenny) I'm
not really on speaking terms with any of them. There's
one attractive woman I'd like to be on such terms with:
she works for some sort of health outfit in the far
southwest corner of this floor, and she nods and smiles
a lot and actually seems to check me out with a flicker
of interest at times, but so far we've exchanged not a

single word. Just as well too, probably, of course,
since she and I both would likely only have certain
delusions shattered. (I do like to note these matters,
I guess, trivial though they obviously are. At least
once every entry something like this in one form or
another. I guess maybe to suggest -- if only to myself
-- that I haven't gone completely dead in that realm.)
      -- Onward now, looping back and uphill and eastward
to the scope mines.

*   *

      -- Step over to the old conference room, worn down
(me) from several hours of punching in edits on my own
work. In here this week's memorial to a reporter who
died last weekend of a heart attack at age forty-four, I
believe it was -- name of Bart Y., originally from the
same upper-midwest city which Rikki and Mischa are
visiting right now (I never met the man or heard his
name before this week; all I know about him comes from
the memorial card) -- it lingers on together with
flowers, photos, trays of crackers, and an official pro
football signed by all forty-plus members -- or most
anyway -- of the newly merged firm.
      For me the man's death meant mainly (and lord knows
I mean him no disrespect in saying this) a week of
excellent eating that didn't cost me a cent. "Help
yourself," said reporter Una (no longer a partner!) as I
came in Tuesday night, and did I ever. For days the two
fridges here were stuffed with trays of cold-cut meat,
bowls of fruit salad, cakes and breads and veggies,
sodas and juices and wines. In one night I wolfed down
more roast beef than I'd consumed in probably the
previous fifteen years combined. The next night I think
I beat that record. And the third night and the fourth
night, close to it. The ham and turkey were also quite
good and I devoured almost as much of them.
      Wotta pig. But I couldn't help myself. I feel
Bart Y. would approve if he knew (from the many tributes
he seems to have been not just a meat-and-potatoes kind
of man but a life-loving type as well).
      I was lucky to catch Una alone in the office that

first night. She was in no hurry to get home and she
obligingly answered all my questions about the status of
grand jury and what might be ahead for Jyzer Ink in its
work for the newly merged so-called super-firm. That
is, she answered all the questions she could answer.

In a nutshell, it's likely but not assured that J.
Ink will still be getting work from the new firm this
fall and on into next year, but if it does, the volume
will almost certainly fall short of what I'd need to
survive on the income from that alone. The grand-jury
contract is expiring in October and Una will be seeking
a renewal under the new firm's auspices. She feels it
will be approved unless some other firm underbids them,
and so far she's heard of no one else who even intends
to bid. She also thinks it unlikely Naomi will return
to reporting. But Verna will become the primary grand-
jury reporter and J. Ink will do her scoping (she won't
be allowed to scope GJ herself at home) and may get some
additional hourly work from the office, maybe even some
additional scoping, because dayscoper Amy will be
leaving at the end of August (yayhoo!) and from that
time on the new firm will no longer employ scopers
except by independent contract and J. Ink will be the
firm's sole scoping vendor holding a government
clearance. Una may even give J. Ink some page-rate
scoping herself when she gets extra busy since Amy won't
be here to do it as she's done in the past.

Upshot: I probably won't need to look for additional
work until after the first of the year. And I should be
able to keep printing my own stuff on the old firm's
system (which they're keeping in downsized form in one
small room here, formerly partner Fran's office, where
from now on I'll be doing all the J. Ink scoping) -- and
this may be so even if the grand-jury contract doesn't
renew, since Una, to repeat, and possibly some others
may be calling upon J. Ink for scoping from time to time
when business gets heavy.

So I'm not displeased. It's about as good as I
could've hoped for. And if Naomi does decide to come
back, as I still think she might, I'll be sitting pretty.

(That is, I'll be able to go on living as I am at
subsistence level without seeking a second job.)

    -- So now the main entrance here bears the new
firm's name and logo. A number of changes have come
down in the way the place is run but they won't affect
me much. The office doesn't even look all that
different, except the work areas are messier because
with twenty-eight additional reporters on the rolls a
lot more pages are going through the computer room. But
most reporters are now scoping their own jobs at home
and "modeming" stuff in, as they say; none even has a
personal desk here. Most of the same desks are in place
as before the merger and people in need of a temporary
spot to work just use whichever desk happens to be free
at the moment. More filing cabinets than before line
the walls and more cups hang on the hookboard above the
sink (and a new auxiliary board next to it) and lots of
strange photos populate the bulletin boards (or rather
photos of strangers -- or to be truly precise, strange
photos of strangers). But everything else seems about
the same, including even the paintings on the walls (in
fact I'll swear to it: they're exactly the same).

    Naomi told me she'd be working into September. So
for two more months I'm hoping to avoid spending any of
my cushion. Then I'll start nibbling away at it (it
will stand at roughly seven K once I've bought a new
toner cartridge and a three-ream box of computer paper,
which I've decided I might as well do, for use with the
old firm's printer) and if the grand-jury scoping stays
at the same level I should be able to hold out for close
to a year. But I won't wait until the last moment (I
swear it!) to start looking for something part-time to
augment my income if it appears to be falling short.

    -- Ten to two now. Best to hit the streets before
the bars close.

*   *

Back home in the same chair where this grand loop-
de-loop started earlier today and dressed the same as
then (gray shorts only, and with private parts hanging
out picturesquely from a pulled-up leghole for airing).

227

[Jyze and Jyze Alone]

I know I've already JIRTed more than enough for this
week's entry and yet more than enough is still not
enough, it clearly needs some kind of capper.

     A wall of heat stood just inside the door to unit
B-2 when I opened it a few moments ago. This wall -- no
surprise here -- turned out to be as wide and tall and
deep as the apartment itself. Now I've got the fans
going and they're pulling in some slightly cooler air
through the window at my side. Delicious night smell to
it. Earth and sea and that greenery right outside.

     These strawberries, the ones I've been carrying
around all day, look good. I ate one -- it was good.
Not great, but better than just average good. After
wrapping up in here I'll core and slice the rest.
Probably my last strawberry feast of the season (but
then I thought the same thing two weeks ago).

     Such a fine night it was for walking. Earlier the
triangle was all athrob, the clubs so inviting with
their doors wide open and many of the partiers standing
around outside. All the skimpy jumpers and sunsuits and
microminis -- almost enough, or rather almost little
enough, to make me wish I were on the prowl again (I can
write this with some equanimity but when faced with the
fleshy reality I was aching every bit as much as I ever
did in the highest of the high-testosterone days, if not
more). Even saw that lovely rainbow-haired server (as
one must say these days -- sounds kind of classist to
me, "server," like a weak euphemism for "indentured
servant") from the digi-cafe, now in tight powder-blue
jeans, glossy red heels, and a little black fringed
halter top -- and she looked right into my eyes just as
she does when she's at work but this time she didn't see
me at all. But then I'll admit I appeared truly scary
tonight and knew I did, all unshaven and greasy-haired,
and for this reason spared her the embarrassment of
saying hello, not to mention directing some of my new
power gleam her way. I think I'm now at the point where
I could bring myself to say to her (if we were alone),
"Hey, you go out with older guys?" But I also want to
spare myself that sort of thing if I possibly can and

for as long as I can. At certain moments I must be
extremely vigilant with myself. Damn it anyway.
     A capper. Should mention I did make it out to the
Yuke to see the foreign film, which wasn't much and also
fell far short on subtitle decipherability. An
interesting moment, though, when I was poking around in
the cafe attached to the theater and was startled by a
glimpse of myself in the lobby's full-length mirror. A
different image, just barely recognizable to me.
Definitely the slightly graying older guy -- sort of
shaggy hip-professional looking, I thought, or could
pass for that with some not-overly-discerning observers.
I kind of liked it. Looked robust, this guy, full of
life, but a bit more seasoned than I'm accustomed to
thinking of myself as being. The new post-zen-marriage
me, that's who. He should have a few good years in him
before he'll be needing another new makeover. (I say
should. No point in ticking off the names of all the
forces he's at the mercy of, now more than ever.)
     -- And suddenly I think I'm finished here. This
was the week that was: the finest of them all, at least
for some time and maybe ever. I've got the plan now.
The big story of my life is finished, ending with the
dissolution of the zen marriage. The cycle. I'm
liberated into something new knowing something big is
accomplished and just what remains to be done, which is,
to be sure, a helluva lot.

25

     Tough to resurface here. (Where? The same green
armchair!) But I mean it's tough to get back into this
current daily life, the one lived smack-dab in the

present -- my cork-lined life as I've been thinking of
it lately.

Not that the toughness of resurfacing is bad. It's
good! It means some hot JIFT action's going down in the
old town these days. It means I'm doing it. It's
happening. It's popping. It's far freakin' out, man.
Can hardly believe it myself.

As for this contemporaneous reality zone (which is
the place where at least for a while longer I want to be
doing all my real-life jyzing, JIRT as opposed to JIFT),
it's marred by the fact that Kar's wedding is today and
I have no choice but to be sitting here (or could be
sitting, standing, lying, squatting, jumping, etc.,
elsewhere in the room) (and might soon branch out into
any or all of those) because I'm waiting for a call to
tell me when I'll be picked up. I won't be attending
the wedding, no, but I will be hitting the reception.
And it damn well better lay out a good spread.

Speaking of weddings: tomorrow would've been the
twenty-ninth anniversary of mine with Lady C if things
had lasted. Of course we didn't even make it to the
first anniversary, except technically. Had we made it
that far, we would've had to last another whole year to
make it to the second, and then the same twenty-seven
more times to reach tomorrow. Hard to feature. What
would we have come up with as an encore in year two for
all the drama of year one, I wonder. No, a single year
was the outer limit and in that sense I'd say we came
very close to realizing our full potential.

I'm still drying off from the shower. Sipping
coffee. Sun's out after several cool, wet, blustery
days. (Used my folding umbrella!)

For entertainment this week I've been going full
bore after the fruit flies. I've knocked off hundreds
-- reminds me of the era of the fruit-fly wars back
when Lady U and I were only beginning to explore the
mysteries of zen marriage. -- Hey, come to think of it,
tomorrow is also the anniversary of our zen wedding! It
would've been our eighteenth if the lady hadn't dared to
say hasta la vista, akachan.

    Anyway, the fruit flies. They're the second big
drawback to opening the window here at chairside, after
the danger of derelicts or desperate or exhausted or
just plain trippin' druggies crawling in. (But it's
still an ideal spot for long-term sitting, I insist now
more than ever.) The expandable screen I put up (this
is the one from my former shed, delivered to me
personally by Lady U) -- this screen keeps most of the
flies out, but hundreds, obviously, still find a way in.
(True, some multiply when inside. In fact probably many
do. These are fruit flies! So let's say scores have
gotten in and I've knocked off thousands. This really
is more accurate, I'd say now, upon reflection.)
    Trouble is, the loose fit between the screen and
the bottom of the sash on the open window always leaves
a few tiny gaps for the more supple of the fruit flies
to squeeze through. And at night I turn on my reading
lamp right next to the window and it serves as a beacon
for any and all creatures of the alley, fruit flies
included to be sure. And on any day when the mercury
rises much above seventy I have to open the window at
least a crack and that goes also for the nights
following such days, even if the nighttime temperature
falls into the fifties. And of course, as it seems I
never tire of mentioning, the garbage dumpster for our
whole building stands across the alley just twenty or
twenty-five feet away. And by one or two a.m. when I
usually get home and need to crack open the window, at
least one of the two dumpster lids has almost always
been left flung wide open by one or more of the long
procession of dumpster divers (Sofie perhaps among them,
though I haven't actually seen her out there yet).
-- No exaggeration here either. Rare is the night when
I don't hear at least one or two divers at work, and
often it's more. If it's less, it's likely because
either the cops or the drug dealers are stationed nearby
and have driven them away. (Sometimes I can hear the
divers cursing out the dealers or vice versa or both at
once. -- Some of the divers sleep beneath the viaduct
on the other side of the fence behind the dumpster, on

the grassy slope above the off-ramp. On warm nights
some come around and sleep right next to the dumpster,
using its bulk to shade the bright crime lights in the
alley -- which cast intriguing shadows on my rug and
couch in here, incidentally, if I don't close the
blinds, especially when the wind gets the vines moving
-- a very bright shadowbox picture, lively, worthy of
an art movie almost, with the shadows of the opened
blinds lending an entirely apt barred effect as in
jailhouse windows, horizontal from the alley's
perspective but vertical from mine where I sit.)
     -- So I leap around wearing just my shorts (usually
the gray ones, though they're about shot now and I'll
soon have to shift to the less comfortable red ones,
once part of our city-league hoop uniforms around the
time Lady U and I met) and I wield a rolled-up copy of
a certain glossy political magazine, or if none of those
are available (they wear out after maybe a hundred
swats), a certain newsprint political magazine. The
glossy mag works better because its paper lasts longer
and, being harder, deals the fruit flies a quicker, more
merciful demise. When my subscriptions to these two
mags run out, as they will any day now if they haven't
already (and I think the newsprint one probably has), I
don't know where I'll turn. Eventually it'll have to be
rolled-up newspaper sections, I guess.
     -- Home delivery of the "indispensable paper" did
start this week, I want to note, and I'm delighted with
it, except for one drawback. By "home" it turns out
they mean outside the building door. Not my room door;
the upstairs lobby door on the "edge road" side of the
building. In other words, prime ripoff territory. But
then by a happy coincidence the paper usually arrives
about one-thirty or two a.m., shortly before I come
hustling back from one office or the other, hideaway or
scope. They stick the folded paper, wrapped in
transparent plastic, down in the far corner of the
floor-to-ceiling lobby picture window, trying to make it
look as inconspicuous as possible -- and it does look
pretty much like the other discarded bits of trash often

rattling around in the drafts out there, including lots
of free advertising circulars -- and so far it's been
there every night. Hasn't missed a one.
     -- Oops, the phone.
                              *

     That was Rob. He and Gail are on their way so I'll
have to put this on hold and go figure out something to
wear. (As if the choice will make any difference! All
my clothes are at the same level -- not of grunginess, I
can't say that since the word's been commandeered by
higher forces -- of subcasualness, I'll go with; can't
come up with anything better under deadline pressure
here.) (Interestingly, Rob and Gail missed the apposite
ferry and so missed the wedding as well, finally
arriving just as it was breaking up -- too late even to
stage a hoax of a last-second marriage naysayer
appearing at the church door -- like, say, the one in
the movie about the confused recent college graduate --
"Psst, go for plastics" -- that first came out back in
the days when I was a confused recent college graduate
myself and also about to get married, to Lady C. "Does
anyone here object to this man taking this woman as the
very first in what will turn out to be a long series of
lawfully or zenfully wedded" -- never mind.)
                    *   *
     Now back and it's one in the morning. What I did,
I frittered away the day. By the time Rob and Gail
dropped me off here (half past nine) it was too late to
get much of anything serious done. So I just read and
shot some hoops, nerf type. It's been a long time since
I've taken a day off. "A day of rest." My feet are
happy to have it. (Yet this week I began running a
little and discovered it actually seems to help them.
Stretches out the tendons, I guess, apparently thereby
easing what sometimes feel like chronic ankle jams.)
     The wedding reception was fine except the spread
was less than hoped for and fell far, far short of the
one for Bart Y.'s memorial at the scope office. I met
Josh and Aaron, Kar's high-school-age kids, and Elaine,
his new wife, all for the first time. Elaine's a

strikingly attractive blond of primarily Scandi ancestry
similar to Kar's (and mine and a lot of other folks' at
the reception), a masseuse by profession, with a flashy
toothy smile and several almost-grown kids of her own.
Savoir faire too; from what she showed today I'd say
she can handle Kar and then some. Mort and Greta looked
surprisingly healthy and generally kept their ultra-
right political views under wraps. (Greta the youngest
of Dad's siblings and the only one still alive.)
Everyone tsk-tsked me for having become such a recluse
but of course the truth is no one really cares one way
or the other and that's just fine with me. I did wear my
engineer boots for the first time in at least eight
years. Nice to get a little use out of them.
     (Where was this? A small hillside coffee shop/bar
about five miles to the north, on the far side of the
big hill and across the canal. Who attended? Mostly
environmentalists and outdoorsy types and Elaine's old
school chums. What anchored the spread? Salmon, of
course, Kar being most recently, until RIF'd, a "salmonid
specialist" and still enamored of the creature -- "This
fish looks good enough to eat!" -- even though he's now
hunting for a different kind of job. Rob and Gail and I
stuck it out until the very end, sitting around with the
bride and groom as they opened their wedding gifts. I
fell into the chintzy group who failed to bring one. In
truth it never occurred to me that a gift was called for.
But even if I'd thought of it I would've opted out on
principle. Once is enough for anyone in a lifetime and
I've already doubled that with Kar. Whereas, if I'm
recalling correctly, he's "gifted" only one of mine --
and that was the zen marriage. And with that, as I say,
I believe he fulfilled his lifetime wedding-gift duty
vis-a-vis me and I just hope he'll view my gifts given
decades ago the same way and not have too hard a time
explaining the matter to Elaine.)
     This week I:
     **   printed up my first batch of pages using the
new paper and toner cartridge (both bought earlier in
the week after a long waterfront hike -- on a dramatic

double-rainbow afternoon -- to an office-supply
superstore a mile south of the southern border of my
regular tripolar turf);
     ** came across the name of Lady V's grandfather in
a book of colonial history about the country of her
conception (he was a prominent figure, a publisher and
political insider, but it appears he was never governor-
general as she told me);
     ** wrangled with the library over misleading info
given out by their tinny-voiced robot (who left a phone
message saying one of my back-ordered books had come in,
but it wasn't there when I tried to pick it up at the
downtown library; and the next day the exact same thing
happened again) (not only that, but I was disappointed
to discover the library's selection of periodicals is
even worse than it used to be -- I was counting on it to
take up some of the slack on my expired subscriptions
but it clearly won't be doing that).
     And not much more did I do. Or a few things, I
guess, noted here just as filler:
     ** appreciated a public art stunt which currently
has its perpetrator locked in the clink (it's the same
bad dude who a year or two ago attached a huge ball and
chain to the immense kinetic statue of the slavelike
kinky-haired black figure pounding away in front of the
downtown art museum) (I agree with him: the statue's
blatantly racist).
     ** ran a full load of laundry for the second time
since moving in, well pleased that the infusion of old
rags from the storage unit made possible such a big gap
between launderings (but the size of the mound of
clothes rising from the nerf court awaiting folding was
formidable and in fact most of it's still there, except
what I'm wearing and/or wore yesterday).
     ** oh yes, and noted a study (which made much less
of a splash than the public art stunt) reporting three
billion people or roughly half the global population
must scrape by on a daily income of the equivalent of
two USAn dollars or less.

[Jyze and Jyze Alone]

26

     Aboard. First crossing in a long time. The hum,
the rumble. For a change I left B-2 early enough that I
didn't have to rush down to the dock (and since the "low
road" is gently downhill all the way, rushing's not
really all that taxing).
     Still in focus. Even more so, I'd say. I've
caught fire and I'm thinking I can keep burning like
this almost indefinitely. Maybe even until I've got one
foot in the grave -- as long as my jyzing hand's still
free and operable. (Depends on the size of any pain
quotient involved, I guess, among other variables.)
     Heat wave all week (but it's cool here -- as with a
mighty toot we're pulling out). Now I'm truly glad I
have the portable fans. The one in B-2 rattles a bit
when it's on "sweep," so I usually keep it stationary.
But it still works well enough, and during sleep hours I
can aim it in such a way that, with a couple of tricky
caroms, a cool breeze washes over my naked and coverless
body up in the loft. And with the fruit flies eradicated
or otherwise occupied at least for the time being, I can
open the window when I get home at night and cool the
place off a bit.
     The eighter that was: a notably different kind. In
two ways. For one: I spent not a single penny of my
weekly cash allotment on anything but groceries. For
another (related) I did breakfast at home every day. No
exceptions. -- Oh, and a third, I skipped lunch every
other day (having decided I need to be both leaner and
hungrier). Thus I'm even happier getting home at night,
because not only is the night newspaper awaiting me in

236

all its indispensability but I can soon chow down again.

Grinding across. Doing this directly below the spot where the full moon hung as viewed from my window last night -- right up that shimmery corridor of glint. "Moonlight on the Bay" -- but it sounds so much better with the second "ooh" in there, "on the Bayou." Which is not to say I'd like to be living next to a bayou, no.

Thinking: just about a year ago this week was the last time I saw my mother alive (I picture her sitting on a chair in the corner of the laundromat a block from her apartment gazing proudly but also somewhat quizzically up at me where I was perched on the edge of a folding table as we waited for our clothes to dry). On "Memorials," by the way, the publisher still hasn't replied to my letter. Worries are mounting again.

Just as last week, I'm scarcely living in the present at all these days. Nor do I regret this fact in the slightest, except in the predictable reflexive ways, which at this point I can easily ignore and generally do. My moods as well as my thoughts depend almost entirely from day to day on what's happening in the universe of JIFT, both in the direct sense (what's doing with the "Jyzer" characters) and the indirect (how's the writing going). (Or should it be vice versa on the direct and indirect?)

What's more, I'm casting about for new ways I might take this J-book right here back into that universe with me. So far I haven't come up with anything that looks workable. (But I have hit on another idea for a JIRT-annal theme. Already in place are "A Jyze Jubilee" and "The Nine Zones of Jyzetopia," which will undertake a truly detailed yearlong exploration of good old unit B-2. The new idea is "The Year of Random Jyze," in which coin flips will determine which day of each eighter will be J-day and which two or three venues from a preset list will be the sites for that day. -- Well okay, it may lack sizzle. But I think it'll work. It'll get me going or rather keep me going.)

Rounding the first of the Z-bends. So steady, so pleasant. The slight rattle. Comforting, like the

clickety-clack of railroad tracks. (And I do enjoy
standing on the footbridge leading to the new pier a
block and a half down from B-2 and listening to
unusually pristine specimens of same as the trains roll
by a few feet directly below.) (And can't resist the
next association: a movie about spotting trains being
the must-see of the day, and it's just too bad "Jyzer"
didn't get to the public first. Not that there's much
similarity between the two -- "Jyzer," in fact, being
more like the antithesis of the train-spotting movie in
story lines, judging from the reviews and a preview I
saw, although both tackle the theme of youthful
rebellion. -- Well, but maybe I'd better see the whole
movie first before spouting off.)

This trip today has no real purpose. I'll be able
to pay my monthly ministorage bill in person and save
the cost of a stamp, but of course ferrying back and
forth sets me back about twenty times what a stamp does.
Then again I paid for the ferry coupon some ten or
eleven weeks ago and it'll soon become worthless if I
don't use it now. So in the end it came down to this:
Did I really want to do it? Last-minute vacillations.
A lot of effort for nothing. Poke around in the ruins
of the old life -- or rather in certain excavated
leftovers and archaeological salvagings of that life.
But -- I'm doing it. For its jyze-friendliness mainly,
I'd say. Today being J-day, I could think of no place
where I'd rather be going at it. "Cool out there on the
water" -- somehow that overheard phrase clinched it.

Still no word from Rikki. But I did finally write
her again, and what started out as a brief note kept
pouring out, ten pages in all, just goofing but probably
it will improve at least a little the chances of her
visiting J-town with Mischa next month (to me anyway
this letter made it sound like so much fun up here). At
one point I was even -- well, but I see it's time to
quit this tub. We're pulling in. "Building on a Proud
Tradition." I'd recognize that damn lying destroyer
anywhere.

*   *

-- Didn't stop to think how hot it might be up in
this unit. Very hot it definitely is. Even hotter it
would be but for a slight breeze which manages to reach
me here at the old picnic table. Blue-checked plastic
tablecloth and all. Loving birthday gift of a bygone
era -- and still dirt-encrusted from that era too, as
well as from the not-so-loving era that followed half a
decade later. The little-finger side of my jyzing hand
is showing some serious traces of detritus. I might
almost be better off wearing the ancient gardening
gloves stored in the box of same on one of the shelves
along the back wall -- which I can even see from here,
the glove fingers sticking up (imploringly!).

The bus drops me off at the mall across the highway.
Figured why not check out the hardware/garden store
there, see if they're carrying any of the hardy fuchsias
I've been hankering after. They're not. But they are,
as always, offering free popcorn, which I'd forgotten
about. At the checker's insistence I helped myself to a
couple of bags (meaning I won't be looking forward to
getting home quite so much tonight). -- Struggling local
hardware/garden chain, they recently filed for bankruptcy
protection. A third of their stores have gone out of
business already and I thought this one might've also.
But I guess the chain gets a big-enough gouge out of the
old home-port crowd to keep it open. In the category of
nongrocery items I'd say this outfit has separated me
from more of my greenbacks over these past seventeen
years than any other peddler of goods except the only
real bookstore.

It's always a kind of shock to see that everything
in the storage unit looks exactly the same as I left it
at the end of the previous visit weeks or months earlier.
A thrill too, as in venturing up to the attic when
you're a kid. (And a good number of items once stored
in the attic at 2015 Gatewood -- Mentoka styling -- are
now stored here. Though of course a great many more
aren't. But the ones that are here, it seems both
utterly normal and yet completely wrong that they should
be here, that is, rather than there.)

[Jyze and Jyze Alone]

      Once here I decided my mission all along must've
been to pick up the big cloth bag containing Lady V's
notes and letters from our high period. Sometime fairly
soon I'll want to be rereading the entire lot, I think.
In any case I'll haul the bag back to the city just so
I can say I've accomplished something today. -- Seems
I'm developing the make-work mentality so notoriously
fitting for members of the part-time winding-down
"semiretired" workforce. (This trip itself really
being little more, as I'm seeing it now, than the
latest move in the ongoing campaign to convince myself
paying eighty bucks a month to rent this place is
justified.)
      Light string dangling a foot to my left, ending at
eye level. Once in a while it sways a little in the
breeze, almost as if a spider were gently "shaking off
the cobwebs." Otherwise no movement in here. Stillness
of the past (though surely wild parties break out when
no one's around, as with those toy-shop puppets after
the shop closes in the fairy tale). Mustiness too,
especially when I open the drawers of the old black fire
safe (which have reeked a bit ever since surviving a
flooded basement back in city rental house number one).
      -- On writing Rikki, I was about to say earlier
that for a short time I thought I detected an aura of
inevitability about it: she and I would become lovers.
Would remain so for the rest of our natural lives. And
I'm not saying now we won't -- who knows? -- but the
inevitability moment seems to have passed. Soon any
such destiny was again starting to look highly unlikely.
Too many barriers. This old dog would be better off
focusing on existing tricks, so to speak. (Hey, tricks
are walking this afternoon, at least on paper.)
      Nonetheless, still and all, I think a lot about her
and for all the same reasons as before. And I'm likely
to continue doing so unless she gives me some more
direct reason not to or someone else comes along.
      (One eye on the pocket watch here. Probably it's a
few minutes slow. It always is, so why not now? -- And
how bad was the evil Soviet regime under which it was

produced? I can hear the joke now: "Couldn't even make their exported watches run on time." -- But I still say this watch was one helluva "smart investment," yes I do.)

All week my big reading project has been a second go-round with a book on the poetics of protojyze. It's a rewrite of a Ph.D. thesis and reads like it, full of academic pomposities and dull explication of tired orthodoxies, not to mention stylistic infelicities to make even me (yes!) blush, and also a great many typos, but even so its discussion of protojyzing from a structuralist point of view is inspiring. It's so rare to see jyze of any kind taken seriously as literature: for that reason all by itself I'm almost in heaven reading the thing. Or no, the real reason I'm there -- in heaven -- is simply because that's where immersion in the astonishingly beautiful protojyze tradition this book focuses on, that is, Lady U's ancestral tradition, "nikki bungaku," always takes me.

Not that I've thought through any of this. Some other time for that. Right now I'd be well advised to close this storage place up for the nonce and start the long hike down the hill (and being thoroughly bathed in sweat from this heated history bath I'll be leaving a trail like a slug).

-- And so for those who'll be remaining here after the door rolls down, prepare to party!

*   *

One of the most powerful moments of my life. Maybe the most.

Already I was in a heightened state after the walk down the hill. Seemed it was all coming together now. Yes, the vision, the era of the east/west wars, the united tribes, the grand synthesis, the internal and the external, the great loves, the revenge of the oppressed, the chronological framework with the attack on the mid-ocean harbor at one end and the eighteen-year mate whose family home overlooks that same harbor at the other (that's Lady U, of course), the sixteen protojyze volumes all at least two hundred thousand words, the

241

[Jyze and Jyze Alone]

fictionized introduction hailing the opening of the Jyze
Age, the series of postscript JIRT annals including this
one right here, the upcoming grand finale of the
millennial apocalypse -- yes, it was all there or soon
would be, a lifework I could be proud of and could and
would devote the rest of my days to completing -- and
all the important pieces were not only already existing
but already written (with the one apocalyptic exception)
and needing now only some shaping, pruning, perhaps some
deepening in places -- or no, some dredging of the
detritus from the already existing deeps.
     Such a clear vision it was. On the wooden bench
where I like to sit in warm weather, and often have over
the past seven years, dockside, the view so impressive
and a cool breeze blowing off the water. And now comes
the handsome old black-and-white double-deck wooden foot
ferry chugging across, and I walk over to board, I take
a seat outdoors on the prow, top deck, just in front of
and slightly below the pilothouse, I'm the only one up
there, and as we pull out I'm fascinated without at
first knowing why by a sailboat that soon appears about
fifty yards ahead of us and maybe ten yards to starboard,
it's tilted at what appears to be a dangerous angle,
well over forty-five degrees, slicing along on a course
parallel to ours at just about our speed -- and it's
white, the deck I'm sitting on is white, the chair's
white -- and the sailboat, which is a fairly large one,
almost a yacht, is far enough away from us that I can't
see anyone aboard it (though I suspect someone must be
leaning out the far side because of the extreme tilt) --
and as so often when I see a sailboat for the first time
in a while I think of Dad dying as he raced aboard his
tiny sunfish -- and now I'm aboard this small ferry which
I also often associate with Dad because it was launched
the year of his birth -- and that white sailboat slicing
ahead of us, such a splendid sight on an afternoon like
this -- cavorting like a porpoise escorting a clipper
ship, I'm thinking, or even more like the riderless white
horse accompanying a funeral cortege (that powerful
symbolism of the funeral procession for the assassinated

242

president rising into memory) -- and maybe it's just
the wind sneaking under my shades causing it but
suddenly tears are streaming down my cheeks (as even
now while I write this they're threatening to well up
again -- as the auto ferry plows out of the twisty
narrows roughly an hour after the sailboat incident) --
and not merely tears of sorrow or mourning but of a
strange and powerful joy, as if old Dad's spirit is
rejoining me here and now, accompanying me, riding
alongside as I travel back to the city bearing this new
vision he'd -- after our long semi-estrangement --
finally find worthy of me and of him.
        -- And all the way across the inlet (on what's only
a twelve-minute voyage for the foot ferry but seemed
much longer) it was affecting me like that, taking my
breath away, infusing me with what I knew with certainty
would be a supreme "visionary" moment for the rest of my
life and indeed one that somehow unified all my life --
and then as we neared the in-transit side with its
lengthy row of gray warships (many in the so-called
mothball fleet hailing from the era of the east/west
wars, even its earliest years, and including Dad's
decade of service therein, although the fleet's numbers
are dwindling now as one by one the old clunkers are
hauled off for scrap) -- then the foot ferry slowed and
turned to port, toward the dock, and gave a toot on its
steam whistle, while the white sailboat glided onward,
finally disappearing from view beyond the bow of the
showpiece destroyer of "phony incident which started the
Vietnam war" infamy. And I gathered my things,
staggered off, found another wooden bench and just sat
there stunned and numb yet also awed, grateful, jubilant.
        -- Too bad this moment's left me in no kind of
shape to write it up in depth. If I could do so it
would be something. Nor is there anything more I can
say about it at this time.

[Jyze and Jyze Alone]

27

    Forgot to put the ink bottle in my bag. Also left
backup J-stick No. 6 on the worktable in B-2. Damn!
    Guess I'll go until I run out and then fill up
again at the hideaway or scope office, in both of which
places I've stashed backup ink bottles.
    This atop the central hill, a familiar tavern. For
old times' sake, though my old times here were strictly
limited. Protojyzed here once or twice over the years
but that's about it. Also stopped in on occasion with
Lady U in the era when she was attending dance rehearsals
at any of several nearby practice venues (including a
large hall housing a number of arts outfits that's
currently controversial for renting space to homophobic
far-right religious groups in the middle of a famously
gay-friendly neighborhood). Or in a later era when we
were early for a movie at the theater a few blocks to
the west. (Where the picture showing at the moment is
also controversial: the one about train-spotting.)
    It's altogether apt I'm up here running an errand
for the same Lady U. Just scored a community-college
catalog for her, as I promised to do when we last met
more than a month ago. Fairly soon now it'll probably
be time for our next get-together. After that, not too
many more, if any. No reason for them, not with my mail
addressed to the old "U Acres" diminishing to a trickle.
Sad, yes, but this is how it is. Wasn't my idea, our
split-up. But there's no longer any doubt life's better
this way, for me and presumably for her as well (she
hasn't said so but certainly seems to think so).
    Warmer today, finally, after a cool rainy spell

that put the kibosh on the dreaded city summer festival.
Hooray! My back's soaked where the pack was pressing
against it during the long uphill trek. As for the
festival, I tuned it out as much as I could, but the
dozen-story-high and thousand-foot-long aircraft carrier
parked right outside my window, almost -- actually two
blocks down the hill -- was hard to ignore, as were the
thousands of gawkers lined up to go aboard for a tour.

I also ignored the Olympics which just whirled to a
close in another corner of the country, except for quick
glances at the sports pages for track-and-field results.
It's exciting, every night sometime between one and
three a.m. my buzzer (as it's called) gives a couple of
honks and I hurry up to the lobby to pick up my hot-off-
the-presses "daily indispensable" in its bright plastic
wrapper (usually blue now) propped in the inside corner
of the lobby picture window (instead of outside, by
agreement with the delivery guy, after I loitered in the
area for an hour one night and intercepted him). See
what's happening out there in the world. Reminds me of
rushing two blocks over to the main drag to pick up the
bulldog edition of a somewhat more dispensable, but
still crucial to me, newspaper way back in the long ago.

What's new? Basically I'm just waiting to go crazy.
It'll be like the so-called "turnover" of the oceans
which, as scientists are hypothesizing these days, may
have caused one of the previous great extinctions (that
is, rivaling the one we're producing single-handedly, we
human creatures, right now) -- and also caused, in a
more confined setting, the poisonous gas cloud that
erupted from a lake in Africa a few years back and
killed thousands of human creatures along with untold
numbers of other kinds.

My current life will be wiped out. Into its place
will move my obsessive fantasy life.

Right now I'm hanging on by a thread. This I'm
doing as a matter of courtesy to Rikki and Mischa in
case they really do decide to show up. (Odds are
lengthening fast now: we're a week into August and still
not a peep from them.) Once they've come and gone, or

once it's clear they won't be coming, I'll let go of the
thread. Or just possibly -- and I mean the chances are
truly slim -- something will start up between Rikki and
me. In which case not even the jyze gods know what
might happen next.

   This tavern. Famous place. Pool players, a couple
of foul-mouthed ex-cons, an anomalous nerdy laptopper
pecking away at the bar, a grandly tattooed woman of
large proportions blazing out a handwritten letter in a
corner booth. Bricks, carved wood, trees thrashing
happily outside industrial windows as city buses roll
by. Peeling brown paint on the ceiling. A detective
novel with this joint's name in the title: I bought a
copy of it a year or two back but still haven't gotten
around to reading it and now probably never will.

   -- These days, though, the reading is good. A
grandmaster in the loft, a grandmaster in the head, a
near-grandmaster on the couch. Poetics of protojyze
sadly completed, now I'm moving back into a magisterial
history of the same literary tradition the poetics book
focuses on, but this time a volume covering the early
centuries. In my bag a contemporary memoir whose
smarmily likable title I'll cite right now (breaking all
rules, seeing as how it's nonfictive): "The Heart Can Be
Filled Anywhere on Earth." Dig it! (This work being of
near-Mentokan provenance and therefore useful from the
fictive point of view as well.) And a nightly dip, time
permitting, into a volume of contemporary lyric poetry,
a collection of short-short stories, and the never-
ending tome of USAn personal essays.

   My life now. The reading is actually more like a
kind of antifreeze -- or the reverse, rather, a cooling
system to keep the engine from dangerously overheating,
as it tends to do when it's engaged big-time in JIFT or
protojyze projects.

   (One of the ex-cons here in the tavern blathering
aloud -- very aloud -- about his four-year obsessive
love. His addictive gambling got in the way and did it
in. Naturally this has me thinking of the inimitable
Lady V and my own addictive protojyzing of the era when

we were together. She, I could say, is the one rising up
to kill off all current life for me. I'm a goner again
on her. This is what love's all about. -- Started with
a rereading of a long letter I wrote her exactly ten
years ago this fall. It went nowhere, that late exchange
of letters with her, but it doesn't matter now. Her
photos are up in No. 225. Paintings too. I'll be doing
everything I can to get all the way back into loving her
with a wild passion.)

     -- And why not? The current scene just strikes me
as child's play. It's kindergarten, folks. I'm not
interested. So much better just to flip out: go on as
long as I can with my own crazy obsessed grandiose
dignity so to speak. Make something huge and astonishing
as my gift for the ages. "Cork-lined life." So it'll
be. -- And besides, I have my two new hardy fuchsias,
each boasting scores of blooms; I lean my head back in
my armchair by the window so I'm looking straight up and
the blooms of the Santa Claus lightly brush my brow and
eyelids (easily imaginable as loving lips to be sure,
those blooms, although this is a notion I'd probably
better keep to myself outside of the JIRT).

     And one day took a hike all the way to the navy
dock at the north end of the main waterfront park.
Walked close to twelve miles that day, I figure. The
great gray grain terminal. The huge spinning globe atop
the newspaper building. The narrow, ugly, nearly
treeless park proper with its endless asphalt loop.
Already I was in an intensified state, sometimes weak in
the knees with longing and anguish. -- Realizing it'll
be manic now with so little anchor in reality, the highs
higher and the lows lower. (That park so scrabbly and
depressing I screamed out loud: "Holy shit, I don't
believe it, I hate this place!" -- And the railroad
tracks running right alongside it, leading straight --
well, okay, rather crookedly -- all the way back to the
fictive province of Mentoka and the city of Wachute
where Dad was born, and onward to the city of Mentoka
Falls where this jyzer right here attended grad school,
and then onward to the capital city, Lahontan, where Dad

and Mom met and this jyzer right here was born, and on
through to Gatewood, where this same jyzer grew up from
age five, and finally terminating in the metropolis
where so many of them do: Centropolis. C-town. Could
hop a freight or one of the daily passenger trains and
be right there, any of those places.)
    My Mentoka-series intro volume, yes, it hurts to
say it, but I'm laying it aside for a while. The main
body of work is more important. The hugest I-novel ever
(using a term from that other lit tradition): got to
whip that into decent shape first. Get the damn thing
popping. "Jyzer," you just take it easy for a while now
and I'll get back to you, you can be sure of that.
    -- Meanwhile thinking, what about money? If I
closed down the Jyzer Ink office and the storage unit, I
could live in unit B-2 for a sum quite close to what I
expect the feds to bestow on me monthly starting at
retirement age. Yes, I'm thinking ahead now. This is
all that matters (of course if I last long enough).
This means I could shift the deep reserves from the
investment group to easily accessible bonds and use not
just the income from the bonds but also chunks of
principal if necessary to supplement any scoping income
and thus not have to take another job. -- See how it
goes this fall once Naomi's out of action. With a
little luck I'll be able to hold out into next year
without having to decide about withdrawing funds from
the investment group. But the point (to repeat, because
for me it's crucial): even with no other income I could
live about seven years on the deep reserves alone.
    Here's an old rock hero of mine, one of the few
still performing at a high level -- on the box. This
place is all right. Better than any of the taverns in
my home hood. If it were nearby I might pop over every
now and then. But basically my nightlife now comes only
in the briefest of inward glimpses from the street as I
trudge by various jumpin' joints. The historic quarter,
the home hood, a few scattered spots in between. (Last
week, first time in a long time, a woman tried to pick
me up on the street. Probably a hooker, but who knows.

[Life of the Jyze to Come]

Either way, I've got no time for such things now.
Unless it's blatant serendipity. Lightning strikes,
fine. Actually I'm in good physical shape and fully
alive and alert. Brain's omnivorous as rarely before.
I'm roaring away in the deeps a lot, amazing myself.
It's been building on itself for many years and now with
nothing standing in the way, no attachments at all, it's
in runaway chain reaction and I'm feeling no limits.
Scary at times but only if I stop to think about it, so
I don't do that if I can avoid it, and I usually can.)
    I'll push on.
                    *   *
    Back home now and fully inked up. Window cracked
open but it's not necessary that the fan be on (so it's
off). Every five or ten or twenty seconds a vehicle
hurtles by in the night. Last week a repair crew was
working on the viaduct out there, traffic backed up for
miles, and I thought they must be smoothing out the bump
that causes the empty trucks to boom out such horrendous
jolting THUNKs as they career around the bend heading up
and out of the tunnel (and maybe sometimes the ones
going down into it do that too). But no.
    Train whistle. Swivel my head forty-five degrees
to the right and here's that cheery Santa Claus fuchsia
again. Kiss me, you beauty! -- But happiness I'm not
in pursuit of, no. The latest psychological findings
(ha!) suggest we all have a happiness "set point"
anyway; we may diverge from it momentarily, up or down,
but it's more or less a sure thing we'll soon return to
our normal level as a matter of homeostasis. So why
worry? And I'm not worrying. But were I down in the
dumps for too long I don't doubt I would. (If such set
points really exist, mine's probably up there pretty
high. If one of the acknowledged prose grandmasters of
our century now ending was the self-proclaimed "happiest
man alive," with him gone maybe I can claim the title.
Or am I being ridiculous? It's just that I had it so
good for so long I almost forgot what it was like to be
unhappy. And too I got a lot of love as a kid,
especially during those famously formative years up to

age three when Dad wasn't around and Barb wasn't either
(nor of course Jeff and Rob) and Mother and her two
sisters and her parents and grandmother, with all of
whom we were living in a single house during the war
years, had no one else to focus on except the grinning
little future jyzer. So I have nothing to grouse about
and that's why I never do grouse all that much. The
exceptions are all self-explanatory. True, I've always
set my goals very high and thus doomed myself to
unhappiness -- except for one thing. I've always known
how absurd those goals are. Or how about this: my
happiness set point is calibrated for having ludicrously
utopian goals.)
     Jyze on O jyze grandmaster!
     All right, I will. And wearing only my gray shorts
(still in action!), and in full sight of four photos of
Lady V in a skimpy bikini looking extremely sexy as she
always knew how to do. Black-and-white photos I took
myself back in the days of the high craziness. -- Is
she still alive? Of course I don't know. She dropped
out of sight -- maybe off the edge of the earth -- after
that last letter ten years ago. I ask myself if I even
want to know whether she's alive and it's a tough one.
I wouldn't go chasing her down unless I had something to
give her -- say a fully achieved protojyze volume
focusing on herself. Until then it might be better to
remain in the dark. But it is frustrating at times.
Chances are fairly good I could determine what her fate
has been through her brother or her son, both of whom
I'd bet are still living somewhere near their old haunts.
Not now, though. I guess what it is, she's alive to me
these days and I want her to stay that way. Learning
she was dead might not kill her off for me as I'm loving
her now, but learning she was alive just might. Better
not take any chances.
     See, I'm out of the loop. I'm done. Like millions
of others I'm dropping out to contemplate the higher
things -- or my navel -- or whatever pops up. Like all
those recluses of a millennium back. Like the idleness
grandmaster of six centuries back, say, the gorgeous

title of whose splendid primary prose production means
"works of calm solitude" (and for years I thought it was
his brush name!). Like all those lyrical hermits.
"Leaving the world." And then once every six to eight
days I rise to the surface (like a submarine
replenishing its air supply, say) to issue another jyze
bulletin. States location and how's the vessel, how's
the crew, takes a quick look around at the vast and
featureless ocean -- oops, time to dive again.

I like "Jyze Bulletins" too. And "Random Jyze."
Not for nothing is this round in the life cycle
called, as Rob reminded me, "The Year of the Joker."
And the next round, due to start up in about twenty-five
days, will be "The Year of the Double Joker." The round
after that might be "Jyze Around My Room," in homage to
the corny rock'n'roll song that began it all, the one
about doing it around the clock.

I like "Jyze Bulletins" too. And "Random Jyze."
And especially "Tell It Jyze," which is a shameless
rejigging of "Tell It Slant" but surely that's no knock
on it. So I won't be running short on titles. As with
many other things -- and even more, of course, because
this is rule No. 1 -- it's just a matter of the jyzer
himself lasting long enough to use them.

Tonight's dinner? Microwaved potatoes. Papa's got
a brand-new bag of potatoes, and this time it's only a
five-pounder because the previous fifteen-pounder lasted
too long: what hadn't turned moldy was growing eyes on
its eyes, whether inner or not. Happily these five-
pounders are available at the public market for just a
buck; no need to be hauling them all the way from the
tripolar north pole, or more specifically, the
purportedly real supermarket.

Waiting now for the honk-honk of the news courier.
A cross between a honk and a buzz, actually, or so it
sounds to me: buzz-honk. So buzz-honk, buzz-honk. And
startlingly loud; it always makes you jump even when
you're expecting it.

What's new in the daily routine? Not a whole lot.
For the second week in a row I ate all breakfasts at
home and skipped all lunches and hit the supermarket on

Saturday instead of Monday because Saturday works out better for the day-old-bread rack. And to any scoffers out there I'd just say patronizing that rack can save you up to a fin a week. (Most people, I've noticed, say "a five" or "a fiver" these days, rather than "a fin," but isn't it better to sound at least somewhat nautical now and then when you live on a waterfront in what many locals still think is an old sailors' hotel?)

Bought two pint boxes of blueberries and a quart of ice cream, so-called natural vanilla, over the past two weeks. My extravagances, paid for, almost, by the savings on the day-old bread.

Also new, a $2.49 mister. Misting the plants becomes part of the ritual: every night when I get home. Clearly they all appreciate it and so I feel better also. Especially on hot days the air in here gets way too dry. It bakes is what it does. The question now being: will the two hardy fuchsias be hardy enough to make it through the winter holding forth right where they're located now? We're hoping so. Knowing absolutely nothing about how to care for hardy fuchsias growing indoors, hope is all we can offer.

Who is this nosistic "we"? Me and jyze, who else. And the hummingbirds too, I suppose I could say. These cheery little wooden whirligigs, much more often than makes any sense at all I notice I'm happy simply because they're around. I gaze at them a lot. Easy to do because, as I'm sure I've noted before, these birds really do stand still. (And today at a shop across from the tavern I bought a picture-postcard portrait of the same twentieth-century prose grandmaster mentioned earlier -- the one who so deftly made the cheery little hummers stand still -- and other postcards featuring several greats already ensconced, as he is, in the Jyze Pantheon. But this one I'm especially pleased to have gazing at me again. His image joins those of the blues heroes and Lady V and the supreme neoprag, among others, at the hideaway. And my mother's too, I should specifically note, with me the euphoric two- or three-year-old kid sitting on her lap. -- So another

extravagance. But this week I'm flush because groceries
set me back less than twenty bucks.)
     All these ghosts love me, I know they do. Then
there's real life where it's just the opposite: nobody
does. It's really true! Nobody! My two brothers love
me like a brother, okay, and I suppose my sister loves
me in her own twisted sisterly way (and I do mean
twisted), and that's it. For active day-to-day love or
even mild caring there's nothing happening right now.
So back to the ghosts. When Lady V looks out at me from
those photos I may still shudder -- I do! -- but I have
no doubt I'm loved.

28

     Fine spot here. Fine day too, though maybe a
little hot. Here in the sun a guy in heavy jeans and a
hickory workshirt -- it's me, folks, J-slinger G! --
albeit with sleeves rolled up.
     Where? The pier? New? And looking straight up
the hill at the bricky old artist-lofts buildings and
the actual back windows of unit B-2? Observation deck?
Several stories above water level? Double-sided
contoured wood-slat bench? Facing the downtown highrise
cluster? Not a cloud in the sky? Scarcely a tourist on
the ground? Big volcano preening off in the distance to
the southeast? Limp flags dangling right here, four of
them?
     Well anyway. (Someone was objecting to the mad
proliferation of rhetorical questions -- in a review of
that book of "creative nonfiction," I think it was.)
     So for news, there is some. Bad. What little
heart I have left it took right out of me, at least for

a few days. As feared, Rikki and Mischa will not be
visiting. A long letter in explanation but again really
nothing personal in it. The car broke down, funds were
scarce and had to go for repairs instead of travel.
Maybe later when new funds come in.

I suppose a single strand of that string I was
mentioning last time remains uncut. I suppose.

(Now it looks like banishment. The setup crew in
tacky black formalwear just marched in carrying crisp
white tablecloths folded across their outstretched arms
like flags as in a raucous British cinematic farce.
This area can be closed off for parties. I was out here
once before when it happened.)

Toot of a waterfront streetcar. It would be good
if a train rolled by on the authentic working railroad
tracks I can see at the base of the bluff half a block
to the east, leading to the tunnel entrance a block
farther south right below the lookout park at the public
market.

Some other day I should jyze here again. A spot to
provoke much thought. From the other side of this bench
I could gaze out at the mountains to the west, the bay,
the sound beyond the bay, the ferries, the big container
ships dragging along their suckling tugs, the shoreline
of the far province where I used to cohabit with Lady U
and the distance between here and there and for that
matter between here and just about anywhere, or at least
part of that distance. Could gaze and gaze, yes.

(Obnoxious military air-show jets were screaming by
about a hundred feet above this spot last weekend. More
summer festival. I hadn't taken seriously the existence
of a second week to this massively exasperating affair.
Huge crowds. Another big warship docked right here,
again almost within arm's reach of where I sit now. And
how proud we all are of being part of the most bellicose
nation that ever was -- just in terms of number of wars
launched per decade of national existence, let's say --
super-heavyweight division I'm talking about.)

-- But...to my surprise I discovered I didn't
really want to go all the way crazy. When I started to

do so it felt bad. So, no, I don't think I'll go wild
with love for Lady V. I'll obsess but I'll obsess on
the art and the characters as a group, and among them
she'll probably be the most important, the one most
deeply and also most self-destructively loved, the one
who most infuriates (as, of course, in real life). But
take up full-time residence in a fantasy world, no.
I'll continue living here and now as best I can.

But...wait. Does this mean I'm not leaving the
world? Not consecrating myself to the god art? No, I'd
say I'll still basically be doing that. I'll be a monk
for art, absolutely. Unless, that is, something else
comes along which looks more interesting, even if only
temporarily. But in the meantime, obsess away. Enjoy.
Go crazy with it but in more bearable fashion. Keep
some kind of tether to be at the end of.

-- Rumble rumble, ding ding, here's that train I
was hoping for. Or no, it's only engines, I see now, in
fact five of them hooked together, the first one gray
and the other four the standard green. Switch engines
all. But gone almost instantly: swallowed by the tunnel.
Lots of power but not a single pound of visible payload.
And what kind of crazy-making pills or powder might be
stashed in the engineer's pocket (as Tom T. the railroad
dispatcher used to wonder)? No way to know.

-- Flags rippling in a saving breeze. Silverware
and plates and wine glasses appearing atop the buffet
tables with those crisp white coverings. Crew of seven
hard at work, at least one of each major human race (so-
called), four women and three men (to my eye). At least
three languages being spoken. This is a cosmopolitan
city! -- But no city flag among those rippling. State,
country, country to the north, and port (which is not
city). And of the six sets of anchored view binoculars
available up here, only one is in use. They're free too,
so this was one of the places to which "the Glunk" was
planning to introduce Rikki and Mischa.

Time'll be up soon. I'll go now and save the crew
the trouble of booting me out. Stagger on down the
waterfront. Still humming Ron C.'s "Pegleg," the

ancient vinyl version which was spinning flawlessly all
by itself in unit B-2 not much more than an hour ago.

*   *

Now the other end of my own personal waterfront. A
vanilla softie. "I'm just an old softie for you." A
seagull perches atop an outdoor table in the fenced-off
customer seating area here at the familiar old ferry-
dock fast-food franchise. Otherwise I'm again alone in
a quasi-public commercial space (as folks clomp by
loudly and endlessly on the metal staircase and the
overhead walkway leading to and from the slips).

Every Sunday I show up here. It's just worked out
this way, but a story of sorts lies behind it. On
Sundays the drugstore on the edge road where I buy a
ritualistic ten-cent mint each day before starting work
at the hideaway is closed, so it's necessary to resort
to a fallback ritual, the fast-food softie cone. And to
get to the franchise at the ferry dock, which is the
best softie source I know of along any of the six main
north-south avenues of the bipolar turf, you might as
well come straight down the waterfront (or what by the
jyze naming scheme is also the very low road). As good
an excuse as any to vary my daily routine a little.

Today's not Sunday, true. But Sunday when I came
down this way the line of festivalgoers at the fast-food
counter was so long I issued myself a raincheck on the
softie. Therefore I'm permitted -- obliged almost -- to
have one today. (No more than one a week, see. For
financial reasons, mainly, rather than nutritional.)

-- For a weekday the crowds are still, I'd say,
quite large. This is mid August and tourist season's
still near its peak. Horse-drawn carriages and bicycle
rickshaws, tour boats and totem poles. Sidewalk T-shirt
vendors galore, many with a shaky personal card table.
Legions of panhandlers. Unfolded maps and puzzled
frowns. Flapping fish banners. Dripping waffle cones.
Buzzing languages of the world. What are these people
really thinking? Life going on and on like this. My
poor dead mother who can no longer join the promenade.
I the peripatetic observer now just a fortnight or so

256

short of becoming her son the full-fledged double joker.
Lazing along with, or at times going a little faster
than, the flow, with the piers to my right and the
street and the opposing flow to my left. "And ever so
it has been and shall be." (Surly slouching teens, for
example.) (But to be sure the opposing flow might be to
one's right in other lands.)
     So I'm asking myself, wandering along, is this,
then, the pathway to salvation? (As a loud bell rings
right now and the automatic black gates swing open just
outside the fence here, meaning the ferry on the route I
rode all those years, the ferry whose basso arrival toot
almost lifted me out of my seat a moment ago despite my
bone-deep familiarity with it, is now unloading.)
-- For the pathway to salvation is what you're supposed
to find yourself on when you leave the world. Or
reworded, can an outdoor seating area at a fast-food
franchise be a waystop on the pathway to salvation?
(For surely it couldn't be the place itself, meaning the
heavenly paradise. Or could it? The Way is everywhere,
so why not the paradise as well? And of course, yes,
fast-food franchises are pretty much everywhere anyway.)
     Or to take another tack on the matter, how much do
I want to renounce? And how much must I renounce? And
how much must I or do I want to try to justify my
renouncing, whether the renouncing itself be willing or
unwilling? -- For, as a great scribbler of the previous
century pointed out (and we're reminded of this in a
fine little story in a current glossy weekly from the
far coast), "After [age] forty there's only one word to
sum up the basis of life: renunciation."
     Or again to rephrase the question I'm hoping to
pose to my own satisfaction (which just might be the
very worst word to use in this context): how much, to
what degree, do I want to, can I, should I, must I,
renounce renunciation? And what will the ramifications
be in the realm of art & jyze?
          -- Feels like rush hour now. Why? Just angle of
the sun? Difference in roar of the traffic? Circadian
vibrations, a stirring hunger? Literary shadows? (All

week I'm so happy (say) reading the massive tome on the classic lit of Lady U's ancestral tradition, I even do it in the tub with the bathboard working quite well to hold up that humongous library volume -- no danger, or anyway much smaller danger, of baptizing it with full immersion as I once did another library's collected works of a great city poet -- my own copy of which I'm also delightedly browsing through this very same week! -- But especially the massive tome for opening new angles on ancient romantic tales -- among them not only the one upon which my own Lady U tale in "Howler" is based but, it turns out, also my "Mr. Decadence" tale and therefore "Jyzer" itself by a kind of back formation. -- And then the same formidable authority on "The Tale of Lady O," which may be the ultimate source of the "Lady" term I first used for Lady U, who in my own private mythology is the last of the angels as well as a moon princess called Kaguya and the coffee picker's adopted daughter. -- What I'm actually trying to say with all this I don't know, but it's hard not to feel things coming together here. Which itself may be an artifact of running up against the big question concerning the pathway to salvation, but no less crucial to grapple with for that.)

*   *

Hey, Lady V, how you doin'?
Also her. For the past couple of weeks so pleased to be greeted by her photos on my desk here in the hideaway. I feel her love, I feel my love, I feel the craziness of it all (sure, after all these years) and still love every last bit of it just so long as I've still got that tether (or better to say it's got me, by which I refer to my back or at least my collar).
Pacing around for an hour or more out in the triangle, just in front of the entrance to this building, with the big totem pole and its oversize faces frozen in agony and horror, among other ways, looming behind me and the bust of the eponymous chief riding its plinth to my right -- the trees, the crowds, the vagrants (for one of whom I'm often mistaken, no doubt, now more than ever,

or should I just say spotted, as with a train? -- the
warm late sun -- and I'm pondering the matters of love,
renunciation, art, purity, morality, community -- all
the really good stuff of this moment -- thinking of
Lady V waiting for me up here and some letter of hers
from long ago accusing me of not wanting to give up
enough of myself and my time to her, to our love, to
meeting what she didn't hesitate to call her "desperate
needs."

     -- And now, is this a clue? Well of course, not
willing to renounce, not all the way. No man could've
loved anyone more than I loved her -- surely not -- but
still even today I sicken if I try to give up all of
myself. There must be a remnant, and not just any kind
of remnant but a deep remnant. The wild and unsocial
and amoral. The true core of pride and being. The
swagger zone. The heart of the artist. Even for art I
can't renounce this. Or another way of laying out the
paradox: "Follow the heart, yes, but protect the art."

     You, Lady V, how I still love you. Oho what an
ache! I'm looking deep, deep, deep into your eyes --
deeper than you'll ever know (or could you imagine such
weirdness as this?). Your eyes of ten years ago. You
in a jacket of what looks like silk, electric blue, no
doubt fashionable, and a red scarf, also probably silk,
and with your hair fluffed up in some chic-salonish way
I never saw you wear it during our time together,
nothing even faintly like it, but -- no matter. Your
broad smile, closed-mouth, those astounding lips. Those
mesmerizing eyes. (And what's that pinned to the lapel
of your jacket? Maybe a button or a couple of buttons,
political type, but I'm wondering if it could be a clip-
on mic.) -- And in the background a celebrated landmark.
You returning in triumph to the land of your birth and
your first fourteen years, give or take: an arc de
triomphant journey. Yes, I'm proud of you too.

     (Never mind what you wrote me ten years ago. I've
reread it several times and still find it bewildering.
Why would you react in such a way to my long letter?
Why the lectures and condescension? It's just about

impossible to fight through the bristling hostilities to
the underlying love, which nonetheless I sense is still
there. As for the mysticism and the advice about
letting all my "little categories" go -- forget it. My
"system." You don't know it but you're actually asking
-- no, demanding -- that I stop protecting myself and
give up my soul. -- You're no longer coming right out
and saying give it up to you, but this is surely what
you mean and always did. You who could not control your
cruelty! And admitted it! And I should give my soul up
to you for shredding? Forget it!)
     -- Though I did try over and over regardless. And
any regrets? None. Did follow my heart. Just know
better now in retrospect how far I can go. And for that
I have you to thank, Lady V. (For true love as I now
know it will always be "impure" enough to grant the other
a soul freedom, an invincible self, an impenetrable inner
turf to love from.)
     Still...how it can ache. It's aching now. I'm
loving your eyes and lips, Lady V. I'm loving your soul.
I'm reaching out for you with all my heart -- I'm
wrapping you in my arms and never letting you go. You
hear? You know? You still know?
     My flaw, I'm well aware. I couldn't and didn't and
won't let go. This is why I'm alone now and also why
I'm the jyzer I am and also why I still love you now and
not just you and it's also why they'll live on, this
love and these loves, after we're all gone, if I can
come up with words accurate enough and striking enough
to make them do so.
     The only salvation. Such as it is. The pathway to
which is for me the only pathway to be on. (And if this
sounds sappy to you, fair reader, up yours! -- That is,
you keep right on going up your own pathway, however
kinky it may be, and godspeed to you as I go up mine.)
                    *   *
     -- Back home. Later. To explain. I should
perhaps not end this entry on such a note, or better
never to have struck it at all, I suppose. But were I
to take such a notion seriously I'd have to tear up a

great many pages.

     (Wish I could have more dialogue in this jyze.
Some way or other. Less monologue, more dialogue. Will
see what I can do about this. -- But probably nothing.)

     As for unit B-2 here, at least no need to worry now
about it getting too messy or where everyone will sleep.
It's all mine now. Mine and mine alone. For jyze and
jyze alone. (Cool breeze. Jazz. Delicious. -- And
hardy fuchsias all still prospering and beckoning.)

     The other night at four-thirty a.m. some drunk
started messing with the buzzer panels outside the lobby
entrance -- trying to play them, it seemed, like a pair
of accordion button-boards. I was just drifting off to
sleep at the time and with so many windows open on that
warm night I could hear the buzz-honks going off in
bizarre rhythmic patterns all over the building. And
then the curses and screams. On and on this went.
Apparently nobody jumped out of bed and headed for the
lobby with a carving knife to chase away the mad
accordionist. Could be most of the tenants, like me,
are just happy to have the illusion someone's calling on
them, even at such an uncommon hour. Maybe for ten
minutes it continued.

     (I didn't mention it before but about ten days ago
I did read through all of Lady V's letters from our high
period twenty to twenty-six years ago (with many low
points and turbulent suspensions included therein).
Scores and scores of these letters and notes and poems,
and only a small fraction dated. I made a start at
ordering them chronologically. A long way to go, though.
In any event: this is what really set me off on Lady V.
She loved me once, she truly did. So much so that deep
down she must still. As likewise, of course, I must
love her still.)

     -- But I'm bad. Each of us is bad, V and I, but in
such preposterously different ways. And for just whom
is this not true? (Never mind. Wrong road to go down
right now.)

     Thumpety-THUNK, a truck hits the BUMP.

     So then what in the outside world do I have to look

forward to? Tomorrow I call the genealogy publisher.
Sunday Mindy, the building manager, is finally throwing
the long-promised barbecue out in the jyzeyard and oddly
enough it will be her going-away party: she's given her
two weeks' notice. I'm supposed to bring a salad.

Any possibility of something positive for me coming
out of this barbecue? Sure. But it's mighty slim. And
I don't think it'll be wearing boxing gloves, no.

Beyond that, just the last badly frayed Rikki
thread and the final few get-togethers with Lady U,
maybe spaced out over six months or so. But both of
these are for all intents and purposes nothing.

So there's the nightly buzz-honk heralding the
arrival of the indispensable news (or the crazy drunk
again, right, about to work up a new commotion).

And brother Rob. Rob will be my last active link
with any part of my former life that's also current.

Almost dinnertime, meaning two a.m. I'm looking
forward to this more than usual because it's albacore
night. The can and the can-opener are both already set
out on the kitchen counter: there's my proof.

29

Wearing this summer's indoor uniform of gray shorts
and green short-sleeve henley -- then slipping on my old
sandals -- I hobbled up the back staircase to the lobby
to check the mail. This just moments ago. Less than
ever am I expecting to find anything for me there these
days, but that doesn't stop me from making the hike.

And guess what: there was something! For me! And
not just a bank statement, though one of those too. A
package! Squeezed into the mailbox and just barely.

[Jyze and Jyze Alone]

Maybe that jar of plum preserves Rikki said she'd be
sending up, I thought while laboring to extract it.
     But no, it's something from sister Barb. Has the
heft and feel of a paperback book or two. Oh god no,
not more religious indoctrination -- another first
thought, and what's more a deistically inflected one.
     Hobble back down (sore right foot lately, maybe
from too much walking and jumping or maybe early onset
of the same arthritis that plagued, though that's
probably not the best verb -- can one say arthed? -- old
Mom's ankles). Green armchair. Sit on pattern of
slatted sunlight. Windowsill row of potted flowers
still looking good, and especially the miniature
snapdragon which has recently presented two spanking-new,
glistening almost, blooms. Fancy geranium good too, and
consistently so, as I keep neglecting to say, yet this
is undeniably important to me.
     -- Well, I'm surprised. Maybe hope can still
spring with Barb. Just this week I was thinking about
what to do if Barb and Keith ever proposed visiting.
First I'd say to Barb, I have an ultimatum of my own:
you must drop your ultimatum. I never welcome a visitor
who has me under ultimatum. Nor would you be under one
yourself, I'd go on, since mine would merely insist you
cancel yours and then would cease to exist unless yours
came back into existence first. (Though I did consider
demanding an apology as well. But why pick a fight?)
     (Pause to punch on the fan. Weather's heating up
again. Hot spell ahead for the weekend.)
     What it is, Barb's package, is a couple of novels
written by the rantingest of the leading Euromanics of
our era. A truly world-class Euromanic, I'd even say,
and for this or any era. Also a short letter written at
my old caffe-with-two-Fs hangout in her city (formerly
my city too as well as old Mom's) bearing no overt signs
of hostility -- a birthday greeting! Hope expressed by
Barb that no aftershocks have followed the breakup with
Lady U. Revelation of a bursitislike shoulder problem
of her own and a request for detailed description of the
magical exercise that cured old Mom's and my bursitis.

[Jyze and Jyze Alone]

Also new difficulties at her job, which she's
nonetheless still hanging on to though just barely.
     Yes, I will have to -- am moved to -- take some
positive step in return. Maybe send her a copy of
"Heart Anywhere" (which I enjoyed flipping about in
while traveling to the storage unit this week). Maybe
even a phone call. For I do have news to pass along.
     News! And more than one item!
     First, and crucially important for me, reporter
Naomi will be returning to work early next year. This
time she's talking about taking off just four months for
the birth! In any event my savings cushion ($6,810 and
change according to today's statement), along with the
income Jyzer Ink will be bringing in for doing reporter
Verna's grand jury, should be more than enough to tide
me over. Meaning: no need to look for a backup job!
     (Strings are still attached, though. The toughest,
most worrisome of these: will the new super-firm retain
the GJ contract? Naomi's early return itself should
help with that, though how much influence her husband
can bring to bear at the Department of Justice (where he
still works as an assistant U.S. attorney) I don't
really know. And best not even to consider the ethics
of it if he did. In any event: my anxiety level vis-a-
vis paid work will now sink to a low unseen in years.)
     News item two. "Memorials" may still be on track!
I finally got through to Suzanne at the publishers
(after a full week in which no one was answering the
phone there -- but just to know it hadn't been
disconnected was encouraging). Poor embarrassed Suzanne.
It seems they've been "bogged down" for the past couple
of months. And she'd been meaning to reply to the
letters of that other GPS (i.e., me) (i.e., her
company's initials are the same as mine, not to mention
Dad's, not to mention those of the Global Positioning
System devised by the ever-vigilant U.S. military -- and
I wonder, did any of these facts have anything to do,
perhaps unconsciously, with Mother's choice of this
outfit to submit the manuscript to in the first place?).
Well, I didn't want to make matters any worse or more

embarrassing for Suzanne. Mainly I wanted to know:
when? When would those bluelines promised so many
months ago be arriving? And she said: about a month
from now. Publication assured for later this fall.
     Hokay. Good. At least now (again) I have
something I can pass along to Barb, Rob, Shar, et al.
     -- And that's it for news items from the world
which I'm renouncing (but with an asterisk referring
down to this footnote qualification: "In my own way.
To my own extent. At my own speed.").
     (Now I'm writing across the pattern of slatted
sunlight -- or with it, rather. If I turn the J-book
counterclockwise about thirty degrees the slats align
with the blue-green lines on this page, superimposed, a
slat falling almost precisely on every other line.)
     The burning house of the world. Abandon it! Even
the hero of the world's very first novel was preparing
to do just that at the end, although he too was taking
his time about it and never did get around to it in the
book itself. (But thinking about this hero I was
reminded of the palace he built with apartments for the
women he'd loved and couldn't stop loving. Isn't this
exactly what I'm trying to do, at least in a way, with
my JIFT? "The Memory Palace of Jyzemaster G." My funds
are a bit short for building a real palace, and I'm not
too sure the beloveds would want to move in anyway, even
with lifetime free rent guaranteed. Even with a
contract specifying extensive if not exclusive conjugal
rights with the jyzemaster himself, or rights to avoid
all conjugality with him or anyone else if preferred.
In our present age the beloveds have better options than
they did a millennium ago in the era of that first
novel's composition and rightfully so and I'm a longtime
supporter of such options. -- But for me the memory
palace is a wondrous place I can retire to at any time
-- to keep the joint up. Improve it. Make it one of
the wonders of the world. Truly this is my pathway to
salvation. Consecrating myself to the god art, yes, but
this is a god of many names and aspects and the one I'm
talking about here is the newly -- as of some twenty-

nine months ago -- primary one for me: jyze.)
    -- And out there in the jyzeyard (visible through
partly canted blinds and luxuriant greenery, and so's
the familiar old redbrick backdrop four stories high)
was there a barbecue last Sunday? Supposedly. At noon.
I don't know, though, for sure, because I split. Sorry,
Mindy, but you should've started with the niceties a bit
earlier and then kept them coming during the final days.
Not for just anyone, not even for someone beating on my
door wearing shades and boxing gloves, do I take such a
drastic step. To me this barbecue began to look more
and more like an aspect of the "burning house" itself
rather than an R&R stop on the pathway to salvation. (I
may not have noted this before: "burning house" is what
ancient poets of a certain religious bent called the
world they were abandoning.)
    Lots of work for Jyzer Ink at the scope office
these days. (One more week and dayscoper Amy's out of
there for good.) Lots to do today, this being grand-
jury week and today a Thursday, usually the second day
of the fortnightly GJ sessions. I'm still faking it in
the same way with the horribly slow but "secure" laptop
which I'm supposed to be using; I'm actually doing all
the work on the much faster and more comfortable office
system, then shifting it back over to the laptop for
storage in the safe. Since no one's around to know I'm
doing this it doesn't seem to matter a whole lot. My
hunch is they're well aware of what I might be up to but
as long as they don't "officially" know, as long as they
can maintain typical high-muckety-muck deniability,
everything's fine. In other words, cover-your-ass time.
    As of this week, though, Jyzer Ink has stopped
paying the firm a dime per page for the privilege of
using its machines for doing their work, the rationale
being that the firm is no longer providing J. Ink with
the specific machines on which that deal was premised.
Also the firm has failed to meet its vow (made a couple
of months ago, to be carried out within a month) to come
up with a better alternative to the laptop. It's a
gamble, but I figure they probably won't even notice the

absence of those payments; and if they do, J. Ink has a strong case to make to them. Meanwhile I as the J. Ink CEO and workforce combined gain what amounts to a thirteen percent raise. (And this in itself is well justified, I figure, since they've boosted their rates by about twice that much since we reached our page-rate deal, which they haven't offered to adjust accordingly.)

 Cheat, steal, rob 'em blind. Is this the only way after all? Strict corporate logic? -- But no, I say what J. Ink is doing is fair. Why should we let the firm be the sole judge? They get away with what they can and fail to keep us informed about it, so we'll do likewise with them. Make the best we can of a bad situation. (But I'm not saying it couldn't be a helluva lot worse. I'm saying we must do what we can to keep it from actually being so.)

 Am I ready to hit the road? Just about. Change clothes, water plants, wind watch. (Still no lunch to pack. Lunch is off the menu and likely will remain so for quite a while. I'm enjoying going hungry. Except when I start feeling weak. Then I sometimes break down and pop another hunk of "day-old" raisin bread in the toaster. And what's more "butter" it with months-old thawed margarine -- which turns out to be not too bad.)

*   *

 -- Back in the slatted-sunlight seat again. Back where a friend is a friend (and what's more is the only friend you got, pal, so be extra kind). But because it's even hotter today the blinds, though raised a third of the way so some breeze can sneak in, are closed tight above that. Ergo at this juncture no slats to align the jyze with.

 A full day later, but otherwise everything's much the same. Blue shorts instead of gray, absence of slats -- that's about it. And today's hobble to the mailbox yielded nothing.

 Too much scoping work last night. By the time I dragged myself home at well past two, exhaustion. Dipping into the stacks of books and periodicals arrayed on the couch, reachable from here in the green armchair

without standing up, was all the system could bear.
(This armchair is it for the rest of the summer. Warm
weather makes the simulated leather of the loveseat too
sticky if you're not wearing a shirt and long pants, and
you'd have to be nuts to dress that way under current
conditions in here.) Still, pleasure almost euphoric,
reading in the gentle light of the floor lamp standing
behind my left shoulder as jazz plays softly at three
a.m., my head leaning back into the ever-growing cloud
of fuchsia leaves and blossoms, the window letting in a
light breeze through trembling fence-borne greenery
which brushes audibly against the screen at times, me
in just the gray shorts (then) with my legs outstretched
and propped up on the wooden footstool (currently
covered with the small frayed golden towel -- for years
a favored bedside "sperm rag" at U Acres but now
deployed to protect my bare feet from splinters).
-- And nibbling from a big bunch of red-flame grapes
resting in old Mom's beat-up tin colander, I believe is
what this contraption is called, which was serving the
same purpose for me half a century ago, almost, may the
gods help me, and especially if they're the jyze gods.

    A garden apartment is what this place really is,
lacking only a door with direct access to the garden
(for that you must tramp about seventy feet down the
zigzag hall) (climbing in and out the window behind the
loveseat would also serve, but even more awkwardly).

    Atop the stack of books another fat volume focusing
on the same lit tradition of Lady U's forebears by the
same awesomely knowledgeable authority. The premodern
era this time, up to a century and a half ago, featuring
some of the major heroes of jyze. This is the last of
the volumes I haven't read all the way through (though I
did bone up earlier on the figures I'm most interested
in) and I'm again using the library's copy even though I
have my own boxed up in storage. It's almost as if I
need the irritant of the book's return date hanging over
my head to spur a front-to-back reading.

    Also at the library I did some preliminary research
relevant to the memory palace. Most of this focused on

an attempt to dig up traces of Lady V's movieland career
after her first two films came out, or say after my last
letter from her when she was about to ratchet down her
career focus and marry the "nice boy." Despite diligent
digging I could find nothing. If she's still alive, and
still involved in film, it's almost certainly not in the
production end, or at least not at the same level as in
previous years. (This in itself may account for her
long silence: embarrassment after all the boasting about
director credits and big exploits ahead. As of this
year she apparently still has only the same two credits.)
     While browsing in the library's computer catalog I
looked up all the people I've known of roughly my own
age cohort who in my estimation might've published
something -- all the ones I could recall, anyway -- and
of these only two had actually done so and had books on
the shelves in the city library system. One was Joyce
A., who's co-authored a couple of books about sports.
And the other, oddly enough, was myself. Yes, the
politics/urban-ecology screed can still be checked out
from the downtown branch. But Lady V, Lady K, Lady C,
Fiona L., Jane C., Ken D., Jim G., Eva T., Marna H. --
no trace. Of all my friends and lovers really only Ray
W., as far as I can tell, has ever accomplished anything
significant as a writer. Though if she'd lived, I don't
doubt that Karen A. would've.
     (Reminding me: Ross W. the poet died this week. I
scarcely knew him, but he was always around during Mezzu
days and he was important to Lady S and comforted her
during our first brief separation there. Later that
same spring I sometimes saw his wife, Lori, a painter,
sneaking down into Brady's basement apartment directly
below mine -- could view her out the window as she cut
across the yard while I sat at my typewriter and could
hear the telltale sounds from below as the classical
music started up. Could also observe her guilty little
grins when she saw me seeing her as she entered or left.
So I must belatedly ask: why didn't she just sneak in
the back way if she didn't want me to know?)
     -- Buck up, pal.

[Jyze and Jyze Alone]

    Thinking of dreams. It could be my love life will
soon be limited solely to the phantoms of the dream
world. And I do mean by intention (though of course I'd
have little other choice regardless the way things have
been going lately). But dream romance does offer
certain distinct advantages. Chief among these is the
amount of time it takes out of your waking life, which
is to say: none. Nor do you lose any sleep over it, or
at least not much (waking up with a start is about it,
along with, of course, the time for getting back to
sleep). It's also attractive in its unpredictability
and variety. Who will show up next? (Last night it was
Monica R. from newspaper days. The night before, Lady U.
A few nights before that, Karen A. in a nightmarish
replay of the hours after the motorcycle accident. But
over the long haul Lady V appears far more than anyone
else, and sometimes in deeply moving ways. And this has
always been true -- for twenty years now.)
    Can I cultivate this dream life? Make something
jyzically interesting of it? Probably the way to start
would be to keep a dream notebook handy up in the loft.
So maybe I'll try that.
    In real life the action does indeed seem to be over.
Again this is so at least partly by my own choice, and
again it's a matter of weighing trade-offs. It's not
that romance is impossible but that I'd have to give up
way too much to boost to a tolerable level the odds that
it would be interesting and fulfilling. The emotional
satisfaction available from concentrating on my work
(and perhaps on my dreams) looks like a far better bet.
-- Nor am I saying this is necessarily for all time. A
literary breakthrough or a stroke of luck could
significantly change the odds. But I intend to act as
if the matter were settled. I don't want to have to be
rehashing it all the time. Of course I may not be able
to stop myself. And if that's the case, so be it.
    Lady U I still haven't heard from. It's been
almost two months now. (Except for the dream, in which
she called my name from a crowded car as it roared by.)
Rikki, nothing more from her, nor have I written back,

nor does Barb's letter mention her, which I'd expect it
to do unless she had some reason to believe Rikki's not
interested in seeing me again, since at prior times Barb
was all but openly urging me to go after her. So I'm
still temporizing on how to handle Rikki. And Sofie,
only in dreams do I see her even though we still live
just a couple of hundred feet apart (or at least her
name still appears on the co-op roster posted by its
street door). In dreams Sofie and I get along quite
well, we're even lovers, although we have yet to be
assigned an erotic scene that I can recall. And
recalling erotic dream scenes is one of my favorite
things to do, so I doubt Sofie's shown up in any.
-- Day dreams, that's different, of course. But here
I'm talking about night-dreams-while-asleep only.
    -- And so. How about some other topic, eh?
    All right. Thinking. For changes we've got the
big dance club two blocks south on the edge road going
under, for unspecified reasons probably having to do
with the numerous drug busts that have taken place in
its parking lot; and so the weekend nightlife scene in
the hood is considerably less hypercharged, though this
is likely only temporary. We've got the wellness clinic
next door to my Jyzer Ink hideaway also closing down:
name scrubbed off the door and suite empty except for a
phony desk setup and a framed print (atrocious water
lilies) hung on the wall and visible through the door
glass twenty-four hours a day above a table lamp that's
always lit (presumably for realtor lease purposes).
We've got a mighty battleship packing up and heading
for the harbor near Lady U's family home, where it will
become a permanent tourist attraction, which to me
sounds like the right way to go for this particular
eyesore, but of course jingo city (a/k/a the transit
port) is aghast to lose it (to which I say, as I always
like to say to that place, Up yours, foul burg!).
    For routines we've got not a damn thing new.
Nothing anyway that jumps up at this moment with hand
wildly waving. Still Saturday for the supermarket,
Monday for the public market, all meals at home, no

cafes or nightlife except for briefly pressing my nose
against various windows on the way home. Certainly no
movies or anything like that. -- Oh, a meekly waving
hand: the milk revolution. To save four bits a week and
cut back on trips to our local grocery store next to the
pocket park I'm now buying whole milk there by the quart
instead of the pint and two percent milk by the gallon
instead of the quart. Before I started taking all meals
at home I couldn't buy the larger quantities because the
milk would go bad. Now I can because I use it up faster.
Significant savings: meaning more morale-boosting impulse
treats can be indulged in, such as this week's big bunch
of red-flame grapes.
    Granted: nothing earthshaking here. But how many
times does jyze want the earth to shake in a single
volume? (Think of the grandmaster of idleness. Think
of the builder of the most famous writing shed of them
all. Think of the celebrated lusty poet-priest. And
while thinking of them, stay mindful of all those
literary terms which can't even be translated -- they
have to be referred to using the original terms printed
in italics. In other words: maintain ties to the long
tradition. Remember "The Account of My This" and "A
Year in My That." -- For these are the matters, people,
ideas, works that come to mind most often these days
when I'm thinking of the fundamental things, meaning
those which may need some shaking from time to time but
by and large do not. But then again, almost proving the
point, jyze wrestled with these very things last year
and the year before, probably using close to the
identical words, so no need to go into them any further
now.)

30

Hold everything. The shining jyzemaster has found
a loophole in his renunciation contract. He's appealed
to the gods of cyberia and received a stay. A pause at
the entrance of the pathway to salvation. A leave in
the world before leaving the world. A last mad dash
into the burning house to see if anything remains to be
salvaged.

And this the act of a newly double joker. Entry
number thirty on another thirtieth that's steeped with
personal significance. (Oyez, oyez.) Here at the old
punk hangout on the route to the north turf pole, simply
because it's become a jyze tradition of sorts to end a
volume where it began, and especially the crucial middle
volume (more in need of a beginning and an ending than
are the beginning and ending volumes, which after all
have a beginning, for the first volume, and an ending,
for the last one, built right in). Or else call this
place the local annex of the most happening club of the
past decade or two on the biggest entertainment strip in
the world capital of mega-cities at least until recently,
since that's the club I've joined as of today. And I
don't mean the 21 club. I'm referring to a studio, yes.
And a fully full deck, both jokers included and all
stoked up, ready for a vigorous shuffling.

-- Thinking the last time I saw my father alive he
was just the age I've turned today. (And how many
chapters in the world's first novel before the hero
abandons, a reader must presume, the world and the
memory palace? The same number as the studio I've
joined today. And how many chapters in that other

ancient novel about an amorous fellow who in the end
sails off to the island of memory? That same number.
So watch out.)

     -- I'm not being coy about this number or any of
the other details. I'm simply following the jyze rules.
Violate a single one and (given my current emotional
state) all hell could break loose.

     -- And thinking this is the first birthday of mine
for which my mother is not present in the world.

     Later a spirit party at the only home I know. For
now this stop on the road to the supermarket. Good
brother Rob sent over a gift certificate for twenty-five
bucks from -- that same supermarket. This is a man who
understands his brother's needinesses! (At four p.m.
only a couple of patrons and a bartender in here, the
self-proclaimed world championship of baseball for teams
of boys thirteen and fourteen years old ("ponies")
playing out soundlessly on all three tubes and an odd
mix of old and new music spinning out loudly on the box.
As buses roll up just outside and discharge numerous
folks and take on a few others and roar away (or glide
away for electrics). This year my big day happens to
fall at the start of Labor Day weekend and thus the
crowds are arriving for the monster end-of-summer music
festival at the old fairgrounds right next door, and
appearing on the main stage there tonight will be not
only an incomparable warbler with her memories of
walking with her baby by the bay of my own late-teenage
swoons but also -- all this live! -- the reunion gig of
the only punk band I ever really listened to. Which
broke up in the very year I was infatuated with that
same warbler just because of what she sang about and
where I was listening to it. Or was that the next year?
-- And did I care yet about the punk band? If so, only
because Lady V did. And do I care now? Same answer.)

     So what's all the excitement about here? Just
this. While nosing around at the library I came upon
a so-called national telephone index, a computerized
directory that allows the user to look up names,
addresses, and phone numbers of anyone with a listed

phone anywhere in the country. I'd heard about this
index before but never checked it out, pretty much
forgot about its existence, though I remained aware the
technology was available. Just -- now I decided why not
give it a fling. (But I did deliberate first, and for
several days. Open this can of worms or not?)

    Wow, instantaneous results. Two big ones. Type in
Lady V's last name (married name) and immediately it's
right there on the screen along with a city name (same
one as before, just as her married name's still the same,
in fact the same since before I even knew her) and a
phone number, but no street address. And then Lady K's
name: a phone number and address. -- No guarantee this
is the same person I knew but the location on the far
coast is the type of place where I'd expect her to be,
about halfway between the suburb where she grew up and
the small city where she went to college and where we
met.

    (Other interesting results included a Briana T.
living near where the Briana T. I knew used to live and
a Chester S. (my own last name!) in, of all places, one
of the real-world models for Mentoka Falls. Addresses
for Ken D., Ray W., a number of old Mezzu and city 2/7
pals. But nothing for Miko, Sachi, Marta R., Patty S.,
Janie T., Jill R. Too many Colleen D.'s and not a
single Ciara D. (both are Lady C, I should note). And
all the information appears somewhat dated: my name
wasn't on there, for instance, but my mother's was, that
is, as a putatively living person.)

    So for the past couple of days since hitting on
this index I've been mulling the key question. What to
do with the new info? Try to reopen channels or not?
Would doing so derail me, my work? Hidden dangers here?
And I've decided what the hell, let's go ahead and see
what happens. I'll give myself until the end of the
year, that is, one full JIRT volume, which of course
will be Book III of this annal. If nothing's there,
return to the renunciation program: use it as a theme
for next year's JIRT annal. Gives me something to fall
back on, look forward to, such as it is and/or perhaps

will be.

Meanwhile, regardless, I'm all set for the renounced life. The new jyze dreambook's in place and though I didn't record any dreams this week, I did coax Lady V into visiting me twice in that realm (in one of them we were trying to decide whether to get married, and unlike the case in real life, I was the one doing the pleading). In rereading a short classic woman's novel I learned that a traditional trick to lure a lover into appearing in a dream is to wear your nightshirt to bed reversed. I'm intending to do just that. I may not even wait until the end of the year to try it.

And the work, my own work, is looking good. The last two years of the chronbook urjyze and the first of the journal protojyze, I checked into all three and came away elated. Some great stuff in there! Possibly this discovery is what's instilling the confidence necessary for me to take on the contemporary avatars of the real-life Ladies V and K. (And should I go for two at once? Why the hell not? We're not talking purity here. It's way, way, way too late for that.)

Rikki too. The plum preserves arrived so I'm not writing her off completely just yet. But no message accompanied them -- not one single word; not even "Enjoy!" -- so my hopes will be as slim as before. No, not true. Even slimmer, because hopes are being drawn off in other directions now and my overall supply is drastically limited.

Shall I wander on? Sun's begun hitting this window booth, late but still hot. Some jagged crude industrial art hanging in the window, colored glass and steel, electrified, not at all the kind of thing you'd want to get cozy with. Still only two other patrons in here, and not the same two as before. Mobs will descend tonight, though, most likely, with the festival drawing tens of thousands within easy staggering distance.

-- And what for my birthday feast? Brother Rob in his card insists I use the certificate on something special along the lines of what old Mom would want for me. Maybe ice cream, shortcake, berries of some kind or

maybe peaches if any good ones are available. Let's
see. Some wine for sure, since I can drink it with Rob
one of these days. (He's decorated his staircase walls
with old family photos and portraits going all the way
back to John of G. That's six hundred years!)
*   *

So here it comes, end of the volume. Home now, the
spirit birthday party. A jazz party and a jyze party
but this year not a blues party. By proclamation. But
mainly because that's just how it happens to be.

Had a hard time finding a match to light the
candle, then worried about the smoke alarm. Meanwhile
gobbling strawberry shortcake here at the redwood table
(specially cleared for the occasion) (and I'll note I
bought peaches too -- first of the year for me -- but
none are ripe enough to eat). The lamp's on and the ice
cubes are crackling quietly in the drink. Only my
second real drink since I moved in (meaning hard liquor
imbibed in B-2) or is it the third maybe?

First birthday in nineteen years for which Lady U
hasn't been present. So let her spirit be among the
invited guests. Mother, Dad, Lady U, Rikki, Ladies V,
K, C, and S, Karen A., Briana T., Tom T., sister Barb
(grudgingly), brothers Jeff and Rob. And son Elgie too,
sure, though he wouldn't even know me. And Unk Erik.
Anyone else? I think not. (A nifty essay in the
current issue of a journal I no longer receive but read
today standing up at the small chain bookstore -- the
chain Rob works for! -- near the north-pole supermarket.
It explored a certain poet's discovery, while writing
screenplays, of exciting uses of self-reflexive voices,
one voice denying what another has said. I too have hit
on this gambit and what's more with no help from
screenplay writing. Certainly jyze, without such voices
and method, would not be jyze.)

As tradition decrees, the array of gifts is set up
on the table just for this occasion. Rikki's plum
preserves, right there. Barb's novels written by the
hateful world-class Euromanic ranter. Rob's card (and
without his thoughtful generosity, no strawberry

277

shortcake and possibly, since my morale might've been
much lower, no party). And finally my gifts to myself,
two more books: one about truth in aesthetics (which is
already looking like a clunker) and the other a
collection of essays addressing the alleged crisis of
the written word caused by the proliferation of digital
technology.

(Am I some sort of Luddite because I have no
working computer of my own, no e-mail address, no web
browser and no interest in any of the above? Not at all.
It's just that for me these items would be pretty much
useless right now and I can't afford them anyway and
don't need the distraction or the excitement -- this
last-named also being, as it happens, the reason a
number of celebrated writers cited a century ago for
shunning the then recently invented dictaphone. -- And
just a few days ago I was thinking that this is really
the first time I've ever had all the major elements of
my life under control, or anyway it's the closest I've
ever come. But now the computerized national telephone
index at the library may've undone all that, who knows.
I who had said I was open to romance but had neglected
to add "if it can find me." In fact I'd written twice
in almost identical language, I noticed in reviewing
these Book II pages, that romance would simply be, in
essence, too expensive. And it may still be so. Guess
I could be finding out during the four months ahead.)
(And all those fine writers who never knew what it was
to be a double joker. Whose decks not only lacked
jokers but weren't even complete. The amorous haiku
grandmaster, dead at a minus playing card. So thank my
lucky stars -- and thank the Old Bull too, standing right
here beneath Mother's warmly glowing table lamp next to
the plant mister and the colorfully hand-painted and
endlessly amusing ceramic-chicken pitcher.)

An hour ago I was hanging out at the digi-cafe, my
first visit there of any kind in maybe a month. Live
jazz, same quintet as before. Very fine. I sat in the
same armchair in the same cluster near the entrance and
sipped from a highly similar schooner of root beer and

dashed off an almost entirely fictive letter to Rikki.
I didn't want her feeling sorry for me, did I? Better
to go out in a blaze of glory. Or at least I was trying.
I gave her a couple of big juicy smacks on the lips (and
since her spirit is here for the party, I'll give her a
couple more right now: SMACK SMACK) but also said in
this letter I recognized we probably wouldn't be meeting
again. I was openly pessimistic about it. And this
represented my true feelings. I intended the letter as
a kind of farewell. The truth is we just don't have
what it takes. Or so it appears to me given what has
and hasn't happened so far, plum preserves or no plum
preserves (though I certainly did thank her for those --
for one thing, they're very tasty).

Before that I called Rob from a booth at the ORB
cafe -- first time I've been down there since the run-in
with the mad newspaper clipper. Rob, still the only
human contact I have with whom I exchange more than a
few words on any one occasion (though he doesn't know
this; for him too I have to contrive some fictions --
though only hinted at; not outright dissimulation -- so
we'll be able to relate in a way not too abnormal).
Talked twenty minutes or so. The poor guy, he was
probably thinking, meaning him thinking about me.
Alone on his birthday. After a traumatic breakup and
relocation. After our mother's death and our sister's
putdowns and ultimatum and all the troubles with his
(my) job. -- So we'll be getting together again next
Saturday night, Rob and I, and already I'm pondering
what he might like to eat. Pea soup with added turkey
ham -- been there, choked that down. Maybe soy
grillers? And the get-together falls on a jyzeday --
the first of Book III -- unless all does not go well.

*

-- Just freshened the drink and also the ink.
Thinking while I was at it: boy, for these last four
pages of Book II have I got my jyze work cut out for me!
And also: would ol' Mom ever be able to make hide or
hair out of this volume which after all is dedicated to
her? Most likely not. (And not to deny, I also

279

wondered: what would Lady K's reaction be? What if I
wrote to her in the same half-crazed free-associational
style I just broke out for Rikki? For sure she would
think the boy has gone through some big changes in the
several decades since our parting. And probably also:
sad, sad, he who at one time seemed to show such promise
(or was that just her hormones telling her so?). -- Of
course she may've tumbled to a few changes herself.
-- And even if this Lisa K. turned up by the phone index
isn't the right one, I think I'll go ahead and try to
track down the right one, maybe through her college alum
office if I can't think of any better way. "Just for
the jyzey jyze of it."

So should I then postpone contacting Lady V? After
all? A special issue of a recent quarterly devoted to
"art and ethics" has helped me to see once again the
links between Lady V's self-justifications for her
spells of extreme nastiness, I'll call them, during our
time together and what one of the writers calls "S/M
nihilism." I mean this is strong stuff we're talking
about here, not just a hiccup or two in some saccharine
pop-song cliche romance. At a downtown chain bookstore
tonight I was checking out several works by the dubious
Hollywood spiritualist whom Lady V was suddenly
championing a decade ago -- found him aptly enough in
the "Guru" section. Would Lady V and I even be able to
stand each other now? Had I not better, after all, take
them, the two ladies, one at a time?

I'm pondering. But I expect I'll just charge
heedlessly ahead. Best to get all this out of the way
so I can return to work on the memory palace. -- In
which Lady U will certainly have a room, by the way, an
"apartment," but for now the unit reserved for her is
uninhabitable and I expect it'll stay that way for quite
a while before I can get around to scrubbing it down and
refurbing it. I'll want to make sure all the other
tenants are comfortable first before I take on someone
new. All the other major Madam Exes, I'm saying.

(Not that I don't love Lady V anyway. Don't let me
lead myself astray here! Of course I do! -- Her one

good film having first borne the more Lady V-like title,
I just learned through my library research, "Red on
Red." After that came "Torn," a title which she
borrowed from me, as I no doubt had borrowed it from
someone else. Then she changed it briefly to "Street
Life," but this, it turned out, had been used fifty
years earlier, and it also sounded too much like the
title of a near-contemporaneous film (which ironically
is about those same J. City street kids I used to have
to elbow aside to get into the downtown mom-and-pop
stores on my way to the scope office), so she settled
for "Torn" after all. -- And then they were advising
her to write a novel about her boggling life. Is that
perhaps what she's been up to for the past decade? I
also wonder, because the phone index comes up with no
hits on her son's name, has he perhaps died? Does she
maybe have AIDS? Has she become some sort of movieland
functionary and thus is ashamed? Why didn't she ever
write back after I sent her that "Star" stamper as a
wedding gift? I must, I absolutely must know the reason
before I renounce this life for good. -- Or maybe take
up exclusively with a dream or a ghost Lady K, who knows.
-- Lady K who is now mostly Lena to me, because that's
who she is in "Jyzer.")
     Whew, vertigo. Birthday entry nearing its end.
Must mention my intention -- and shrug off the lapse
into doggerel, because I'm on a birthday high and I
ain't just second-jokering! -- Intention to -- what?
Think. Drink. No. Think? Can't. -- Confusion
flapping in....
     Okay, got it: intention to lay out for the ghouls
my last will and testament. (Isn't "last will" enough?
Or just "will"? What's this with "testament"? Or is
that, could that be, jyze itself? As in some funky
quirky jyzey testifying?)
     Any rate, this I must do sometime soon before
setting off down the pathway. (Does the woman whose
work I'm about to read, she being eight hundred years
dead and yet another stellar product of Lady U's lit
tradition, choose the same pathway? Don't know yet, but

I'll be surprised if she doesn't.) Soon otherwise how
will anyone know anything, given my intended absolute
reclusion and renunciation -- all else failing, of
course -- but failing how? This "how" always -- of
course! -- the only matter of real interest anyway.
    Egad, what a way to end this one. End this first
day of yet another new age. Flying out of control, yeah,
but following the pathway regardless, I do hope and do
so intend, at least to the extent one can testify to
one's own true intent (and why the hell not try?).
    Happy birthday, Jyzer G!

BOOK III

[For Jyze You Know You Must]

31

          "Hey man, what you want?"
          "Slab'a jyze t'go."
          "You got it."
          Nah, nobody's ordered up any jyze. Not yet. But
I'm rehearsing just in case.
          -- This on the historic front steps. Totem pole
and all, and the black iron-grillwork gate behind me is
closed because today's Saturday, though come to think of
it the gate would be just as closed at this hour any
other day. Dinner hour. Also about an hour before
brother Rob's due to meet me here. Pigeons staggering
around at my feet. Jacket laid out across my bag -- for
the first time since spring I've been carrying it with
me all week, and have even worn it a few times. New
forest-green hooded canvas jacket. (Still a thrill.)
          But oh what a wrenching week. Talk about
staggering. Not until yesterday did I find some
equilibrium again.
          Agonizing over what to do about the jyze -- the
jyze -- what's the word? (It's lost. Not revanchism.
Not -- oh never mind what it's not.) -- But what to do
about contacting Ladies K and V. Charge heedlessly
ahead on both, as last entry I said I thought I might?
Rethink? Take them seriatim?
          (Meanwhile it's possible I'm about to embark on a
long vacation, say about four or five months. Reporter
Naomi is going in Tuesday to give birth, cesarian I
presume since it's scheduled in advance (duh). Reporter
Verna, meanwhile, Naomi tells me in a note, has backed
out on doing grand jury, so most likely ex-partner Una

                            285

will be filling in while Naomi's away. But it's not at
all certain Una will want to use Jyzer Ink for GJ
scoping, especially now with -- here's another reversal
that's bad, bad news -- my nemesis, dayscoper Amy, hired
back on for the new office crew. And given the horrors
of scoping Una's stuff I'd say J. Ink would almost
rather do without the business. But then I'd have no
legitimate excuse to go in to the scope office --
instead would have to sneak up there to use the machines
for my personal work or just give up on doing revisions
that way for the interim, the four or five months.
-- Oh well. Some other time for chewing on this.)

So Labor Day weekend I agonized. Did none of the
real work at all. Realized I could easily lose my
balance once again just as in the old days. -- Wrote
Lady V a letter while riding the ferries to the storage
port, even resolved to send her a passage from last
month's jyze (the one in which the jyzer talks to her
picture) but then while leaning against the railing
along the new jingo-city boardwalk (where the blackberry
festival was in progress and the warships all spiffed up
for the occasion) I realized I couldn't go that route.

So at the storage unit later that same afternoon I
dug up all of Lady V's letters from the post-breakup era
and reread them. Some dozen or so, and to my surprise
they didn't come to a complete stop until seven years
ago, just about when Lady U and I were taking up
backcountry living. But I was also reminded of why I
might've suppressed all memory of those last few years
of letters (which is to say, the last few letters). The
tone she took with me. The kind of person she seemed to
have become. Name-dropping show-biz jet-setter Lady V.
Her wild exploits so tackily boasted about. Her failure
to respond in anything like an equivalent way to my long
letters -- including a sixteen-page critique of her
"Still Crazy" screenplay, typewritten and single-spaced
with tiny margins and done at her urgent request.

(Atavism is the word I wanted back there near the
beginning. Jyze atavism. -- Spacing out the word is
itself a kind of atavism, feels like. -- And it's a

word that might someday prove useful with Lady U also.)
     But no, I didn't want to plunge into anything
"still crazy" with Lady V now in my year of already
sufficient existing craziness. I wanted to proceed much
more cautiously. So I hit on a different kind of plan.
The twentieth anniversary of our parting would be coming
up in late October, so I'd hold off for six weeks and
use the anniversary as a pretext for getting in touch
with her. And I'd keep the message real simple. A
short note, maybe some flowers. And wouldn't even
include my address; make her work a little if she wanted
to reciprocate. Let her request it from telephone
information for my city (since the postmark would reveal
the city of origin, and it's the same one I was living
in when she and I were last corresponding) or she could
call sister Barb to get it (as she did once before,
initiating the six-year series of sporadic letters).
     (The retro lounge's sidewalk cafe fully occupied to
my right. Two new tour groups just trooped by, one
right after the other. I can hear the spiel directed at
the second group now gathered around the near end of the
pergola and gazing up at the great white antiquarian
skyscraper. -- And see by my pocket watch it's only
half past six, so I have more time than I thought. But
then again Rob's probably busing in, so he could appear
at any moment. -- And for dinner I'll be offering him a
choice of tuna helper, grillers, chicken patties, or
chicken pot pie (to tie up a loose thread from last
time). -- And then blackberry shortcake. And maybe
we'll work up some sort of card for brother Jeff, whose
birthday falls next Sunday. -- Using for this purpose
the new tempera paints I bought this week so I can make
posters featuring jyze titles for the apartment walls.)
     So I came up with a tentative message for Lady V.
No question I was under the influence of the poetry
tradition of Lady U which itself was and still is under
the influence of Lady V's own tradition (on her mother's
side, that is). In any case the first attempt was way
too sappy and provocative, not to say ridiculous:
     Twenty years today since I last saw

[Jyze and Jyze Alone]

          your tear-stained face. -- With fierce
          love always.   -- G
Through a series of modulations I've wound up with this
(shorter, safer, blander):
          Twenty years ago today we parted.
          Hope all's well with you. Peace & Love.

                         -- G
It was rediscovery of the unfailingly useful all-purpose
counterculture-era sign-off "peace & love" that somehow
brought things back into balance. -- Of course further
changes in message may lie ahead. And I may or may not
throw in some flowers. And I should check the phone-
index number for Lady V to see if it's really hers.
(One possibility just occurring to me: the number might
be for a message phone. She could be living part or
most of the year on the other side of the world. Who
knows. Anything's possible. This is Lady V!) -- But
basically the whole business is, to repeat, going on
hold for a month. See how it sits.
      (A little chill creeping into the air. Also a few
dry brown leaves scraping by. Football season getting
underway. From the convenience store several doors
down I can hear the owner's exclamations as he watches
a game on the tube. "Aigoo!" (Yes, as in Lady S's
ancestral lingo. "Ouch!" would be my translation.)
-- And the presidential campaign's starting up in
earnest (so to speak). And a powerful hurricane is
battering the far coast. And in the past few days our
cruise missiles, this country's -- my country's! -- have
leveled targets in yet another far-off land as part of
our outrageous never-ending world-domination crusade.
-- And enough for that line of thought.)
      -- But I still like this scene here. A bunch.
Feel I fit right in. Big trees, slow traffic,
cobblestones, old brick. Leaning against the cement
base of a marble column, part of the arched doorway
frame: it is, I am.
      So then. (Soon I'll have to be abruptly cutting
this off, I expect.) So then -- Lady K. Yes, better to
try her first. Reach out for her. I thought about it a

288

lot and could see no reason not to go ahead. Especially
I like the symmetry, the formal neatness, Lady K
appearing in the very first entry ("chron") of my urjyze
life and now again in its "mature" form after it's
morphed twice, first into the daily proto stage and then
into true jyze (and true jyze in both current forms,
JIRT and JIFT, since as Lena she remains a key character,
along with Lady S as Yo, in the fictojyze "Jyzer"). ---

*   *

  This is not how I expected to be doing it next.
Nor is it the mood. Far from it. But maybe in a mood
like this, jyze, refracted through it, can prosper.
  At what I'm calling the worktable. Same one where
I was celebrating last week (the party of the second
joker). And last night too, with Rob, right here, it
being now almost a full day since he strolled up as I
was jyzing on the hideaway building's front stoop.
  Certainly it's not Rob's fault. The other half of
the Jyze Brothers duo. He even told me I don't look
anywhere near as ancient as I've just become (though we
passed most of the evening talking wills and testaments,
and specifically what he's to do if I croak unexpectedly,
since he's now the best one to do it -- in fact pretty
much the only one). Chicken pot pie, peach (not
blackberry) shortcake, chardonnay courtesy of Bart Y.'s
memorial a few weeks ago at the scope office. And right
here on the worktable are a couple of Rob's pipe
cleaners, the same kind I delighted in fashioning into
stick figures as a kid when Gramps was the supplier.
Rob brought me his copy of a volume of classic protojyze
from a century and a half ago and I gave him my copy of
a different protojyzer from roughly the same era and an
adjacent land (a used copy I'd just bought for him this
week because I'm reading the library's copy and, though
I'm only about thirty pages into it, I'm impressed).
And here are the jars of tempera intended for decorating
the card to Jeff we never did get around to working up.
(Rob had already bought a card of his own for Jeff -- a
second copy, he confessed, of the one he'd sent me, but
he couldn't help himself because he liked it so much.)

289

[Jyze and Jyze Alone]

    So it's not Rob's doing. Not anyone's! Just mine.
Sometimes you turn grumpy, who can say why.
    (The ceramic-chicken pitcher with its bright yellow
beak. The Old Bull. The fat dictionary. Various books
I've been chipping away at. Gramps's brass ashtray now
bearing Rob's pipe cleaners and some spindly blackened
dead matchsticks. Two place mats. Two wooden
candleholders. Emergency radio that still doesn't work
even with new batteries. Cigar box containing all my
personal correspondence of the past six months, leaving
lots of room to spare. Supermarket flyer with coupons
waiting to be clipped. Salt and pepper shakers devoid
of salt and pepper, as I was surprised to discover when
Rob asked if I had any. Dish of hard candies, dark-dark-
cherry flavor, one and only one doled out per day,
ritualistically, always a quotidian high point. Pathetic
package of cheapo brewery coasters with Rikki's name
written on it, originally set aside in anticipation of
the promised visit which she scrubbed last month. Jar of
ballpoint pens and felt-tip markers, most or maybe all
being of the almost-defunct type you can neither use with
confidence nor throw out without doubt. Oh, and the
community-college catalog Lady U has still failed to pick
up or even ask about.)
    -- As lists go it may not be up to those of the
masters but it's the very best jyze can do under the
time/space/mood constraints of this entry.
    So Lady K. I was talking about the appealing
symmetry of getting back in touch with her. A couple of
times I dreamed about her. More to the point (what
point!) I fantasized embracing her, for a long time and
silently, standing, and in my own mind it was to be
happening right here, behind where I sit now, center of
the room, the nerf court, and my fantasizing self was
observing this from the green armchair, and with my eyes
slightly narrowed it almost seemed I really could see it
happening out there. This obviously deeply attached
couple in which I myself made up roughly a two-thirds
share (bulkwise) was swaying and slowly moving about
with tiny dance steps inside a square no more than

eighteen inches on a side. For some reason I was
wearing a white dress shirt open at the collar and brown
"slacks" (a word I can't even say with a straight face
anymore). She was in that little powder-blue dress I
always liked so much. It looked to me as though we were
having us a wonderful time. I'm not kidding: it nearly
brought tears to my (wondering) eyes.

So I did send off a letter to the Lisa K. I found
in the phone index. Quite a goofball production it was,
the "That Lisa K." Sweepstakes ("That" underlined), an
explanatory letter with a postage-paid card enclosed on
which to check off the appropriate box, then mail back.
"Yes, I'm that [underlined] Lisa K. and please send me
my prize right now." Even a box for writing in a
personal detail known only to the jyzer ("U-pick-it")
and thus "proving" her identity. And I figure the reply
could come any day now -- maybe even tomorrow.

But, alas, I already know this Lisa K. won't be
"that" Lisa K. Further investigation via the phone
index revealed that the Lisa K. I was writing to lives
at the same address as one Anthony K., same last name,
probably her husband, so almost certainly K. would not
be the probable wife's maiden name. The Lisa I know has
no brother and her father's name is not Anthony (it's
Phil or Herb; at this point I can't remember which is
his real name and which is the fictive name I use in
"Jyzer"). I suppose a slim chance exists that this
phone-index Lisa could be "that" Lisa with Anthony being
her son or a relative. But this chance is so slim, and
so many other Lisa K.'s and L.K.'s are listed, and the
likelihood is so great that the real "that" Lisa has a
different last name now and can't be found through the
index, I'm planning to call her college alum office this
week and see if I can talk them into divulging her
whereabouts. (What'll my cover story be so they won't
think I'm some sort of stalker? Don't have one yet.
-- But a stalker is most assuredly what I am, though of
a somewhat offbeat and presumably harmless variety.)

Going the alum-office route, however, is not
appealing. I like the phone-index approach much better,

the sheer serendipity of it as well as the directness.

    A frightening thought: had the kid been born on
schedule, the one the real Lisa and I conceived, he or
she would be turning thirty along about now, i.e., this
month. (And sure, maybe the kid is out there somewhere.
Maybe the abortion never really took place. What proof
do I have?) And at my age plus eight months what would
Lisa herself be like now? Would she too be fortunate
enough to have a sibling say she looks much younger than
her real age? (Rob also said, when I revealed my plan
to contact Lisa, that she was "the first of your
girlfriends I fell in love with," which I thought was
truly touching, since he was only eleven years old at
the time. And in turn I recalled how fond Lisa had been
of him, especially during her weeklong visit to Gatewood
the summer after our graduation. And the modest and
tactful Rob replied, "That was only because I reminded
her of you.") -- But I'm afraid she'll have become a
suburban matron. I'm afraid she'll view me as having
become all the things she most feared I would become and
least wanted to have anything to do with. The virtual
derelict. Living alone, broke, unloved and little
published except for journalism, and worst of all not a
single white picket to my name (for the fence around the
suburban yard, I'm talking, the one she so insistently
let me know she couldn't live without).

    And as Rob pointed out (not that I hadn't thought
of this on my own) it's quite possible Lisa has chosen
to make herself scarce to her alum association, just as
he and I have done with ours.

    But I'm determined to give it a try. And it's
likely this determination is somehow a source of my sour
mood. I just sense it.

    -- Meanwhile someone did try to get ahold of me by
phone this week. Bizarrely, sort of, this was also for
anniversary purposes going way back, and for the very
same number of years: thirty. Saundra N., I think was
the surname initial, an employee of my old muckraking
counterculture/antiwar "alternative" newspaper, wanting
to update her info on me for a "Where Are They Now?"

feature on the occasion of the paper's thirtieth
anniversary. Two calls, in fact, two messages, and I
returned neither, and then presumably the deadline
passed. -- Of course I'm too embarrassed to let them
know what I've been up to and even more what I haven't
been up to since leaving the paper. I shouldn't be but
I am. I'm also feeling freshly maltreated by the
editor/publisher (still the same Mike M.) simply because
I've recently reread parts of my protojyze account of
that period. Totally unjust of me to feel this way now,
or at least seriously outdated. But this is how it is.
     Another source of sourness? I'd say so.
                         *
     I dunno. Just cracked open a package of fig bars.
Jumped around. Brooding: do I really even want to
bother with all this real-life contacting of the ancient
loves? Or wouldn't I rather just settle in upon myself,
as it were, and work very, very hard? See where it
takes me? Do the best I can to avoid all distraction?
Do whatever I must to stay afloat financially? (But
maybe preferring to spend a chunk of the deep reserves
to pay for the writing time rather than hunt up another
job, should that seem to be the only other choice?)
     Jyze gods, tell me what to do.
     With Ladies K and V too, as with the old newspaper,
I suppose the real catch is I don't want to reveal
myself as a failure -- not a failure in my own current
terms (or at least let's say not) but in my former terms
as revealed to them back in the ancient days, or maybe
just assumed by them and never quite denied by me. The
hitch. That's as close as I can come to explaining it.
     Steer clear of the old excitement? I'm glum about
this too. The jyzemaster again eyeing the exit. Ready
now after all? The truly cork-lined life, the dream
world, the memory palace? Not a single goddamn thing to
look forward to above the level of, say, this week's
swap of the red coffee thermos for the black-and-white
coffee thermos shaped like a penguin? The two a.m. buzz-
honk of the newspaper courier? (Because there's no
point in looking forward to or praying for acts of the

gods.) Meanwhile wait for my hair to turn the rest of
the way gray and/or fall out? For the cancers (or just
the Big One) to start or maybe just continue growing?
The joints to accelerate their arthing? The memory to
start or increase its failing? The eyes to go?

Or live now? While I still can, maybe? Grab that
brass ring? Party hearty?

-- Of course I don't have to make my choice this
very moment. But it seems I'd like to. And it doesn't
have to be such a stark choice. Yet it seems I'd like
it to be. (Rather than go for, say, renunciation lite.
-- But in truth I could never go for true all-out full-
bodied renunciation anyway. Mine will be a lite form,
there's no way around it. What I don't want it to be,
I'm saying, is a wishy-washy super-lite form.)

This leaves me once again in an undecided state.
No sooner do I think I find equilibrium in this or that
crucial concern than another frame, and usually an even
larger one, starts shaking. More brooding and mulling
ahead, I guess. Geez, I mean, I hate to just give up on
everything. Seems that's not like me at all. Yet on
the other hand -- and so goes the internal dialogue.

-- Almost sunset. Trees and bushes rustling
uneasily outside the windows. That kind of day, season
of storms coming on. Fitful. Moody and broody. A
basic grimness somehow revealed, as no doubt must happen
from time to time no matter what, even if it's only
weather that's doing the revealing, the pathetic fallacy
after all being as likely to reflect a psychological
reality as any other type of fallacy or for that matter
any other type of reality. (At the very least -- but
also at the very most -- one can try to come up with
some fresh jumblings of the language to describe all
these primal truths.) Meanwhile the fan keeps spinning
and the room becomes palpably darker and this one lamp
turned on, here atop the worktable, grows brighter and
warmer and incrementally more reassuring. It's the jyze
light, folks.

Rarely have I stuck around here this late in the
day. Next I shove off for the hideaway, then on to the

scope office to do the very last corrections for Naomi until her return next year. (And what if she changes her mind and decides to retire for good? This could well be my last night ever as a scoper.)

So this is how it is now. -- For even the masters of jyze, the grandest of grandmasters, must occasionally have a really bad day.

32

From an outdoor seat at the bar with the art shtick. Yeah, same one. Again. Looking straight into the sun so I can sit with my back to the wall (right next to the weakly glowing red neon of a beer sign in the window). More likely this way to minimize any hassles with the sidewalk traffic here at "ground zero" of the old crime turf. (Where else for an artfully authentic art bar?)

So I'll start with this. Again I consulted the jyze gods, and this time the jyze gods spoke. And they said: Let there be an explosion of jyzos. And there was an explosion of jyzos. All J-week. "Jyzos Bustin' Out All Over." "Whole Lotta Jyzin' Goin' On." "Delirium Jyzens." "Extinctions of the Jyzonian." "The Construction of Jyze Reality."

And what exactly is a jyzo? Well, best I can tell it's the title of a hypothetical future jyzebook, and the only rule seems to be that it contain the word "jyze" in one inflection or another (or more than one). Further, many of the titles will go on a series of painted jyze posters resembling hand-decorated book covers. And all will appear in the catalog of the House of Jyze Publishing Company, which will include current

hardcover titles, paperback reprints, a full backlist,
and remainder-table bargains -- because we're talking
great swarms of jyzos here, that is, "The Jyzos They
Just Keep A-comin'." Suddenly I understood (as I never
did before) how it was that certain short-form poetry
masters could pump out hundreds and sometimes even
thousands of their specialties in a single day. Simple:
you can't turn the damn things off.

And I still can't do it. Stopped a dozen times
during the walk over here just to jot down new ones.
The three very latest: "Feast of the Fallen Jyzers."
"An Outdoor Seat at the Jyze Cafe." "Jyze on Up to Papa
G's." -- So quite obviously it's still not over. "By
Jyzos Possessed," that's me. (An hour earlier two of my
favorites so far popped up: "Jammin' at the Jyze Spot"
and "Y'all Got Jyze for Her But Not for Me." -- In
general, though, I try to keep 'em short and punchy.
("Jyze Cummin'!" Or maybe not so punchy even if short
and to the point: "Halt Jyze Pleonasm!")

So a splendid eighter, more than offsetting the
miseries of the previous one. For the jyze gods also,
being in a mood of vatic expansiveness (as the cosmos
only knows I am right now down here at street level),
advised me to this effect: nah, don't renounce the world
just yet. Don't give up on contacting the old loves.
Be bold. Risk it all for jyze. And I will. And I
have. And I am. "For Jyze You Know You Must."

But I still couldn't face calling Lady K's alum
office. So instead I wrote and asked them to forward an
enclosed letter to her, and I noted the appropriate
class and dorm references. I figure today's the first
day she might be able to respond -- say by calling
information to get my number and ringing me up (my
letter does mention I'm in the phone book). Of course
we're talking vanishingly low odds here, and even at
their peak a week or two from now they won't improve all
that much. But no matter: a new excitement enters my
life. The thrill is not gone. The thrill is back!
"Got My Jyze Flaps On!"

-- Mostly it's a waiting game right now, to be

sure. Lots of waiting and the waiting's of many kinds.
Still don't know whether I'll have any scoping work at
all this fall (day after tomorrow I'll learn more; and
that also happens to be the day when the supreme leader
of all of us USAns will be coming to town, so we're
already seeing lots of gimlet-eyed tough guys snooping
around down here -- he'll be stopping in at the public
market -- just as when my strictly mythical jyze prez
comes to town in "Mentoka Ghosts" -- but the real prez
won't be dropping by for a quick one here at the art
bar, I'd wager, though he does do that at Nick's J&B
there).

(-- The thrill is back also, a different one, as
of a moment ago when a guy unloading a keg from a pickup
truck bumped a little red sports car parked some nine or
ten feet of sidewalk in front of me and set off the
car's alarm. The godawful whooping and wheeing --
though plenty exciting -- made me consider moving inside
the bar, so raucously did it persist -- but in time it
stopped. And not too long after that my pulse started
the slow drop back to normal.)

(Wow -- tall, long legs, miniskirted business
outfit cut just as foaming-edge fashion decrees, I do
believe -- strolling by. I'm roiled by her scent
currents. Which is to say: pulse is up again. She
maybe six-one, two, and sure can strut that runway
stuff. The pretty women of this city, unlikely as the
notion may strike me (because this is glamour on the
sashay right here, right now, quite a bit of it, in
fact, at office-closing time: this ground-zero block
oddly being maybe the one place in town to boast a
noticeable fashion-model presence -- and possibly this
is related to the reason art is colonizing here and
apparently jyze is as well).)

So, waiting. For others too, and especially Lady
V, but relations with her I've rethought again and
accordingly I've dropped most of that protective "peace
& love" coloration and seen the remainder go through a
series of new permutations. One featured "Sorry to hear
about your sad news" and worked up a whole spiel based

loosely on that theme, but I quickly realized I don't want to be playing that kind of game either. Now I think maybe I'm returning to the "tear-stained face / fierce love" message, but with this difference, for which I can also thank the jyze gods: with my temperas I'll slash the words out on newsprint want-ad pages and add some Fauvey painted flowers and mail off the ensemble. (Now see how that steeps for a while.)

Iz some news tho. In a couple of realms my waiting is over. -- But the specifics on these had themselves better wait until later, because I've got stops to make before the shops close at seven. A coupon to cash in for apple juice and another for yet more canned tuna. Also an envelope to drop in the mail, my quarterly payment to the tax authorities, four hundred bills -- just a wild guess on the amount I should be prepaying since I have no way to know how much work J. Ink will score over the next three months -- but due today. And by an odd coincidence the check I'm sending them is numbered the year of my birth -- when the jyzemaster's agonies began ("The Agony of Jyzemaster G") on this hard-to-renounce planet ("Along Came Jyze!").

*   *

Might as well continue here. "Punch G for Jyze." Got detoured into my former prime haunt, the cafe in the basement of the only real bookstore (ORB), lair of the mad newspaper clipper. But he's not here tonight and a good many friends of Jocelyn I. are, as is the woman herself. Until a moment ago she was sitting just the other side of the wooden central staircase from me. And several of her friends being, like Jocelyn I. herself, strikingly attractive and spirited and well-spoken females, I found myself lingering.

(Applause in there now as she launches into her presentation. A new book, a fine one I'm sure, like her breakthrough novel, but not jyze, though closer to it than are most fictobooks I know of written by others.)

She I guess being a racial mix but from most angles looking almost my kind, long-faced and that signature close-cropped blondish (dyed?) hair. Our eyes caught

once and the room burst into flame, I thought, but even
if it didn't the moment quickly passed. Nonetheless it
left me feeling I know her on a first-name basis and
something even beyond that. So I took the liberty with
the moniker "Jocelyn I." and the jyze rules be damned.
Truth is, even if our eyes have met, we haven't.

Now this room is almost empty. Someone left a
plate bearing an unfinished veggie sandwich on the table
here so I'm good without even buying anything. Instead
drained a glass of water from the spigoted cooler at
Jocelyn's left hand, inches away. (Sexy voice she has
though. Unexpectedly rich and warm, a little thrill in
it. Not the hardness or decadence you might expect from
her prose. Or put it this way: "Mama Got Jyze Pipes.")

I'd been thinking next stop the depot. It would be
even emptier than this room is now, most likely, and
feel much more so because the quantity of emptiness per
capita would be far greater, and applied to that as well
would be the higher multiplier assigned to lonely depots
as compared with sad cafes. Also I'm now starting to
squirm over the taboo aspect of being here. "In the
Cafe Jyze Renounced."

-- What started all this jyzo business, or rather
got it really rolling, I've been wanting to say, was the
effort a week ago today to paint for Jeff the card Rob
and I failed to come up with a week before that. Not
only did I produce such a card (again, tempera brushed
on newsprint classified ads) but also the first dozen
jyze posters. And loved their look, even the bad ones.
Right up on the wall and the back of the bureau they
went (the back of Jim Q.'s old bureau, this is, which
stands between the closet and the staircase end of the
loft, blocking off the dressing area except for a narrow
entrance, and blankly faces -- the back of the bureau
does, or did, because now it's covered with posters --
faces the middle of the room, that is, the nerf court).
Looked just as I'd hoped and dreamt from the start!
-- Though soon the newsprint will yellow and then I
don't know what I'll think. Would some preservative
spray help and could I afford it? Do I maybe have an

old can of it stashed away somewhere?

   "The Old Man Crazy about Jyze" grabs the laurels
among the posters. "Jyze Me Right There" and "Jyzey as
I Can Be" both look good. "A Jyze Manifesto" is
probably my favorite as far as the artwork goes.
"Jyzelby the Scoper"'s pretty damn fine as well. "Jyze
Shoot Off its Mouth Again" is the rawest. "Jyzo Ergo
Sum" and "The Critique of Pure Jyze" will surely appeal
to ontologists. And "The Memory Palace of Jyzemaster G"
simply repeats a key theme of the current era. (I for
one know I can hardly wait to show these posters to Rob,
the only other living person on this planet with any
idea what jyze is (other than Lady U, who of course
could care less) (and other than Tom T., a little).

   As Jocelyn I. moves into her question period. Lots
of laughs in there. "A Good Jyze Room." (Even for
near-urjyze -- or no, a distant cousin of JIFT or maybe
call it standard fictive prose with a few jyzey touches
mixed in -- I'll still say she can pump it out.) "The
Jyzeness of You" -- that kicked up by the mere word
"near." So many totally unremarkable words are doing
it! "The Jyzer Who Fell into Grace with the Jyze."
-- And next month the old Mentoka Ghost himself, Ray W.,
is due back on these premises to take the same podium
where Jocelyn I. is now holding forth. "Jyze is Back in
Town." "In Search of Lost Jyze." He'll also be among
the literary stars at the annual book fair next month,
which this time around maybe I'll try harder to attend.

   -- Surprise, looks like the reading's over already.
Yup. First runners bounding up the stairs two at a time
like reporters scampering for the phones.

   On the Lisa K. front, nothing. If I don't hear
before much longer from either her or her alum office, I
don't know what my next step will be. The options are
few. Try somehow to come up with the alum directory?
Or try to call the alum office? Hmm, ex-aunt Polly
attended the same college, so maybe I could seek her
help. But just the thought makes me queasy. My high-
school classmate Sue B., also a graduate of that college,
is a possibility, likely reachable through our most

recent class booklet (if I could find my copy), but --
too much awkwardness there too.

   -- Meanwhile speaking of jyze. No. Of bookstores.
Or both actually. Anyway, I happened upon a review of a
new novel set in Mentoka, and much of it in one of the
two main real-world physical models for Mentoka Falls.
It uses a lot of the historical material I'm deploying
myself in "Jyzer" and "Mentoka Dreams" (in theory now, I
have to say, since they're both on hold at the moment).
It also deploys real historical figures in fictive ways,
though not in my own preferred fictive ways -- in a
fashion, in fact, that I dislike, the "omniscient" way,
ostensibly getting inside the heads of people who have
really existed or at least are alleged by more or less
reputable contemporaries to have existed. -- And one
of these days I'll start reading this novel. But a few
quick glances were enough to convince me it wouldn't
steal much of whatever thunder I'd be able to convince
the jyze rainmakers to grant my own work. Still, I had
to have it on my shelf. Laid out the bucks. A last
extravagance of the birthday period. Last for a while.
(Except for a roll of orange Danish pop-out pastry still
to bake up.) (And bought a sackful of ultra-cheap
brushes for the next jyze poster session, but that was
so well planned for, I even had the money set aside.)

   My forbidden pleasure, watching them straggle out
from the reading room one by one or (more often) two by
two. This country of ours where two by two is the rule
just as for the Ark. ("Jyze from the Ark." "Raiders of
the Lost Jyze." "Bring Me Your Jyzers.") Guilty
pleasure. -- Nah, not really. To repeat: from the
second-joker perspective it's okay to gape and ogle as
long as you're discreet about it. ("Jyze Pervs Out.")

   -- Chairs in here starting to jump atop tables and
quiver upside down with rigidly spread metal legs almost
like tuning forks but two forks per critter. Talk
continues at the far end of the reading room. Suppose
it's time to mosey on. "Jyze, You Outta Here."

   But first for Jocelyn I.: "(Ooh Baby) It's Jyze
like That."

               [Jyze and Jyze Alone]

                     *   *

     And back in the hideaway. "Jyze Writ Twixt Twin
Desk Lamps." -- But no, on the way over I suddenly
realized the jyzo brainstorming session is over. I've
had my fun. -- "Got to Hide Your Jyze Away." -- "Smoke
Rises from a Jyze Crematorium." Fact is I've already
got enough jyzos to be churning out jyze posters from
here to J-day and well beyond. (For instance, this:
"Licks from a Mean Jyze Stick.")
     Stop!
     "Can't Stop Jyzin'."
     -- Can stop with the jyzos, though. Or I think so
anyway.
     So relax then. A deep breath. I've been so jyzed!
(And will be again!) ("Keep Your Jyzos Back now!")
     -- Almost forgot about the suspense set up earlier.
Two things I was waiting for I'm waiting for no more.
Neither one was Rikki replying to my birthday letter or
Barb to the one I sent her (two to her actually) (but
how Rob howled with strange glee while browsing through
one of the rants of the world-class Euromanic -- "Listen
to this!" -- and then seemed startled to hear Barb had
turned seriously religious, though I thought we'd talked
about it at length before). Nor was it the city utility
getting around to sending its long-delayed bill, which
by now must've grown to gargantuan proportions (but on
the off-chance they'll forget permanently or forgive
some of it -- out of well-earned shame for being so
irresponsible, and this a public agency! -- I'll keep on
keeping quiet). Nor was it the "Memorials" bluelines
coming in. Nor was it -- but I guess that's all the
main stuff available for what it wasn't. And so:
     Yes, a contact from Lady U. Or Madam Ex. (I'm
often tempted to go back to the Madam Ex lingo but
better not: it's too confusing with the other ladies
also exes.) -- But a few days before the quarterly tax
was due she finally managed to send over the new forms
the feds had mailed weeks earlier to our old (and her
still current) street address. Also in the envelope was
a hastily scrawled two-sentence note on which she didn't

even waste a stickie; a ragged triangular scrap torn
from the flap of a used manila envelope was good enough.
She hopes all's well with me -- the very words I settled
on to replace "tear-stained" on my altered note (still
unsent) to Lady V. Carefully chosen for their bland
neutrality! And she has more mail for me and I should
"let her know" -- about our meeting again, I guess.

So now I'm taking my own sweet time on contacting
her, even though I'm only hurting myself by still
further delaying her delivery of whatever it is she has
for me. But probably I'll try to set up a meeting for
this weekend. And I wonder what she'll say about
failing to pick up the community-college catalog I went
way out of my way to run down for her. By now the new
semester has already started! (And then there are all
the things I don't even want to know about, though I do
wonder about them. Her parents, her love life, her
health, her "career choice." I can't imagine Mama and
Papa U approving of her living alone out in the woods
for much longer. -- But never mind. Just more sorry
thrashings.)

And then the other one I was in some sense waiting
for, Sofie. Of course! Wouldn't ya know. Last
previous contact with Sofie was the same week as last
previous contact with Lady U. 'Long about summer-
solstice time. And now it's almost autumn equinox --
which "falls" this coming weekend. And the day Lady U's
letter arrived and the day I saw Sofie again were the
same: last Friday. Friday the 13th! (Though I must
confess I didn't put all these pieces together until
moments ago.) And again with Sofie I was totally
ignored. We were walking straight toward each other on
the diagonal cement path crossing through the pocket
park, almost on a collision course. She didn't look
good, as if her asthma had been kicking up again and/or
she'd missed lots of sleep recently. I couldn't prevent
myself from staring to be sure she was who she seemed to
be. But then I was sure, and by that time she was about
five feet away. In black denim pants and a tight white
T showing her busty torso to notable effect. Talking

with a tall thin Cawk guy, probably about her age or a
few years younger, possibly her set-designer boyfriend.
Gesturing the animated way she does, gripping his arm
for emphasis. (I like that warmth in her. She showed
it to me too, early on.) -- And she never saw me! Or
if she did, it was before I saw her and she then shifted
into ignore mode. As they sailed by I could easily have
bumped both of them into the puddly badlands of the
sandbox; just a little elbow flick would've done it.
    I figure it must've been because my hood was up.
Sprinkles of rain were floating about. Maybe she
doesn't know how I look hooded. (And later the
sprinkles turned into a hard rain. My shoes got soaked
and probably lost a month off their useful life. And
the air inflow from the windows in unit B-2 took on
enough chill to induce me to don sweatpants in the room
for the first time since April.)
    It still hurt. How did she strike so deeply in me
with such short exposure? All a function of the
crazedness of my state at the time, I suppose. My
hurtin' heart. Still, although this equinox stab seemed
at the time to go nearly as deep as the solstice stab
had, the recovery was much quicker. I must be healing
across the board. And I must be wising up too,
adjusting, learning better how to live the reclusive
life. It's an art, really, and requires practice. It's
not just a simple matter of always being ready to jump
into a cold shower. Many little foxy tricks to being a
hermit in the city, not just one big hedgehog trick, and
more tricks still when you're a hermit no longer young.
Or maybe that's turning it around. Maybe fewer tricks,
now that I think about it. It's just you reach an age
where the hormones will permit more of the tricks to
work. That's the commonsense view anyway and it looks
dead-on from where I sit. (Just for an example, as one
no longer young you really are better off if you avoid
looking in the mirror too much, with a single important
exception. When the hormones start coursing, look. Be
reminded. Stand corrected. Stand humbled. Off their
feet they will not be swept. You got to give it up.

[For Jyze You Know You Must]

"You better leave my daughter alone!" -- a warning
you'll no longer be hearing, and regardless you already
know how to act with that daughter. Young blood, huh-
uh. Blood, go old. "Don't be a hip dip, go old."
"Don't Be a Sham Sam, Go Jyze.")
     Otherwise, though, you can fool yourself into
forgetting this inconvenient fact of life a good solid
ninety-five percent of your waking hours. Dreams, all
the rules are suspended, including the rules that make
the tricks work. But no need to delve more deeply into
such matters at this time, because for now the move into
the dream world (floating world, could say) is itself
pretty much suspended. A few doozer dreams during the
eighter, true, and certainly welcome at the time, but I
can no longer provide details on content. The dreambook
up in the loft remains blank. I may even be developing
a kind of twilight-zone phobia about recording anything
in it, as if by doing so I'd be admitting defeat.

33

     No, can't keep the jyzos down. Haven't been able
to all week. Roll over, amorous haiku grandmaster.
"Mama I Wanna Jyze." "Papa's Got a Jyze Bag." "Jyze on
Up." Literally thousands and thousands of the jyzey
little things. "I Lost It to Jyze." (But here in the
jyze itself I'll ruthlessly clamp down. Surely I can do
this for an hour, maybe even an hour and a half.)
     Where? Cafe in the Yuke. And outdoors too, on the
veranda raised a foot or so above sidewalk level, and on
an early autumn day with classes just starting up and
the avenue here predictably aswarm. Man, if I were
living up in this area again I'd never get anything

done. Would do nothing but sit right here and gape and
ogle. Waste enormous amounts of energy, no doubt, just
trying to be cool about it. -- Or say ruthlessly clamp
down but do it in the hormone sector.

    Yup, autumn came right in. The prez dropped by --
did the old in-and-out on us. To hear him talk you'd
think all's going as it spoze to, not even a slight
wobble in it (talking about this planet of spinning
blades, this monster whirligig).

    Except -- I'm on a badass kick. Right now I mean.
First I blew almost twenty bucks on two good-quality
watercolor brushes. Then upstairs (this at the U
bookstore) in a serendipitous moment -- while searching
for the proper reference book in which I could check on
the exact number of the grandmaster's one-day haiku
record and also see whether haiku was actually the form
he was working in, or was it some kind of waka (or am I
just jivin'?) -- I suddenly found myself face to face
with a book I've been trying to locate for years. On
"experimental autofictions"! It's true! I couldn't
help myself, I yanked it out for inspection and knew
right away it was a keeper. Not only that, but
serendipity doubled: on my way to the cash register I
ran smack-dab into a copy of a newly translated work on
the sociology of aesthetics! For which I've also been
waiting for years! This one I didn't even have to yank;
it jumped into my hands and, defying immediate
inspection, spurred me on to the register. Before I
knew what had hit me I was out in the street, almost
forty dollars poorer and yet immeasurably richer
(eyeballs roll -- but I mean it!).

    -- And then crossed the street to pay a visit to
brother Rob. I feared it was his day off but it wasn't;
he was up shelving in the newly inaugurated music-books
section (near where I might've found him stocking
classic vinyl albums a decade ago). Long hair, T-shirt,
ratty jeans, some classical ditty playing (maybe "Jyze
Air for G Strings"?): ah, the perks of a job in a
franchise record shop! Last week I sent him a copy of
Volume 1 of the jyzo list and now he said he liked it,

his favorite being "What's Jyze Got to Do with It?" I
thought he might see me as some kind of nut if I told
him that since then the list had reached Volume 15, so I
kept this as my own little secret. Nor did I tell him
about the notion that struck me in the shower the other
day: starting up a "Top Ten Jyzos" feature for one of
the local weeklies, with little jyze stories provided
for each one. I have no doubt it would be a sensation.
But...no. Jyze is more serious than that.

Rob never seems especially welcoming when I see him
at work. But then that's just how he is. Work too is
serious business! He was no different even when Mother
popped in there during her visit to J. City with Barb
eight years ago this month (hard to believe). -- So I
rather quickly was outta there. Letting him know first,
though, I'm expecting him to come by sometime before his
birthday in mid October because a gift is awaiting him
("Uh-oh," he said) and also I want to show him the new
jyze poster gallery -- and every last poster featuring a
jyzo he's never seen before! (A jyze poster gallery no
one but the jyzer himself has ever seen, is it still a
jyze poster gallery? Of course it is!)

And meanwhile the waiting. All of it. In this
realm I know not one damn thing I didn't know a week ago.
But each day is exciting, I mean truly wracked with
suspense (yes, really truly). This week the odds for a
Lady K reply are highest, I'd say, and they'll be almost
as high next week. Her alum association hasn't returned
my postage-paid card with the checkoffs for indicating
why they couldn't forward my letter to her, so the
chances seem fairly good they've indeed sent it on (as
opposed to the other obvious possibilities -- not least
that the whole schmear is moldering in an in-basket
somewhere). So each day my heart pounds -- ain't
kidding -- as I head upstairs to check the mailbox.
(I've fairly well steeled myself to wait until three
p.m., the latest hour the mail's likely to arrive,
before going up. And this even though some days it
comes in before noon.)

Today, however, is different. I wanted to document

in jyze -- docujyze? -- what the suspense is like, so I
left the building a little before three without checking
the mailbox. Intentionally. Only when I go home
tonight will I open the box. And then report the
results, of course, in these very pages.

What could be in that box? Anything! (Including,
I want to mention, a letter from Rikki or Barb or Tom T.
-- to whom (Tom) I did send off several jyzo lists this
week -- and even the "Memorials" bluelines maybe, who
knows. Possibly even, shudder, the city utility bill.)

Absurd, all this, to be sure. Lady K likely a
fusty little old granny by now. Why shatter my image of
her from our salad days -- which were so long ago I'm
not even sure the term itself is in play anymore. I
mean, she might be thinking something like this herself,
or if not yet, soon (maybe); and for the same reason I
might want any new photo of myself intended for her eyes
to be carefully posed on a dark afternoon and shot sans
flash. -- But no, I don't really think that way and she
probably wouldn't either. Nonetheless it's far from
likely we'd still have enough in common -- not to mention
enough mutual allure -- to sustain a correspondence for
long. Not to mention (say it again, sure) an actual in-
person encounter.

This is the sort of thing I'm doing way too often
these days, trying to prepare myself for disappointment.
Just superstition, of course, is impelling this. It's a
kind of ritual incantation or rather a series of such.
(And later, most likely, it'll be the same repetitious
drill with Lady V. Or I could simply say it's a way of
easing myself through the days. -- And for Lady V, in
this week's new wrinkle, I've refined the "tear-stained"
painting idea a little further, going back to a "peace &
love" sign-off but adding a kind of marginal comment or
postscript, an antic arrow pointing up to the Fauvey
flowers from a cache of words: "Shadow of the main
squeeze unforgotten." Or this may be too ridiculous, I
suppose. Further refinements or radical changes are
still possible and even likely.)

-- Meanwhile the shadow of this cafe has crept all

the way across the street and is starting to edge up the
brick facade of the copy shop on the far side (the
magazine shop to its north, my next stop, is already
completely shadowed by the larger building to our north
on this side, and this larger building happens to be the
one whose second floor is the dance studio where Lady U
rehearsed and taught up to twelve hours a day (unpaid!)
when we lived roughly five blocks to the west of where I
sit now -- and by the way, I've put off calling Lady U
for another week -- because in truth Lady U no longer
dances in my heart -- though I don't doubt for a moment
she'll someday dance there again, perhaps even joining
Lady K and Lady V -- and Lady S too, absolutely -- and
Briana T., can't suppress her even though she bailed on
me before reaching lady rank (that is, we never lived
together) -- and of course Karen A. -- all six of these
worthies breaking into a kind of jyzey heartbreak
kickline). -- And a chill has crept into the air and I
suppose I should consider packing it in.
     First, though, say this. I'm liking it here.
Other veterans of roughly my vintage lurk in these parts.
Not many, but a few. In that respect it certainly beats
my current home turf. -- Okay, enough, until later when
I'll at last be ready to break the unbearable suspense
about what's lurking in my mailbox. (Ain't kidding!
-- But the word "unbearable" occasioned more right now
by my need to hit the head fast.)
                    *   *
     Surprise. No letters in the box. Suspense over.
Just a bank statement in there along with a quarterly
from a city on Mentoka's eastern coast.
     So down to unit B-2. Unlock double lock. Flip
interior hall lights on. Set bag and package down on
worktable. Flick radio on to jazz station (rabbit ears
still working; record player still working too). Unpack
all the shiny new material items, including -- not
mentioned before -- a box of long tan recyled-paper
envelopes for mailing out jyzo lists, among other things,
and four boxes of my favorite kind of gingersnaps, each
box of which lasts about two weeks at the usual allotment

of three snaps per night (they're very thin). Strip
shirt off, one of my two new ones from last spring,
both khaki. Strip off turtle pendant too. Twist
worktable lamp on, a soft glow to make the jyze poster
gallery on the walls above look good -- which it does.
Terrific! Can't stop checking it out!

Chomping away, meanwhile, at my allotted three
cherry tomatoes and one fig bar (since now it's past
midnight and I haven't eaten at all since noon except
for the daily midafternoon ten-cent drugstore mint).

-- But wait. Always upon returning home I
immediately check the answering machine in the loft room
and today the dial read "02"! A true rarity. Prior to
today my only call in this week when in theory any ring
might've been Lady K (albeit showing uncharacteristic
initiative) was once again the robot at the library
phoning to say a book I'd placed on reserve had come in.
Now today, of the two messages waiting for me, I knew
what the first one was because I'd heard it come in
shortly after I woke up. It was again Saundra N. at my
old newspaper. I figured that solicitation was all done
with, but no, it seems they weren't working on deadline
after all. (But my intention remains the same no matter
how diligent they become in their pursuit: I'm lying low.
In abject shame too, no denying. -- The other day Mike
M. was extensively quoted in an article in the night
paper -- for completely arbitrary reasons no longer to
be dubbed "indispensable" in these pages -- on the
alternative-paper wars. He sounds in fine fettle, and
so at least I don't have to worry the old rag will
suffer even slightly from my spurning them again.)

But the second call? Could it be? Just maybe?

Of course it couldn't. If it had been I'd've
mentioned it long before now. No way could I have kept
it under my hat this long (what hat?). No, it was once
again the same Saundra N., this time phoning earlier
tonight. And for the first time she got a little
personal (though still managing to sound as if she were
peddling kitchenware): said she'd just been talking with
Peggy R. (Mike's wife still, I presume, and in any case

still going under the same work name) who'd said to
Saundra, who repeated to me, "You're one of the ones
she's most interested in knowing what you're up to." I
bet! The one whose crazy girlfriend Lady V threatened
more than once, and quite seriously, to turn the paper's
offices into a smoking ruin!

Nope. All this serves only to make my shame still
more abject. The only way they'll nail me is by posting
someone at both entrances to our building here in Jyze
City to catch me as I try to sneak in or out.

So with all suspense now unsprung, I offer myself
up to the embrace of the green armchair and I -- jyze.
"Yet Again for Jyze." (Up in the loft, by the way,
what's new is the college dictionary I brought home from
the hideaway. It's more useful here. In both places I
have an unabridged but here when I'm in the loft it's
too much trouble to clamber down to look something up,
the B-2 unabridged normally resting on the worktable
beneath a major part of that fabulous -- looking up here
to admire it once more -- jyze poster gallery.) (So
warmly lit, that gallery. So colorful! So hilariously
funny, I still chuckle even at my ten-thousandth
exposure! "Ol' Jyze Keep On Rockin'." "Treat Your
Jyzer Well." "The Jyze Within.") (-- And also up in
the loft I wore sweats again this week for sleeping. So
another sign of the inexorable grinding of the seasons,
regular allusion to which is called for by one of the
auxiliary jyze rules I'm still doing my best to follow.)

I did glance at the bank statement before sitting
here. Nothing unexpected in it. By the end of next
week, though, I'll have to start drawing on the savings
cushion for the first time. At this point I still don't
know about scoping work for the rest of the fall. Talk
about being dissed! Was grand jury canceled last week
(maybe because of the president's visit and the colossal
traffic jams it caused)? Or was the reporting of GJ
farmed out to some other firm because ex-partner Una was
out of town (on a cushy overseas job) and reporter Verna
didn't want to do it (though two weeks ago the docket
showed she'd be taking it, and then the whole entry was

scratched) -- or what the hell's going on down there? I
don't know, that's for sure. What's more, on the usual
GJ night I walked in the door and found virtually
everything in the office shifted around again. No
warnings, no explanations. But I did eventually manage
to locate the workstation assigned to vendor 273 (Jyzer
Ink) and figure out how to hook it up and I did keep
sneaking in late at night to use it for cranking out my
own stuff (though I'm trying to confine this to weekends
until the scoping picture clears up).

So now onward to -- what? Look up, the couch (that
term synonymous now with "loveseat" on the B-2 furniture
list). Stacks of books and mags, journals, reviews --
all the usual, and this where visitors would ordinarily
sit were any such to arrive. New to read is the
library's copy of the book on postcultural anthropology,
as I think of it (it's the one the robot called about).
Still to be gotten through are the library's copy of the
protojyze classic from a century and a half ago (which
is turning out on the whole, despite a number of
enviable passages, to be way too abstract and
religiously oriented for my taste) and the thirty-year-
old book of poems about Lady U's culture of ancestry,
written, as it happens, by Karl M., Lady S's former
teacher, advisor, and wannabe and maybe-was lover who in
fact, and to his immediate regret, and in some sense to
mine as well but later on, introduced her to me.
Earlier this week I returned the library's copy of this
same Karl M.'s posthumously published childhood-years
autobiography, recently released, which I did read in
full and enjoyed more than I expected to, though my
responses fluctuated wildly just as they did to the man
himself in real life and for the same reasons, pretty
much, and I guess there's really no point in trying to
go into those now. (Better to save all that for the
fictojyze, mostly "Jyzer," specifically for the Karl M.-
like character who introduces Jyzer G to Yo there.)

Also arrayed on the couch, copies of two articles I
first read standing up at a magazine rack. Great stuff!
I'm planning to reread both, however, so until I've done

that I'll withhold all comments. And most likely after
that too, right, but still great stuff. I now try to
hit one of the two main downtown franchise bookstores
every other afternoon since extended browsing is a bit
more comfortable there than at the only real bookstore,
where the magazine racks are located directly in front
of the main sales counter, and to the people who work
there I'm sort of a harmless eccentric and I don't want
to alienate any remaining affection they may have for me
(or even any remaining indifference) and certainly don't
want to be taken as a neighborhood crazy like the mad
cafe newspaper clipper.

Let's see. Nice euphoric walk home tonight.
"Night and Jyze." Straight up the edge road from the
hideaway, popping on all cylinders as I often have been
for weeks now. It's doing weird things to my mind, this
reclusive celibate life, and I like it, I like it. If
only I can keep resisting the temptations! One of whom,
by the way, I learned during this walk, will be moving
from room 205 to room 207 at the co-op at the end of
September, according to the new resident list posted by
the front door, and therefore my torments will continue
and I should be grateful, I guess, for in their perverse
way they still help fill my need for hope. "Abandon
hope all ye" -- but cain't. It's not even amputatable,
it seems. Rather I have to use the very quality against
itself jujitsu fashion if I want to keep it off-balance
and distracted. (On the wall in the kitchen nook I've
taped, next to the maps, a copy of an intriguing photo,
taken 130 years ago and recently rediscovered, of the
downtown area of this city. It shows, from a rooftop
perspective near where the only real bookstore now
stands, the very turf I call my own, the bipolar part,
including the stretch up the edge road which lately I've
been walking twice almost every day, though today I did
it only once. Also plainly visible in the photo are the
sites of the hideaway building and the B-2 building,
with not a whole lot of development in between but a
very good view of the edge itself, the waterfront bluff
in its near-primordial state. Fascinating. One of

these days I'll probably have heaps more to say about
it. -- Because once the excitement of seeking to
reconnect with the lost loves dies down and I move back
into the memory-palace groove I figure I'll have a
crying need for things to jyze about. Old photos, Karl
M., good magazine articles, the true story of what
happened in that run-in with Lady S, Karl M., and Karl
M.'s nemesis Lee C. thirty years ago that also plays a
big part in "Jyzer" -- I'll be needing 'em all and
much, much more, most likely. Unless, of course,
something unexpected happens. And -- something might.
Just might. Hope, always hope. Slice off another arm,
still hope. Even go eunuch, still hope.)
     Also to mention: This week one of the ferries I
used to ride regularly ran aground in the Z-narrows near
where the head-on collision occurred a few years ago
while I was aboard, and in a similar heavy fog. A big
media commotion over this latest incident, but "only" a
quarter million in damage done and a five-hour delay for
the four hundred passengers stranded aboard before
tugboats could refloat the old tub.
     And...I exchanged a stack of antiquated postage-
short aerograms for current stamps featuring mythical
culture heroes -- several of which are now glued herein,
this J-book, the front inside cover, including the
lumberjack with the blue ox and the mighty slugger who
struck out -- this signaling the true end of the long-
running correspondence with Fiona L., for which the
aerograms were originally intended. It's just not
something I want to keep up anymore. (Abject shame
again? That may play a part.) And...I did heat up
those orange Danish pop-out rolls for a birthday last
gasp and they were damn good and while wolfing them down
I seemed to be recalling every single one of the
thousands of pastries of that type I've consumed over
the years and the circumstances for each, so strong was
the deja vu. And...I chased several wild ideas off into
the bush one at a time and emerged a few hours or days
later feeling in each case a bit closer to grasping the
secrets of my personal corner of the universe. One idea

has to do with the role of competition, another with the importance of voluntarily limiting oneself to being only slightly hip (hop to it!), and a third with the notion of a large cavern riddled with subcaverns and subterranean passageways serving as a (hackneyed no doubt) model for the psyche. And there's a fourth, the disclosure of which I'll have to save since I'm running out of time and space and I'm getting too hungry to continue (and I can't remember what it is, that's true too -- though it still might pop up).

Like stage dialogue. Like my mind's broken a number of tethers and is wandering at will in dark subcaverns even though unknown reserve tethers remain in place and will cause quite a tangle in the deep passageways one of these days, no question. But it's still fun. It's jyze. "A Séance for Jyze Antiquity." (Because I had to squeeze in one more jyzo. And now can call it a night. -- But as a final note mention that the tangle of reserve tethers when diligently unraveled may still enable me to find my way back out of the darker realms of the cavern.) And all this dithering demands an encore jyzo: "You Jyze Too Much!")

*

(And I ask myself: do I know I've pretty well flipped out at this point? And answer: of course not. Because if I did, that would be a clear indication that I hadn't -- because otherwise how could you know? And that to me sounds not just paradoxical but, yes, twisted. -- As defined for all time by she who also asked, several decades later, in an inspired cover of a tune by another highly admirable female vocalist but of the R&B type, "What's Love Got to Do With It?" Most likely not knowing -- either of them -- she was talking about jyze too and thus giving me the jyzo brother Rob likes best and is also one of my faves. -- And now, finally, chow time.)

315

[Jyze and Jyze Alone]

34

    Midnight more or less. Could be I'm all stroked
out. Let's see. (Best shot. Let it fly. No
obligation but why not.)
    At the worktable. Jazz piano on the radio and
arrayed around me the six watercolor bowls for a jyze
poster session, all with colored water now gently aslosh
from table movement caused by the act of jyzing itself.
Red, blue, yellow, green, white, black. How primary can
you get? And the brushes soaking in the bathroom sink.
    Nine posters. Tonight's production. Leading the
pack, the title of an earlier jyze volume, conceived
long before jyzos had a name: "Theory of a Unified
Jyzefield." Most of the others trail badly. "Tailings
from a Jyze Countershaft." "All Jyze Is True."
"Jyzosophy." -- Think maybe I'm starting to take myself
too seriously. The art for "A Jyze Mazurka" ain't bad
though. (Also did first runs on the posters for Rob and
Lady V. His is "Jyze Bros Jyze Again," though I'm
hoping to come up with something better. Hers is the
"tear-stained" message exactly as it was last week.
It's corny and gooey -- at once! -- but what the hell.)
    Then again here in the JIRT taking myself more
seriously may be just what's called for. Myself and
everything. Last week I let myself get carried away --
too much. And now as I start living on savings my life
itself is taking a more serious turn. (Nor should I be
using the term "savings." It's part of what ol' Mom
left me, the cushion though not yet the deep reserves.)
    If Jyzer Ink were to be receiving any grand-jury
scoping work this fall I'd probably have heard something

about it by tonight. Today was a GJ day. But since my
talk with ex-partner Una a couple of months ago neither
she nor reporter Verna has tried to reach me. As Una
and I left it back then, J. Ink would be doing the
scoping for whoever wound up handling GJ. They just
haven't bothered to inform me of the change in plans,
whatever it is. Obviously a change has occurred.
Somebody has to be reporting GJ. Unless they somehow
lost the contract to some other firm (as they did once
before) and haven't told me about that either.

A week ago I went through a sleepless night over
this. Ridiculous. But the picture of what I'm up
against twisted more clearly into focus. If I earn no
money at all through any kind of work, the cushion funds
will keep me going until roughly April 1st. This is
only if I live within my budget, of course, though I'll
have an extra $200 or so to cover at least some of the
all but inevitable surprises and impulses and slipups.

I'm keeping an eye out for part-time holiday work.
Chances are slim, but if something good comes along
I'll probably take it.

Barring a major change -- another one -- in
reporter Naomi's plans, she should be back in harness at
the new firm a month or two before I run out of money.
For now this is what I'll be counting on. In the
meantime I'll try to keep the focus burning as fiercely
as possible on my own work. (Isn't that what I wanted
to do in the first place? It is!)

As for Lady K, nothing. Angelface. "A Jyze Too
Far." Is she out there somewhere agonizing over her
options? I'm plenty unhappy with her alum association
for failing to tell me whether they forwarded my letter.
(It just started to rain. The drops are plopping
noisily against my jyzeyard windows. Since last jyze
until an hour ago nothing but fine early-autumn
weather.) -- As of now I'd say the odds of hearing from
Lady K are starting to decrease. Pressure will be
building to shift the Book III spotlight to Lady V.
It'll be wrenching to give up hope on Lady K. It's
true, true, true: I'll miss her. These past couple of

weeks it's been almost as if she were walking at my side
wherever I've gone. I talk to her frequently in my head
and sometimes out loud. Must sound crazy as hell,
though I try not to let my lips move too much when
anyone's within earshot or eyeshot.

A sad trip to the home port too. Or storage port
now, yes. In any event, by any name, the atmosphere was
right for it: heavy fog all the way, the normal one-hour
auto-ferry crossing taking closer to three (and riding a
smaller, slower ferry to start with, a substitute for
the regular vessel still laid up for repairs after the
grounding). Then as I was trudging up the big hill, the
sight of a guy whizzing by on a bicycle jarred loose
memories of the days when I was biking that route myself
-- what a pleasure it was coasting that last mile at
tremendous speed after the long pull over the killer
central hills -- and that really set me off. First time
I've ached so badly over losing Lady U since -- well, in
a way since I moved out. (Possibly I should've focused
more on what it was like pedaling back up that same hill
in the mornings on the way home.)

But the mailbox finally did yield something good.
"GPS," a manila envelope -- not the bluelines for
"Memorials," sorry to say, but a proof of the cover and
title pages for me to sign off on, and also material
samples to choose from. So it would appear they'll soon
be moving on the printing itself. About time! (One
irony: the spine bears only the title of the book and a
big "GPS" at the bottom, making it appear I'm the author.
Could be it's the closest I'll come for a while, if not
forever, to having my own monogram appear on a book
spine in the way it's done for the true lit heavies.
-- Though I'll publish the Mentoka series on my own dime
if that becomes necessary and if the time ever arrives
when I can dare to use my own dime that way -- or Mom's
dime really -- which most likely it won't. But if it
did, I could do the publishing with GPS publishers and
thus be doubly sure I'd get a monogram.)

All those others I have letters out to, still
nothing. It's bizarre, as if a classic conspiracy of

silence were at work.

     Surely I'm not failing in my attempt to sound more
subdued and serious this week. Let's see, what else
will go with this mood? A health report maybe. But
happily there's little to report. My whacker's elbow,
the left one, finally seems to be on the mend, though I
must still be careful with it -- mainly be sure not to
move it too quickly or abruptly and not attempt to lift
anything heavier than a glass of water. Otherwise
nothing to grump about. Feet okay. Some real spring in
my step these days. My hair still seems to be thinning
gradually (though perhaps less gradually than a few
years ago) and yet somehow I've still got what appears
to be a full head of it, or almost, if you don't look
too closely, or even if you do and your standards aren't
too high, or better to say too thick.

     -- Going back to developments at the scope office,
one night last week I arrived there at eleven p.m. with
a big sheaf of edits of my own work to punch in and I
got a shock: the computer I usually do my work on was in
restricted-access mode. I couldn't log onto it, and
that's the only computer in the office I can use other
than the godawful laptop locked in the safe. "I'm
fucked!" I screamed: in just those words too, which
hardly ever pop out of my mouth. No more could I print
my own work on the office printers, neither the old ones
nor the new ones, or at least not until Naomi's return.
I'd have to change my whole M.O.! Maybe even buy a new
computer and printer for home use! (This incident also
contributed to the sleepless night mentioned earlier,
which was that same night.)

     But I lucked out this time. The very next day a
back order came in for Naomi. The firm (actually
dayscoper Amy, the same horrific Amy) had to allow me
access to the computer after all. Nor did I fail to
take advantage of it: while scoping the job I also
printed up all the proofed pages I had on hand, a total
of almost five hundred. True, I used my own paper and
toner, so I didn't really get away with much. Still I
felt, yeah, pretty damn slick. (And the back order

earned me enough to pay for those two books I bought on impulse in the Yuke last week.)

I don't know yet if Amy will be cutting off my access to the system again. I expect she will, just out of her sheer orneriness. If she does, I'm thinking I'll try to make do with that loathsome laptop to keep up on my proofing. I might even take the laptop down to the hideaway for the weekends and then I won't have to worry about someone barging in on me. I can be almost certain no one will be needing the thing, which is basically obsolete (why else would they decide to have Jyzer Ink do grand jury on it?). And I'm fairly sure I'll be able to hook it up to the firm's printers for cranking out my own stuff. This weekend I'll see. It'll be a real pain working on the laptop -- it's bogglingly slow and the ergonomics are preposterously bad no matter what kind of chair you're using. But it still beats buying a new computer and printer. Beats it by a J-town mile.

All week, meanwhile, more jyzos. I've now got literally a thousand and one of the damn things -- I mean good ones! (Well, if "Jyze Me, She Murmured" is good. Or "Squeaks of a Jyze Couch." Or "You Don't Know Jyze Like I Do." Like that. "Man's All Jyze." I'm looking at the new posters drying on the floor.) Lots of mad cackling down here. "Please Mr. Jyzeman." "A Jyze Bestiary." "Can Too Jyze."

For me the best way to test the titles is to read the long lists of them out loud. "It Jyze It Jake." "Be Good To Your Jyze." "Jyze on the Up and Up." "There You Go Pimping My Jyze." Book II's title winner, "Life of the Jyze to Come." After a while I get to laughing hysterically and have to shut down the reading. -- But I think the jyzo storm has probably just about blown itself out. The last couple of days I've made it all the way from here to the hideaway without stopping more than a few times to jot down new inspirations. Therefore: "Jyze Done Lost Its Pop."

Meanwhile tearing off big chunks of the postculture book. A delight. Had it not been for the fact that I couldn't afford to buy it I might never have gotten

around to reading it. Going through the library forces
me to tackle immediately the books which are hard to
track down, like this one.

 After a month or more of quiescence, this week one
of the windowsill impatienses produced a bloom, a single
one, almost certainly its last for the year. It's a
salmon-colored beauty with nifty red streaks. Meanwhile
the fuchsia are still hanging in there and in more ways
than one. I get lots of pleasure from them, especially
the Santa Claus with its dozens of red-and-white paper-
lantern-like blooms (the round kind, size of a ping-pong
ball or slightly smaller: maybe a "boulder" marble).
And the fancy geranium. These are my only real "flesh-
and-blood" companions these days, that is, the only ones
that are not ghosts. But they won't be lasting much
longer, I'm sure. The seasons. The changes. All much
in evidence. Tourists mostly vanished from our city.
Fallen leaves rattling along in gutters. Sidewalk cafes
moving back inside. Sunset rapidly backing up --
suddenly one day it was dark before I even made it down
to the hideaway.

 As of a couple of days ago I've now been living in
this unit B-2 for six months. If I'm not confused, that
is. (And why should I be?) So I suppose it's only
right that some of the excitement's wearing off and
along with it some of the self-protective effect of that
excitement. This life right here is not an aberration;
this is how it's gonna be. And it's how I want it to
be! So whatever's tough to take about it I must be able
to take regardless. (Just keep working at it, that's
all you can do. But often I think of ol' Mom starting
to live alone in her new city after Dad died. Lots of
similarities, some quite surprising. Probably -- no,
almost certainly -- the radio station I'm listening to
is the same one she'd be tuning to if she were here.
And when Dad died she was only a year and a half older
than I am now. So two years older than I was at the
time of the "death" of my own mate late last winter.)

[Jyze and Jyze Alone]

35

    A dry run I guess this will be. Here in the
hideaway. Because -- because there's been a change. A
major one, at least by current jyze standards.
    A few moments ago I was nibbling on a bag of
popcorn at the railroad depot. Or more than just
nibbling; I was shoveling it in. And the depot was as
crowded as I've ever seen it. Then everyone went out to
board one of the regional trains and by the time I
finished off the popcorn I was the only non-employee in
the room, except for a couple of sparrows hopping along
the floor pecking at spilled popcorn, no doubt including
some of my own. Then two janitors appeared on opposite
sides of the room and came sweeping and mopping toward
me in a kind of pincer operation, closer and closer; and
a cocky cop (who looked and walked like Lady S's
weightlifter brother Nim and reminded me of those nasty
soldiers at the airport when I arrived in her country
for the first time a couple of decades ago) -- the cop,
he took to loitering meaningfully nearby, sending
frequent bad vibes my way. So to the hideaway ho.
    On this, another jyze poster night. In my bag a
couple of new jars of tempera and a new cheapo brush
(but not the new nerfball I'd hoped to find at the big
toy store downtown, to replace my two considerably
shrunken mainstays, the red and the purple). In my
shirt pocket a list of new poster ideas to play around
with, including double size and greeting-card size, and
the one for Rob's birthday still to do (though his
visit's been put off a week because his daughter's in
town this weekend). "So You Think You Know Jyze" tops

322

the list. Others: "Deviant Jyze Readings." "Hymn
from a Jyze Pavilion." "That Good Jyze Moan."
"Everybody Got Jyze But Me." And new just now way
down at the bottom: "Jyze Hideaway Ho!"

(And here I'll note the job-placement service is
moving into the suite which shares my foyer entrance.
Currently they're holding down the suite around the
corner, so maybe they're expanding and will occupy both
suites. Snazzy dressers every one, at least by my
standards, and from their accents I'd guess several are
recent immigrants from various far-off lands. Should be
interesting -- although I hope not too interesting.)

But the big change. Actually it started with the
decision to postpone contacting Lady V. Forget about
"the last time I saw your tear-stained face." Don't
fret "peace & love." -- Or anyway not for another year.
True, a year from now I'll be (if I'll be at all) a year
older, a year grayer, a year less springy-stepped. But
by then I should have some recent work I can proudly
show her, or at least have a better idea whether I ever
will have anything recent I can proudly show her (not
that I'm saying I have anything old I can proudly show
her). -- And even so I may not want to contact her then
either.

How come this reversal on Lady V? I don't really
know. Reading through the bound version of "Notes on
Ending with R" (the fictive V) probably had a lot to do
with it, as did a delayed reaction to rereading her
letters from a decade back. Delayed chills. Her cruel
streak. The way she just dropped me flat six years ago.
More than anything else the sense -- much as with Lady U
-- of our interests having radically diverged. And...I
just don't want to go crawling back to her under such
circumstances.

(Meanwhile, I should say, nothing from Lady K this
week. So it would appear hope's just about expired with
her as well. Only minor twitches and tingles now as I
approach the mailbox. Maybe she'll send a card at
Christmas? Maybe I should make another try to get
through to her? -- But not likely, no. And this too

has something to do with the big change.)

Next step, I swung by the scope office on a Saturday night and checked the job docket and the safe to see if I could figure out what was happening with grand jury. And an answer emerged. Simple. Reporter Verna is shafting me. Again. She's taking grand jury but now is scoping it herself. Her own laptop is in the safe along with the one I use. I guess she needs the money pretty badly, and I don't really begrudge her that. But you'd think she would've at least told me. Called or left a note. Or ex-partner Una would've. How could they not have felt some obligation -- both Una and Verna -- after assuring me earlier the work would go to Jyzer Ink?

The ingrates! I was cursing and blowing hard for hours. Now I found myself truly up against it: J. Ink would have (just as I had feared) no more scoping work, except possibly an occasional back order from reporter Naomi, until January at the earliest, and I might well learn before then that it, and I, would have no more scoping work ever (should Naomi change her mind about returning, as I continue to hear she might).

Or another way of looking at all this: I'd have the next three months free. Might be my last chance to focus exclusively and full time on "Jyzer" or any other JIFT project, Mentoka series or otherwise.

But was I ready to? I started turning it over in my head. And lo and behold, the jyzo blitz came rushing to my rescue. Suddenly I saw how I could incorporate something much like it into the "Jyzer" story and how it would fill a gap in the weakest section. And then (while pacing around in the hall outside the hideaway here at a late hour when apparently no one else was present in the whole building) I stumbled upon (as it were) a new narrative approach which I'm calling retroJIFT or maybe reJIFT (though I've used both of these terms before in different ways), and instantly I knew I now had enough to go ahead and give "Jyzer" another whirl.

So I'll do that. Starting Monday. Will sweep aside all else except for the usual JIRT sessions every eighth day in this J-book right here. ("Jyze! Jyze! Jyze!" "Daddy Don't You Jyze So Fast." "Jyze Fool You." "Too Damn Jyzey in Here!" "Squirt of Jyze on Top." -- All from today's list.)

Every day I'll be going at the retroJIFT/reJIFT here in the hideaway. In a little under two months I should have a draft finished. And beyond that I don't want to be saying much of anything about this project. Don't want to queer it by jyzing about it.

And that's it. The big change. No Lady K, no Lady V, no Sofie, no Rikki, no anyone else -- except for whoever pops up in "Jyzer." (And of course I know just who that will be. We've got Lena (the fictive Lady K), we've got Yo (the fictive Lady S), we've got Mija (another fictive version of Lady S). And for pals we've got Tom T. and Ken (the fictive Ken D.) in beefed-up roles. And for murky villains we've got Karl M., P.Z.W., and Lee C. And to top it all off we've got the whole Sandefjord clan, including several closetfuls of little-known but still usefully disruptive family skeletons which in my own Mentoka days I didn't even know existed.)

-- Meanwhile another back order came in from reporter Naomi and so I was granted a second crack at the new scope-office system. This time I typed up my "1,001 Jyzo Hits" and printed them in nineteen lists of fifty and one of fifty-one. Personally I think they're funny as hell -- I might even want to append them to "Jyzer." At the very least they'll be adorning the walls around me in one form or another for the rest of my life (barring some other big change of a type that as of this moment seems highly unlikely) -- not all of them, of course, but eventually maybe a couple hundred. "Dude You Get So Jyzed," for example, and "The Godelian Completeness of Jyze." And: "Rubbings for a Jyze Genie." "Bucket for an Old Jyze Pump." "The Origins of Jyzemania." "You Jyze Me So Good." -- All from the most recent volume of "1,001 Jyzo Hits."

To plunge into this new "Jyzer" effort I don't really have to do much rearranging of my life. My daily schedule should be just about exactly the same. Up at eleven, to the hideaway around three or four, back to unit B-2 around midnight, to bed at four, with all meals taken at home and grocery-shopping on Saturdays and daily browsing at magazine stands on the way down to the hideaway. "And on the Eighth Day He Jyzed" -- in here, the JIRT kind, that is, real time. And that same day also a day of rest from the retroJIFT/reJIFT (or I think I'll just call it reJIFT now that I've made as clear as I can -- or will ever want to -- what it really means).

As for Lady U, I've decided not to see her for a while. She waited more than two months to contact me, so I'm in no hurry to get back to her. This week the post office mistakenly forwarded to me the water-district bill for U Acres, so when mailing it back to her I'll add a note saying I'm on a roll right now and hope she won't mind putting off our next meeting for another month or two (and meanwhile would she please keep tossing any periodicals coming in for me under her name into a box for future exchange). I'll suggest we get together sometime around Christmas maybe -- for what I expect will be the last time ever.

Decks cleared. Right here it'll be happening. And this is how it should be. If ever I was ready, I'm ready now. Got the place. Got the story. Got the time. Even got what I think are a number of hot new ideas (yeah!). Even got a new connection with current jyze preoccupations so I can feel I'm doing what I know how to do and love to do and thus keep an old, old promise to myself. "Jyze As It Oughta Be."

-- So now home. Watercolors. And back for an encore later. "The Way You Jyze Tonight!"

*   *

Better get on this before I'm too tired. Too tired to jyze. Could it happen? -- But of course, and it has many times. What's good, though, it leaves zero tracks in the jyzebook (usually) when it does.

Same place as last week and I think the previous week too. The redwood worktable, the lamp, the paint bowls, the posters drying on the rug. Three a.m. "Jazz

After Hours," I think the show's called. The DJ's voice always brings Tom T. to mind. -- And Tom did write, by the way. Squeezed out a page which showed up in my box in real life this week. Said he was "greatly amused" by an old protojyze excerpt I sent him. Didn't say a thing about the "50 Greatest Jyze Hits," Volumes 1, 2, and 3, so I guess I'll have to see if the complete set of twenty volumes will spark a reaction.

Tonight I devoted mostly to touching up old posters. Tomorrow night for new ones. After that I don't know how long it'll be before I get back to them. Maybe not until Christmas-card time. (At least one card will say on the cover "I'm Dreaming of a..." and then inside in big red glittery letters: "Jyze Xmas!!" That would be Rob's, though it could be Tom's too. I keep forgetting: my jyze audience has doubled now. Or considering that Mother's gone, I could say tripled, Lady U being the only other living member.)

My jyzing muscles are worn out from all the poster daubing. Hard to control the J-stick here as it careers along. This pleases me in the same way sore muscles do, or did rather, after hoops. Or after some acrobatic balling (going way back now, and using a term that seems to have gone completely out of fashion -- except in the hoops realm, that is -- and since hoops is often called balling now in street talk, I guess I can say I've been balling all along -- since I was about six years old).

I'm always happy doing watercolors. Even as I'm doing them I like to picture myself doing them, sort of like an action painter flinging down the paint. This isn't to say they're much good, these posters, as works of art, although some of the lettering may be okay (thanks to all my years of practice with an almost-brushlike pen on blank-book protojyze pages).

Barely awake. The window washers came by this morning, startling me into maximum vigilance at eight a.m., which is to say: the exact middle of my night. Never did get back to sleep. Turned out my windows were the first they did in the entire building.

Wondering what I should touch on real fast now to

be sure it gets in before I conk out. "Hold Up Your
Jyze End." Yeah. So then how about the bloody red moon
of a full eclipse, one evening a couple of weeks back.
Everywhere I went downtown that night scores of heads
were tilted skyward: a strangely disconcerting scene.
It reminded me of some old sci-fi movie where the crowds
were all staring up at a slowly descending spaceship
stuffed full of alien -- what? -- jyzers maybe.

And the planning meetings I missed, one each for
the two main polar zones of my inner-city turf. At one
point I was determined to attend both but eventually I
pulled back on both. Civic-mindedness just doesn't fit
in with the person I want to be right now. I ought to
be brooding over my work, not attending community
meetings. But yes, I still believe in such meetings.
One day I'll start paying my dues again. But now, like
I say -- and say and say -- fierce focus on "Jyzer" is
what it's all about, and more than ever.

Slanting autumn light. Presidential debates. The
snide and sarcastic right-wing warhawk who reminds me
way too much of my father at his worst. Interesting
review of a book about killer chimps. Reprint of an
inspiring antiracist rant from an obscure radical
journal, "Why Be White?"

-- And the stock market keeps going up. Longest
bull market in history, so they say. Every day on my
hike from hideaway up to scope office I pass by the
local office of the brokerage Lynn hired for me (well,
no, not every day now; did before, though) and I'm
reminded of ol' Mom's sacrifice, my good fortune, though
I also find it awkward to be part of the stock-owning
"rentier" class (by whose standards my deep-reserves
stash, while still a good piece of change, would
certainly be nothing more than change). This week's
report from Lynn's group crowed about their selection by
Pure Greed Magazine, I think it was called, or something
similar, as one of the two hundred best investment-
advice firms in the country. I'm not getting rich or
anything, but in six months my deep reserves have grown
from 66K to 69K and they've also paid out -- to me! --

almost $2500 in quarterly installments.
     Lost a button off one of my new shirts from last
spring. That shirt's now out of action until I can find
the time to stage a major domestic repair session.
Shoe-gooing will also be part of that session.
     Must stop. Must. "Jyze the Hard Way" -- halt!

36

     Always wanted to go at it in this joint.
-- "Always" hailing back a good three, four months now,
maybe even a little longer. But it's the cine-cafe in
the north tripolar zone. "The village." About two
blocks from the supermarket, which I'll be hitting next.
And what's more, it's north of the supermarket, meaning
this is the new turf's end. Farther north than this I
don't get, or at least not without transgression.
     A round table right by the door, which at this
moment stands wide open. Sun again! After a week of
miserable storms and drenchings, thunder, lightning
flashes on the inner walls of unit B-2 (pulsations
similar to those of the Fourth of July fireworks but far
brighter). And under the glass tabletop here, a print
of a nude female figure study by "Tal 9/33." I like it.
Mixed chairs, colorful carpet, movie posters ("Because
of You"), a lazily spinning wooden ceiling fan, warmth
and intimacy, decent prices, delicious aromas, a window
flowerbox aburst with late blooms at my right elbow --
welcome all this collectively, sez I, to the list of
top-ten jyze venues, and I mean with a bullet.
     What news? Main thing, start-up of the "Jyzer"
reJIFT has been postponed, until roughly day after
tomorrow. This because I needed time to rethink some

plot elements and get everything set for the big push
(I'd thought I was set, true, in that first burst of
excitement, but on second thought some adjustments were
necessary). Then too, the "Memorials" bluelines arrived
-- finally! -- and I've had to devote about twenty
hours to those and I'm not finished with them yet. Then
too, I have a new romantic interest.

What say? Come again? Yes, true, someone new, but
not much to report about it. An impulse. A regression.
What's more, it's something I doubted I would ever do:
bite on a classified personal ad. But there I was
glancing through the personals in a national literary
review at two a.m. and the name of a city a mere 140
miles from here jumped out at me. Short ad, someone
who's (as I recall now with no copy to refer to) "witty,
kind, attractive," an "SWF" in the decadal age cohort
one behind mine (meaning she's four to fourteen years
younger), self-proclaimed bibliophile and cinephile,
attends readings and goes for walks, and at the end she
queries, "Correspondence, visits?" On the spot I dashed
off a letter, a four-pager but the pages were small, and
had fun doing it, and sent it off the next day.

Why so? Guess I needed something to help keep my
spirits up and to fill the gap left by Lady K's failure
to reply (which remains the case) and my own decision to
postpone for at least a year any attempt to get in touch
with Lady V. And by my own earlier vow back in August
that I won't be ready to go full renunciation -- or even
renunciation lite -- until this volume itself is full
and this year we're in right now is over. -- And I
think it's working: that is, my spirits are on the rise.

The chances of anything actually coming of this
personals venture are slim indeed, but that there is any
chance at all -- and surely there is -- may be enough.

I did hesitate to do it. Mainly I was afraid I
might somehow be distracted from the reJIFT push. Was I
sabotaging myself here? Just in case, I made clear in
the letter that I'm committed to a "writing project" for
the next couple of months. Meanwhile how about we
exchange some letters? -- And to my surprise I'm

finding this hope that a correspondence will result does after all fit well with the reJIFT project itself, because there too my fictive narrator (none other than the familiar Jyzer G, of course, but with a few new quirks and foibles grafted on and some others chopped off) is involved in a romantic correspondence and wondering what will come of it once his own jyze project is completed. And ironically enough in his case the correspondence is with the very Lady K -- in her fictive Lena form -- with whom the version of the jyzer sitting right here today is also trying to get a correspondence going, in real time, right now, though with rapidly diminishing hopes of success.

More later on this new venture? Maybe. Eventually for sure because the letter can't be called back (nor would I want to have it back if I could). But now time's short. Rob's due to show up at B-2 at five to look over the bluelines and be the first to inspect the jyze poster gallery, which is up to thirty wall-mounted and four back-of-bureau-mounted works, with eighteen of the earlier hangees demoted to a storage portfolio, so fifty-two in all. And I've got a new one for him too as a birthday present, No. 53, framed and gift-wrapped: "Brother, Can You Spare a Jyze?" (A change from the "Jyze Bros Jyze Again" I'd originally planned to do for him.) The five o'clock arrival time is a concession to his new schedule; he must be up at six a.m. tomorrow for the long crosstown bus ride to work.

And already it's -- what? The watch! On its chain! Yank it! -- Sez, when I push the windup knob down and the red-starred lid pops open: 3:27.

Very likable spot, this. Neighborhood folks in and out. A row of little shops across the street to the west and the start of the big hill across a different street to the north, site of the renowned counterbalance (a kind of cable car) in days of considerable yore.

Same question for Rob's visit as the last couple of times: what's for dinner? Will it be chicken patties to go with the two big bakers? I guess. And cake and ice cream because this is also a birthday celebration. I

already have candles for the cake, leftovers from my own
over-the-top private birthday celebration. (And Rikki
still hasn't replied to the letter I wrote her that same
night. It might even have offended her. More likely,
though, she's got other matters to tend to and it's hard
for her to whip off a quick reply. She's not the
spontaneous type. Seems to labor over every word.)

Eyes of the frowsy little naked lady peering up at
me, but upside down, when I slide this J-book out a
little farther to squeeze in these last words at the
bottom of the page. Hello! Standing on her head no
hands! Like a parrot swinging under its perch -- or a
sassy sixty-niner smiling back through spread legs!
Yes! Memories flash! -- "Beep My Jyze Horn," he urgeth.
"Honk honk," she replieth between slurps.

*   *

Midterm at the deli U. Just walked Rob to the
downtown bus stop (seventeen stories directly below the
scope-office windows) and as I hiked the middle road
back toward home a screeching band working out on the
tiny stage just the other side of the storefront picture
window here snagged my attention and I thought -- why
not. Go ahead, blow the buck and a half.

Am doing so. Bottle of draft root beer. But I'm
not sitting in that performance room. Too dark for
jyzing in there anyway, but that's not the real reason.
The screeching band is gone but a maximally affectless
guitar-strumming folksinger is now doing her thing. A
dozen people listening, or at least physically present.
In some sense listening if not deaf or earplugged.

I attended only the one reading here. Never did
return. But since I've been nowhere else in the interim
-- no other clubs in the evening, except the birthday
stop at the digi-cafe -- my failure to show up again
might not appear to reflect on the deli's readings. And
maybe it doesn't; how could I be sure? In any case I
doubt anyone will ever be able to drag me into that room
over there for another reading. -- And does this hold
true even for the dedicated reading-goer of the
personals ad to whom I have a letter out right now? I

say it does, yes. But perhaps I should be ready to bend
a little. (Only a little, though. Bending a lot would
require an extreme depth of incentive or inspiration or
need. Fiery infatuation at the very least.)
     Four and a half hours with Rob. We couldn't talk
much; he needed most of that time for double-checking
the bluelines. He's willing to pay for another round of
corrections, so unless this would delay the printing too
much (and raise our fears that the company itself might
fold in the meantime) we'll go ahead with it. The cost
will be over two hundred dollars, maybe closer to three.
Rob's take on it: "It's not my money anyway" -- that is,
it's Mother's and she'd want those typos cleaned up.
And he'd be troubled by the thought of some great-
grandchild of his coming across them a century from now
and thinking how careless the compilers must've been.
(I don't disagree. But given the nature of the
publisher I'm pleased we've reduced the number of
glaring errors to a few dozen. The first time around
there were literally thousands.)
     Popeye would've been delighted, Rob and I concurred,
to know two of his grandsons were poring over his
manuscript more than four decades after his death.
     The jyze posters had Rob chuckling. Liked "A Jyze
Mazurka" best (an excellent choice!), then "The Love
Song of Jyzeslinger G" and "Jyze What You Got," with "A
Jyze Manifesto" garnering honorable mention. Insisted I
do too have artistic talent, saying he'd been aware of
it ever since the days of the sundeck murals when we
were living together a quarter century back. I aw-
shucksed. I can letter a little and that's about it (I
repeated); the rest is a step or two removed (at best)
from blind paint-slinging and I have no illusions about
that. -- A single candle on his birthday cake. His
hair's thinning too, he said, and I could see this is
true. Nutshell, the Brothers S. (a/k/a the Bros Jyze)
are making ready to limp off into the sunset. -- And at
his request I offered my view of why it is Barb's so
inflexible and hard to get along with, the sibling-
theory version focused on the very early years. It

seemed to help him some. At bottom, though, we're both
still perplexed and probably always will be.

(Sibling theory. This week a well-known shrink's
new book on that very topic is drawing lots of media
attention. We firstborns do not come off well in it --
not unless you happen to chime with rock-ribbed
reactionaries, which according to the book firstborns
tend to be. If not for Lady K and the counterculture I
might've gone down that path myself. Plenty of us
exceptions hanging about, though, in my generation -- so
many we might almost disprove the rule.)

-- The chain of mediocre folksingers here at the
deli continues unbroken. Some a lot worse than others.
But hearts are in this and art of a sort is being made.
People cheer and applaud. An authentic jyzer's
meanwhile hard at it in the other room and no one knows
(this room's empty -- has been the whole time).

No alcohol here. Probably this is why the place
always goes dead so early. Regardless I'm happy such a
spot exists in my hood and I'd like to see it prosper.
(You don't have to be a fan of any particular art to
want arts-oriented joints like this one to do well.
Spirited. Offbeat. -- As now, a poetic rapper. A
surprise. High-school girl, hip-hoppy, an out Afrusan
lesbian, to summon the old Mezzu lingo yet again. Looks
a little like Marna H. of my muckraking days and her
voice even sounds like Marna's: rich and cheery and
melodious, seductive, young even for her age. "We're
going out of our minds tonight -- that's where we're
going." Whoops and cheers. Hey, me too! Take me
along!)

-- Well, but the jyzer's still alone in the outer
room, de facto guarding the deli counter. Out of his
element. "Jyze What You Got," yes indeed, and he'll
keep on striving to do so. But the world might no
longer be providing the kind of element he's most
comfortable in and can also afford. And yet if that's
so, so what? The task is still the same, in one's
element or out -- still elementary. Fundamental.
(Meanwhile, close this book and head the jyzer on home.)

[For Jyze You Know You Must]

                    *   *

     -- And as I walked those four or five blocks I
suddenly realized why I'd been feeling so low earlier.
It was talking with Rob about Lady U. He was saying he
could understand how painful the breakup must've been
for me. And I was finding myself unable to go into it,
except haltingly and stupidly. The wound. This must
have had Rob thinking either I'm pathetic in my
woundedness or I don't care enough about him, feel close
enough to him to be able to open up about it. Or maybe
I just appear to be a monster of unfeeling, I don't know.
Just a typical callous male of this culture or any
culture or maybe just a typical callous human being,
period, yeah. -- But which of these is true, if any? I
can't say. What I can say: I'm deeply saddened by it
all, by the breakup itself and by my inability -- indeed,
lack of desire -- to come to grips with it.
     Another sadness too that was related to aging in a
more direct way. Telling Rob about the time shortly
after my college graduation when Mother, as she and I
were driving downtown to meet Dad one evening, said --
blinking back tears -- that she wanted me to remember
her the way she looked at that moment, not how she'd be
when she was old. She wanted me to appreciate her when
she was at her best or at least not too far removed from
it, as she had failed to do, she said, with her own
mother. And I'd been reminded of this tonight because
at that time Mother was exactly the age Rob just turned.
(And she was all dressed up for a big night on the town.
And I do remember how she looked then as she sat in the
passenger seat: terrific. What a mom! No wonder all
her kids are so screwed up! -- Not that Dad played no
role in it. -- And not that we didn't ourselves, we
sibs, whether in ways currently theorized or not.
-- And of course society and the times and for that
matter a permute and combo of marauding deities and
vengeful spirits no doubt chipped in plenty too.)
     So these two sources of bone-deep sadness. On a
Saturday night. (Barb, by the way, sent Rob a birthday
card with a short note saying she'd taken two months off

from work -- on disability -- and wasn't at all sure
she'd still have a job when she tried to pick up the
traces again at the end of October. And her live-in
partner Keith was spending the entire month on the far
coast, presumably readying the family home for sale
after his father's death (just as I did with 636 in
Gatewood twenty years ago). Yet I've heard nothing from
Barb in reply to my two letters and the birthday gifts I
sent her in late August.)

    -- A grievance here? Am I whining or something?
Nah. Or at least no more than usual. At heart it's a
matter of puzzlement. A sadness. One more lousy
sadness. And me a jyzer full of life with lots to do.
A jyzer in "mature" disguise, yes. -- And right before
my eyes a couple of walls magnificently bejyzeled, so
why even a puzzlement? "Jyze Hits the Wall." Dig it!
Hit it again and again! Then do a jyze mazurka!

    But I'm still grumpy, okay. Maybe because tomorrow
I'll have to grind out that promotional piece for
"Memorials." Rob and I had planned to work it up
together tonight but we didn't get around to it. "Guess
you're going to have to do the whole thing all by
yourself," he chortled as we packed up to leave. Ho ho.

    Wall heater on; I can hear it. The new season
truly demanding its use for the first time. Soon the
vines on the fence outside the window will be withering
and my private life will gradually expose more and more
of itself to the eyes of bypassers in the alley (very
tall ones especially) as well as those of jammed-up
drivers out on the viaduct and also those of occupants
of the upper-floor studios in the brick building across
the viaduct. So then will I be feeling less lonely?
(But who's feeling lonely now? Except for rare isolated
moments, not me. Or anyway not usually.)

    -- Because I did come up with a new pair of
nerfballs. Must work in a mention of those right here
before I crash. An orange one and a blue one. I might
even spring for a couple more next week (at a discount
joint in the storage port) and thus make myself
virtually immortal in terms of nerfballs.

[For Jyze You Know You Must]

37

    Aboard. A brilliant autumn day. A terrific chance
to see if the old stuff will still jyze in the same way
at the start of yet another new era: era of the reJIFT.
    Yes, it's underway. Just barely. (Like the ferry
itself right now. And it's my old regular vessel, the
grounded one, back in action after its reruddering,
aptly enough.) -- Feeling my way on the thing.
Realizing already I won't be able to make some of the
hoped-for changes but also seeing some new possibilities
opening up. Working very roughly and spasmodically so
far. A raw draft is what it's supposed to be, though,
and I'm intending to keep going at it in pretty much the
same raw fashion all the way through to the end. Which
will be, if all goes well, December 10th. Forty-four
days from now. Just as in the story itself (that is,
fictive G supposedly churns it out on, but not in,
forty-four days, meaning they're not consecutive).
    Today being J-day, it's also my off day. R&R. Hop
on that ferry and ride. Hike up that mean milelong hill
double time just to show I can still do it. Buy a
couple more spare nerfballs in case they stop
manufacturing the things. And later, back in the city,
using a free pass Rob gave me, take in the movie about
spotting trains. Cousin Georgie, who's connected with
the movie industry in some way I've never understood,
sent him a batch of these passes and he and Gail won't
have time to use them all. Rob and Georgie became
friends during Rob's university days in Lahontan and
they've kept in touch over the years. (To me it's a
surprising connection; until recently I didn't even

know it existed.)

So all eyes are on the reJIFT. Turn the heat up high and stir for forty-four days -- of which actually just forty-one remain -- and see what we've got.

The start itself was the hardest part. Three straight afternoons I marched down to the hideaway "fiercely determined" and the first two I found I still wasn't ready. Something felt wrong. Finally the third afternoon it was going to happen or else. And did, though not until several hours later, as the band blasted away down below (mostly old imported rock stuff, itself rehashed -- which is a lot like reJIFTed -- and electrified blues, both of which happened to sync well with the original era of the story). Except for me, the office portion of the building (the upper five stories) was empty. Or maybe Byron J. was hunkered down in his own hideaway two stories up quietly churning out another prizewinning play, who knows. If he was, he probably knew someone was hard at work down on the second floor, because every now and then I would burst out of my office and pace around in the hallway for a while, maybe even mazurka in place and emit a few yowls to put to shame those coming from the band one more story down.

Meanwhile the book fair's in session and Ray W. is the poster boy. He's back again! So old this is getting. But just as with Lady V, I'm not about to reopen our acquaintance unless I have something in hand, meaning something newly published which at this point would just about have to bear the title "Jyzer." (And if this reJIFT works as I now think it will, Ray W. himself will feature as a key character in the second and third volumes of the trilogy: "Mentoka Dreams" and "Mentoka Ghosts.")

Here's the turn. (The very old lady sitting in the booth behind mine lost an earring -- it fell off and I heard the tinkle as it hit the deck -- and a little girl sitting across the aisle dived under the bench and found the bauble right next to my foot and for this heroic act the woman gave her a dollar as a reward. For a moment it appeared it would be a fiver because the woman

couldn't find any singles in her purse and she'd already
promised a reward and the little girl was jumping up and
down in wild anticipation. She's six years old. Just
happened.) (If I hadn't been too wrapped up in this
damn jyzing I could've had that buck for myself.
Could've easily kicked the kid aside.)

Looking back on the J-week I don't see much other
than the reJIFT struggles. Mailed off the corrected
genealogy bluelines via a parcel service, lightening my
wallet by a sawbuck (do they still say that?). It
would've been a twenty but I sent the package second-
day delivery when they told me the cost of overnight.
As if one day or one month or even one year matters now.

Then I wrote Barb to let her know the second half
of the "Memorials" bill needs to be paid. On the way
back home after mailing the letter I decided she in her
prickliness might find a couple of mildly joshing
sentences in it offensive, so I called her. We talked
for an hour or so -- on my bill! No breakthroughs. She
seemed irked when I urged her to keep working at the
exercise which cured my shoulder problem a few years ago
(and Mother's a quarter century ago). Otherwise, okay
talk but majorly constrained. Will she ever bring up
her "you're a liability" ultimatum from almost a year
ago now? "Say only the kind of things I approve of or
stay out of my life!" Probably not. Ever withdraw it?
Almost certainly not. Therefore it's not too likely
we'll be seeing each other again anytime soon. If
something had developed with Rikki we might've been
drawn back together despite everything. But it hasn't
happened.

(Regarding Rikki Barb said, "I just have no idea
what's going on with her." Obviously they're not the
best of pals. She also said, "Whenever she gets one of
your letters she just glows. She always asks if I've
heard anything from you." -- But it's now been almost
two months since my last letter to Rikki and she hasn't
replied. And I'm into the reJIFT now. All romance is
on hold. -- Not that there is any romance, of course.
But the hold is ready just in case.)

[Jyze and Jyze Alone]

    As we pull in. This is the last weekend until next
summer for riding the foot ferry free. It's also the
last weekend for riding the state ferry on my current
coupon book. But I'll be coming over once more this
winter, as it looks now, to pick up my mail and say one
last goodbye to Lady U. For that, aptly enough, I'll
have to pay full fare. In December most likely.
                    *   *
    Did I say brilliant autumn day? That was then and
this, though only a couple of hours later, is something
completely different. Gray and gloomy and soon rainy.
It blew in from the southwest as it usually does over
here. The Stygian express. How well I remember them
roaring up and engulfing our backwoods town.
    The birds are liking it. They figure it must be
dusk and so are preparing to bed down in the trees and
shrubs, meanwhile chirping up a mini-storm of their own.
    Storage unit. Garage-style door rolled all the way
up, naked dangling bulb shining high overhead. The old
birthday picnic table. Both drawers to the old fire
safe wide open to let the old manuscripts and notebooks
(and whatnot) air out, though I doubt it does much good.
Too much oldness in there. And everywhere else in here,
yes, except attached to these bones (the ones working
trusty old No. 5, the J-stick). Renewable flesh -- ha!
    Anita, co-owner with her husband of the storage
franchise, was holding down the front desk. We jawed
the usual way as I paid my November rent. She saw Ray
C. at the summer concert series in the city, she told
me, and didn't think too much of his show. I told her
I'd seen it just a mile or so from where she saw it --
but several decades earlier. She told me about her
problem with shingles, the disease kind. Talk about
old! (And I've got a few years on her, I suspect.)
    -- Rode over on the historic wooden double-deck
foot ferry. Every time I come here now I think of that
remarkable epiphany a few months back, Dad's spirit
sailing on ahead. Also thought of the anguish caused by
the sight of that guy zipping along on his bike as I
trudged up the same way again today, the long pull. But

I'm almost invulnerable right now, absorbed in "Jyzer."
And no doubt for that same reason I'm scarcely noticing
the expected lonely-guy pangs. It becomes easier to see
how fictionizing, for some writers anyway, could be a
substitute for socializing (as proclaimed in a fine new
book of essays, several of which I read standing up at
the ORB last week) (and yet this way of looking at
writers has always bothered me: it condemns you to being
seen, and seeing yourself, as a social failure -- which
might not be too terrible at my stage in life or that of
the author of the essays but can hurt plenty and maybe
do a lot of long-term damage when you're, say, twenty-
two, like fictive G in "Jyzer").

Bought two more sets of nerfballs at the discount
store across the street here. Also noticed my favorite
brand and type of soup was on sale (and one of the best
flavors too: country vegetable) and sprang for half a
dozen cans. Clearly I need to be on guard -- as before,
only more -- against doing too much of this impulse
bargain-buying. I'm now up to about thirty cans of soup,
all but two this same brand and type and most the same
flavor. How long does the stuff keep, I wonder. Got to
be at least a year. Or so I hope.

Big load off my mind earlier this week, finally
opening the way to attack "Jyzer": I wrote the text for
the "Memorials" publication notice. It's what I was
working on exactly a year ago when Mother's health took
its sudden turn for the worse. Her very last letter to
me contained half a dozen suggestions for the notice.
(I wound up rejecting them all. But I'm sure she'd be
happy with it regardless. Not least, I managed to work
in the word "distinguished.")

-- It's still not raining. If I wrap this up now
and hurry down the hill I may be able to avoid a soaking
(though I did bring a folding umbrella, as always, and
I'm wearing the hooded green canvas jacket; but neither
of these will help much if it's wind-driven rain, and I
suspect that's what it'll be).

Talk about funereal. So dark now the birds have
fallen silent. And it's only four o'clock, official

sunset time still hours away.

*   *

Man that was ugly. The movie, the walk through the mean streets. Now back in my own little B-2 cell of innocence and sorrow and undeniably relieved to be here.

It's like last week's jyze session or the one before, the sadness at the end. Stupid nostalgia, grief for a lost life. All those prior visits with Lady U, probably a score or more, to this same theater where the movie was showing tonight. The many film-festival screenings we attended there. The night she and I saw a romantic farce there shortly after Marco had left town and her return to me had begun but was far from assured -- inauguration of a whole different kind of life for us.

So all that's history now anyway, sure. The pain wells up and then it ebbs. My note told her I was on a rewrite roll, maybe we could get together in late December. But now I'm thinking I might let that one slide by too. The ache, though, to know she'd rather go off into this new life she's chosen. The concern too, the fear. What'll get her first: dope, AIDS, brain-death? Agony to think of it. Her preference though, I must keep reminding myself over and over.

And my tightly constrained little jyzeworld. My preference.

The movie -- well, obviously my judgment's warped. Decadence and cynicism and ugliness and fatalism but at times some of these artistically conveyed. Powerful moments. Clear connections with our city's own smack-ridden punk and grunge scenes, among others. Stirs up the old paranoia, and it's not really paranoia either: wondering what lurks around each corner on the mostly deserted back-route late-night streets.

I wish now I'd stayed a while at the coffeehouse at the east pole (so to speak) rather than just ducked in for a moment on the way home. Candles, a good crowd. Jyze this jyze of mourning there and it would probably come out quite different. -- Two blocks past the coffeehouse, glary concrete avenues, the low-income

342

highrise where I might easily be living now had I not
flipped through the booklet at the housing agency and
come across the photo of this place right here. That
highrise dump by the freeway makes this lowrise dump by
the viaduct look like paradise. And that coffeehouse
scene, fine as it is, I'm sure would've soon been eating
away at me if I'd become a regular, just as the digi-
cafe scene was soon doing here.

Nope, carry on my own way. Resolutely working to
keep ties with the past alive -- that is, keep my heart
alive -- and to live up to the old hopes and dreams.
Sappy, I'll be the first to agree. Meaning, then, I
think life could do with being a little sappier in some
respects? Something short of cartoon theme park though
maybe? (And this week a leading business magazine rates
our city the most livable in the country. How's that
for cartoon? Think about the trade-offs here! Think
about all those gloriously triumphant selfish genes and
memes! -- So then it's either greed or smack?)

No. Of course it's not. Keep on battling.

-- I even did my laundry so it would be out of the
way. Even walked up to the supermarket at ten p.m. two
nights ago to get a leg up on the weekly provisioning
chore. Clearing all decks and keeping them that way to
the extent possible.

Nothing from Lady K. But some good corn toaster
muffins slathered with spun honey. Not a single visit
to the scope office. But a couple of good stiff drinks
here in B-2. "This is it, pal. Now or never. Maybe
never another chance like this for you."

-- And last night the time change. Six different
clocks I've moved back an hour -- and without a single
hitch! Coming up fast is Halloween, bigger now than
ever in this era of metastasizing social anxiety (when
we all know in our guts unimaginable ecohorrors loom and
what's more here comes that scary millennium!). -- And
for further distraction, this will be the week when the
SWF of the personals ad might get in touch. Or maybe I
should say the chances, however slim, will peak.

Guess I can handle it. This emaciated reed. Of

hope. And when it's gone, if it does go, then what?
Don't know. Looks grim. But worry later, in about
forty-one days. For now, get out there and -- zurk it!

38

It's been a hard struggle, still ongoing, or rather
about to start over, but today's different. A letter.
From Lady K. Just came in a couple of hours ago.
I'm agog over this, turned upside down. My latest
restart on the reJIFT will be postponed for a day or
two. (Tomorrow was to be the day -- election day. The
incumbent supreme leader ten or fifteen percentage
points ahead in the polls, which, speaking now of the
other kind of polls with actual voting booths, I once
again won't be visiting, and for all the same old sorry
yet still wholly legitimate, I do believe, reasons.)
Today my lucky day? It all turns around for me
right here? Maybe so. One good omen: after reading
Lady K's letter I headed out on my way to the south pole
and at the corner stoplight nearly bumped into Sofie E.
She was crossing in the opposite direction, too lightly
dressed for the chill wind, moving fast with her arms
folded just beneath her breasts (which made them look
almost alarmingly bulky), but she said hello as she
passed next to me. In reply I worked up a weird left-
eyed wink, which I don't think I've ever done before.
Any kind of wink at all for me is extremely rare, but
left-eyed? -- And kept going. No break in stride, hers
or mine. And that was it for Sofie until the next
sighting, which by the law of averages will be sometime
in January or February.
But Lady K. (Lisa B. it is now, though, so should

it be Lady B? I say no. Lady K once, Lady K forever.
And Lisa K. too, not Lisa B., except for strictly
practical present-day purposes such as addressing
letters. And of course still Lena P. in the reJIFT.)
     First thought, even before I opened the envelope:
could she have married Jesse B., my college classmate
with the same B. surname? The return address stamped on
the envelope is far coast, of course, within fifty miles
of the town where she grew up. (I'm looking at the
envelope now. This account going down in the pit, as
I'm thinking of it these days, meaning the hideaway,
where I swear to the gods I'll have churned out a
complete draft of "Jyzer" -- co-starring Lisa K. in her
Lena P. form! -- by the end of December or have ground
myself to mulch in the attempt.)
     A short typed letter, one page. It's funny and a
little sassy and a little bristly but not really
unfriendly. From it I learn she's currently living with
a younger guy, apparently not bearing that same B.
surname, but who "adores" her and has been doing so for
the past seventeen years. Unmarried, I gather, because
she says she didn't do well with marriage, using the
past tense, though she has two fine sons, presumably by
the B.-surnamed man: one now a musician and writer, the
other a lawyer (or at least a law-school grad and from a
prestigious law school too, upper five percent of his
class as I recall she said -- I'm doing this from
memory) (meaning that, although the letter's right here,
I'm not reopening it just now, and I don't know why not
except I don't want to be distracted by it -- start
reading it again and lose my train of thought).
     Most interesting, she's a published writer -- of
business and technical writing guides! And travels all
around the world giving classes and consultations in
those same kinds of writing! And pronounces herself to
be a fine and funny teacher -- as well as gorgeous and
immensely successful -- and though this self-evaluation
is partly, to be sure, tongue-in-cheek, it's more like
tongue-sticking-out, as she acknowledges herself,
declaring she has every right to be "snotty." (Nor am I

345

about to disagree. Not now and not ever. Fire away,
kid -- just don't hang up. Or don't take me out of your
sights. Or however it happens to be you're looking this
way, right.)

She wonders what suddenly made me think of writing
her. A "life change" maybe? (Bingo.) She's surprised
I'd give a damn. In an intriguing sentence or two she
refers to having once "revered" me. She says she wishes
me well. She makes fun of me for having signed my
letter to her with just my initials. (Why did I do that
anyway? Was I dreaming of author monograms again?)

That's about it.

-- So on the way down here this afternoon I stopped
in at the library. Sure enough, there she was on the
national phone index under the B. surname, and I added
her phone number (which she didn't include in the
letter) to my brand-new address-book entry for her. The
index mentioned no one else as living at her address, so
I learned nothing more about her sons or the current
seventeen-year man in her life. She wasn't listed in
Who's Who or the authors index, nor had any of the men
with the B. surname appearing in either of those sources
married a Lisa as far as I could make out. But the card
catalog did note one book of hers (just as it does one
of mine, I was amusedly recalling). That book's mind-
blowing title: "How to Write a Great Annual Report."

The irony of this -- it'll have me chuckling and
shaking my head for years, I just know. -- Well, of
course I just know! I know I know! I'm cracking up!
I'm losing it right here and now!

Lisa the poet. When we split up I too was teaching
-- business writing! I too have taught technical
writing "around the world" (it could be said, since I've
done it in cities seven thousand miles apart). The
parallels are boggling. I too have a male offspring,
not two of them (so far as I know) but at least one. I
too was a flop at marriage and then got together with a
younger person of the opposite sex who was "adoring" for
exactly the same period: seventeen years (our eighteenth
year, of course, was a whole different story -- and the

346

fifth and a few others weren't too stellar either).

And one might also ask: Is her writing a how-to book about business practices any more mind-blowing to me than my writing a book about politics and urban ecology is likely to be to her?

Or this: In a sense haven't we both wound up in the field of annual-report production? Hers having to do with business results and mine with personal-life results? I mean, what else is an "Annal of the Jyze Age" if not an annual personal-life report, albeit one featuring incremental updates every eight days.

So I found Lisa's book up in the business section on the second floor. Had to maneuver past a couple of grizzled gents sprawled on the floor to get at it, but pulled it out, opened it to the inside back leaf of the dust jacket and there she was. Instantly recognizable. And is so right now as well, in front of me here on my hideaway desk, because I checked out the book. A small black-and-white photo of Lisa as she looks at age -- what? This edition of the book is seven years old, but an earlier one preceded it by eight years. She looks quite young. Lovely. Intelligent and serious as only befits a world-trotting author. Light brown hair with blond highlights, shorter than I've ever seen her hair (collar length and curled inward) but with full bangs down to just below eyebrow level. Round face, smooth complexion -- scarcely a wrinkle. Wonderful lips. Smallish hoop earrings. She could easily pass for mid to late twenties. Yet when this photo was taken she must've been close to forty. In short, same Lisa: "angelface." Same one who flummoxed the age-guesser at the Centropolis amusement park, he hazarding sixteen when she was actually twenty-two. (And mine he missed by just a few hours, guessing twenty-two and that's what I was about to turn at midnight that same day.)

From the bio beneath her photo I learn damn little. She scored a master's in psychology from a very good school and "...gives highly regarded seminars for [a national management association]."

My father's jaw would drop a foot. As no doubt

her father's would also, and likely did.

(Not much else has happened this week, by the way.
It's all been impassioned grapplings with "Jyzer."
Later I'll try to get back to describing those and to
anything else I can come up with. "Run It Through the
Jyzillator." -- A few things maybe.)

The burning question now is how to respond. She
doesn't openly discourage a response. The return
address is there. She does ask a question ("So -- what
makes you look back?") which can be interpreted as being
less than wholly rhetorical. But she doesn't explicitly
encourage a response in any other way, and as I recall
my letter to her, it specifically inquired as to whether
she might want to start up a correspondence. (Which
reminds me: my response to the personals ad, the one
placed by the SWF just a 140-mile sprint down the road,
still hasn't drawn a reply. I've pretty much written
the whole thing off. But then before today I'd written
Lisa off too.)

What makes me look back? What indeed. A truly
frank answer would admit I'd like her to dump her adorer
of seventeen years and fly out to see me at the first
opportunity, just on the off-chance we might still spark
each other off in person as back in conflagration days.
But best I not say this. -- Or should I just say it?

No. Of course not.

But what should I do?

Her last paragraph is worth quoting in full. (I've
pulled out the letter now. And it is distracting in
just the way I expected.)

So -- what makes you look back?
Perhaps a life change, or even a lingering
memory of a time when you were revered.
Thomas Wolfe notwithstanding, many can and
do go home again. I move forward only,
with no curiosity for what was or might
have been.

Hoo boy. This is the Lisa I knew all right, the
one who talked tough from very early on about, among
other things, either we must marry or we must split

up. I suspect she gave this paragraph considerable
thought. (Maybe she gave the whole notion of answering
my letter considerable thought. She doesn't say when
she received it, but I sent it to the alum association
in early September and her letter is dated October 29.
Of course she might've been off consulting somewhere, or
the alum association might've been slow in forwarding my
letter, or both. So who knows.)

I am grateful for that "revered" line. It's good
to know she wasn't so badly hurt by the way we split up
that she's had to repress everything or regard our time
together with open bitterness. Mutual reverement it
was, then. (Or: mutual first love and other sorrows.)
And I note also that in letting herself use the phrase
"when you were revered" she's directly contradicting
what she says two sentences later, "I move forward
only...." This may not be hugely significant but it
does suggest she's not quite as all-business as the last
sentence of that same paragraph implies. (No curiosity?
Not even a tiny twinge of nostalgia? -- Which, after
all, is an indulgence in, a curiosity about, what was
and might have been. Is it not? Should I ask her?)

No doubt what I'll do is just dash something off in
my usual haphazard fashion. "Slapdash." "All Jyzed Up
Over You." -- And damn the consequences. Which will
probably therefore be negative. -- But in any case I
won't push openly for anything beyond a simple friendly
correspondence. Try to be humorous. Let her know I'm
busy too. Feel her out but not aggressively. Don't
come on like a homewrecker. "He Don't Jyze You Like I
Do" -- no, no, no. Make light of it all. Hang loose.
Hope for the best and expect the worst and -- wait a
second, hope for the best? Don't even bother. Just
hope for another reply. Fantasize all you want, but
keep any serious hopes on a very low simmer.

However, it does give me something to live for on
a day-to-day basis. Outside of the reJIFT, I mean.
(Will my extreme neediness shine through no matter how
or what I write her? Probably. Nothing I can do about
it.)

[Jyze and Jyze Alone]

        Gives the old JIRT a shot in the arm too. And so
far, at least, it sure does beat renunciation. The
memory palace -- now I'm glad I stopped at the door and
decided to take one more spin around the grounds and up
Lady K's alley before locking myself in for good. And
if upon further reflection I decide to lock myself in
anyway -- say starting January 1st -- I may still want
to keep a line open to the real flesh-and-blood Lisa of
the present era. This might even make consorting with
her ghost a shade or two (groan) more intriguing.
        So now, yes, I think I'll grant my overworked
jyzing hand a short break and then see what I can crank
out in the way of a response to her.
                    *   *
        -- It came to eleven pages, but the narrow
reporter's-notebook kind. Plus I enclosed a postcard
showing the historic hideaway building and also a full-
page ad which my former newspaper happens to be running
in today's night paper. (A juicy coincidence, that ad.
No longer am I upset with the gang down there.)
        All in all, without trying to make myself look too
good, I endeavored to paint my condition as being
somewhat less pathetic than it actually is. Most of all
I tried to write a lively letter she'll want to reply to
in hopes of receiving more just like it. But I'm
probably hoping -- that word again -- for too much. On
rereading her letter a few additional times I fear even
more strongly that her current man will be opposed to
her becoming pen pals with a former big love (as I'd
certainly be if I were in his shoes) and she'll respect
his wishes (as, again, she certainly ought to do if
they've been adoring each other for seventeen years).
-- And I wonder: Did she let him vet this letter to
me? I wouldn't be surprised. But then did she have to
override his veto to get "when you were revered" in,
even if only in the passive voice, the identity of the
reverer or reverers unspecified (a fact which I hadn't
really noticed before now)?
        Regardless, three a.m. and I'm still in a state of
jubilation. "Baby Get Jyzed!" I've even skimmed

through her book. Feeling sorry for her, mostly, that
she had to grind out such a thing. It could've happened
to me too, easily, so the sympathy flows extra strong.

A few more rereadings of her letter (still more)
and what struck me with gathering force was the
defensiveness hiding behind all the strong statements.
The vulnerability. Again, it was exactly this
combination of qualities (along with a whole bunch of
others, of course: beauty, wit, smarts, sass, literary
talent, warmth, sensitivity, sensuality, sexuality, on
and on and on) -- this combo, I say, that drew me to her
in the first place. (All that and nothing more? What
about the ineffable Lisa gestalt? You cad you!)

So will she turn out to be a neocon? This is quite
possible too. And maybe it would be good if she did.
At least my interest in her would cool off fast.

*

-- Just retrieved tomorrow morning's night paper.
I guess they don't buzz-honk anymore. A new courier?
If so, no problems thus far.

Election-day paper too. So great was the incumbent
high honcho's lead in the final pre-election polls I
half-expected the headline to declare him the winner.
In a few minutes the first polls will be opening for
actual voting. (My old paper endorses the major third-
party candidate for president. If I were voting I'd be
going for him too.) (-- I'm so tired it's all but
certain some extremely dubious comments will be popping
up in here. Jyze blushes but urges me onward regardless.
-- "For Jyze You Know You Must," yes. And that means
right now! Just jyze it!)

What would I be focusing on had Lady K not written?
For one thing, on the question of why she still hadn't
written. Beyond that, on how this would've been the
week to send off the "tear-stained cheeks" anniversary
watercolor to Lady V. (Now I'm doubly glad I decided
not to.) Beyond that, on how I dropped my favorite
coffee mug this morning -- the one featuring the cheery-
flying-violinist knockoff -- and it broke into exactly
five large pieces (and not a single chip to be found).

[Jyze and Jyze Alone]

     What else? The two aborted "Jyzer" restarts. One
was forty-two pages, the other fifteen. I'm flailing
wildly as I try to find the right tone. This next go-
round will attempt maximum sincerity and it'll also
experiment with telling the story backwards, meaning the
narrator will write the story from memory but in reverse
chronology, the ending first and working backwards week
by week. Strangely enough I think this kind of twisted
telling might solve some of the tone problems. No
longer will I have to worry about how much of the story
narrator G knows at any one point since at all points
he'll know it all. But will new problems arise -- of
course they will! -- and will I be able to handle them?
     Damn well better.
     Or if not, on to the next round, even fiercer and
more desperate.
     -- And anything else? I would've jyzed in depth
about an odd flashing light on my walls. At this time
of year as the sun sinks the last few degrees to the
horizon, it shines through a gap between the two large
buildings directly downhill from mine, its rays reaching
obliquely deep into B-2 along the south (jyzeyard) wall.
But every time a large southbound truck or bus or tall
van goes by on the viaduct the rays are briefly blocked.
Cars don't have this effect at all, only those larger
types of vehicle, but enough of those appear that the
wall sometimes seems to be throbbing or palpitating or
maybe flashing an elaborate message in Morse -- or
Norse? -- code. (If not for Lady K's letter this
phenomenon might've merited half the entry.)
     And leaves, fallen kind, many more of them than
you'd expect in the middle of a city. Cluttering up the
sidewalks along my usual tripolar routes. Mostly small
yellow maple leaves. (Outside a certain fancy French
restaurant a few blocks up the street I almost always
encounter a mound of ice shavings dumped in the square
of dirt at the base of one of the maples shedding its
share of those same abundant leaves and I love to stamp
a footprint in that mound. "The Tread of the Jyzer.")
     And I'd better leave that footprint as the end of

the trail for tonight. Deserted by inspiration (but so
pleased, not to say downright amazed, to find myself
aligned in a whole new way with the universe, including
a big chunk of my own past). Gotta sleep now. ("Thomas
Wolfe notwithstanding" -- that still has me blinking.
Did she forget he wrote most of his stuff standing up?)

39

     For once the jyzemaster can report all seems to be
going well. The new draft of "Jyzer" (the reverse-
chronology reJIFT approach) is now up to page 47, one
day behind schedule, it's true, but nonetheless chugging
along under what at least appears to be a good head of
steam. The incumbent president's back in office for
another term and our state's new governor is likewise a
moderate from the more centrist of the two so-called
mainstream parties and also the first of Briana T. and
Lady V's (half) racial/cultural ancestry to win the
office and that's certainly good except for the
"moderate" part, as opposed to progressive or liberal
or at least a little leftish, in both cases. And --
what else? Can't think. (A book club meeting's getting
out of hand a few tables away. Got to refocus.)
     On "Jyzer" I extend a vote of thanks to Lady K.
Her letter jolted me into a new way of seeing our
fifteen months together or close ---
                         *
And the noise back there jolted me into moving.
New members arriving. Cries of joy, and this of
course is as it should be. Raucous laughter of true
book lovers about to savor communally -- or maybe to
savage communally -- the week's offering.

[Jyze and Jyze Alone]

          -- Wait! Now I see the whole club's leaving!
Trooping up the stairs! Going to, of all things -- if I
heard right -- a movie! -- So no one's back there after
all and it'll probably turn out to be noisy here where I
am now. And that's my favorite table back there. And
hanging above it is an acrylic painting, primitive and
colorful though also more than a little cutesy (but I
still go for it), called "Spring Flight."
                              *
          So now I've flown back. Midautumn flight. To the
brick alcove. To the pipes. A few onlookers must think
I'm wacko to be flitting about like this but then -- I
am. Finicky too. For me this combo is fairly unusual
and I think it must have to do with the reJIFT state I'm
in. The intensity. The hyperfied monomania. And I'm
loving it. A good thing I'm not living with anyone,
though. If I were, I couldn't possibly allow myself to
push this hard. Therefore I must extend thanks to Lady
U as well. (She who finally faced up to her own desire
to live a more normal life. Little did she realize my
own life with her, as I saw it, and even though I
usually liked it well enough, was still much too close
to her idea of normal.) -- But then I also had to wait
for my hormones to ease off just a bit, I think, before
I could go it alone as I'm doing now.
          Except for Lady K. I've clipped her photo from the
dust jacket (who could possibly ever care?) and I often
find myself ducking under the loft to gaze at it. Even
more often I break into semihysterical laughter at the
absurdity of our present state of affairs. -- Didn't
mention this in last week's entry, but the big bold
headline on my former paper's ad, the one which appeared
in the night paper's national edition the very day Lady
K's letter arrived, read "Thirty Years." It was
announcing the anniversary issue, the same one for which
they'd been attempting to solicit quotes from former
staff members such as myself. Clip out a coupon from
that ad and for just three bucks you'll be sent the
three issues detailing the paper's history. And I
wonder: will Lady K bite on the offer? Or maybe should

I bite on it for her? After all, she last knew me when
I was at Mezzu, and (as I mentioned in my letter to her)
I went straight from there to the city where, just a few
months later, this newspaper came into being (though I
didn't join it until four or five years after that).
What's more, when Lady K and I met I was editor of my
college paper and that may well have been what gave me a
leg up with her in the first place.

Yes, bizarre. The very same day!

Sister Barb, I must report, is not at all impressed
with Lady K's photo, a photocopy of which I sent her.
Lisa looks like "just an ordinary person now": that's
how she put it. (True enough if by this she's referring
to the way she's dressed, her makeup and hairstyle; but
there's nothing ordinary about her looks. This is
especially true of her eyes and lips, which I'd defend
all the way to the stake as being truly -- extraordinary.
Like Lady V's, yes, but -- different.)

Barb says she hopes I'm not thinking of starting
anything up with Lady K. Ha -- as if the lady would let
me! As if in my utterly unpresentable and
unaccomplished condition I'd have even a slight chance
with her! No, nothing's changed here; I'm just hoping
she'll prop the door open to a correspondence and
therefore to a continuing fantasy on my part which I can
use to keep the romance machinery occupied. -- Not that
the fantasy wouldn't be based on a true hope, even a
desperate one; it's just that it would be all but
impossible to realize. And I'm well aware of that.
Even in our jaded era we might want to admit that the
troubadours of old knew a thing or two about what really
matters when it comes to romance (the most celebrated
troubadour of all, as an instance, with his own
impossible Lisa/Lena who went by Laura and was married
and utterly unobtainable for a mere troubadour).

(Will Lisa keep the door open to a correspondence?
My view on this now is a little more positive than it
was. Probably what I should fear is a crisis not too
far down the line, one of the shit-or-get-off-the-pot
variety. Even more than she did thirty years ago Lady K

looks to be, and certainly sounds to be in her letter,
the no-nonsense type. "Marriage or nothing." No
dawdling. She'll suspect she's being played with.
-- This is my fear, yes, as I just said and now repeat.
But I do expect to hear from her again. I do expect a
correspondence to develop. -- So go ahead and prove me
wrong, Lady K. Make the jyzemaster look bad right here
in his own home (and only) arena: the jyze.)
     Otherwise Barb's letter had little to say. A
report on her Day of the Dead quest for marigolds to
place on the final resting place of our one and only
mama-san in her scattered ashen form. The gardening
crew had been through up there and the area where the
ashes fell had been weeded and raked -- as the return to
"mother earth" continues apace -- and a couple of
nearby trees had been cut down. I may be wrong about
this, but my understanding is that the Day of the Dead
amounts to a pagan ritual for propitiating the spirits
of those unhappy dead you fear will come back to haunt
you. And if spirits really did work this way -- and
who's to say they don't? -- Barb and I both, and Jeff
for sure and probably Rob too, might have something to
fear where Mother's spirit is concerned (though in the
end I believe her love and strong empathic powers would
prevail). -- And likewise in the end, surprising myself
a bit, I'd say pretty much the same for Dad.
     Oddly enough this matter of propitiating the
spirits of the restless dead plays a key role in "Jyzer"
as it's developing and this week I've been working on
one of the chapters where such a propitiation takes
place (of Roar and Sadie's spirits and also that of the
kid aborted from Lena -- from Lady K, of course, in real
life -- and fathered by fictive G, that is, me, and also
the suicide of the fictive Ryu Mija, who is, to repeat,
a split double for Lady S, from whom a kid might've been
but was not aborted some nine years later -- and that
kid, of course, would be Elgie -- and so, yeah, I can
relate to this Day of the Dead mythomania).
     Another oddity, this week our overwhelmingly
vanilla and notably unreligious city is suddenly

thronged with folks of Lady K's ethnic and religious
persuasion. "The tribe." Some sort of council of
national tribal branches is holding its annual
convention here and it's drawing thousands of delegates
from around the world, including the egregiously right-
wing head honcho from the biggest and baddest such
branch of all, and no doubt this convocation will be
getting lots of play in the (back to being
indispensable) night paper which Lady K probably reads
devotedly just as she always did -- and I'd bet she
still faithfully watches TV news too -- and who knows,
the way things have been going it's entirely possible
she'll see me trudging along in some footage of
delegates taking in the sights at the public market or
the historic quarter. In passing through both of these
prime tourist venues on my way down here tonight I
encountered big crowds, klieg lights, TV crews, and on
one occasion in each venue a network camera which seemed
to be pointing more or less in my direction, perhaps
because they saw me as a bit of local color or (more
likely) a typical member of the slogging local masses.
And even if I don't make the six o'clock national news,
I ought to be able to milk this nifty little coincidence
for a few good lines in the next letter to Lady K.

     (As for that lonely SWF of the personals ad,
meanwhile, forget it. Seems I didn't even make the cut
for callbacks with her. Guess I must've overdone the
offbeat approach. Perhaps it's not wise in such
circumstances to admit up front one is wary of self-
proclaimed intellectuals and one is also just barely
scraping by financially. My letter at least tried to
show her a little of the wit she called for, but even if
it succeeded, it could be wit was not what she was
actually seeking. Or rather: not wit alone. Wit
combined with the standard material attractors, perhaps,
or say wit displayed from a kind of glittery
superstructure atop those same attractors. -- And why
should I be surprised by this? Yet truly I am. I
honestly believed my letter would catch the woman's eye
if not win her heart. Provisionally, sure, but she

wouldn't be able to resist. "This jyzeslinger guy I've got to meet."

-- In three days Dad's birthday. Way back in January when I roughed out my jyze schedule for the year I was congratulating myself because I thought I'd nailed it: J-day on the old man's B-day. So why am I always thinking it's on the 12th rather than the 15th? September, October, November: all three feature a family birthday on the 14th or 15th or both, culminating in Dad's. That fact, should it not be mnemonic enough?

The "Jyzer" schedule, I'll mention here, has now been extended to the last possible date, December 30th (the 31st being a J-day). Go any further and I'd have to break my vow to complete the raw draft this year and also risk facing distractions and disruptions from the restart of scoping work.

Nonetheless I've already checked the calendar and noted that January 1 falls on a Wednesday. This means it's unlikely grand jury would meet until the following week of the 6th and therefore unlikely reporter Naomi would call on Jyzer Ink before then (and that would be the very earliest she might do so; more likely it would be later in the month or sometime in February -- and I'm just hoping she'll call on Jyzer Ink period, anytime. -- So perhaps I'll extend the reJIFT schedule still further at some point, a week or two into the new year. But only if truly and utterly necessary. As of now I'm sticking with the fierce concentration and fully intending to finish the draft by year's end.

Rain tonight. Lots of it recently. A hole has opened in the sole of my right shoe, I just realized this afternoon while hoofing it down the puddly edge-road sidewalks. Shoe-goo time for sure. Gotta do it! (I've rearranged a few items on shelves -- and hung the metal blue dragonfly from the top rail of the loft -- but otherwise accomplished little in recent days in the realm of home improvements or domestic caretaking.)

On cornflakes I'm now extremely well stocked: fourteen giant boxes bought with supermarket half-price coupons, all stacked proudly almost like bars of gold

bullion in B-2's internal hallway. Yesterday I wore a
long-sleeve henley for the first time this fall. The
small maples standing in the jyzeyard and on the other
side of the chain-link fence behind the dumpster have
finally turned handsome shades of yellow. The Santa
Claus hardy fuchsia is still producing new blooms --
miraculous! What a buy! And a postcard came in from
Tom T., currently visiting Mentokaland during a break
from dispatcher training in Centropolis: he knew I'd be
all but derailed by the nostalgia the card would evoke
(picturing a steam engine huffing mightily at the main
depot in downtown Lahontan: the city of my birth and
site of two key scenes in "Jyzer").

     Sounds as though I'm wrapping this thing up and
indeed I'm doing just that. But not for the night.
Just for now. More to say, I'm sure, later, after
finishing off the reJIFT prep work for tomorrow at the
hideaway and walking home with one foot (at least)
squishy cold.

*   *

     Oh yeah, most excellent bowl of country-vegetable
soup. Now for dessert the usual three gingersnaps but,
of course, no pudding, for this is a Tuesday. Every
other day for the pudding but every day for the
gingersnaps, which do quickly go stale once the package
is opened, even if I immediately close it tight with two
wooden clothespins, which I almost always remember to
do. Ironically, though, it's the gingersnaps I should
be rationing; just this week I discovered the drugstore
chain which appears to be the only source of this
particular brand within hoofing distance is no longer
carrying them. "And so the cookie crumbles." (Damn!)

     Arrayed on the carpet below are the freshly unboxed
soccer shoes from this past summer's shoe-sale binge,
the dark-brown ones with black trim. I'll be pressing
them into service tomorrow. The shoe-gooing will have
to wait a bit longer. For one thing I need to let the
sneakers with the right-sole hole (with me it always
seems to be the right side where things go bad these
days) -- let them dry out for a while.

359

                    [Jyze and Jyze Alone]

     It's been a week of idea uproar. I meant to note
this earlier. It's mostly Lady K's doing. The jolt.
The whip. Spurs digging in deep. Hop on this thing and
ride like hell while it's still snorting.
     A couple more ironies and these I plan to tell her
about. First, most days I walk by the site of the
drugstore owned by the family of one of her college
classmates, the very one who was her predecessor with
me, romantically and sexually speaking: Renee D. (though
to my knowledge she's not living in this city anymore
and never has been during my second time in the area,
and I didn't know her yet during the brief first time).
And second, I'm living less than half a mile from the
spot at the fairgrounds where I met Renee D.'s
predecessor, Kristi K., some six months before I met
Renee herself roughly three thousand miles east of here.
-- And an irony I surely won't be mentioning to Lisa, at
least not early on, is that Kristi is the one girl I saw
(balled, yes, it's a fact) between the time I met Lisa
and the time Lisa and I became lovers -- when Kristi
visited Gatewood for a few days while Lisa and I were
both home for Christmas vacation in our separate cities
eight hundred miles apart and we both thought it was all
over with us. (Last thing I heard of Kristi she was a
grade-school teacher at a U.S. military base on Guam, I
believe. -- And neither Kristi nor Renee turned up in
my phone-index search. But even if they had I'd've
still tried to contact Lisa first, no question.)
     Jazz on. A while back the grooveyard jock offered
a bit of cracker-barrel wisdom quite possibly apropos to
my situation with Lady K and/or hers with me: "Better to
have loved and lost than to have loved and won."
-- Reminds me of a dream I had the other night. A Lady
U dream. We're living at the last of our city rental
houses and her parents are visiting us (which they never
did at that location in real life) and she takes me
aside and whispers, "There's a new development," and
leads me out into the backyard and across to the barn
(the saggy cedar one magically transported from the "U
Acres" property we moved to later) and points through

                            360

the window at a guy lying on the bed in the guestroom
(which her parents at one point were planning to put in
that same barn but never got around to). The guy looks
exactly like her father did in pictures I've seen of him
as a young man and to a surprising extent still does, or
at least did as of last year. He's wearing just red-
checked boxer shorts. My eyes ask her if she means this
is her new lover -- the one she's throwing me over for
-- and she nods proudly.

Prophetic? Or so laughably Freudian it might've
been scripted for a parody of a dream textbook? Maybe
I'll find out in December or -- more likely now with the
possibility of an extended "Jyzer" schedule, though
still not very likely -- January.

(Regarding the Kristi K./Renee D. tales involving
Lisa, it's resoundingly true I'm relishing the storybook
aspects of this atavism or recidivism or recrudescence
or whatever it is that Lisa's reappearance in my life
represents. Since otherwise jyze is totally bereft of
plot for this year -- next year too, of course -- I want
to milk them for all they're worth. The title for the
combined annals three and four might someday, who knows,
demand to be something like "The Jyze of How I Got Back
with My First Big Love." -- But that's not too likely
either, no.)

Also this week I sent Lady U a clipping of a
newspaper feature story about Paul A.'s latest opus.
This one, following hard on his bestsellers about slugs,
geoducks, and abominable snowpersons (that's three
different bestsellers), looks to boast the greatest hit
potential of them all: it's about cockroaches. Two
hundred eighty pages!

Another idea popped up for a future year's quota of
jyze. It's basically a steal from a new book in which a
fictionmeister hero of my youth (when he wrote fiercely
about first love) grapples nonfictively but still
powerfully with his own expected upcoming death from a
terminal illness. If I were granted enough forewarning
I might try to do the same and call it "Late Jyze" or
maybe even "Death Jyze."

[Jyze and Jyze Alone]

     (This jyze right here I'm merrily pumping out at
the redwood worktable beneath the jyze posters and
suddenly I'm wondering if I should send Lisa photocopies
of certain posters. Would she appreciate the jyze
concept? Would she see the jyzo as being a form of
poetry sort of like haiku or Korean sizo? I have my
doubts on both scores. But maybe "Think You're So
Jyzey." -- Or no, first "No Way To Get Jyzed." Then
"Jyze Says You Do." Or better, "Jyze Me Tonight," then
"For Jyze I'll Do That," then "A Jyze Supreme." -- But
more likely to be apt, no way around it, at least at
this point: "The Things Jyze Makes You Do.")
     Meanwhile my wall of posters has stopped magically
palpitating at four-forty every day, but this may be
simply because the weather's been heavily overcast all
J-week in typical November Jyze City fashion.
     I should note that the man we've just reelected
will be the country's first president of the twenty-
first century and the new millennium, though in both
cases only for slightly more than a year. And I've had
some moving moments going through old photo albums and
Dad's babybook. At certain times, I discovered, he
looked and acted a whole lot more like me than I'd ever
realized before now. -- But most of all I was stunned
once again by the photo of Lady S sitting on the bench
with me at a lakeside park near Mentoka Falls shortly
before our first parting (that same picnic for students
from her sizo-mad country serving as the model for a
similar scene in "Jyzer"). Could there be a man alive
who wouldn't lose his senses (even give up a woman like
Lady K, as I eventually did) over the Lady S in that
photo? If there could, and is, that man is definitely
not me. -- Or in any case is definitely not as fickle
as I am, I suppose I could say with the delayed wisdom
of a whole lot of perspective. -- But am I trying to
suggest I regret my time with either of these women? No
way! (Some of the side-effects or sequelae, though,
yes, for sure.)

[For Jyze You Know You Must]

-------·

40

-------·

    I may roast here but otherwise it's a great seat.
Front corner of the same cafe as last time out in the
Yuke, away from the entrance, indoors but just behind
the outdoor veranda seat of that earlier visit.
Northeast corner this would be. And a large ceiling-
hung heater blasting away about three feet above my
head, therms coursing downward. On a snowy, cold day,
and I see no other heaters in here. But no other free
tables either, because at this hour -- it's right around
four-thirty -- lots of students hit the nearby streets
these days, and probably always have. (I should know,
at least concerning the past couple of decades, but I
don't specifically recall. Gut instinct says yes.)
    A bench seat with my back to the wall so I can look
out over the assembled multitude. The usual student mix
with a few townies sprinkled in, including a white-
bearded, bald-crowned elder in raggedy street clothes
leafing through a newspaper two tables away. Apart from
him it appears I'm the ancient in here. At the next
table down the bench, tickling away at a fancy laptop, a
sharp-looking guy who resembles Lady V's brother Armand.
Here two shelf-mounted table lamps, one perfectly
positioned for the jyzer's jyzing convenience, a warmly
glowing yellow shade casting a horizontal hemisphere of
ideal size and luminance in which to lay out a J-book.
    Paradise -- of a sort. (Just at dusk. Sidewalks
showing signs of early festive holiday mood. Tolerable
grunge-neopunk fusion playing in here and not too loud.)
    Came out to the Yuke on a bus and also on a lark.
Why not? It was J-day. What else did I have to do?

363

(Other than lots of prep work for the next three days of "Jyzer," true, but I'd still be happy to have a place to visit for tending to the JIRT, the real-time stuff.)
     Comical slip-slidy trek on icy sidewalks to the underground station. (Yesterday the first snowstorm of the year hit -- a total surprise to me -- and when I awoke today the still-green-leafed vines outside my window were packing seven or eight inches of fluffy white stuff.) Then rolling northeastward along the familiar transit route. In summer, with the same number of riders, the bus might've been only half as crowded, everyone aboard today being almost absurdly bundled up, swollen to twice normal size, myself included. -- The overdressing not truly absurd, really, because given this city's predictably hysterical reaction to snow and ice you never know when you'll be marooned owing to tied-up traffic, quite possibly having to walk miles to get home. It's happened to me several times over the years, once entailing a seven-mile in-city walk and on another occasion, in the far province across the water long before it became merely the storage province, an epic icy-hilled ten-mile trek in more than a foot of snow wearing my usual lightweight sneakers.
     And at the U bookstore did find a copy of a quarterly I've been looking for. Then at the cash register, while handing over my check and ID, was asked by the midlife longhaired male clerk as he examined them, "Would you happen to know someone with your same last name whose first name is Rob, or Robert?" Turned out the guy was once employed across the street at the record store and knows brother Rob quite well (though perhaps not well enough to be comfortable trying to pronounce our surname). -- And as far as I can recall, this was the first time in all my years here in Jyze City and environs I've come across anyone unknown to me who's recognized me solely by surname. That is to say: it's doubtful any quest for anonymity has ever been more successful than mine. In fact, before today it's impossible; my record has been perfect. (Unless I'm forgetting something. And maybe I am. Even so, the

feat still looks pretty damn impressive to me.)

A little overheated -- shirt halfway unbuttoned -- but not roasted. Had the storm not persuaded me to wear a heavy long-sleeve henley for only the second or third time since last winter I'd be perfectly comfortable now. (Sitting under this heater reminds me of the many times I intentionally hunkered down directly beneath an overhead ferry heater after getting soaked by frigid windborne rain while waiting in line outdoors to go aboard.)

Nursing no-cal cola in a can -- more than half of it still remaining, so I'm doing well. The one guy in the room who's clearly my senior is still here; in fact he just carried away the wooden folding chair standing on the other side of this table. "You're not using it, are ya?" he asked with a cackle. What he's using it for, I see, is a low table-side shelf on which to stack newspapers. He's also nursing a paper coffee cup which he refills from time to time with water from the fountain in back. The guy's probably hanging out here to stay warm. Gets away with it because he looks harmless and almost professorial and not too many others are trying to run the same scam at the moment. Non-U-looking folks, I mean. This whole time most of the seats have been occupied but not all; the crowd flirts with capacity but never quite reaches it. And so: no heavy pressure to move on. As I was saying last time I was here, the joint's ideal. Wish we could call in a building-mover and transfer it as-is down to my home hood. Locate it around the corner from the coffeehouse and also the bar I want moved down there from east hill.

"Jyzer," I'm up to page 125. It's hard work. Just yesterday I killed off Mija (a suicide, based on that of Jang's -- i.e., Lady S's -- dance-world friend Sun Hee) and found a ridiculous tear trickling down my cheek. It seems now I'll be able to keep charging ahead all the way to the end -- or charging backward to the beginning actually. Or plodding. But it appears to be a fairly good bet I'll finish the damn draft. I'm only two days behind schedule. Still struggling with tone,

though. I know I'll need many, many drafts. Yet it all
seems promising, and I mean by the highest standards.
So maybe I'm finally in the process (early stages, to
repeat) of churning out something I can be proud of.
(And if not? Can't bear to think about it.)

In other news, short letters came in from Tom T.
and Lady U. I replied to both immediately, as is my
new, or rather newly reinstated, policy. Lady U's was
just briefly thanking me for sending over the article
about Paul's cockroach book. She said she's completed
her first computer class and she's discovered she loves
computers. She also said she traveled over to the city
to take in a concert involving her favest-rave indie
anti-machine band of them all and she loved that too,
which to me sounds like she's got loves in conflict.
But maybe not. Maybe computers aren't machines to her?
I for one can't feature either of these loves for Lady U
as I've always known her. But my reply to her simply
suggested, with a show of old-school savvy, to ride that
passion, grrrl. Ride it until an even crazier one roars
in and snatches you away (or you snatch it).

She also included a packet of my favorite powdered
guava drink, which is impossible to find around here.
(Mama U often sent us whole boxfuls of the stuff and
apparently is still doing so even though I'm no longer
on the official recipient list. And even more sadly
that's also true for the splendid coffee beans she's
always regularly sent.) -- Otherwise no further
information. Still, I sensed a slight warming trend in
the lady's prose. Maybe deep in the wintry nights she's
starting to feel a few pangs of regret. (No, wait, this
further bit of info: all the cats are doing well. But
I'll also note she didn't go so far as to say any of
them miss me -- which used to be a regular line of hers
when she called me every single night at the scope
office for all those years.)

Tom T. now holed up in Centropolis for dispatcher
training. Checking out what he presumes is my old turf
in the city of my youth. The museums, the jazz clubs.
Most of the places he mentions I don't know much about,

but I'm enjoying the vicarious learning experience.
     And a brief crisis blew in over "Memorials."
Suzanne at GPS called saying they couldn't start rolling
the presses until the final payment arrived. Barb was
supposed to have sent this weeks ago, so I had to call
her to find out what was going on. Turned out Keith had
advised her not to send it, because in the high-powered
world of textbook publishing in which he once wheeled
and dealed you don't pay until you have the printed book
in hand. Okay, fine, but shouldn't he or she at least
have let me know they were overruling my request? (But
I didn't protest too much. No need to be antagonizing
either of these touchy folks over such a minor matter.)
Outcome: Barb agreed to overnight-mail the check to GPS
the next day and thus the presses should soon be gearing
up. -- Unless, that is, this episode shunted the
project onto a sidetrack at GPS where it'll get lost
again or, god forbid, permanently derailed. (I also
okayed the draft copy of the publication notice and this
boosts my hopes that they're seriously intending to roll
those presses and our ordeal is close to an end.)
     Barb, I'll note, remains unimpressed by the photo
and dust-jacket bio of Lady K that I sent her. "What's
happened to her!" -- Thinks she must've gone straight.
May have become a suburbanite, yup, or even worse.
Nonetheless I'm intending to give Lady K a chance if
she'll give me one, and I don't care if she's joined a
militia, I'll still keep writing if she'll keep writing
back. But will she? Other than to kiss me off? On
this I go back and forth. At this moment I'm leaning
toward expecting a "get lost" missive.
     Rob not at work today. The guy up in classic told
me he's on a new schedule. Ed, his friend at the
bookstore, says Rob's relations with his new boss are
near the breaking point; Ed's thinking Rob might soon be
working the next register at the bookstore. "Really
good fringes here," Ed said. In that case, I told him,
Rob and I might be applying as a team. (For, yes, as my
own crunch time approaches I'm starting to worry again.
I may soon be facing some hard choices. Even if

reporter Naomi does come back, and early enough that I'm
not yet broke, I'll still be needing extra money, either
to replenish the cushion -- which I'd need to support
the sporadic kind of work I'd be doing -- or to
supplement a not-quite-adequate scoping income. -- Just
today, by the way, I came across a figure for the median
individual annual income in this city, and it's now
reached $37,000, or roughly four times what I project
Jyzer Ink will bring in next year from Naomi. Even with
my annual $3300 booster from the brokerage added on I'll
be lucky to reach a third of the median. On the other
hand I should have no trouble continuing to qualify for
subsidized housing.)

    -- I've held forth so long here, I might as well
push on a few more pages and have done with the JIRT for
this round. The other ancient's still present, still
working his way through the stack of papers on my former
chair and nursing the same bottomless cup of water. Is
he actually reading? Seems to be. But the stack stays
the same size. Looks like maybe he lays the section
he's just read on top of the pile and then pulls out
another section from the bottom to read next, thus
making the stack even more inexhaustible than the cup of
water. Perhaps he has short-term memory problems and by
the time a section works its way to the bottom it's
fresh again? Except for his, though, all faces at
nearby tables are new. And yet they're also quite
similar to each other and to their predecessors, in most
cases belonging to a twenty-something shaven-headed male
student in jeans and flannel shirt and/or sweatshirt.

    About Sofie E. I was wrong. Already I've bumped
into her again, and with identical results, except this
time I didn't wink, left-eyed or right. It would seem
even my unconscious has wised up. A skeptical nod and
that was it and if I can help it that will be it
forevermore. What a disappointment she's turned out to
be! I was pleased to note, though, it's been several
weeks since I've checked out her second-story window
while walking past the co-op. I'm not even entirely
sure which one's hers now, though I'd guess the new digs

(207) are west of the old ones (205) (but it's
undeniably the case that those two numbers are burned
into my brain, just as is the number of the room I was
rejected for there: 201, which is east of 205).

The snow, it also encouraged me to break out my
engineer boots for only the second time this year (and
also this decade). Clomping down through the public
market at half past six p.m. I found the place eerily
deserted and snow-frosted. Clomping back home from the
hideaway at one a.m. the whole mile-long stretch of the
edge road was carless, truckless, busless. Two or three
human figures in sight, and those out in the road itself
and looking like mountaineers staggering around on a
glacier. The boots, meanwhile, were mangling my
tootsies with their stiffness. Possibly my feet have
expanded while wearing nothing but those same low-cut
canvas sneakers for so long. On the way down a pebble
trapped inside the left boot was bothering me, but no
way could I stop to take that boot off (it's a major
operation now and requires my feet to be elevated for a
while first, and especially the left one). Also I have
trouble walking normally in the boots because the
increase in heel height over the low-cuts means I lose
some lift-off power in my weakened left calf and, unless
I concentrate on compensating, start limping noticeably
(I can see it in my shadow and the window reflections --
sometimes even when I'm trying to compensate; but then
it just becomes a different kind of limp: the
overcompensation type; but either way I'm always
reminding myself of the guy in "Of Human Bondage").

And these days the cold forces me to fire up the
heater in B-2. Does this mean a utility bill will
finally be arriving? Yet I've been using electricity
all along for other things, and water too, of course,
including heated water, and sewer services as well (and
again of course). But still no bill. No doubt a hefty
one will show up just at the moment it'll hurt most.

One change in routine: I've begun buying all my
bread at the day-old stall at the public market. It's
more expensive -- a buck per loaf as opposed to thirty-

nine cents at the supermarket's day-old rack -- but the
bread itself, one of my longtime favorite local brands,
is excellent, and it's always available. It tends to
mold up fast so I keep it in the refrigerator, thereby
freeing up a kitchen drawer for overflow miscellaneous
items, meaning in turn I have more room on my desk in
the inner sanctum. "Boy, you eat a lot of bread," said
the counterman at the public-market stall. He rarely
rips his eyes away from the sports channel on the
overhead TV, so I was surprised he'd noticed.

     Also I've started hauling home the old Mentoka
newspapers from the hideaway, one batch at a time as I
finish the chapter draft related to it, and I'm stacking
the batches along the east wall in B-2's interior
hallway right next to the cereal. I'll do the same --
but on the other side of the cereal -- with the boxes of
"Memorials" when they arrive. Eventually, however, I'd
still like to line that hallway with bookcases. It's
wide enough that I could install them floor to ceiling
on both sides without inducing too much claustrophobia
in visitors -- such as pest exterminators, say, not to
mention the pests themselves. (This week I was again
mulling the wisdom of closing down the hideaway office
after I've finished "Jyzer." It's clear now I could
easily fit everything there into B-2 and still have room
to do what needs to be done, including, crucially,
nerfhoop workouts. This would be one way of dealing
with the upcoming money crunch. But I love that
hideaway office and would hate to give it up so soon.
Probably won't do it unless it seems I've run out of
options.)

     -- Turn me over, slice me open, slather on butter
and bacon crumbles: I'm baked to the core. Outdoors
I'll leave a swath of melted ice behind me -- "like a
human zamboni," as I for some curious reason just can't
resist writing. (Anything else I should touch on before
closing up here? Probably. Surely. As for squeezing
it in at this late stage, though, no. -- Except to note
that the old white-bearded guy's still present and still
busily reading, the same stack of house papers piled on

my former chair and the same water cup riding the table.
-- And is this any different from someone, for example
myself when visiting the ORB cafe, reading house papers
threaded through wooden split-sticks and nursing a can
of soda which is sometimes not even his own but an empty
left unattended on a nearby table? Clearly not much.)

--------·

41

--------·

    "Can't go on. I'll go on."
    Another crisis of faith. On this the first
anniversary of Mother's death. More or less it's that.
The actual date was a year ago last Sunday and the day
we scattered the ashes was a year ago tomorrow and the
day when I'll feel it most will be day after tomorrow,
"Black Friday," the current popular appellation for the
day of the week on which she died, tomorrow itself
being, of course, Thanksgiving (except I see we're now
a minute past midnight so Thanksgiving and thus also J-
day are already officially here).
    Stormy night. Strong winds rattling the B-2
windows and sometimes making the walls creak. Hard
walking in a straight line coming up the hill on the way
home, especially at cross streets. -- And I'm in
despair over what's happening with "Jyzer." I'm losing
my grip -- tonight barely even managed to eke out a
skein of fragmented (highly) sentences and told no story
at all -- just filled pages. Desperately seeking a way
to go on. So I'll go on. Didn't I say that already up
there at the top? But must be believing in what I'm
doing or it'll just be a charade. And even if it's no
more than that I'll keep grinding away until the end.
    Mood might change. What I've got so far is not so

371

good but I can layer it over time, fifty drafts or a
hundred and fifty. As do fellow scribblers of serious
intent such as Lawrence J. and Warren E., to name just
two. As no doubt's true for a great many others. But
then a crucial question arises: will the final result
be worth doing all that?

Two days off here, long planned. A chance to
revive my vision. (What vision? I'm working with a
"plot" I've labored over for years but is it inherently
ridiculous? Is there perhaps something about our
uniquely perilous era that's making all "plots" (that
is, contrived stories) preposterous? Other than this
"plot" I've got nothing but thousands of pages of notes
about places and history and people I knew and a passel
of other things. Mere trappings, all these, to hang on
a risibly absurd "plot"? -- Or a select few anyway?)

Just read another article on the alleged crisis of
serious literature (appearing in, of all places, our
local weekly indie-oriented rag). Interesting stuff but
my own crisis has little to do with it. Mine is one of
getting it written in a way that's convincing to me, not
one of finding a market for it or, heaven forfend, high-
culture approbation. (Jyze could possibly meet a need
in the larger crisis. I'd like to see the concept move
out into the real world. But if I can't get it there
through "Jyzer" I doubt I'll be making any other kind of
effort to do so, or at least not anytime in, say, the
next decade or two.)

It's just me now. I'm so utterly alone in this
struggle. "Unloved." Aww, says the chorus -- but that
doesn't change anything. And would it help if I were
loved? Probably not. Hasn't in the past. Just made me
feel better when possibly I'd've been better off feeling
worse (easy to say now -- but not easy to believe, no.)

At this point I'm three days behind on my self-
imposed schedule. Not too bad if the writing were any
good. But it's not. Something over a hundred and
eighty pages of gobbledegook. Like an idiot I flipped
through and read some pages from earlier chapters. And
if I dwell too long on their badness I'll give up

entirely. Got to press on. Because who knows: maybe a
karate chop in just the right spot during the rewrite --
first, fiftieth, a hundred and fiftieth rewrite -- will
flip the whole thing to goodness. To virtuosity even.

So many writing crises over the years. I still
want to believe I can pull through by focusing fiercely.
Purity and intensity of intention. Wordslinging
fanaticism. (I also must believe that writing like this
about it will help somehow. Lord knows I've indulged in
this kind of self-reflexive harangue often enough. And
obviously none of those indulgences have really helped,
other than maybe as a temporary morale booster. At the
time they always feel extraordinarily powerful -- as now
-- but inevitably in retrospect they look like nothing
more than vapid peptalks.)

Crisis point in the JIFT and so crisis point also
in the JIRT. That's what it feels like. A crack in the
JIRT of the year jyze three. Never again a JIRT annal
like this! Can't let it fall apart now!

*

Tomorrow, or actually later today, bus to Rob's
house about six for Thanksgiving dinner. Turns out this
particular route originates just two and a half blocks
from here, up by the parking lot where I once watched
aid-car workers grimly pulling on latex gloves before
tending to a fallen near-fossil who looked a lot like
me. So it's good to know they've got the area covered
in case the bus never shows up. It's not really the
kind of corner you want to be standing on for a long
time in the dark on a holiday when the streets and
sidewalks will likely be much emptier than usual.

Still no Lady K reply. Too bad. Maybe I'm
speaking too soon, but it appears we're not about to
become pen pals after all. My guess is she fears that
starting up a correspondence with me, however platonic
and harmless it might seem at first, would be to venture
out onto a slippery ledge overhanging an even more
slippery slope. She always did see consorting with the
likes of me, and even more with me in particular, and
still more particularly with me in the flesh, as a big

risk. And lord knows she wound up getting burned the
first time around. (Landed so deep in the fiery pit I
should be grateful just to know she was able to escape
it eventually. And I am. And I'm equally grateful, or
even more grateful -- admit it! -- to have escaped it
myself, assuming I actually have.)

Just me and the obsession. Me and the jyze, ficto
and otherwise. Truly. Guess I'm having a hard time
believing it or I wouldn't keep saying it.

And in a sense it all started with her. Simple
truth. With Lady K, I mean, but of course it's also
true of old Mom -- but quite young Mom then, yes.

So am I flaming out now? Is this how it ends? I
ask myself the question quite often. And almost as
often answer it in the probabilistic affirmative. Yet
I'm still able to force myself to struggle dumbly and
numbly onward. So far I'm able to, that is. But how
much longer? As an authentic double joker I have no
choice but to ask myself this question.

"Dogged." I still can't accept the term (Barb's)
to describe my efforts to come up with a decent piece of
fiction -- I doggedly resist the term, yes -- yet surely
I've gone far beyond mere doggedness in these efforts by
now.

I knew, I knew, I knew I shouldn't flip back
through those "Jyzer" chapters.

(Other notes before I rustle up some dinner?
Sighing heavily. "Don't mistake difficulty with
suffering." What, me suffer? When all this is so
comical and ridiculous? -- I do like my cut-rate brown
soccer shoes with the black trim. I do frequently thank
my lucky stars I've been able to hang on to most of my
health. Apparently. Energy's unimpaired, improbable as
this may seem. Just -- to harness it, there's the rub.
To make it move the one thing whose movement truly
matters to me. Or better to say: matters by way way far
the most of all the many things that still do matter.)

*   *

Next afternoon. That is, afternoon of the turkey.
I've just stepped out of the shower. And there I made a

gruesome but useful discovery: with a tricky little
press-and-countertwist maneuver you can remove the drain-
stopper mechanism and thereby finesse the need to call
in the housing-agency plumber. I hit on this maneuver
and then dug deep into the newly exposed drain with a
carving fork and hauled out a shrunken head with lots of
black hair still attached to it, headhunter type, so it
seemed, except no skull was in there: just a hard knot
of hair. "Hair all the way down." Now my tub drains
swiftly for the first time since the move-in and also I
know that the previous occupant of this unit, or at
least the most recent previous one who took showers
and/or baths, had long black hair. (Or maybe not, true.
Maybe the most recent previous one who took showers
and/or baths was bald and it was the one before that who
had long black hair. Actually the possibilities are --
many. Not infinite but certainly numerous.)

Also a sense, as I say, of accomplishing something
useful. I even managed to reinsert the drain-stopper
mechanism. Everything's hunky-dory with the drainage
now. Trouble is the tub itself is quite dirty --
encrusted all the way around inside up to near the rim
-- mainly because it was filling to that level even when
I showered and then taking forever to drain and/or
evaporate dry. In order soon, therefore: a big tub-
scrubbing and crust-chipping project. Or will I put
that off, as I'm doing with everything else not a clear
necessity, until after the "Jyzer" draft's done?

Scrub, scrub, scrub your tub -- but when?

Right now the worktable. Hair wet, old green
terrycloth robe on. (Or maybe not terrycloth. Towel-
like material, though, with one of the two belt loops
missing, or rather hanging uselessly by a thread, as
it's been doing for at least two years. -- So also put
reattaching that belt loop on the list of household
projects. Surprising I didn't think of it before. But
of course I've only recently begun wearing this green
winter robe again after going with the lighter blue-
checked yukata all through the warmer months. -- And it
was Mama U who bought me both of these robes as gifts

back there a good long while, when all still looked rosy
with me and her daughter. Which was very kind of her to
do and I probably didn't thank her anywhere near enough.)
(Wonder what she's thinking of me now. Nothing too
positive, most likely. Not too many regrets regarding
the banishing of the zen son-in-law.)

   Closing in on four p.m. on a gray day, although we
did have a few minutes of sunbreak back around two. The
winds have died down. According to the paper, last
night's gusts hit fifty-seven miles an hour. (Last
week's big snow, I should note, took about four days to
melt away entirely. It provided the raw material for a
huge snowwoman (inflated green condom tips for nipples)
in our neighborhood pocket park. And on the other side
of the mountains to the east it turned into mainly an
ice storm which many are calling the worst ever in that
area: it toppled or uprooted countless trees and left
virtually everyone without electricity for several days
during sub-zero weather. Thousands still lack power
today. Even here everyone's talking about it.)

   This day a decompressing one for me, at least in
theory, during which I try to get my act back together.
Last night a fine Lady V dream; maybe it's a good omen.
In any event, I've noticed whenever I go into all-out
fierceness mode it's apt to summon Lady V onto the field
of dreams. In this one she agreed to take me back and I
held her face and head in my hands up close and told
her, eyes burning into hers, "You know how much I love
you." Fiercely. Truly fiercely. I mean this!

   As Lady K fades, Lady V will return. I suspected
it would happen. And I hope it keeps happening, and
most of all I hope the dreams are truly vivid like last
night's. In real life, though, no movement toward Lady
V. Only if I complete "Jyzer," and maybe not even then.
Next appearance before the parole board is roughly nine
months from now (for my Lady V love, that is, appealing
to be released back into real life) (trouble is, as an
habitual offender this love is too likely to reoffend
and next time, who knows, maybe lethally).

   Well, but here's a philodendron leaf rising

impressively, almost cobralike, from the vine winding
along the tabletop. And dust, I notice, coats the
varnished wooden ledge riding the bottom lip of the
horizontal slot or gap, about eighteen inches high and
maybe seven feet long, in the wall dividing the kitchen
nook from the rest of the room. A light coating, like
frost. Reach out right now and inscribe a letter in it
with my finger. Now more letters. So that confirms the
matter of which I have no doubt nor ever have, nor
should anyone else: "Jyze, I Will." Writ in the dust.
A reply to the command of the jyze gods I was hearing
just then: "Jyze, We Said." (This right above the left
horn of the ceramic Old Bull, size of a pug dog,
representing Dad. And to the left of the black tin,
painted with quaint countryside scenes, which I bought
with the intention of humorously personalizing it as a
gift for Lady U, back when we were first considering
moving to the outback; but I never did personalize it,
and now I store sugar in it and am always reminded of
Lady U when I scoop some out (and also of one of the
finest living jazz/blues singer/pianists who's almost
daily letting me know via the radio she too wants some
sugar in her bowl). And to the right of the pair of
ten-ounce veggie-juice bottles containing water and
philodendron cuttings which actually I made at the
hideaway about six months ago, following tips supplied
by Lady U during her visit there. Soon it will be time
to toss out some of the annuals occupying my west window
ledge here and use the pots for replanting these
cuttings, which seem to be doing fine so far. -- And
put this replanting, too, on the to-do list. -- And
consider this entire paragraph, in fact this entire
entry, a kind of exploratory preview of next year's
"Jyze Around My Room," that is, annal number four. Or
"JAMR Jyze," I might call it, acronymically, with a nod
to those activists aiming to do the same -- jam it -- to
out-of-control consumer culture as a whole. -- Or maybe
just "Jyze Jam"? -- Or "Jyzer Jam"?)

*   *

Too sated for further jyzing, but why not take a

crack at it anyway. What's more after washing down a
big rich slice of a formidable contemporary writer and
critic. Such a wordmaster, but I always wind up feeling
a single well-aimed hammer tap could shatter his entire
oeuvre. Hailstorm of gravelly glass, and opaque too.
Good for faux aquarium seabeds maybe.

Traditional Thanksgiving dinner in Rob's kitchen.
Surprisingly his two kids were present, in from the
small town 350 miles due east where they live with their
newly remarried mother, good old Marcia. Since I last
saw them several years ago Zach has become hefty and
shaven-headed and surprisingly sweet, Emily blond and
nubilely aburst and startlingly reminiscent of Marcia in
many ways: appearance, mannerisms, voice, accent. Emily
on the phone most of the evening; first thing in the
a.m. she'll be off to the mall with girlfriends in mad
pursuit of boys. Zach sticking around at the table to
talk, which is something. He'd even done a watercolor
especially for his Uncle Glen, a handsome grove of fog-
shrouded evergreens, quasi-impressionistic, and I've
just now set it up atop my bureau. Looks good there, I
think. Reminds me of ferry trips to the storage
province before storage became its main function for me.

(Why so drowsy? For the simple traditional reason
of tryptophanic gorging. Trad eats all the way through,
even fruit salad and rolls, pumpkin pie, the only slight
variation a different sort of stuffing: rice-based.
-- And then snatched away from the table while sipping
on after-dinner decaf by the realization that the last
bus would be rolling by outside in just eight minutes.
We three males standing at the stop right across the
street from Rob and Gail's small house with the big firs
arrowheading up out front. Under a cloud-wreathed half
moon swelling toward gibbous -- a term Rob the
meteorology freak was surprisingly unfamiliar with.)

The gallery of ancestors lining his staircase is
admirably done. Some forty framed photos and paintings
more or less in triple tier paralleling the steps, each
frame with a neatly typed and matted label beneath it or
on it. Rob's garret study, always a pleasure to poke my

nose in up there. Old wooden desk of Popeye's, worn
carpet, long row of protojyzebooks, big racks of classic
music albums, stacks of not-yet-read books (many being
gifts from me), stereo, a good-size potted plant, desk
chair, reading armchair, pipe rack, tchotchkes galore, a
dozen or so of his own paintings mounted at eye level on
the slanted ceiling and elsewhere. Rob touchingly proud
of this compact and cozy retreat and rightfully so.
Close to the ideal garret study, I'd say.

No chance to talk about anything too serious. A
relaxed family scene. I was grateful to be basking in
it. (See, you're not really entirely alone even when
you're most feeling you are. And I believe Rob and I
are gradually working our way back to the old closeness.
And I enjoy the wordplay with Gail, her quickness at
it.)

-- It's just a matter of mood right now. Pleased
to be here but anxious to get back to the main task.
Possibly feeling refreshed, revived, rededicated. (Have
I maybe picked myself up off the floor?) -- Have fun
with the damn thing! Confound expectations!

*

In Gregorian terms it's now the day after
Thanksgiving, as of an hour ago, and I'm feeling it.
The death-anniversary part. Rob suggested calling Barb
earlier tonight and I think I inadvertently vetoed the
idea. I told the story of the unsent "Memorials" check.
Somehow the talk turned elsewhere after that and Rob may
have thought I was weighing in against calling her, but
I didn't mean to. I just failed to be alert enough to
realize what my words might seem to be suggesting. And
I regret this. Then again maybe Rob didn't really want
to call her himself. My sense, though, was that he did,
maybe hoping a chance would arise to improve his own
relations with her, which at the moment are at least as
poor as mine or maybe even poorer.

Yes, I think I'll be able to make a wholehearted
effort to push ahead on "Jyzer."

It's hard work. Have I mentioned this before? The
writing itself might take only four or five hours a day,

but the preparations require close to twice that. Other
than flipping quickly through the day's newspapers when
I get up I have little time for anything else. Review
my notes from two until six, hike down to the hideaway,
reacquaint myself with the old Mentoka newspapers for
the week to be written about, write until midnight or
so, hustle home and start in on reorganizing notes for
the next day's work, this carrying me until bedtime at a
little after four a.m. (and right through dinner break
to the extent I can manage it). Massive amounts of
material to digest, to synthesize, to try to find an
angle on, one that's both emotionally true and fictively
compelling. Invariably I fall short on these goals --
no surprise there -- but at least some of the failures
have at times seemed promising.

All-night jazz but not all-night jyze. Not this
time. "Run Your Jyze on Me." Lots of little items I
might mention if only I could work up a bit of energy.
Can I do it? Certainly not at this moment. The loft
stairs are beckoning more and more insistently, albeit
silently and also, of course, as always, woodenly (pine
in this case, although the uprights there, like those
for the doorway jambs at the other end, are hemlock).

Mother's memory. Rob had the date of her death
wrong -- acknowledged it was the 24th after all. I
added a few new photos to my own small hideaway gallery,
including two showing her with Dad during their happier
days together. (And a review of the photo albums as a
whole reminded me of something: her own remarks of last
year notwithstanding, most of their days together were
by and large happy ones. I don't believe I'm deluding
myself in saying this. They kept falling for each other
-- they needed each other. I tend to forget it at
times -- mainly because I'm trying to focus (for fictive
purposes) on the sources of the serious conflicts they
also had -- but I was there for the majority of their
years together and I saw it and I know it in my bones.
-- Which isn't to deny for a moment it's as well
something my bones are wanting to believe.)

And now she's been gone a full year. I've missed

her maybe even more than I expected to. With her still
alive I never felt truly alone in the world and now I
often do. And...so it is.

(The "Jyze, I Will" writ in the dust with my finger
this afternoon, I notice a few new motes are starting to
fill it in already. Like footprints in a light snowfall.
"Jyze Tracks Filling with Dust." Or yes, her ashes like
a light snowfall on the hillside eight hundred miles to
the south one year ago as of today, the Thanksgiving Day
just now ending.)

Much to do and each day the motes in the air
thicken and this jyze becomes ever more maudlin, and how
can I...well, never mind. In a word, I can't. Best to
stop right now, that's what, while I can at least
believe I'm, maybe, if only just slightly, ahead. And
believe I can go at things with some gusto tomorrow.

42

Bound for the supermarket on a rainy gray
afternoon, I hoped to stop in along the way at the new
retro "cocktail nation" lounge where the punk bar used
to be. But as of four p.m. it's not open and won't be,
I'm just now hearing, until five. (This going down in
the spiky little postmod restaurant next door, of which
the lounge is "still sort of a part," says the rooster-
haired guy -- the bird is orange -- in the kitchen.)

Window booth. Disabled trolley bus sitting outside.
A white one; not one of the newer forest-green-and-gold
coaches slowly being phased in (and still new enough to
catch your eye -- or mine anyway).

Push it. Push it. Sweep aside the damn detritus.
Of news, something good. It's now confirmed

reporter Naomi will be returning to work, and she'll be
doing it at what for me will be just about the ideal
time: early February. This means I'll have close to two
months to repad the financial cushion before it would
otherwise thin to vanishing in late March. It also
means I can cut myself a month's slack on "Jyzer" since
I won't have to be scoping in January. It also means,
barring a major change, Jyzer Ink will have scoping work
for at least the next several years (the grand-jury
contract which Naomi will be handling through the new
firm has been renewed for three years).

So why am I not ecstatic? Maybe I am and I just
don't know it yet. But in truth I continue to be caught
up in a death struggle with "Jyzer" and all else seems
to be happening in the shadows. (The bus is still
sitting out there but it's not fully disabled, it turns
out; its lights are on -- I realize now as dusk deepens
-- and its doors actually open and close. Yes, I've
even seen them do it. Both. -- And at this very moment
up rolls a huge transit tow truck with its yellow beacon
flashing, making the boothback opposite me pulsate. And
also the whole facade of the dark four-story apartment
building across the street: more throbbing yellow.)

Before the Naomi news broke I was deep in the
glooms. The lonely life. Trudging through the crowds
of cheery and/or driven downtown holiday shoppers had
become just about unbearable (and that hasn't changed).
The worn old rationalizations were not, and are not,
having the hoped-for effect. Yes, I'd rather go down --
fail -- as a fictojyzer than succeed at anything else.
Nonetheless going down remains massively unappealing.
(There it goes: the tow truck pushing the bus not down
but off the right side of the gritty urban screen made
by the greasy and scuffed-up picture window. Such hokey
symbolism in all this!)

Am I really going down? Maybe not. "Jyzer" is
still reasonably close to being on course in its odd
backwards production. True, I've abandoned the goal of
finishing the draft before year's end -- settling now
for a January 10th deadline -- and also yet again shaken

up the story, a/k/a "the plot." I still feel confident,
at least in certain ways (but not all that certain, no),
that I can complete the draft. So then what, if I,
Jyzer G of the here and now, may ask, is the problem?

Just the quality of the writing, that's all. And
this time I haven't even glanced back at any of it.

-- But something new. An acceptance of sorts, I
guess it is. A voice in my own head letting me know
it'll just suspend judgment and I should be content to
carry on with whatever I actually do produce. Layer it
later. Jack it up section by section. Have faith in
myself as a "long-form," as they're calling it now,
editor. "The joy of endless revision."

Going inward, then, let's say. Even more so. Next
year, it's becoming quite clear, will be the year of the
truly deep weirdness. Nose to the grindstone. "The
School of Hard Jyze." Jyze confined to the room (and,
as a kind of extension of the room, the hideaway, as
long as I have it, and maybe the storage unit, via the
occasional ferry excursion). Reclusion. Isolation.
Solitude. Dream states. Maybe even, who knows, an
authorized bout or two of lonely-guy melancholy here and
there just for the helluvit.

(In the deathless words of an immortal early rocker
whose work was playing on the box here a moment ago:
"I'm a lover." And I say what goes for him goes for me
as well. And therefore doing without love -- doing
without loving someone even more than being loved by
someone -- can be torture. But in my case anyway it's
at least in part self-torture, self-imposed, and I'm
usually well aware of this, and thus I hope I can
continue to wrestle down most of my ad nauseam
complaints about it.)

Other than reporter Naomi, no communications with a
human being or for that matter any other kind of critter
for the past several days. Nada. Literally not a word.
The orange-rooster dude in the kitchen here was the
first since Tuesday, I think. And today is Saturday.

And then there's this. It's probably time to
abandon the last remaining hopes of establishing a vital

link with Lady K. If she were interested in any kind of
connection at all she wouldn't be waiting more than a
month to reply to my letter. So -- bye-bye, Lady K.
(And no regrets, on my side anyway, about reopening the
wound. On hers, maybe a few. Otherwise I doubt she'd
just drop me flat like this.)
     No other romantic hopes. Rikki, done. Personals
woman, done. Sofie, very very done. Lady U, forget it.
     The end.
     -- Resurrection of some sort at some later time?
Say a year or two down the pike? That's about the only
remaining -- not hope. Shred-of-hope maybe. (Should I
be counting the days? The months? Maybe it's best just
to drop the whole matter. Probably that's what I'll try
to do. Let dreams take over, yes. Renounce. Suppress
all, if there is any, real-life competition, even in
shredded form.)
     Today, I should not neglect to note, is my
conception day. A simple fact, well documented, as
reconfirmed just last year by Mom herself and also by
her diary from her early twenties. Not much else to say
about it, though, or at least not this time around.
(Now here on the box comes a certain sonorous crooner
with that ultimate nostalgia-wringer about what a very
good year this is. This year, that year, a bunch of
other years. Not a single rotter of an annum in this
vile man's bunch! And the retro lounge's mirror ball is
spinning, spinning. The corny violins, my god. It's
like a whole series of "great annual reports" drawn up
in pure schmaltz! "But now the days are short / I'm in
the autumn of my years" -- someone kick that thing!
Stomp it into tiny plastic shards!)
     Holidays, yeah. Should I make up some cards after
all, maybe, now having a little slack to work with
schedule-wise? For purposes of boosting my own morale?
(If cardmaking would indeed serve such a purpose. And I
think it probably would, much as making jyze posters
always seems to do.) -- And I do get to take in the
extravagant downtown holiday decorations. A tree of
white lights twinkling like a unicorn horn atop the

city's iconic six-hundred-foot-high golf tee. The gaily
spinning carousel at the triangular central plaza with
all the authentic (or so it sounds to me) children's
laughter ringing out. The white star flashing above the
grand harbor staircase. And for that matter the small
tree with the steady white lights I keep finding my eye
drawn to in the farthest right but one of the second-
floor windows across the street from where I sit right
now. (Of the eighteen or so apartments visible from
here in that building, only this one shows any sign of
being decked out for the season. A reminder that in
noncommercial realms the season's scarcely begun.)

Cards, I don't know. Possibly I'd need to feel
just a bit more inspired. But I do have some blanks
left over from previous years and I do have the paint
and the brushes. Just for the hell of it I could try to
crank out a few -- maybe even do a few jyze posters
while I'm at it. Either way, tonight would probably be
the best time.

Will ponder.

*   *

-- And hours later still pondering. In the
meantime, though, why not one last stand at the cafe
ORB. For the next year at the very least jyze will be
otherwise occupied and therefore this cafe must be,
without question or exception this time, off limits.

The bricky and brown-pipey back corner. Dark-brown
root-beer bottle. Black backpack. A big framed canvas
entitled "Flame Hues, Circular Variation" hanging above
my right shoulder. On the table my shameful impulse
purchase of the evening -- of the week, I almost said,
but there was another, even more dubious, just a couple
of nights ago. This one's a current special issue of a
lit quarterly on "The Future of Fiction," with most of
the doyens of the metafiction gang present and accounted
for in their astoundingly verbose ways. Reducing me to
speechlessness, almost. But not quite.

Asking myself: does studying the cerebrations of
this wonky bunch seem likely to help my own work in any
conceivable way? Knowing all too well the answer is

most likely no. But since "Jyzer" tackles many of the
same issues indirectly I guess I ought to try to keep up
with the pronunciamentos of the hot young fictionists of
the age -- "The Writer in the Catastrophe of Our Time"
-- and never mind how few their readers compared with
the hot young-'uns of earlier ages, meaning the
predigital era. And regardless of "ought" I like to do
it, though maybe only because I'm usually left feeling
that my own confusions on the matter under discussion
are not so extreme after all.

Today's idea salad. More than ever I'm just
plucking out a few juicy-looking delicacies (cucumber
slices, tomato wedges) for sampling, just to prove I've
put in an appearance at the lit gathering. In the past
couple of weeks these samples have included critic A on
the alleged inability of today's writers to "have fun"
(he's doing the alleging but in doing it he's utterly
somber and untrustworthy); and critic B (Ben D. of my
college days) on the laughable mainstream push for
"civility" (as in let's all be nice to the masters as
they screw us over or they'll screw us over even more);
and -- and what? Not much else comes to mind.

*

-- Just a moment. Just a moment! What is this
slop I'm ladling out here? For sure it's not jyze. I
want nothing more to do with it. What's happened?
Somehow I've relapsed into some bad old habits.

Reportage. Who needs it? Touch on what really
matters or touch on nothing. Spin. Wheel. Do
cartwheels and wagonwheels and wheelies. Glug down root
beer. Schoon, baby, schoon! But instead I'm letting
these absurd cogitations bog me down.

(Try lonely guy again. Recall a fact: fully a
quarter of this country's households, so-called, consist
of people living alone. Twenty-five million of us, and
not just the absolute number but the percentage is
growing fast. Which is to say: we who are alone are not
at all alone in at least this one sense. And not only
that but we're less and less not alone in this same sense
-- or no, make that more and more not alone. -- But

nonetheless I'm alone. To indicate just how alone, on
Monday unit B-2 had its first female visitor since Lady
U dropped by some months ago, and it was a tenant from
down the hall who'd locked herself out of her room and
needed to use the phone. A morose little meanie, it
turned out. No fun at all. Then the very next day
another female visitor, this time the new manager,
Rebecca, accompanying, yes, the exterminator on his
quarterly rounds. -- And this visit was welcome, even
though I once again had to get up at eight a.m. to host
it, because on Sunday I'd seen my first roach in the
unit. -- And on Saturday, outdoors, crossing the steep
street a hundred feet to the south ("sluice street"), I
was nearly bowled over by a pair of very large rats
scampering across right behind me and headed in the same
direction, almost as if they were following the Pied
Piper of J-town -- and then surging ahead of him after
deciding he wasn't moving fast enough. (Rats of a
species named after the land of my paternal ancestry too,
I suspect, but don't actually know.) -- And further,
concerning lonely guy, every time I return to B-2, no
matter how short the period I've been away, I check the
answering machine, and owing to a peculiarity in the
electronics of the display panel the double zero
indicating no calls often seems to read "06" or "08,"
and though I've never had more than two or three calls
at a time backed up on the tape, and rarely more than
one, and in fact usually not any -- especially if the
library robot is excluded -- I always take a couple of
steps closer to make sure I don't really have six or
eight calls awaiting me. Today by itself I've done this
twice already and I'll probably do it again when I get
home tonight. -- End of lengthy lonely-guy digression.)
     However grotesque, it's life. Keep it lively!
     -- The barista in the beret, he slipped back here
and quietly, as if to avoid disturbing the jyzer at work
-- or was he putting me on? -- set the chairs atop all
the tables in the back section except this one. So
should I go then? Don't really have to. That's what he
said. "Take your time, man, take your time." So then

mention first my bartender-approved free acquisition of
an ashtray bearing a tobacco-company logo from the retro
lounge next to the postmod cafe and then my purchase of
a set of preloaded salt and pepper shakers at the
supermarket, thus remedying in a single trip the two
prime deficiencies of my B-2 pad insofar as entertaining
brother Rob is concerned. I also bought toilet paper
for the first time since the week I moved in. And a new
sponge to replace the one that disintegrated in my hand
as I tried to scrub-a-dub-dub my tub last week.

   Now I feel better. I've made my point. Can move on
at peace with myself. "Shove On Jyze." Not only will
bus my root-beer bottle; might even put my chair atop the
table all on my own just to show I'm not really one of
the bad dudes (like the mad clipper, say) just because
for so long tonight I failed to take the hint to vamoose.

*   *

   And home. B-2. Still pondering the Christmas-card
project. Meanwhile open the bottle of bourbon and bring
the lippy "o" at the top up close to my nose and breathe
deep. Why have I never thought of doing this before
today? (Think of all the times I did something similar
with a pack of smokes back when I was trying to quit
that nasty habit. -- Hey, and I succeeded!)

   Again cap off, again breathe deep. Bottle lip this
time pressed firmly against my nostrils -- now a reddish
arc imprinted on the column of skin rising between them
(is it part of the septum?). I know, I can feel it,
even, almost, the alcoholic-like redness of this mark.
Reminding me: how easily I could've become a lush myself.
Except for the consequences, just about every known
addiction is appealing to me. So how is it I've managed
to avoid a good number of them and to overcome all but a
few of the ones I haven't avoided (jyze, to be sure, and
its forerunners being the prime exceptions)? Not
discipline, exactly, but more like a talent for self-
punishment. Had I been more successful as a commercial
fictionizer -- monetarily, I'm saying (not that I ever
really tried, since I never felt my stuff was good
enough in that respect) -- but if I had tried, and

succeeded, I never could've resisted a whole raft of
vices or kicked them once acquired. (Or so I imagine.
Then again maybe I'm just phobic about thinking of
myself as being highly disciplined or Boy Scoutishly
wholesome.)

     Lady K, you let me down. But yes, I'll say it
again, I forgive you. And I still wish you'd get drunk
some Saturday night -- like, say, tonight -- and ring me
up just for the hell of it. Of course I know it won't
happen, now or ever. For one thing it's a few ticks
past three a.m. back where you live. But if you sent me
just a plain old Christmas card -- even one with no
personal message at all and your signature commercially
embossed on it in gold -- I'd find a way to wriggle out
of any vow noted earlier in these pages to abandon all
hope of reconciling with you. I might even send you a
card of my own making regardless. A brief message
starting out something like this: "Dang it anyway, Lisa,
looks like you're not going to reply to my letter of" --
and so on. (Allowing myself this recourse on the
ludicrously slim off-chance that my second letter to her
-- the reply to hers -- got lost in the mail and for
that reason alone, thinking I had blown off her "revered
you once" missive, she decided not to contact me again.)

     (Now on the weekend grooveyard show comes my
longtime favorite jazz singer of them all. Yes, the
very one whose current hit inspired brother Rob's early
favorite among all jyzos then extant: "What's Jyze Got
To Do With It?" So many thousands of times did I play
those half-dozen albums by her trio, even her scarcely
recognizable voice of today still strikes deep. (Wow,
now she's doing a new version of her big hit from back
then -- and it does indeed sound better, even more
twisted, as if this one's being performed by an
anonymous vintage bag lady who just happens to have a
great set of bogglingly weathered pipes.))

     -- Thinking of all the places I might be stepping
out tonight. Having a real good time (especially if
accompanied by the right avatar). -- Not the deli U,
though, because it's closed down, maybe permanently or

maybe just for remodeling. Can't really tell. But if
it were merely a matter of remodeling, wouldn't they put
up a note or a sign to that effect? Well, maybe not.
In business smarts that joint always seemed sorely
lacking. And that, again, argues in favor of closure
but also in favor of their hearts being in the right
place, if I can let myself put it that way one more time
(and by jingo I've just done that!).

     And an amusing moment at the only real bookstore
tonight after I left the cafe. One of the workers saw
me gazing at the beat-up "Fiction" sign he'd just
replaced with a new and better one. Maybe he sensed the
intensity of my desire to have my own works displayed
under that old sign (which I'm pretty sure has graced
the fiction section there for all the years I've been
haunting those aisles). Said he, "You want that?" Me,
stunned almost to silence: "Uh...." "I was just going
to throw it out." "Well...okay, sure. You know, I can
use this. Hey, thanks, really."

     So now my manuscript shelf at the hideaway might be
mistaken by some for the fiction section at the ORB.
The sign's already up. Gazing at it in its new location
makes me smile maniacally. For real!

     And I'll note this in truly bathetic follow-up:
I've succeeded in clearing sufficient space in the
fridge vegetable bin here in B-2 (that is, I've consumed
enough butterscotch pudding) to store most of my
potatoes there. This should cut way down on formation
of those annoying eyes. You can break them off before
baking, sure, and I do, always, and never fail to take
sadistic pleasure in doing so, but in many cases you'll
still have an inedible lump formed inside the potato by
the root, as it were, or the stalk of the eye, or what
some might want to call the inner part of the eye or
just -- I can't resist! -- the inner eye. Yes.

     And: the Santa Claus hardy fuchsia is still
producing new blooms. Even in bona fide Santa season.

     And: I've solved the mystery of the disturbing
"burning plastic" smell. Numerous times this noxious
odor has vexed me, usually late at night. I searched

all over for the source. It might've been coming from
anywhere. The refrigerator motor? The microwave? The
answering machine? At times it was driving me crazy
because I couldn't escape it. It was even getting on my
fingers, yet I couldn't pin down where it was coming
from. Then one night while stripping the blue plastic
wrapper from the "night paper" I happened to lean down
close to the wrapper itself. That was it! Stinko! And
I'd thought the smell was everywhere simply because it
was on my fingers! Every night! For months!

43

   Nine more shopping days until Christmas. This is
assuming all remaining days are shopping days. And was
there ever really a time when a remaining day was not a
shopping day? (But I remember! Yes, there was!)
   Ensconced. Armchair. Late afternoon. At loose
ends. "What's with the Jyzer?" It's J-day but it's
also Christmas-card day, the latest one, except now I
guess it isn't: I've just about decided to take an extra
day off tomorrow and do them then. Seventeen in all, or
listed anyway, but six are fully provisional (write only
if written to, and I haven't been written to yet) and
two others contingent in a lesser way (write for sure,
but wait until after Christmas to do it).
   And just an hour ago this year's first card came
in. Turned out to be one of my own cards, the ones I
sent out last year (the ones with the bohemian-looking
Santa, almost a double for the white-bearded elder who
sat near me at the cafe in the Yuke a few weeks ago) (I
knew I'd seen that guy somewhere before!) -- but perhaps
surprisingly, to me at least, this isn't a card I sent

to myself, like, say, those calls I made months ago to
my own answering machine (and which I'm almost ready to
start up again). No, this is an extra card I sent to
Rikki a year ago (though I have no memory of doing so)
and now she's sent it back, enclosing a long-promised
copy of the photo of Mischa and me taking a break from
loading the big yellow rental truck outside their place.
The message acknowledges that I am myself the source of
the card. It also states that the birthday letter I
wrote her, mailed three and a half months ago and to
which she's never replied until now, was tough to read,
especially in the latter parts as I became more
inebriated. (Thus it may have struck her less badly
than if she'd been able to decipher the contents.)

And how do I respond now? I don't. I say too late
this card. Way too late. Because I'm giving up on this
relationship. Already have.

And the same with Lady K. I refuse to impose
myself where I'm not welcome. If I don't receive a
letter from her by year's end -- a reply in kind to my
own, now presumably in her hands for more than six weeks
-- I'll send her a New Year's card in which I'll
"withdraw my candidacy for pen pal" (or some such
message). Nothing rude or crude, certainly not, but
it's time to beat as graceful a retreat as possible.
Admittedly I'm disappointed. Admittedly I'm also
somewhat shocked she hasn't even bothered to reply, if
only to say "I prefer not to."

(Nor do I like the photo of myself with Mischa.
I'm not that guy. "The Glunk." My self-image is far
zestier. Therefore I suspect I'll be ripping up the
picture or maybe cropping it and keeping the part with
Mischa and a small portion of the truck's hood.)

Will jyze be turning sour now? Has it done so
already?

More hard times for the soul this past week. Blame
for these can fall neither on any failure to churn out
pages for "Jyzer" (I'm up to 275 of the damn things,
past the halfway mark in terms of the outline) nor on
failure of the printed copies of "Memorials" to arrive

(they haven't come in, no, but Suzanne did call to say
they're ready and looking good -- I wouldn't expect her
to pan her own product! -- and she'll be mailing me the
first box this week). So what's to blame then? "Jyze
why Thy Sting?"

   Same old stuff. Just some additional seasonal
twistings of the stinger, I guess.

   -- The couch nearly buried under stacks and mounds
of books, clips, binders, magazines, journals. A quick
count, I can say eight Santa Claus blooms still dangle
on the hardy fuchsia above my right shoulder. Shimmer
almost, like so many little round paper lanterns in a
frisky breeze, all thanks to the vibes from heavily
loaded trucks or buses passing by on the viaduct.
Ironically (after this miracle of longevity, at least by
the standard of my own expectations -- because what do I
know from hardy fuchsias?) -- ironically, I say, the
Santa Claus will probably stand bloomless at last just
as Christmas arrives. -- I did hang a few Christmas
ornaments and a red Christmas stocking on the main loft
bookcase this eighter, two of the ornaments being
Christmasy miniature cable cars Mother sent me over the
past decade. (Did she bring one up for the holiday
visit with Barb fourteen years ago this week? Possibly.
I'll say this: since it turned out that was our last
Christmas together I'm doubly glad I put so much effort
into making it a festive occasion. -- And I was already
plenty glad of that well before I knew it was the last,
which of course was not until this past Christmas.)

   (If I want to get to the public-market newsstand in
time to do a little browsing before it closes at six-
thirty I'd better start packing up. This time of year
the holiday bustle and decorations make it a whole
different experience down there. Cold feet too, and
hands, and possibly one's own vapory breath obscuring
the print of whatever one's trying to read, if, that is,
one's not merely pretending to read while scoping out
the crowd. Or of course one might be both reading and
scoping out the crowd, alternating the two: and that's
me at most times.) (The new edition of the newsstand's

annual calendar is splendid -- size of a large notecard,
with individual photos of all the workers superimposed
on a collagelike photo of the newsstand itself -- but
this year I won't be sending it to anyone. What's
Christmas without breaking a few Christmas traditions?
I won't be making my own cards either. Disinterred a
cache of leftovers from previous years going all the way
back to my first year with Lady U and I'll be deploying
some of those -- the ones I can bear to part with.)

*   *

By main force I've dragged myself over to the
laundromat cafe four blocks due east of B-2. Why, I'm
asking myself. And the short answer, I've decided, is
simply that I've somehow persuaded myself I ought to be
here. And just how, one may ask, did I do that? Well,
by recalling that in two more weeks I'll no longer be
able to take the JIRT thing out into the world, and on
the two J-days remaining before then, both of which fall
(by design) on a holiday, I might not want to leave B-2
at all and this joint here might not be open anyway. So
the long answer's pretty short too. And this is how I'm
deciding a lot of things these days.
"Jyze in the Lime Light." A lamp with a lime-green
bulb stands at my right elbow, making for somewhat dim
and shadowy scribbling. (Suddenly I'm thinking jyze has
gone down in here once before. Has it or not? Certainly
I've at least sat in here thinking about it. Without
doubt I've been here several times before, including
once with Lady U. It's more her kind of hangout now, I
suppose, the atmosphere being late grunge or alt or
indie (or whatever's right), catering to pretty much the
same crowd that patronizes the music venue/cafe Lady U
likes so much, and that's just around the corner and two
blocks west. -- Which goes to show that, if nothing
else, I'm becoming a bit more familiar with what's where
in the hood. I didn't even have to consult the map in
my head first before locating that joint relative to
this one. Not consciously anyway.)
Looking straight into a Christmas tree with strings
of glary medium-size bulbs in the usual holiday colors

flicking on and off in waves. Another kind of shimmer
effect. It's a shapely tree about six feet tall and
maybe ten feet away but under a fourteen-foot ceiling
it looks rather stubby. And that combined with the
general brightness of the room makes the tree appear to
be trying too hard with those lights. Overexerting.
Showing its sweat. Which I'm pretty sure is not so cool
in a joint like this. Or -- I could be wrong about
that. Hard to say. Could even be I'm not cool enough
myself to know. (No!)

Black and white checkerboard linoleum floor. Lotsa
chintz (worn) in here. Kitsch too. Lamps that might
hail from any number of Gatewood living rooms of the
jyzer's acquaintance back in his sprout days. Unframed
oil and acrylic paintings crowding the walls, mostly
portraits of icons from the golden era of rock'n'roll.
Or maybe they're just people who somewhat resemble those
icons and therefore their portraits were snatched up at
garage sales and resold at a huge markup as kinky
amateur paintings of actual icons. Bizarre snakelike
wires, frozen conduit, descending from way up there on
the ceiling to power the table lamps, one snake per
lamp. About half the tables occupied at the moment,
mostly by indie, I'll call them, or semi-indie types
roughly one generation behind mine (give or take a
standard deviation or two), mostly in pairs or small
groups. Indie music too, I'd say, most of it not much
good to my cranky ears, and none of it familiar enough
to me that I could name the tune or the band.

But it's all right. Not terrible. Another era,
that's all. Too punky and in-your-face misogynous,
though, the music, for me to get truly jiggy with it,
now or ever.

(I'm plagued by the notion I've written all this
before. So I probably have. In any case I've thought
about it plenty. And if not here, in a number of other
settings much like it, but lacking a gimmick as fine as
the one here, the attached laundromat. Not to mention
the splendid live-music room in back (alas way
overpriced).)

[Jyze and Jyze Alone]

    My new life of grim resolve. In a way it should
fit right in here. Yet I have no interest in trying to
make it do so or figuring out why it won't. (In truth
the reasons are too obvious. Therefore I must have
better things to jyze about.)
    Conclusion, while walking back from the north
tripolar zone (carrying the week's groceries), ten p.m.:
I'm doing this to myself -- this renunciation bit --
simply because I'm unwilling to give up that last shred
of hope. Unwilling to kiss off the dream which hails
from way back in my teen years. (I don't modify that
with "yet," but I might at any time. It almost seems
implied. Even so I doubt I'll ever really let
renunciation have its way with me in its all-out form.)
    I ask myself if grim resolve might not be enough to
cope with the pain. (What pain? The pain of having no
life!) Admittedly the time may come when I'll have to
seek some sort of relief. A group activity perhaps.
Book club? Dance group? Folksinging entourage wowing
them at local nursing homes? -- Thank god this time is
not yet. Surely I can hang on for another year. After
that, reevaluate if necessary. In the meantime eat the
pain. Chew slowly. Savor the subtle flavors, the full
palette. Then jump on the dancefloor and stomp out
another goddamn solo jyze mazurka (jyzurka?).
    If I ever do give up the notion that I can write
fiction, I'm sure I'll be able to come up with a life
again. Even the nasty obstacles posed by aging I think
I can deal with (short of finding my health compromised
in some serious way). I have no complaints at the
personal level about contemporary life (which is just to
say I know I could find plenty to keep myself happy
with, including efforts to make life beyond the personal
level better or at least slightly less apocalyptically
threatening for others as well as for myself). -- But
again, I doubt I'll ever give up on writing fiction.
    What prompts all this grumping and kvetching?
Beyond what I've already said, nothing at all. Which no
doubt is a big part of what makes it hurt so bad.
    -- Ach, they're closing in on me again, chairs

going up on tables and rap music taking over the sound
system, and it's loud and it's ugly. They're doing this
intentionally, of course. "Time to clear 'em out. Put
on the clear-'em-out rap."

*   *

    Back. Warm again. How fortunate I am to have this
unit B-2! Streets crawling with men as lacking in a
life as I am but also hungry and homeless and probably
in bad health in any number of ways. Tonight one's
sleeping on the cement of the covered entranceway
outside our building's front lobby and two more on the
asphalt by the dumpster in back. And it's cold out
there. "Bone-chilling" -- the jazz-station DJ just used
that very term. As he does quite often in fact.
    Deathful thoughts. This week I read that a man my
age can expect to live twenty-five more years. Will I?
It's doubtful. I may be in better physical shape than
many of my male peers and probably eat more healthfully
as a rule, but on medical care I'm way behind and likely
on genes as well (considering that most of my recent
male ancestors have died relatively young). I'd think
of myself as being extremely fortunate to come within
five years of the average death age for my cohort (which
is to say, to live about as long as my mother did).
    Carlos N. of Mezzu days only made it to seventy-
two. He kicked it this week, his obit appearing in the
night paper. The beard gone gray but the eyes still
twinkly as before (this in the file photo taken two
years ago). I have lots of good memories of him but
also one very bad one right at the end when I failed to
write a promised paper for him. Certainly his
encouragement (together with Lawrence J.'s) had
something to do with my irrevocable decision while still
in school to stay with fictionizing forever. His class
on one of the modernist fiction grandmasters influenced
me more than I realized at the time. His own writing,
though, I never much cared for. (I wonder what Ray W.
would say about Carlos's influence on him. -- Whatever
he'd say, I'd almost certainly puzzle over it at length
while strongly suspecting the opposite to be more true

for me.)

I've decided what my own deathbed words should be, just in case I get to utter some. Or if I don't, here's what they should've been: "The jyze [cough cough] -- cue the jyze!"

Preparing to die. In recent days for the first time ever I've been feeling this is truly what my life is about now. And will be about from now on, however many years I may have left (or months or weeks or days, hours or minutes or seconds). I could even say this is what the jyze of annal three has taught me or made me realize -- that is, how it's changed me. -- Although, true, the year's not over yet. This is just, in a sense, a preliminary finding. But then again I'm not expecting it to alter in any significant way.

Going back to the question of whether I'll actually have a life at some point during my remaining time on earth, another way of putting it is this: my best chance by far to become a lover again is to first become a hermit until such time as the Mentoka trilogy is complete -- or not the whole thing, maybe, but at least a single volume of it about which I can be proud. In essence I'm locking myself into my own fire tower and vowing not to come back down the mountain until this single work is ready. Which is just another way of saying I don't know whether I'll ever be coming down.

It's almost as if my motto were "only disconnect." But no, scratch that; that's far from the case. My failure to succeed thus far in my life in sustaining deep emotional connections (loves) is now forcing me to take measures a lot more extreme than I'd prefer -- that's all. Unfortunately what results looks like something beyond even narcissism, so say sheer solipsism. (Is it just a coincidence that solipsism is what our times seem to be driving a large number of scribblers toward? Alas, it probably is. -- And not just scribblers either. Many kinds of folks if not most. Some synchronized swimmers even. Seriously. I read something to that effect in yesterday's night paper.)

Solipsism is just about the last thing I want for

myself. But if it, or a life which seems to approach
it, will enable me to avoid the actual last thing I want
-- which is failing to give this long-planned fiction
project my absolutely best shot (and if it doesn't
produce a fine piece of fictojyze, it can't be my
absolutely best shot) -- then I'll reconcile myself to
it. And at times I think I may be well along in doing
so already. But to admit that outright is a jyze no-no,
so scratch it. Another wasted sentence right there.

The struggle with myself to hold to the main vow.
Some days are so hard. The weakness and longings.
Weepiness almost. Catatonia. Downheartedness. Zeroed-
outness. Pain to the bone. Sorrow like a lead quilt.

(Can jyze itself survive this? Jyze of the JIRT
kind as opposed to the JIFT, meaning real time versus
fictive time? I believe it can. At most times it
serves as my best antidote. "All The Things Jyze Is" --
and this may be the very most important of them. I
doubt jyze only when I cease practicing it and fall into
old protojyze habits and expectations. But no, I refuse
to let jyze go down. "They Can't Take Jyze Away From
Me." Period. Exclamation point too. Yes!)

-- Speaking of fire towers, though, the big
excitement of the J-week was a fire alarm which emptied
the B-2 building one morning shortly before noon and
turned out to be for real: a mattress smoldering in an
empty room, lots of smoke. I stood alone out in the
courtyard; everyone else, I learned later, evacuated to
the sidewalk in front of the main lobby. Then I was
joined by a handsome Afrusan woman close to my height
and maybe about Lady U's age whom I've noticed several
times at the mailboxes; this time she was wearing a
semi-sheer powder-blue bathrobe with matching slippers.
We introduced ourselves. My big chance, I suppose, and
of course I completely blew it. Came up with a couple
of lame jokes, one of which might've sounded leering
(about the bathrobe). Oh well. "Ain't That Just Like
Jyze." (And if I'm a social misfit now, what'll I be a
year from now? Ten years from now?)

Did some reading too. Too much reading. The whole

of "The Future of Fiction" issue, which was depressing
indeed (until I remembered I'm just trying to write what
I consider to be good fiction and I don't care what
other writers or critics think -- and especially I don't
care what the so-called metafiction bunch dominating
this publication think). Also browsed in the protojyze
sections of a newly released volume of collected letters
and prose works by the great USAn poet who was Lady K's
favorite -- subject of her senior paper -- back when she
and I were together. His protojyze entries, which stop
completely in his midtwenties (with I think two
exceptions), give no hint at all of what was to come in
the poetry. And such formality! Such humorlessness!
And in his letters to his future wife (whose profile
graces a USAn coin still occasionally encountered in
circulation), such impersonality, even during their
courtship days! -- Yet I still liked him better after
doing all this browsing, which went on and on: maybe for
close to three hours (at both downtown franchise
bookstores, moving from floor to floor, bench to bench).
(Whether Lady K still sees this poet the same way after
all these years I have no idea at all. Nor will I ever,
I'd guess now. Too bad!)

     And dreams? Read a long review of a biography of a
certain logical positivist of known satyric propensities
and that same night dreamt he was trying to fuck -- me!
Yes! (What's more, apparently he was hetero through and
through.) (And apparently I am too, damn it all anyway.
Things might be a lot simpler if that weren't the case.
-- Except they wouldn't. AIDS just for starters. But
at least the pool of candidates for a love/sex gig would
be considerably larger, especially within the bounds of
my tripolar zone. Then again this would just mean more
temptations to resist, so never mind. -- But if I
thought it would help me survive the pit I'd try it
anyway. -- But it would only deepen the pit.)

[For Jyze You Know You Must]

44

    Jyze does Christmas Eve at the public market. Or
the day's first installment anyway. Surely another will
follow at B-2 later. Seems it's almost required.
    A seasonal scene. The bar & grill, window counter
looking out from second-floor level at the market's main
entrance. Over to the right the big pink neon public-
market sign and the clock. Rows of potted evergreens
line the tops of the first-story overhangs, and this
year those trees are decked out with strings of blazing
white lights. A drizzly late afternoon, closing hour
for the shops. A few last customers cluster at the
brightly lit fish market beneath the pink sign. Lights
still shine at the newsstand under the overhang directly
opposite us here. Glistening bricks of the roadway in
between reflect all these lights in intricate ways, and
also the lights of the nearby skybusters to the south
and southeast which in turn fade into a dark foggy mist
about fifteen stories up. (And a horse-drawn carriage
clip-clops across those same bricks like something right
out of "A Christmas Carol" -- except for the driver's
fancy pink sombrero.)
    A special occasion or I wouldn't be here. Gave the
jyze-venue question quite a bit of thought as I wandered
around amid the downtown crowds. Stuck my nose in at
the art bar but there it didn't feel seasonal enough.
("Heavenly hosts sing hallelujah" -- it's playing in
here right now, the ancient pop version performed by the
prime makeout crooner of my high-school days.) Visited
the market newsstand, the bookstore, the day-old-bread
shop, the cash machine for this week's hit (three days

early, true, but I may not get another chance before
Friday). Wandered from one produce stall to another
until a big red apple caught my eye and I bought it and
then, even though my gut's been in an uproar all day,
chomped it down to the core in the heated stairwell
leading up to the bar & grill as hoo-hahing partygoers
stomped by. -- All this in truth mainly just to have
something to do in the late afternoon of Christmas Eve.

Offering all those delinquents a last chance to get
their cards to me, I tramped up to the mailbox at three.
Unsurprisingly it was empty. Nor did I find a stickie
notice saying the manager's office was holding a package
for me. Nine days now since "Memorials" was supposed to
be mailed.

"Silver Bells." Yet another velvet-voiced crooner
of yesteryear. Five out of the seven booths in here
occupied. A scuzzy bloke sporting a withered sprig of
mistletoe pinned on a shiny black costume-shop top hat
-- everyone's giving him a wide berth for sure. All
three wall-mounted TVs (seems it's always three)
offering the same sports channel, a scoreboard show in
progress at the moment, lots of football action clips,
sound turned off but the gist is still plenty clear. A
string dangling like a parachute ripcord right in front
of my nose; it leads up to the street-facing neon beer
sign clinging to the glass in the middle of the big
arched window here and is presumably for turning the
sign on and off (but I'm not tempted because I like
having the glow up there and also the way it makes
these pages blush a faint but still festive rosy hue).

Flashing memories. How many Christmases could I
dredge up with authentic specifics? If I really worked
at it, at least a score or more. Of those, half a dozen
reign supreme. They're not from childhood but college
and grad-school years, plus the last year in Gatewood
after Dad's death and then the year Mother and Barb
visited Lady U and me here in Jyze City at our second
rental abode ("Looks just like a gingerbread house!").
But the Christmases of my childhood were wonderful.
It's undeniably a matter of shame and embarrassment that

I'm doing so little to carry on the tradition. But so
it is. (I made my choices: oh yes I did.)
     Down in the market now just a few stragglers are
hurrying along. Most of the individual stall lights
have been doused but the gates remain up. -- And here's
the young woman who was peddling "real sterling" jewelry
down by the market bookstore. I mean she's entering the
bar up here. Taking a seat at the very far end of this
window counter maybe ten or twelve feet to my right, her
wares rolled up in a sleeping-bag-like parcel similar to
the one sister Barb carried around during her own
jewelry-peddling era. She orders a cup of tea to warm
up. Our glances met briefly and locked even more
briefly -- or maybe not at all -- but just in case I'm
now avoiding her eyes. All the seats between us are
empty at the moment. (Another lonely soul? I have to
be careful. I'm preposterously vulnerable these days.
"Needy" with a capital N -- to the Nth!)
     Time to toughen up, yeah. In fact this is what
I've been telling myself all week. Surprisingly it's
seemed to help. A couple of new crises on "Jyzer" and
I seem to have come out on the far side of those with a
workable plan for pushing on. More "midcourse
corrections." "Snatch It Back and Hold It." Yeah.
Gonna do that. Or else.
     On Christmas matters I broke down. Took another
day off and wrote out a dozen cards. Even sent a check
for twenty-five bucks to Mischa and Rikki ("Go wild
mama") and a subscription to a literary quarterly to
Barb. Largest breakdown of all, I wrote Lady K again,
just a short note on an old handmade card but it took a
full night's agonizing before I was able to scrawl out
something I could live with. I convinced myself I'd
regret failing to attempt a second approach. Did she
perhaps, I predictably enough asked her, not receive my
letter of early November? (If she does wind up replying
to this latest effort, maybe I'll let her wait a similar
period before replying myself. -- And so far, obviously,
nothing from her. Nor do I expect anything. Except
very, very slightly. And that's just a product of the

general seasonal longing, I suspect.)

Cold here. It's the windows. They radiate winter inward and set drafts to swirling. (Two guys, sitting a single empty stool apart at the bar, are wearing identical Santa caps but ignoring each other.
-- Molasses brain I've got right now. Shivering too.)

*   *

That was slow jyze. About as slow and laborious as it gets. "Jyze Down Slow." -- So now let's see if I can't at least quicken it a bit. "Jyze Can Do That" -- can it not? May make no difference, though, especially in the reading of it. Slow dance, fast reactor (as in splitting the atom) -- so what's to choose? (Huh? What he say? "Doo-Wacka Jyze.")

Came home. A few street drunks -- strode past them. Suffering beings. In which doorways will they curl up on their grimy cardboard on Christmas Eve? Most of the good doorways, I noticed, were already taken. (This larger, extended doorway, so to speak, called unit B-2 in which I now sit so privileged, this relatively deluxe one with its own hot water and heater, wasn't occupied yet -- but is now. Luckily, and I do mean very, very luckily, I happen to have a key for it.)

Checked the mailbox one last time on the way in. Maybe the post office was running exceptionally late on Christmas Eve this year? Yup, maybe so, but if so, still nothing for the jyzerman.

(Now five minutes until midnight. Pride of place for the run-up to the magical hour on the jazz station goes to a supreme scat singer's carefully enunicated non-scat version of "The Christmas Song.")

Yet the unexpected. Not for long am I back home again tonight before the telephone rings. And it's -- "Rikki, your mother's downstairs neighbor." As if I don't know who Rikki is! But this call's a joint project: Barb and Keith are joining Rikki and Mischa for dinner and they're all sitting right there. Fondue's on the stove.

Almost instantly I become high-spirited. Pull it off all right I do believe. I joke about hopping on a

404

flight and arriving in time for dessert before they hit
the midnight service at the waterfront church (Barb's
idea but I'm sure Rikki's down with it too).

(So now it's the day itself. The grooveyard jazz
jock is the first in with official Christmas Day
greetings at 12:01 a.m.)

Anything there with Rikki? Any interest on my part
in her? Or first, any on her part in me? Slight, maybe,
but not enough to bump up my estimate of our chances.
Evidently she's alone on Christmas Eve -- unescorted --
yet still doesn't risk saying anything that might be
taken as even faintly encouraging. And so of course I
reciprocate. (I learn she's got one more semester to go
on her master's. Comprehensives coming up. It'll be
tough to study for those while taking two courses and
also teaching. And meanwhile raising a seven-year-old
kid, so active he's driving her crazy. Or by now he may
be eight. Lord help her.)

So Barb came on. Good of her to instigate this
call, as I'm sure she did. Her gnarly big brother,
truly alone for the first time over the holidays in lo
these many years. No doubt she's trying to light a fire
under Rikki too. A hopeless cause, I'm afraid.

I learn Barb's bad shoulder isn't much better.
Also, she's now become a permanent part-timer at the
same job she was previously doing full time, and the
hourly wage is the same -- twenty-five hours a week --
and though I think she should be pleased with this setup,
she seems not to be. (Keith cackling impishly in the
background.) Also I'm teasing her a bit about her new
religious leanings coming in handy for celebrating the
season -- being very careful with this -- and she seems
to be taking it well enough.

For her gift this year she sent me two tins of
home-baked Christmas cookies of various varieties, most
of them tasting remarkably like the ones old Mom used to
make which I scarfed down in such great numbers as a kid.
They arrived last week and I demolished them all in two
or three days, each cookie a proverbial depth charge of
sugary sweetness freeing up whole reefs of old Christmas

memories. (And then yesterday a box came in from Rob:
more cookies. Two dozen large snickerdoodles. This is
why my gut's been in revolt all day. And again is at
this moment, with the apple from the public market
providing a kind of sur-churn.)

I'm grateful for such thoughtful treatment on the
part of my siblings. More so, in fact, than I want to
show, and I do try to show as much as I can (and
probably show even more than I intend, and it's probably
pretty goddamn pathetic, all of it, and certainly not
least my spasms of overearnest sputtering thank-yous).

A batch of cards did come in over the past week.
Is half a dozen a batch? In addition to Rob, Barb, and
Rikki: cousin Kar, Aunt Shel, and Aunt Shar. And Tom T.
So seven in all. Am I loved? Am I loved?

But not by Lady K. Not by Lady U. Not, of course,
by Sofie E. of the co-op. Nor, for that matter, by Aunt
Greta and Uncle Mort, nor by cousin Greta, nor by
brother Jeff (though a couple of weeks ago he told Barb
he'd be calling all of us, so maybe later today for
that). Nor by the U's. Nor even by reporter Naomi,
though she did leave me half a pan of her excellent
homemade brownies when I cranked out that last back
order for her.

Nor by Jim Q. I should've asked Rikki if he's
still hanging on as part of the scene down there.

-- So here's my little stained-glass Christmas tree.
Six inches tall. Can't light a candle in the holder at
the back for fear of triggering that hypersensitive fire
alarm. (In this building I judge to be about a third
full tonight. Only about, again, half a dozen windows
in the whole building -- that is, of the fifty or sixty,
seventy maybe, visible to me from in here -- show even a
trace of seasonal decoration.)

Cousin Kar, it turns out, has been in the area all
fall. Right after the first of the year he and Kerani
will be moving to the same university town where Lady U
and I once intended to live, a few hours' drive south of
Jyze City. There he'll become CEO, as he says (with no
detectable irony regarding the corporate-speak) of "a

very large and successful river-conservation group."
(Who's Kerani? It's Elaine, his bride of last summer,
after her recent name change inspired by her years-ago
stay in India. -- And the newlyweds are therefore, yes,
Kar and Ker (rhymes with "care," not "cur"), and clearly
delighted to be so.) -- Kar called after receiving my
unknowingly obsolete "Xmas Kard for Kar & Elaine" and
we'll all be getting together at Rob's on the 26th,
which is to say, tomorrow, since it's already Christmas
Day right now, technically, by Gregorian measure.

So after hanging up the phone I did some drawing.
Not too inspired though. Of a bath is all. Hot water.
Sitting by that cold window at the bar & grill chilled
me to the bone. And then emerging an hour later warm
and refreshed from the bath I decided it was time for a
snooze. Mounted the loft staircase and enjoyed a fine
"long winter's nap" of ninety minutes or so (and with
the lamps down below glowing the whole time, the jyze
posters illuminated, the radio softly playing old-timey
Christmas jazz). Lately I've been napping again after
pretty much kicking the habit for the first eight months
of my return to city living. Not too surprisingly the
current bouts of intense work on "Jyzer" often leave me
feeling exhausted. -- Gratifyingly too. I like to
think I'm pushing myself to the limit. Suffering. (And
am suffering. But mainly because, to say it again, the
"Jyzer" results are falling so far short of what I so
badly want them to be. Though I can't be totally sure
of this because I'm holding steady on resisting the urge
to check out -- as before -- the pages piled up so far.)
Regardless: "Got My Jyze To Keep Me Warm." 'Cause
I'm: "Jyze To The Bone." But: "Who Do You Jyze?" (Got
jyzos? Stick 'em in!)
My great success of the week, no question, was
keeping the Santa Claus fuchsia picked free of those
tiny yellow lobsterlike mites. In response it's budded
again and will soon burst into glorious bloom. I'd
hoped it would make it by Christmas Day. It won't, not
quite. Thursday or Friday maybe. (Heavy emotional
investment in this particular real-life Santa Claus.

Among other reasons, because it's right there, next to
where I almost always sit when I'm here, unless, as now,
I'm jyzing away -- or at other times brushing away on
the posters -- at the redwood table. The couch, see, is
unfit for sitting; it's again become an upholstered
workbench stacked high all the way across with books,
binders, magazines, research folders and the like.)
     "I Saw Daddy Kissing His Santa Claus Hardy Fuchsia:
a Jyze Fable."
     Soon I'll try to eat something which is not a
cookie, a brownie, or an apple. I'll start gearing up
for the project right now. (Knowing tomorrow's special
treat will be pop-out cinnamon rolls. Another sugar hit
but then -- it's Christmas!) (I wanted orange Danish
but the supermarket no longer carries them. I didn't
have the energy to try the other big markets in the area.
Nor did I know then I'd be stuffed to the gills with
cookies and brownies this week. And now that I've
bought the cinnamon rolls I can't relinquish the thrill
of baking 'em up. Unthinkable. Heart set on those
rolls. Mouth watering even this instant at the thought
and never mind the gut in clamorous insurrection.)
                    *   *
     Day of the day itself.
     As quiet as it ever gets around here. Earlier this
morning especially: scarcely any sound at all, inside
the building or out. A rarity for a vehicle to pass by
on the viaduct (so much so you start noticing the
whooshes again when they do). A small explosion of
scraping sounds from the west windows: could be the wind
agitating the vines still clinging to the fence,
rattling the few remaining leaves, but in the absence of
other wind-related sounds (flapping of the kitchen-fan
gate, moaning from the vent shaft) it's probably a bird.
-- And it is a bird! Just as I think the thought the
perpetrator itself magically hops into view! Small,
maybe a sparrow or finch (what do I know anymore, if I
ever did, about bird IDs?). -- And regardless it's
winged off already.
     A morning good for sleep. And then an afternoon

good for maundering through the pages of thick holiday newspapers while sipping coffee (I've now officially gone over to making twenty-four ounces of coffee daily, which is two large mugs, or -- and when I think of it this way I'm startled myself -- the same as two standard twelve-ounce cans of cola; and the only coffee I ever buy now originates half a world away from where Papa U himself used to pick the beans of my favorite type, the cost of which has risen far beyond my current means -- but that's the ur coffee experience for me, the way I first learned to drink it -- and I still make it strong: two tablespoon scoops of cone-ground beans for every six ounces of water; and today I threw in an extra scoop beyond that just for the down-home holiday buzz of it).

The particulars of daily living, even if today is highly atypical. Jyze's fate for the next year on every kind of day: detailing the diurnal. The quotidian. Measuring out my life in coffee scoops and sliced half-thawed strawberries. (And once in a great while will materialize among these fragmentary noun phrases, if grotesquely, a verb.) But as for the rest of life, a voice asks, what of it and how will the average reader of jyze -- this jyze right here, say -- know? By some imaginative legerdemain peer through the chinks in the wall, I guess. As the jyzer willfully slides back into the shadows. Even before age forces me to, I'm retreating. "Take one giant tactical step backwards." "Jyze Gods may I?" "Jyze Gods say you freakin' better."

Maybe it's martyrdom. Surely it is, at least in part. My degree, after all, is an MFA: Martyr of Fine Arts. Regardless, the martyrdom -- or better yet, call it "artyrdom" -- will attempt to be a happy one. That failing, at least a lively one, within its severely constricted bounds. (And hey, isn't this the very thing you wanted, O Jyzemaster? It is, it is!)

But I'm getting ahead of the self who was just boasting about being ahead of the pack and this is not good. Can't help myself, however, and thus this foretaste. The coming year in jyze. ("And now this.")

The cinnamon rolls, even though adequately prepared

-- and giving off such mouth-watering fragrance while
baking in the toaster oven -- were not so tasty. The
orange kind is worth the extra effort, I now know: four
to six extra blocks' walk, extra time and planning (yes,
you do have to plan these on-foot supermarket visits
with the same sort of care you might lavish on, say, a
just-in-time assembly line if you were an industrialist
-- or say the interrogation of a grand-jury witness if
you were what I might so easily have become, following
in my father's footsteps and his father's before him: a
mouthpiece, legal type. -- And then in a different and
diminished way, and also a far less remunerative way,
did become, sort of (myself, I'm saying): a scoper of
testimony mainly for legal proceedings).

    -- Looking over my shoulder because I sensed
movement back there, I see I left the lamp on in the
loft room. With dusk creeping in, the light brightened
by contrast and the change registered suddenly as
movement at the periphery. But I do like the look of
that loft when it's lit from within, seen, as now, from
the diagonally opposite corner of the room, the internal
lamplight glowing through the serrated spaces between
the tops of the rows of books and the shelves above them
(like city skylines reflected upside-down in a dark
lake). Looks like it must be a good place to work in
there, though so far in its unit B-2 incarnation it's
rarely proven to be that. At the moment I'm still
liking this old redwood table much better for such
purposes. (And will soon be launching a major effort to
reduce the clutter here on the table, much of which is
attributable to the Christmas-card binge. But then even
more of it can be traced to the jyze-poster sessions and
I expect another one of those will be striking up soon.)

    And now I've inadvertently raised yet again one of
the big questions for next year. Will I be keeping the
hideaway office? I love having it, yes, but maybe I no
longer need quite so much the psychological boost it
provides. Could be the monthly rent of $165 I pay there
would, if I could use it for other things, make the
difference in my being able to live within my income

next year as a part-time nightscoper. Or, alternatively,
if that nightscoper income were to prove sufficient when
supplemented by the quarterly brokerage checks to pay
for all the basics, then the recouped $165 would buy a
lot of books and subscriptions. I'm beginning to think
I'd prefer having the books and subscriptions. The
question then becomes: just how valuable is it to have
this other place, "suite" 225, to go to? It does draw
me out of B-2. It does increase the likelihood I'll get
enough exercise. And yes, it still does provide a
psychological boost. "My own private office." I'm not
just a guy stuck in a single room in a city-subsidized
low-income apartment building.
     Not a trivial matter. I'll continue mulling it.
May go back and forth on it. Don't want to decide too
quickly. Moving my stuff out of 225 -- transferring
some here, some to the storage unit -- would be a big,
big task for me.
     (Now I look up to the right, out my courtyard
window, and see not a single window lit up in the older
part of the building, all four stories. This degree of
lifelessness I've never witnessed here before at such an
early hour.)
     So today I'm kicking back. Next on the docket is a
long hike, first up to the north tripolar zone and then
down to the opposite zone, south tripolar, mainly for
the purpose of walking off some of these cookies and
brownies and cinnamon rolls. Maybe buy a jug of wine
if I can find the right kind of place open, which is to
say: one selling the truly cheap stuff. Then back home
for a note-organizing session in preparation for the
next round of fictojyzing. Read some more. I could
take in a movie -- using one of the passes Rob laid on
me -- but in general these days if I'm not writing I
want to be reading. Limit moviegoing to the must-sees,
and I expect those will continue to be few and far
between. Read, read, read. Write, write, write. And
of course jyze, jyze, jyze. "Got To Have More Of Your
Jyze." (Hit it, Sam!)
     As for romance -- what, this again? -- I'm saying

any remaining candidates have one last week to turn me
around. Rikki? Lady K? Act now or forever pine away.
Sez I. Knowing well -- of course! -- I'll almost
certainly be the only one to do any pining. In any
event expect absolutely nothing. And yet acknowledge
that even on the far side of the New Year's border I
might change my mind. Will deal with any such matters
on a case-by-case basis. But the bias will be toward
maintaining a good healthy productive "artyrdom."

I have no plans for New Year's Eve. As I go around
town I catch myself peering at signs announcing various
bashes. A number of these I'd love to attend, including
live blues with dancing at two clubs in the historic
quarter and a third at the public-market bar & grill
(Isaac S. and his band) and other kinds of live music at
the art bar, the punk bar, the pizza bar at the market.
But they all cost plenty, at least by my standards --
between ten and twenty bucks a head at the door, and
then five bucks or more per drink -- and without someone
to accompany me, acccch, who cares. Maybe I'll wander
down to the fairgrounds for the symbolic ball-drop-cum-
fireworks from the iconic golf tee (if there is a ball
drop this year; I haven't heard yet yea or nay). Or
maybe I won't. I'll play it by ear, that's what I'll
do. Improvise. This is jyze!

45

Last J-day of the year. Last day too, so eve of
the next, and that's next J-year as well as next J-day.
It's about half past five in the afternoon, and it seems
the place to be (I know not why) is the digi-cafe. So
here I am. Overhearing the surprising news that

tonight's shindig on these premises will be sans cover
charge. Could mean I'll stop by again later.

A table for four near the entrance where the
light's good. The venerable schooner of root beer. A
young couple playing a board game at the next table (had
Lady K and I visited a place like this on New Year's Eve
back in our high-romance period we might've been doing
something similar -- and immediately I find myself
wondering if I want to say I'm embarrassed by the
thought -- but also wondering if I really am embarrassed
by it, which I suppose must mean I'm not, or at least
not very much, whereas just a few years after the
breakup with Lady K I would've been for sure).

But what a week we've had (and then: what a year).
Week of massive snowstorms, the worst to hit this region
in decades. And now another's predicted for tonight or
tomorrow, though they're saying after an hour or so of
heavy snow it'll likely turn into a rainstorm with
extremely high winds. One thrill after another!

Roughly two feet of snow with a good deal of rain
mixed in and quickly turning to ice -- the sum so far.
The first round on Boxing Day (the 26th) and the second
forty-eight hours later. At the start abnormally large
flakes were fluttering down like huge moths or even more
like battered cigarette-paper airplanes (a mesmerizing
sight viewed against the brick jyzeyard wall). The
nearly empty building became unusually cold, to the
unheard-of extent that my wall heater could not keep B-2
tolerably warm. For the first time I broke out a
blanket for armchair sitting (in the window reflection
becoming a granny jyzer). And over the next four days I
did a lot of such sitting. The scheduled reJIFT
sessions had to go on hold (and probably would've anyway,
at least partly, given my state of mind). The streets
and sidewalks were close to impassable. Bus service was
shut down. (One day I did hike up to the supermarket
for supplies. Lengthy safarilike lines were trudging
along everywhere -- or mountaineerlike rather, lacking
only the ropes linking climbers, which everyone could've
used owing to the treacherous footing.)

[Jyze and Jyze Alone]

    Today all but a few traces of the ice and snow are
gone. Bananas and cherry tomatoes are marked way down
at the public market, freeze-damaged, also getting old
in many cases because so few customers have been around.
    And in the midst of this, two back orders, reporter
Naomi phoning from out of state. I've done one; the
other I'll be going in to finish tonight (New Year's
Eve! -- but it should take only an hour or so).
    The get-together at Rob's had to be postponed owing
to the weather. We'll try again tomorrow. But Kar and
Kerani are scheduled to begin their big move day after
tomorrow (the van due to arrive at their house at eight
a.m. sharp), so I'm half-expecting another cancellation
even if the new storm turns out to pack less punch than
advertised.
    For several days I thought I'd lost this J-stick.
Searched everywhere to no avail. Finally resigned
myself to going with one of the backups, the stiff-
nibbed No. 6. Then at the larger of the franchise
bookstores yesterday this one here, the first-stringer,
stalwart No. 5, tumbled onto the carpet from somewhere
inside my black coat. I didn't see or hear it do this
but fortunately a friendly woman standing nearby did.
Apparently the pocket clip of the J-stick caught on the
netted lining of the coat (recalling the way the pocket
clip of a previous brand-X fountain pen caught on a
thread of yarn in a scarf of mine and rode around
attached to it like a sunfish on a hooked line for a
long period -- was it ten days?).
    Other than the phone conversations with Rob, Kar,
and Naomi I spoke with virtually no one this entire J-
week. Nor was there any mail. Lady K did not come
through, nor did Lady U (who's surely been without power
much or all of this week if she's still staying in our
old U Acres place, which I assume she is), nor did Rikki
or anyone else I was hoping to hear from. Nor did the
box of "Memorials" copies arrive. Nor, for that matter,
did a single issue of either of my two subscribed
newspapers show up for four days straight. (But the
power has stayed on the whole time in our hood and

that's what really matters. Living in the city helps.
In some suburbs and outlying areas it's still out now.)
     So what did I do all this time? Read mostly. And
one of the major reading projects was jyzebook No. 8
overall -- this J-book right here, that is, along with
its two predecessors, the three also constituting, of
course, books I, II, and III of this annal. In short, a
review of the third year of the JIRT version of the Jyze
Age. I even took notes, thinking I might refer to them
while having at this final entry. But now I doubt I'll
do that. I've already pondered them quite a bit and
that oughta be enough.
     But what a year. Year of transition. Year of the
joker and then year of the second joker or the double
joker. (All this retro music they're playing here at
the digi-cafe this evening is nicely apt. Here's that
same sonorous crooner (the sumbitch!) belting it out
about that toddlin' Centropolis of the jyzer's youth.
Before that, a reconfigured and mildly funkified version
of the one about the man with the golden finger.) Year
of mourning and losses. First full year I've lived
without my mother existing on this earth other than in
boisterous spirit form. Year of numerous preposterous
missteps and setbacks and humiliations, many in all
three categories self-inflicted. First year I've gone
entirely without balling of the sexual kind since I was
eighteen -- or without any sexual contact whatsoever
since I was fifteen. First year I haven't lived at
least in part with a woman since I was twenty (except --
what am I saying? Lady U and I did live together the
first three months of this year, if only nominally).
     Year, though, in which I lucked out. The apartment,
the hideaway, the tripolar order: I'm still thinking I
couldn't've done much better. I've managed to hang onto
my Jyzer Ink scoping work, and that work -- that kind of
work -- continues to be just about perfect for me. I
have a financial cushion backing me up (though it's
rapidly shrinking) and deep reserves behind that (still
growing!). I'm in good health as far as I know. I'm
working hard. I haven't lost the grand vision. I'm

alone but -- so what if I'm alone.

So now in a way I'm back to where I was in late August. Then I paused at the door of the memory palace and decided to take another spin around the grounds before entering -- that spin being Book III of this year's jyze. And now Book III's just about full and the year's just about over. Or call the spin a detour. Nor am I sorry about taking it. But given its success (in the sense of reestablishing contact with Lady K) it turned out to be a lot more painful and frustrating than I might've expected. I got dropped flat -- again! Proving merely, I suppose, that Lisa is still Lisa (and for that matter Lisa is still Lena of "Jyzer," and not only that but Lena of "Jyzer" is still Lisa of real life). At least she helped keep things interesting in these pages for a few months, and at minimal cost (as far as I know) to herself. If she ever wants more contact with me, though, she'll have to take the initiative. "The ball's in her court." I plan to fall silent now, with her as with everyone else except Rob and Gail. Maybe a card to Lisa next Christmas, or maybe not. Worry about it then.

(They're still playing the board game. Mixed couple too. She looks to be of Lady U's ancestry, though possibly of Lady S's or or the maternal half of Lady V's; he looks quite a lot like my own cousin Chad during his later college years, that is, hayseed Norski to the max. Trombones gamboling meanwhile, some sophisticated big-band blues from around the time of my birth or a few years before (same fine tape I've heard here several times before). Sound of fingers whaling at computer keyboards but not too many or too loud. (Earlier in the crowd near the public-market newsstand I spotted a Briana-class smile which then no doubt by sheer coincidence flashed my way for a millisecond and I was transfixed for -- seemed like hours.))

No speculation here about what jyze might become next year -- not to mention the fate of the jyzer himself. That's for tomorrow or maybe sometime in the eighter following, the new volume, the new annal, looking forward. Consequently, though, I'm feeling a little hamstrung right now. Seems I'm not much in the mood for looking back anymore. "Just Can't Get Jyzey Tonight."

Or maybe later. For now I'll move on and tend to the night's scoping work. (Quarter past seven. Rain streaking the industrial windows. Streetlights of the middle road shining steadily outside. Each of the two large windows consists of a mosaic of smaller panes, some seventy-two of them if my count is right (yes, eight panes on the side times nine across the top, just double-checked). Were each pane a year in the life of the jyzer, imagine the visual effect -- most of them already painted in, unless the jyzer were one far-off day to become a centenarian plus ten, in which case one could retrospectively say "most" was incorrect. Ratio of what's happened to what's happening and what maybe will happen -- well, but best not get too mathematical here. -- Press my nose against one of the clear panes representing this coming year, though, and what will I see?) (Just checked again. "All The Jyze I Got" -- not. Just all the usual out there plus an overhead view of a matched pair of red knit caps with white cotton balls on top -- just like the ones I saw at the bar & grill counter Christmas Eve -- but here they're bobbing along two or three feet below window level, moving in close to each other as in an affectionate nuzzle and then back out, passing from left to right before exiting the frame, or rather the many frames. -- Pretty sappy way to end this but I'm ready to exit the many frames myself, and via the door.)

*   *

-- The projected hour at the scope office stretched to three. A fast-talking neurologist with a strong Pakistani accent Naomi had a tough time deciphering, and so I had a tough time unscrambling what she wrote (and even tougher, guessing at what she wasn't able to write). Now it's a little past eleven and the new storm is here. It's rain only, though, so it feels more like relief, especially the warm southwesterly winds.

[Jyze and Jyze Alone]

    Folks out wandering New Year's Eve fashion. At one
of the bus stops on my way home I saw a young, but fully
grown, trio dressed in pink rabbit costumes hopping about
as they awaited their coach. Whether the giant golf tee
will be dropping its ball tonight I still don't know. I
do know I'm going nowhere. This is it right here, the
redwood worktable. "Home Jyzin'." (From time to time a
string of firecrackers or maybe a volley of cherry bombs
detonating. The jazz station is broadcasting "coast-to-
coast live" from our zone here after earlier stops for
more eastward zonal celebrations. I'm planning nothing
special. Dinner will be leftover chicken soup, the broad-
noodle kind. Maybe a drink or two. Lean back and mull it
all a bit one more time, this extraordinary year.)
    I didn't mention it before, what I'm proudest of in
jyze year three. Sheer survival, someone might guess.
All right, I'll admit there's that. But in addition: I
came up with a pretty damn good way of living. Did it
almost from scratch. And now it's proceeding quite
smoothly. I'm prospering at a bare-bones subsistence
level. I see no reason why I can't continue doing so.
    Looking back, what else? Year of the protojyze and
essay grandmasters. I keep plugging away at both (I've
reached Volume IV of the protojyze and page 640-something
of the essays). Neither inspires me much, although the
essays do finally seem to be taking off. Steadiness,
dependability, determination to set down some words about
surrounding life as well as the author's inward life and
to keep on doing this no matter what: for these qualities
and aims I honor these two worthies and hope to emulate
them the rest of my days. But I want to do it with a
spirit much less establishmentarian than either of theirs
(one a mayor, the other a secretary of the navy!).
    Year of the booming stock market. Year of the
burgeoning internet and web. Year of sadly little of
real interest in the world of politics. Political life
is spiraling off in directions which make me deeply
uneasy and yet at the same time raise jaw-cracking yawns
because most of it's so predictable. As far as I'm
concerned only one really compelling new idea, political

or otherwise, has made the scene in the past few years, and that happens to be the jyze idea itself. Of course I would think that! In theory, at least, through jyze one can try to make a difference in other dimensions without becoming totally bored with itself and/or burned out in doing it. Or if not make a difference, at least make a record. An annual report, yes, gathered in six-day or eight-day increments. And I thank you again, Lady K, for that gift of the annual-report concept. May all of your own personal annual reports from here on in bear nothing but great tidings and inspire your stock price to rise ever higher -- not that I have any reason to think it needs to rise at all. I'll even say I strongly suspect it's already way up there.

Twenty-two more minutes and this year's done.

(At one point I was planning to head over to the storage port today so I could finish up this annal where it began the year: in unit 161. The image of the J-master blazing away at the picnic table in the unit there seemed so structurally right as well as transitionally apt. The miserable weather, however, scotched that plan. -- And also caused the shelters at the storage port's marina to collapse, I might mention, doing millions of dollars in damage to the scores of pleasure boats moored there, no doubt including at least some belonging to the bellicose denizens of my old way station the jingo lounge. Fortunately for them, insurance will cover most of the losses and, according to a news report I heard, in many cases help the owners move up to an even higher level of luxury craft.)

More than anything else what comes to mind from my rereading of this year's annal is a single phrase jotted down in the very first entry of Book I and never used again: "Joie de Jyze." An early or proto jyzo, yes, and one that expressed what I'm aiming to achieve in the volumes to come -- acknowledging the task may be far from easy -- and also what I believe I've pretty successfully maintained so far in the wider jyze realm -- not everywhere and at all times, to be sure, but enough. And about this I'm very pleased indeed.

[Jyze and Jyze Alone]

    Year of changes. Year of mourning. Year of the
shaking out. Year of the shaking off of old
attachments. Year of jyzomania. Year of wandering
around muttering to myself about fierce focus. Year of
jyze mazurkas galore and all of the year one big jyze
mazurka and especially the opening two thirds of this
last volume. Year of euphoria and dysphoria, madly
fluctuating manic extremes, bipolar and tripolar orders
and disorders.
    My steady wooden wall clock (ol' Mom's clock) says
three minutes to twelve. Steady but maybe steadily
wrong; best to go by the radio instead. Then at the
ball drop: close this book for good. Also for bad.
Also for indifferent. Move on to whatever's next.
"Jyze Pounds Down the Stretch." Also vamps for time: a
very jyzey thing to do because it's the very way jyze
started up back in the weeks before page one of annal
one went down. -- But now a chorus of foghorns is
sounding from the harbor and, yup, on the radio here it
is -- one last jyzo -- "Auld Lang Jyze!" Phlzzzzzzz,
right. But cheers anyway to all! Because it's now
jyze year four!

                    END